SEDUCTION AND SURRENDER . . .

"Go back to your ranch, Logan," Maggie said finally. "There's nothing for you here."

"Nonsense, Maggie. I plan to camp out in town until I have you where I want you."

"You'll never get me anywhere I don't want to be, Logan Ramsey."

"I wouldn't issue such challenges, Maggie; I can be pretty persuasive."

His words sent a shudder through her.

"Persuade someone else then. You want a ranch woman, Logan, not a town woman who's used to running her own life. You need someone to share your life, not fight it."

"Are you going to fight it, Maggie?"

His question hung in the air between them. If only she could tell him: she wanted everything . . . and nothing. If he could possess her without conquering her, if he could love her without needing her always, if he would just kiss her. . . .

He didn't even need an answer. His mouth found hers unerringly and she sought him with equal eagerness. She held him for the moment, demanded his kiss just for the moment, and savored him as if she were going to die tomorrow. . . .

FIERY ROMANCE

CALIFORNIA CARESS (2771, $3.75)
by Rebecca Sinclair

Hope Bennett was determined to save her brother's life. And if that meant paying notorious gunslinger Drake Frazier to take his place in a fight, she'd barter her last gold nugget. But Hope soon discovered she'd have to give the handsome rattlesnake more than riches if she wanted his help. His improper demands infuriated her; even as she luxuriated in the tantalizing heat of his embrace, she refused to yield to her desires.

ARIZONA CAPTIVE (2718, $3.75)
by Leree Bryant

Logan Powers had always taken his role as a lady-killer very seriously and no woman was going to change that. Not even the breathtakingly beautiful Callie Nolan with her luxuriant black hair and startling blue eyes. Logan might have considered a lusty romp with her but it was apparent she was a lady, through and through. Hard as he tried, Logan couldn't resist wanting to take her warm slender body in his arms and hold her close to his heart forever.

DECEPTION'S EMBRACE (2720, $3.75)
by Jeanne Hansen

Terrified heiress Katrina Montgomery fled Memphis with what little she could carry and headed west, hiding in a freight car. By the time she reached Kansas City, she was feeling almost safe . . . until the handsomest man she'd ever seen entered the car and swept her into his embrace. She didn't know who he was or why he refused to let her go, but when she gazed into his eyes, she somehow knew she could trust him with her life . . . and her heart.

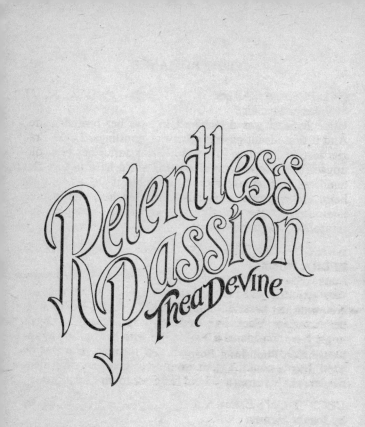

Relentless Passion

Thea Devine

ZEBRA BOOKS
KENSINGTON PUBLISHING CORP.

ZEBRA BOOKS

are published by

Kensington Publishing Corp.
475 Park Avenue South
New York, NY 10016

First printing: November, 1989

Printed in the United States of America

To the best of all mothers-in-law,
Angela Devine

And to John,
for all the reasons he knows

Chapter One

It was a year to the day that Frank Colleran had been shot to death, but the first thing that Maggie Colleran thought about when she awoke that morning was that she had not seen Logan Ramsey in a long time.

It wasn't necessarily that she wanted to see him, she thought; it was just the idea that he existed and that he was in Colville, and that sometime she would see him, or he would see her, or he would come if she were in need, as he always had.

Thinking of Logan made her smile because *he* always smiled; he almost always found humor in everything—except when Maggie lost the baby—Frank's baby. Logan had stayed by her bedside and held her hands to infuse them with his warmth and strength, and with the confidence in his sky-blue eyes that could never lie to her. He had said she would be all right, and she had been.

And when Frank had died so mysteriously, so violently, he had come and held her in his arms, had told her that he knew she would get through it, and she did. Then he had gone away for all this time, and yet she found comfort in the knowledge that he was somewhere close by. For some reason she needed to remember that this morning.

But there was nothing much different about this morning than any other morning. She thought about what was to come in the day ahead. She would arise as usual at six, dress, and go downstairs to the office, make the coffee if A.J. were not already there, and she would spend the day dealing with the thing that had occupied most of her waking hours recently: the coming of the Denver North railroad extension.

It was not a solvable problem: the surveyors would come and they would find everything feasible and there was nothing she could do about it. Nothing. But she had to try. She felt like a helpless moth, futilely beating her wings to avoid the inevitable.

She was cursed, she thought, with the ability to see the negatives when everyone was lauding the positive aspects of the trunk line passing through Colville. The worst of it was that she was one of those who stood to gain the most: the Colleran ranch was right on the survey route, and Denver North wanted it badly.

That she could do something about; it gave her a sweet feeling of power even though she still did not know what she was going to do about it.

She never heard the brisk rap at her door and was startled by the sudden appearance of her mother-in-law, looking like a venomous black crow in her mourning clothes, fully dressed right down to the somber black bonnet with its concealing veil draped over the broad brim.

"Of course you're preparing to attend church today," she said testily as she barged in.

Maggie rose slowly upright against her pillows to give herself time to figure out what Mother Colleran was talking about. "I expect," she murmured as she wrapped her arms around her legs, "that *this* morning I will."

Her mother-in-law stared at her suspiciously.

She stared right back.

Mother Colleran said finally, coldly, "The memorial service for Frank was listed right in the church notices that *you* wrote yourself."

Maggie's heart dropped for a split second with unrepentant guilt as her mother-in-law had obviously intended; she *had* forgotten the date. "Of course," she said coolly, "and I remembered all about it."

"The *early* service."

"I suggested it myself," Maggie said calmly, not moving a muscle. "I will be ready to accompany you."

"I sincerely doubt it," her mother-in-law muttered. "I just hope to God Reese gets here in time for the service." She eyed Maggie distastefully. "Just wait until Reese comes home."

A flash of anger rippled over Maggie's composure and she ran a tense hand through her wildly tumbling black curls in order to give herself time to quell it. "You've been threatening me with that for months," she said finally. "I can't imagine how you think things will change when—and if—Reese Colleran turns up in Colville."

"They will," Mother Colleran stated unequivocally, as if by force of her will it would happen. "Reese will make everything right."

Maggie froze. "Make everything *right?*" she repeated incredulously, feeling pushed to the limit by this unusual confession. "Make *everything* right? Make *what* right, Mother Colleran? *What?*"

She pushed back the cover and swung her legs over the side of the bed. Her smoky eyes turned stony as they narrowed on her mother-in-law, and she began to walk forward to press her advantage, filing away for future reference Mother Colleran's horrified expression as she backed away from her.

"What can Reese Colleran *do?* He can't bring back Frank."

9

Her mother-in-law recoiled as though she had been struck physically.

"He can't bring Frank back from the dead," Maggie repeated willfully, and her mother-in-law turned abruptly and fled from the room, slamming the door emphatically behind her.

Maggie leaned the weight of her slender body against the door wearily. What *had* she been planning, she wondered; what was she hoping? And why would Reese Colleran suddenly decide to return to the family fold after all these years, when he had been the one to leave when his shenanigans had finally been too much even for his indulgent father?

More than that, why did her mother-in-law think that the threat of his return would scare her?

She walked slowly back into the room and sank onto her bed. Damn! she had forgotten about Frank's memorial service. How on earth was she going to get through this day? The whole morning would be devoted to eulogizing Frank, the man she had married and come to hate.

Twenty minutes later, dressed in a dark gray velvet suit trimmed in black, she ran downstairs with just enough time to take a sip of coffee while she tried on and discarded several matching hats. Nothing pleased her. "Damn," she murmured, throwing off the last one.

"A.J.," she called through the connecting door to the office.

His kindly face appeared immediately. A.J.'s bulky body was encased in a rusty black suit. His white hair was combed punctiliously back from his ruddy face, which was lined with years of experiences about which she would never know. His watery blue eyes crinkled up into a smile. "Ma'am?"

She looked at him helplessly, holding a black velvet hat by its frail netting in one hand and her cup of coffee in the other. She didn't know why she had called him, but it occurred to her suddenly that she could not ask him to make the choice for her. Frantically she searched for another reason for her summons. "Is there a notice up that the office will be closed?"

"Yes, ma'am. Right on the front door. Says we'll be closed till noon. Jean made it up yesterday and you didn't have to worry none about it," he assured her in his softly slurred voice that was so formal and courtly.

"I suppose I didn't; no one would dare want to do business when he could attend Frank's memorial service," she said, more to herself than him. "And how will you go?" she asked him, knowing full well that Mother Colleran would never permit men whom she considered no better than servants to share a carriage with her. The matter of their loyalty to Frank and now to her held no weight with her.

"Jean hired a buggy, ma'am. We can splurge a little on this special occasion. We'll be there, ma'am, don't you fret none about that."

She nodded, set her coffee cup down, and turned back to the mirror as he withdrew.

"I *have* to wear a hat," she told herself grittily as she jammed the scrap of velvet onto her tightly braided hair and tied it under her chin. How different she looked, all constricted and constrained by combs and velvet ribbons and buttons to her neck, and by the tight black velvet waistband encircling the fashionable narrowed skirt of her suit.

When she finally pulled the veil forward to obscure her features she felt as though she had created a Maggie in Frank's image of her, someone who could hide behind the stiff contours of her clothes and the soft impenetrable folds of the gauzy veil that she arranged so

11

carefully around her squared shoulders.

She looked, she thought as she surveyed herself in the hallway mirror one last time, like the woman that Frank Colleran had assumed he was marrying.

The woman she had never been.

She turned away from the image abruptly, picked up her cape, and made her way to the side entrance by the carriage drive where Mother Colleran awaited her.

The old woman stared at her disapprovingly as the driver helped her in. "Never," she snapped, "do you ever have a sense of the appropriateness of things. This is Frank's memorial service, for heaven's sake. You look like you're off to do a day's work."

"So I am," Maggie said quietly, folding her hands on her lap and surreptitiously clenching them.

"Are you indeed?" Mother Colleran's eyes narrowed. "Then I say again it's good and well that Reese is coming home. I count myself fortunate that I was able to contact him before he took off for some other God-forsaken part of the world."

Maggie's flinty gaze swung back to her mother-in-law. *She* had summoned Reese Colleran? This was news, and not welcome news either. Why would her mother-in-law need this ally so badly that she would stoop to begging him to return to Colville after all these years?

"I still can't imagine what Reese Colleran could have to do with me—or you, for that matter," she said coldly, and turned her head again to stare out of the window as their hired driver snapped the horses into motion.

Damn Reese Colleran, she thought viciously. There hadn't been a day that Mother Colleran did not throw his name up to her, *every* day, it seemed, for the last few months.

Or had it been since Frank's death?

No. She swung her gaze back to her mother-in-law. The old woman's face held an expression of smugness.

12

What *was* she expecting of this outcast son?

Maggie made a mental note to ask Dennis Coutts and turned her attention to the scenery as the carriage began making its way up the ridge to the church, which hunkered like a huge stone giant on two large plots of land in the center of the residential district.

The town fathers had planned its location to be well within walking distance of town. Nonetheless, this day the long narrow road up the ridge was clogged with horses and carriages as well as people on foot, and Maggie made an impatient sound as the carriage jolted to a stop just within sight of the five towering trees that separated the church from the rectory and the cemetery.

Still further on she could see the milling crowd moving along almost as if it were one body. The number of people astonished her.

"I'm walking the rest of the way," she announced disgustedly.

"You will not," Mother Colleran contradicted. "You will not turn this ceremony into a travesty by *walking* up that hill with that crowd. You are Frank's *wife,* and you will not disgrace him—or me—today."

Maggie pulled herself up stiffly and opened the door of the carriage. "You, of course, as the mother of the man, *should* arrive in state, Mother Colleran. *I* would rather just get there and have this ceremony over with. Do excuse me." She swung herself out the door and gracefully descended. She never looked back as she strode up the ridge.

There was a crowd in the church as well as outside. A buzz greeted her as she entered and took her place in the Colleran pew. She never was sure when her mother-in-law finally arrived; she felt her heavy presence suddenly and heard her slightly labored breathing. Within ten

13

minutes she was bored with the Reverend Dailey's speech extolling Frank Colleran's virtues, and she was almost sure she could hear her mother-in-law purring with delight as every one of them was meticulously ticked off.

Yes, yes, Frank was a community leader, and not coincidentally a regular church contributor, an exemplary husband and son. Every one of them thought so; there wasn't a person in Colville who did not idolize him for his good works and his fellowship.

Maggie made a good pretense of listening as she surreptitiously glanced around. Everyone had come, all the townspeople and the neighboring families she had grown up with—the Rennerts and the Perezes, and Annie and Sean Mapes, both of whom acknowledged her with a nod that told her they had come to the service out of respect for her and not Frank. Up front, Dennis Coutts signaled her with a raised eyebrow as he caught her glance, and further back, in a corner, she just glimpsed A.J. and Jean Vilroy, uncomfortably dressed up and squeezed in next to Harold Danforth, chief proponent of the railroad expansion. Danforth looked pompous and full of himself, and not happy that he had not gotten a seat up front as befitted his standing in town.

All of her old friends had come, in fact, except Arwin Bodey, who ran the general store, and Logan. . . . She felt a little trip of her heart as she realized that Logan might not come at all.

The service lasted a full hour and a half. Afterwards, Reverend Dailey came immediately to her side, feeling he also must minister to the grief he knew she must be feeling. She was thankful her veil still shielded her face as she answered his solicitous inquiries with barely concealed impatience.

"I assure you, I'm quite fine."

He looked shocked. "But—"

14

She had to amend that impetuous statement quickly. "I have thrown myself into my work," she explained further, "and that has mitigated a lot of the pain. I have tried to carry on as I thought Frank would want me to," she added. As usual, the talisman words worked, reassuring him as they were intended to do. She went on with a touch of irony, "It has helped me to feel closer to him. I felt—" she paused a moment before uttering the final lie, "he would want me to."

In point of fact, she thought bitterly, he had never wanted her anywhere near the newspaper office. If he had been able to have his way, he would have immured her at the run-down shack that was the Colleran ranch.

Reverend Dailey reacted just as she knew he would. "Only, of course, until you find someone to take over for you. Yes," he murmured sympathetically, "I'm sure that was exactly what Frank would have wanted you to do. Not to mourn but to carry on. That was the kind of man he was, Maggie, as you know best of all of us."

Maggie smiled. "Except of course Mother Colleran," she interjected smoothly, turning to her mother-in-law and handing the minister into her clutches.

She turned away quickly before Reverend Dailey could include her in the conversation, and almost skewed into Melinda Sable.

They stared at each other for a long moment, Melinda looking perfectly blonde and perfectly dressed in black, her face pale and her wet brown eyes resentful. She moved first, tossing her uncovered blonde curls, daring Maggie to send her away, to say she didn't belong there, to claim that Frank Colleran could never have loved *her*.

Maggie lifted her chin, raised her eyebrows inquiringly, and turned her back abruptly on the woman she knew had been with Frank on the day he had died. She had nothing to say to Melinda Sable.

But others had things to say to her, things she had to

listen to patiently because they had adored Frank and because she was "Mrs. Frank," and they wanted to tell her, and show her by their presence today, how much they revered him.

She said all the right things because she knew how they felt, but only Mother Colleran was enjoying the attention. She herself wanted only to escape it as soon as possible.

She made her way slowly through the crowd outside, feeling impossibly alone even as she was surrounded by the warmth of a community that had adored her husband, and by extension her, murmuring thank yous and how-kind-of-yous as she tactfully avoided detaining hands and tried to find a moment of privacy.

But Dennis Coutts was following her, and as soon as she became aware of it she stopped to wait for him.

"Well, you don't seem too sad," he commented, his open, bluff face expressing his pleasuring at having this spare moment alone with her.

"No, I haven't time to play the grieving widow," she said shortly, and then added in a softer tone of voice, "I wish everyone had not made such a fuss, actually. Although Madame Mother seems to be enjoying it." And then, after a look into his eyes, she added sharply, "This is no time to discuss business, Dennis, or what might be your pleasure."

He laughed. "Dear Maggie, believe me, you are going to have many proposals, and very soon, I wager." He had enough presence of mind not to add that his would be one of them. His whole concern, since Frank's death, had been taking care of Maggie, whose abruptness and real courage shielded her softer nature, a nature, he believed, that desperately needed a strong male hand to guide it. For if Frank had left her the burdens of his business and the responsibility of caring for his mother, Dennis Coutts

16

considered that in a very real sense Frank had left the care of Maggie to him. He was Frank's executor and most trusted legal advisor, and he had a firm knowledge of Maggie's entitlements through Frank's estate.

And he felt a great deal of gratitude that they shared this link to Frank.

Dennis believed that Maggie had loved Frank, as he himself had, as had anyone who had known him. The outpouring of grief today was witness to that, and Maggie could not help but be moved by it, Dennis thought, though she made a very good show of sloughing off her own pain. She had thrown herself into working at the newspaper and had become its guiding force in that short period of time. Nonetheless, it was understood that when Frank's successor was found, Maggie would step down.

At least that was how Dennis understood it. But he wasn't so sure Maggie would move aside so easily now that she had had a taste of power. However, her ongoing battle with Harold Danforth wasn't winning her any supporters.

He took her arm gently and they began walking back down toward the church and the milling crowd. Along the way he exchanged a brief nod with Harold Danforth, a greeting Maggie did not miss.

"I was supposed to have been coercing you to see things Harold's way," Dennis explained conspiratorially.

She liked him very much in that moment. "You certainly may say you did, and how much trouble I gave you, if you like. You had to twist my arm—with words, that is. But I won't retract anything I wrote, Dennis."

"I wouldn't expect you to," he said placatingly, "although Harold would like a public apology. However, an equal amount of space for him—in print— preferably on the front page so he can give his side of it, is acceptable reparation."

17

Maggie considered this request for a moment and then sighed. "He's a vain and foolish man. I hope to heaven this whole thing fails—but of course it won't. All right, but not the front page. Not even my editorial words command the front page."

"You'll print whatever he writes?"

"I will. And I'll let him mire himself up to his chin in his own stupidity," she said venomously. "And he will. I know he will."

"And we'll let him," Dennis agreed gravely. "I'll tell him."

She watched him move through the crowd purposefully and then turned to speak with another well wisher, fully aware of Mother Colleran, deep in the crowd, holding forth with gusto on her favorite subject—her memories of Frank when he was a child. Beyond that, she felt nothing but an ineffable sense of loneliness.

On the other side of the church grounds an elegantly dressed gentleman stood among the dispersing crowd on a slight rise that allowed him to look down on the chapel lawn.

There were so many people. He shook his head in wonder, hard pressed to figure out, in the sea of black clad women, which one was Maggie Colleran.

He strode further on down the incline, looking for a likely person to ask, one who would not question his curiosity.

"Pardon?" He tapped the shoulder of a tall, thirtyish, weather-beaten looking man who was not dressed for a church service. He too was standing and staring into the crowd intently, and he turned with the abruptness of a man who has faced enemies in blind corners. His sky-blue eyes assessed his questioner sharply from beneath a

18

battered stetson.

"Stranger?" His voice was deep and rough and burnished as fine wood.

"I'm looking for Mrs. Frank Colleran," the stranger said, not even looking at his informant but rather shielding his eyes against the sun as he looked down into the crowd. "Do you know her? Can you point her out to me from here?"

"I know her," his informant said shortly, his eyes narrowing. He pulled the brim of his hat down over his eyes and turned to the crowd. "She's by the church door there—the woman with the dark hair, dressed in gray."

The stranger tipped his hat. "'Preciate it," he said, moving away slowly and finally turning and squinting so he could see her clearly.

She was bathed in sunlight as she moved from the doorway down the two stone steps that gave onto the walkway, and her intelligent face, the features of which he could not see distinctly, was bent attentively toward the person to whom she was speaking. Her dark hair glinted blue in the sun, and once he knew who she was he saw that she could never be missed, not even in a crowd this size. The elegance of her posture and the way she held her head as she moved through the crowd told him more about her than any description.

She had a smooth grace and a manner that hid her firm determination. He could see it in her walk and in the way she tactfully turned aside this person and that, obviously saying a personal word to each in a gracious way that made them smile and nod as she passed them. She was heading toward a closed carriage as she impatiently untied the ribbons of the hat that was dangling down her back, pulled it off, and began twirling it insouciantly by its ties the moment she thought she was out of sight of the crowd.

My God, he thought, my God. The she-cat his own

dragon of a mother had written him about endlessly. The scheming Helen who had trapped Frank and ruined his life forever. The rustic jezebel who had lured Frank in a way his mother had never understood.

That gorgeous, unexpected creature had been Frank's wife. Frank's *wife*.

Chapter Two

As the carriage drew up with a flourish in front of the newspaper office Maggie pushed the door open, leaned out, and then jumped back as if she had been struck. Just for one moment she had the stunning feeling that it was Frank awaiting them in the shadow of the office door. She couldn't see his face, only the bulk of his body, his stance, the way he held his arms loosely at his sides.

And then he moved forward and she met the cool, pale blue gaze of the elegantly dressed man who must be Frank's brother. Behind her, Mother Colleran made what sounded like a joyful noise in the back of her throat, and then squelched it, as if she had revealed too much to Maggie too soon.

Maggie leaned forward again. This was not a moment to show uncertainty. This expensively dressed stranger was the mysterious Reese, the threat of whose appearance was supposed to bring her to heel somehow. He *was* rather formidable at first glance, and as different from Frank as night from day. He was broader, leaner, sun-browned, extravagantly dressed in a black form-fitting coat that seemed to barely encompass the width of his shoulders. He wore matching trousers and a stark white shirt adorned with a formal stock tie. The unrelieved severity of the colors threw his tawny hair and pale blue eyes into high relief against his tanned skin. His expression was mocking, as if he were waiting for her to speak first.

She took all of this in with one smoky gray glance. In that instant she read the challenge in his eyes. He expected her to know who he was, if not why he had come. Her lips tightened imperceptibly and her chin lifted resolutely in a way that dismissed him as clearly as if she had spoken.

He would not let her do it. "Ma'am?" The tone was respectful, if his manner was not. His voice was deep and strongly accented.

"I know who you are," she said calmly, not allowing him an inch to maneuver. He was right in her way and she did not know quite what to do to budge him. She felt as if he had cornered her, and she was caught fairly between mother and son without an inkling which of them was the more dangerous to her.

All he said was, "Allow me to help you down."

She wanted that least of all, but she acquiesced and he held out his arms to her as she pushed forward, grasping her around her narrow waist and lifting her easily from the carriage. He looked into her eyes closely, assessingly, uncomfortably.

She wondered what he saw as her own hands grasped the hard muscle beneath his tailored sleeves; then he set her on the plank walk and turned to his mother.

Maggie did not wait to speak with him. She rapped briskly on the door of the office. A.J. opened it and she disappeared quickly inside, where the smell of ink and the mustiness of the room were a welcome substitute for the close, tight atmosphere from which she had escaped.

Oh no, she would not allow the appearance of Reese Colleran to disturb her. The only remedy for unresolvable burdens was work, and she headed quickly toward the hallway closet, where she stripped off her cloak, hung away the bothersome little hat, and took out the voluminous leather apron she habitually wore in the office. It covered her pristine gray skirt to the knee and hugged her bosom protectively. The faint smell of ink emanated from its pores, and in its pockets were three pairs of ink-stained gloves in various stages of disrepair.

The apron definitely gave her a businesslike air. She had only to braid her hair into a loose plait, and she would be ready to put the exigencies of the morning behind her.

It was just not possible for her to pretend, as everyone seemed willing to believe, that all her thoughts centered on Frank Colleran today, nor was it possible to pretend that she had loved him to the end and that she would mourn him forever. She was sure everyone assumed she had returned from the church and gone directly to her room, prostrate with grief. Instead, she was so full of energy she felt like bursting. There was no way, in as public a place as a local newspaper office, that she could resume any of her duties without causing censure and alienating her small group of supporters.

In any event, the office was a good place to avoid having to deal with the sudden appearance of Reese Colleran, she thought mordantly as she entered the room. She didn't even have to change her clothes. She didn't have to do anything she did not want to do in *her* workplace.

She loved this room. It contained all the motion and life that anyone could desire. To her right, near the door, was Jean Vilroy's slant-topped drafting desk and the massive parlor stove that was the focus of the center of the room. To the front on the same side, behind a wainscotted divider with its little gate, was A.J.'s battered cylinder desk, a flat-topped desk with a typewriter on it, and behind that, opposite the stove and Jean's drawing board, was her own desk, its back to the front of the office, the high roll top concealing her completely. On the wall above was a painting of the office building executed by Jean Vilroy, and alongside her desk there was a table where she wrote articles and edited copy.

On the opposite side of the room stood Frank Colleran's desk, now an ornament, unused, shining with wax and reverence, glowing walnut of a dozen shades pieced together in a highly ornate style, the best he could afford. Maggie's portrait hung above this.

It had been his idea. He had insisted in spite of her protestations and she knew why. He had wanted to be a martyr because he knew he had forced her to lie: he had wanted her to be only what he wanted her to be. When she failed he had not punished her—he had punished himself—or perhaps he had thought he was punishing her.

From where she stood by the door she could see the portrait clearly. She had never liked it. He had chosen the dress, the artist, and the pose. The only thing about the portrait that remotely resembled her was her eyes. The artist could not disguise the overwhelming life in her eyes.

It was time, she thought distractedly, to remove that portrait.

She moved quietly past Jean, out of the back hallway where the stairwell was located as well as the second-hand steam driven press Frank had installed two years before. Near the window stood the tall row of print cases where she would be spiking type for the next edition in three days.

For just a moment her feeling of high exhilaration faded and she felt tired and not a little restless. Something was not quite right. It had nothing to do with Reese Colleran's presence or Harold Danforth's vituperative article, or even with her problems with her one unmanageable reporter, Arch Warfield, who thought he ought to have been named editor when Frank died and who never hesitated to remind her of the fact in subtle little ways.

She didn't know what it was that was bothering her as she seated herself at her work table and picked up the first sheet of a stack of papers that awaited her attention.

Her reaction was immediate. "A.J.!" she called stridently.

A.J. came immediately from his front desk, where he was orchestrating the first inrush of customers, advertisers, and neighbors who had come just to gossip and find out the latest news before it was even published.

"Ma'am?"

She handed him Warfield's preliminary article about the arrival of the survey team. "A little too editorially pro railroad, wouldn't you say? Everything golden and rosy for the future, no negatives at all. Nothing about whether this town has the capacity to handle the new population, or the temporary housing these workers are going to have to accept, or all the other things that follow workmen and railroads. Damn, it sounds like an addendum to Harold Danforth's heavenly vision. I have to give *him* space, but . . ."

"Now, Mrs. Frank . . ."

"Please, A.J.. Frank is dead and gone and I'm sick of being labeled with his name, as if I don't have a life or a will or an intelligence of my own."

A.J. stared at her. "Yes, ma'am."

"A.J.—"

"Whatever you want, ma'am."

"And *don't* call me ma'am!" She spun away, utterly irritated with him and Arch Warfield and everything, and stood with her back to him, her arms wrapped around her waist, giving him time to read the article and herself time to regain her frayed temper.

"I see what you mean, ma' . . . am. Look, I have to call you *something*," A.J. protested.

"I think," she said, turning back to him with a faint smile on her lips, "I think you can call me Maggie."

He shook his head doubtfully. She had always been Mrs. Frank, and he already knew he was going to stumble a hundred times on it before he remembered to put it out of his head. "I'll talk to Arch, Miz Maggie." Yes, that sounded right, he thought, respectful, not too forward, not too informal. "I'll talk to Arch."

"Yes, you do that. Now, Jean, do we know when the survey team is coming in?" She was back to business again, pivoting toward the Frenchman who, with his quick hands, was aligning type for the advertisements that had been bought for the week's edition.

He shrugged. "Could be today," he said noncommittally.

She stood behind him watching, admiring his deft movements and his sense of composition. He was an itinerant artist whom Frank had given work, and he had stayed these four years for reasons she could not fathom. He was not paid well, in fact, he did not particularly like the work or the town or the time he had to devote to job printing, which had become his specialty. He had virtually no time for his art, and he could have picked up and gone at any time, she thought, and yet he stayed, for Frank—who had known how to be mighty persuasive. After Frank she had never had to say a word to him.

She wondered how persuasive she could be after all if she could not talk the town fathers into at least considering the ramifications of this northward linkage of the railroad line.

"I'll check that out. A.J., did the readyprint bundle come in from Denver? Anybody check out the express office yet?"

"No, Miz Maggie. I reckon I'll go if you want."

"No," she said instantly, seeing yet another way to

26

delay facing her mother-in-law and her unwanted guest. "I'll go. I need air. I need action," she added, more to herself than them, and within moments she was out in the crisp spring air, her cloak wrapped around her leather apron.

On the street, her sense of expectancy quickened. She loved her home town. She had been raised here and knew everyone. As she walked over to the express station she greeted a dozen people with a nod and a quick hello. They all knew her. To them she was not Mrs. Frank. She was Maggie Lynch, who had married Frank Colleran and now ran the newspaper.

Everyone knew it, the open secret that was never concealed by the fact that A.J. Lloyd's name appeared on the masthead as the editor and that the paper was published, ostensibly, by the Colleran estate. It was Maggie's paper and no one denied it.

"Hey, Mrs. Frank, wasn't that a service for Frank today?"

She waved.

"'Afternoon, Maggie, how you doin'?"

"Just fine, Colbert," she called back. "How about you?"

She grasped another hand in passing, then poked her head into the general store to greet Arwin Bodey. "Heard anything yet, Arwin?"

He waved his arm from the rear of the store. "Nothin' yet, Maggie, but that don't mean there ain't some news over by the stage stop."

"I'm on my way there."

"Let me know then."

She waved and went off down the plankboard sidewalk toward the express office. "My delivery come yet?" she demanded, opening the door.

"Freight wagon ain't due in till—oh, five or so, Maggie."

"Okay, A.J. will come by then."

She closed the door and turned toward the stage office that was directly across the crowded, dirt-dusted street. A little knot of people stood outside the door, old-timers with little to occupy their time, delivery boys, a ranch hand awaiting an expected guest.

Her senses prickled suddenly as she spotted Arch Warfield in the small crowd.

"Oh Lord," she murmured out loud, checking her stride as she was about to step onto the street. And then, "Oh Lord," again as her gaze flashed by a tall familiar figure walking purposefully toward the stage stop.

He didn't see her, and she had several long unimpeded moments to just look at him and to know that he was all right, and just the same.

Perhaps, she thought, not quite just the same; he looked thinner to her, and she could not see his face, except for the set line of his lips and jaw. And then someone spoke to him and he immediately stopped and turned his attention to his questioner in that attractive way of his she knew so well. It was a stance peculiar only to him, a stance by which she could have picked him out from a thousand other men—a slight leaning forward of his body toward the person who was talking, coupled with an air of intense concentration.

He pushed back his hat at one point and she could see his face clearly, his furrowed, well-shaped brows, the unruly curl of sable black hair that drifted onto his broad forehead, the exasperated twist of his firm lips that reformed into a brief warm smile.

Not a handsome face, she thought critically, savoring the sight of him when she had not seen him in so long, but the proportion of it was perfect—for him—its narrow length in flawless symmetry with the long lean line of his body.

Then he looked up and she could have sworn that his penetrating sky-blue gaze rested on her for a long critical moment before he looked away. Her heart reacted with a

28

furious thump, so totally unexpected to her that she could do nothing but continue watching him for a few minutes more.

And when she finally turned away she felt a curious awareness of a slight feeling of release that she could not consciously define, as if the sight of Logan Ramsey were the one thing she had been waiting to see on this one particular day.

Finally she wondered about Reese Colleran. Two hours later, when she made her way upstairs to her living quarters over the office, she found him exactly where she expected him to be: ensconced in her parlor, being entertained—or was the word fawned over?—by Mother Colleran, who made no move to rise from her comfortable tufted chair. She merely folded her hands complacently on her lap, and her gleaming black gaze shot back and forth from one to the other as she waited for Maggie to try to oust Reese from the apartment.

"I never did express my condolences," Reese said after a long moment of silence, during which Maggie had walked into her bedroom to take off her apron and then had returned to the parlor.

"I'm sure your loss equals mine," she said prosaically, but she saw her words made him uncomfortable, as if he hadn't considered that he had lost anything at all.

"You'll be happy to know," Mother Colleran broke in, "that Reese will be staying in Colville."

"How nice," Maggie murmured, and turned toward the kitchen area to pump up some water to wash her hands.

"With us," Mother Colleran added loudly, with just a touch of malice.

Maggie whirled. "No."

"My son is . . ."

". . . perfectly welcome to stay at the perfectly good

29

hotel in town," Maggie said, keeping her voice neutral and continuing into the kitchen.

"I will not turn my son out of my home," Mother Colleran called after her adamantly.

Maggie reappeared instantly. "It is *my* home, and Mr. Colleran is not welcome to stay here." She rested her stormy gray gaze on Reese Colleran, daring him to intervene, to countermand that decision. His face hardened perceptibly, dangerously; he was not accustomed to hearing refusals.

"I will not have the whole town saying you turned my son out," Mother Colleran contradicted shrilly, knowing exactly when to hammer home a point.

Maggie's ears pricked up. What if the old witch had deliberately arranged to have Reese come home this day of all days just to push her into a corner because she knew that Maggie was not proof against the town's opinion?

"How can you be so callous as to send him to a hotel when you know Frank's room is available? What would everyone say if Frank's only brother had to put up at the hotel for weeks—months, perhaps? As usual, you're not thinking of anything but your own comfort."

Yes, she thought, not even responding to this assault, what would everyone say about a young, attractive, and presumably unattached male living with *her?*

"Frank would turn in his grave at your rudeness and thoughtlessness," Mother Colleran went on, her voice rising slightly. She was getting to Maggie, she could see it in her stony expression, always a sure sign of Maggie's anger. "If Frank were alive," she concluded triumphantly, "he would have found room to accommodate Reese."

"Yes, as close as they were," Maggie muttered angrily, now truly backed into a corner. No one but Mother Colleran could have engineered such a situation and have expected Maggie to make the negative decision.

She was reveling in it, Maggie thought, because she knew exactly who was going to take the criticism for either decision, and that person was *not* her mother-in-law.

But what difference did it make to her, after all? She could sleep in the office if it came to that. Whatever Reese Colleran's purpose in coming to Colville, she did not have to be a part of it by choice. He would have to fight her every inch of the way—assuming that he and Madame Mother were, somehow, plotting against her. Perhaps, she thought with grim humor, it would be better to have him right underfoot where she could see at all times exactly what he was up to.

"Perhaps Mother Colleran has a point," she said grudgingly, and noted immediately that Reese's pale blue eyes glinted at this reluctant concession.

"Then I guess you've got me," he said in a faintly caressing drawl.

His presumption fired her anger. "*I* don't want you," she hissed, as much in reaction to having given in as the undercurrent of meaning in his words.

"But I predict you will," he said insinuatingly, and his goading words sent her into a spasm of rage that she fought to conceal from him and her mother-in-law. She turned away from them and slowly went back downstairs to the office, mindful as she did so that she had forgotten her apron and wouldn't be able to accomplish much anyway, dressed as she was.

Her feeling of contentment utterly evaporated. The room downstairs was noisy and crowded. Nominally, it was the place to be three days prior to the publication of the paper. Jean Vilroy was in the thick of it, taking and laying out advertisements right on the spot. A.J. was to one side, taking notes on something someone was saying.

"Miz Maggie—" A.J. motioned to her, and she moved quickly to his side. "This here is Dodd, ma'am, come right from the stage posting."

"Howdy, ma'am." Dodd was a small man, unremarkable and unnoticeable with his sandy hair, tanned complexion, and dusty clothes. He was someone's cowhand somewhere, Maggie surmised, and he picked up a quick two bits here and there by nosing around for information he thought A.J. might be able to use.

The news today she had already conjectured, but A.J.'s gloomy expression confirmed it. "They've come," she said, a statement of fact, neither bad news nor good.

"Stage just arrived up from Denver," Dodd elaborated. "There's three of 'em, and all the equipment, and they're stayin' by the hotel, ma'am; names are Bollar, MacNeil and Wayne, railroad men, by the look of 'em, with money to spend to get the job done."

"I see," she said neutrally. There wasn't anything to be said. She could not have stopped them with her words. There were land barons whose interest went beyond the good of the community; they would not be stopped.

Ironically, she was one of them, a fact that continually burdened her. For a signature on a piece of paper, she and all the rest of them could retire with untold wealth and do whatever they wanted to do. She could leave Colville; buy a house in the big city; travel; buy a husband, come to that, if she were in the market for one; buy a business; anything . . .

It pleased her instead to hold onto the Colleran land with two tight fists and an immovable stance about the coming of Denver North. The anomaly of it infuriated the Harold Danforths of the town, a fact that made her feel even more powerful.

In this matter, "what Frank would have wanted," which everyone, from her mother-in-law on down, tried to convince her *was* the northward linkage of the railroad line to Cheyenne, left her cold, and no one could understand why she wouldn't want to comply with what her deceased husband would have done had he been alive.

But she knew. Frank had bought the town, and everyone revered him and thought he had their best interests at heart, when actually Frank had had his own best interests centermost all the time. But who would have believed it?

"I expect that's that," A.J. said, his gentle voice interrupting her reverie.

"Maybe not. Arch Warfield was waiting at the station. I wonder what information he'll come back with."

"Now, now, Miz Maggie, if it ain't right, we'll fix it."

"'Ain't we always fixing it?" she asked tartly.

"He's all we got," A.J. reminded her.

"We've got me."

"Miz Maggie, you go on and fire us all and do the whole thing your own self, and I'll come visit you in Doc Shields' office in about two weeks' time."

"I wish we had . . . well, I wish I could go out and do it all," Maggie said wistfully. "All right. Enough. The survey team is here, and you can bet I'm going to survey the survey team. Is that your copy, A.J.? Why don't I rough it up before I start the page layouts, and then you can go check the express office. We'll close early, and the devil with the deadline."

She watched A.J. pay his informant and then begin the subtle overtures that would sweep the office clean of loiterers in a matter of moments.

He was so good at it. He couldn't write; he wasn't a reporter or a manager; he was just A.J., who knew how to handle people and get information. His value was unquestionable, and indefinable.

She took his page of notes and made her way to her worktable. She was most at home here, with a pencil in her hand and words at her command. She could always make words do what she wanted them to do. She wasn't nearly so facile with people. She was too blunt, too curious, too apt to ask for whatever she wanted. She didn't know how to circle around things or to pretend. She had never mastered the kind of comaraderie that made people beholden to her. But Frank, Frank had been very good at that.

He just hadn't been very good with her.

She shook away the thought. Not even a year could wash away the betrayals and disappointments. She had been sure she had buried all that with Frank.

A commotion behind her told her that Arch Warfield had just burst into the room. And wasn't Arch a prime example of Frank's ability to handle people? She couldn't manage Warfield and all his resentments, even after a year, the way that Frank had. Arch wouldn't let her fire him, and he stayed around and sulked. It was almost as if he believed Frank had not died and would walk in the door in the next moment. All his loyalty lay with the man who had hired him, and if he and Frank had had some secret agreement, she knew nothing about it. When Frank died, he had been free to leave, and still he remained, waiting, irritating her, handing her biased copy he knew she would immediately rewrite.

"There it is." His voice came from over her shoulder and simultaneously his hand thumped down his notes.

"There what is?"

"The lowdown on the survey team. Got everything you wanted, lady boss. Every detail, fairmindedly as possible, just the way you like it."

She slanted a look up at him. "How refreshing."

"Don't get smart, Maggie mine."

"I'll get even smarter, *Mr.* Warfield. I already have the report, down to the names and the room numbers at the hotel. You're late, and we paid less for the information

34

than we pay you, Mr. Warfield, and somehow I think we got a better deal on this one." She turned back to her papers. "I think that's all."

"*You* think that's all," Warfield sneered. "That ain't all, Mrs. High-and-Mighty-Frank, not by a long shot. You don't know nothing about what's going on with this Denver North project."

"And of course *you* do, Mr. Warfield. I've noticed how diligently you've been expending your efforts on behalf of the paper. Perhaps there are other interests that might be willing to pay your salary."

"Oh no, Maggie Colleran, you don't get rid of me. Frank promised me, wrote me out a contract—"

"Which no one has ever seen," Maggie put in, unperturbed by his vehemence. She had heard this story before and had provoked him in this very same way innumerable times, always with the same reaction.

"And I ain't leaving, Mistress Maggie, no matter what you say."

"The day may come," Maggie muttered, tired of his theatrics. The story never changed. The contract existed, and his blackmail rested solely with what the townspeople would think if Maggie fired him. They would believe in the contract, even without the evidence, and the fact that Frank had hired him. She had never heard of a more gullible herd of cows than the townspeople of Colville, she thought exasperatedly.

She felt the urge to let them reap the reward of their own stupidity. Who was she to be their keeper when they had the likes of Arch Warfield to show them the way? Damn, why couldn't he just leave?

He left. Somewhere in the midst of her vitriolic reflections, he skulked away. The office got emptied, the outside light waned, and a welcome quiet descended around her.

As Jean moved back to his desk to lay out the advertisements she heard A.J. leave through the front door on his way to the express office, the sound of Jean's pen as he worked, and the flick of a match as he lit a lamp.

He was not a talkative man, she thought, pausing for a moment in her furious rewriting. He was calm and temperate, spare and fastidious in his work and his person, as unlikely a person to find in a small town newspaper office as Frank Colleran had been, and as successful in his way as well.

His was a solid, reassuring presence, and he never left the office before she did. Of course he could not know that she did not wish to leave the office tonight to face her self-satisfied mother-in-law and her cocky brother-in-law.

She turned to tell him that she would be staying late, and her heart jumped into her throat.

Logan Ramsey was sitting at Jean's drawing board, one of Jean's pens in his long fingers, his face in shadow once again so she could not see his expression, and his lean body totally relaxed.

It was stunning to see him sitting there as casually as if she had seen him yesterday, when she had not seen him in so many months. Her composure totally deserted her.

She couldn't say a word, and neither did he for the space of several long, intense moments. Then she finally managed to push words out from her dry throat.

"Hello, Logan." That was fine and conventional and just what a widow of one year should say to an old friend. She put down her own pen for want of something to do until he spoke.

"Hello, Maggie."

She didn't expect to have such a reaction to his voice. A rush of galvanic heat spurted through her body and settled in a knot in her stomach. She couldn't think of another thing to say, and it confused her. It had to be because she had been thinking about him today, nothing else, and she was so glad to see him.

She *was* glad to see him. "You weren't at the church today." Her words sounded awkward, grasping at any topic to fill the silence between them.

"Did you think I would be?" There was a repressed violence in the question. "Did you honestly think that I, of all people, would want to memorialize your four years of hell with Frank?"

His vehemence shocked her, but even she had no cause to know that it was compounded not only of his utter hatred of Frank but also his knowledge of the fact that Reese Colleran had come to town.

"Perhaps you could have come merely to support me," she suggested, her tone faintly acid because of the wallop of disappointment his words sent right to her gut. "*I* had to go through it, damn it." She wheeled her chair away from him. "Is there anything else, Logan?"

"I thought there was," he said sardonically.

She swiveled around to face him. "That wasn't an apology, obviously."

"No, I won't apologize for that, Maggie. I'm sure you were surrounded by strong arms—and strong stomachs. I could even make a winning wager on who did attend."

"Fine. I leaned on Dennis and Sean Mapes instead. They liked Frank, but they like me more." She waited to see how that played with him, and she wondered why she was goading him like this.

"Who doesn't?" he said simply, and that infuriated her more.

"*Was* there something you were going to apologize for?" she asked sweetly, too sweetly, as something welled up inside her akin to a childish feeling of aggressiveness; she recognized it from a time long past in her life, and she clamped down on it violently, even while she remembered the exact moment she had first felt it. She had been with Sean and Logan both, and probably Annie at the

37

swimming hole. The boys—and they had been boys then, seventeen or eighteen maybe, had rigged a rope and had been having a high old time swinging out over the water and taunting her and Annie, who was a year or two older than she, that they were skittish girl cowards not to attempt to have the same fun. She wanted it desperately, that same male freedom to compete with rambunctious exuberance.

And she had done it, in spite of her skirts and the jeers of Logan and Sean and the fearful whining of Annie Mapes.

She had been all of eight, and she never forgot the sensation of the competition. She felt it now, and the tension between her and Logan strung out in the silence of the room. She reveled in it and did not know why.

"I don't believe I have anything to apologize for," Logan said slowly, his voice deepening with some other kind of emotion that had nothing to do with the surface conversation. "Except maybe one thing."

"Only *one?*" Maggie chided. "What could that be, I wonder?"

"Oh you damned fool, Maggie. I should have come after you a damn lot sooner," he said roughly as he abruptly stood up. "Well, I'm here now, Maggie, and nothing is going to stop me."

"Stop you from what?" she asked perversely, not liking the way he purposefully moved across toward her.

"Oh, I think you know, Maggie," he said, perching on the edge of her worktable.

But she didn't know. Who was she to predict his feelings or even be able to sort out her own? Already she felt too much was happening in one day.

"I've come for you, Maggie," he added quietly, when she didn't say anything. "And this time, I'm not going to let you get away."

Chapter Three

Surely she had not heard him right. "But I'm not planning to go anywhere," she said reasonably, with a contrary note in her voice that sounded reckless in her ears.

"Well, isn't that nice and convenient."

"For what?" Oh Lord, she had to control her unruly words.

"For this," and he leaned over and covered her treacherous mouth with his own, a move that was at once shocking and desired, as if it were culmination of some kind of battle she hadn't known she was fighting.

She felt his hand cup her cheek and an unfamiliar heat and voluptuous wetness suffuse her body. Oh yes, she remembered that, only not with Logan Ramsey, never a hint of it with him. His mouth was so gentle on hers, so insistent, trying her, tasting her, inviting her . . . to what? Very slowly, he pulled away from her, savoring the texture of her lips, sliding his hand down her cheek and along the firm line of her jaw.

The touch of his long fingers thrilled her. It had been so long . . . but then, that was an impossible thought, and if the loving kiss went any further it would trespass into something forbidden, something she did not want to pursue any further.

But she had been thinking about him so hard today, she couldn't bear to end the caress. It was part of his ability to sense when she needed him: she was willing to believe she had needed his kiss today and that he had come just as he always had done.

He said, "Five years ago I thought I had come to town to court you, Maggie. At the very moment Frank Colleran settled in Colville. He dazzled you and your father. I decided I wanted you a week too late, a month too late, I'll never know, Maggie, but I came too late. That's what I do know. And now you're out of mourning and I have a second chance and I swear by God this time I'm going to win you. I don't expect it to happen in a day, maybe not even a year, but I do expect it to happen—in spite of you, Maggie."

"No." The word, a reaction of pure fear, echoed like a gunshot in the room.

"Or don't you know what your kiss did to me and what it was doing to you," he persisted.

"I won't."

"Won't what, Maggie?"

Even she didn't know; she only sensed that she did not want anything to proceed beyond this point in this room with him. She couldn't lose him. She wanted him exactly the way he had always been, and it scared her that he wanted to be her lover. But she had had enough of that. *That* she did not need ever again.

"I'm very happy the way I am now," she said finally and with great difficulty. "And with the way we have always been."

"I don't believe it."

"Believe it. I don't need another husband and I surely don't want anything else. I like my life just the way it is, Logan."

"I don't like mine," he retorted grittily. "I need you,

and I have always needed you, and I won't give up."

"I won't give in."

"I lived in hell for the last five years, Maggie. I can wait."

His certainty was like a wall between them. Everything was changed now. He wanted something she could never give him, something she had never known.

"I wish you wouldn't."

He stood up and looked down at her. "No you don't."

"Logan—"

"Maggie—" He wanted to shake her for her stubbornness. But of course it was too soon. All he could focus on was the way the light reflected in her dark hair and the shadow of her thick lashes on her flushed cheek. The taste of her lips. The ache in him that had always always desired her.

"Maggie!"

Another voice, deep and vaguely familiar, called from above, and a moment later a well-dressed stranger appeared in the doorway from the inner hall. "Maggie, there you are. Mother . . . Hello . . ." he pulled up short as he caught sight of Logan. "I'm sorry."

"No need," Maggie said curtly. "This is Logan Ramsey, an old friend. Logan, this is Frank's brother, Reese."

Reese extended his hand and Logan took it warily. Reese didn't recognize him, he thought as they shook with a kind of taut cordiality. Reese dismissed him the moment they acknowledged each other and waited politely for him to leave.

He looked at Maggie and she nodded imperceptibly. As he took his hat, he reflected that his gut instinct had not failed him: he had come for Maggie not a moment too soon.

*   *   *

"I think we should get to know each other better, Maggie," Reese said without preliminaries, hoisting himself onto the very edge of the desk that Logan had vacated. "You look just like a skittery mare, for God's sake. I'm not going to eat you."

Maggie sent him a crooked little smile. He was so right. He wasn't going to do anything to her. She was just a little shaken by Logan's sudden reappearance.

"Yes, I think we should," she said easily, folding away the papers she had been working on and turning to look at him. "What do you suggest?"

"Mother suggests that she have dinner sent in and you and I go to the hotel."

"That's fine." Why not? It would be far easier to keep Reese at bay than Logan, who knew her better than she knew herself. "I'll just tidy up a little." Truth to tell, she did not need any tidying up anywhere but in her confused emotions. It would be almost restful to shift her attention to Reese, about whom she had no deep feeling other than a vague distrust. He might reveal something in a relaxed atmosphere over dinner. He might tell her more than he thought by a word or gesture during the course of the conversation.

Or else, she thought a little later as they were seated by the hotel hostess whom Maggie had known for many years, or else Reese Colleran was a very clever man, prepared to deal with her on a level that did not preclude deceit.

He was utterly charming, and that shocked her after her initial impression of him. He could discuss any subject at length, including his fabled whereabouts, which had been bemoaned by his mother all these years. He laughed off Frank's old imprecations and dismissed them as boyhood jealousy for a peripatetic life that Frank knew he could never emulate.

"Oh, he was always the serious one, Maggie; everyone

42

just knew he was going to do big business."

"It's rather amazing he wound up here then, don't you think?" she asked.

Reese shrugged. "Maybe he saw opportunities no one else did," he said lightly.

"Well, the town newspaper is not exactly the *San Francisco Daily Examiner.*"

Reese threw her a startled look. "It's curious you should say that," he said slowly. "You know of course we come from San Francisco, but I wonder if you know that before the war, Frank was engaged to marry the daughter of the scion of another newspaper dynasty. The *Herald* it was, but it folded just about the time Frank came west."

"I didn't know," Maggie said, keeping her voice neutral. Why should she have known? The Frank she knew had begun and ended in Colville. It was as if his personality had been invented the moment he set foot in Colville—she remembered it well—and bought the land where he built later that year the Colleran ranch.

She could even visualize the notice in the paper and remember the first time she had seen him, city slicker to the core, complete with neat dark suit, celluloid collar, and coordinated tie. He had come up from Denver, inoffensive and dynamic all at the same time, and everyone had been fooled by the clothes and the polite West Coast manners.

He was slicker than they knew, she thought, but she had known nothing of another woman in his life before he came to Colville. He never talked about it, although when Mother Colleran had come to live with them after their marriage, she became aware of faint hints that Frank could have had more, could have been more, hints she always ignored because it had been Frank's choice to come to Colville and Frank's decision to take over the reins of the Colville *Morning Call* after her father died.

And Frank's determination to exclude *her*, she thought

43

bitterly. What had he given up for that? What had he gained?

"Her name was Priscilla."

"He never talked about his life in San Francisco."

"He had one. Father struck gold, you know."

"No, I didn't know that."

"And bought businesses and struck more gold. In fact, he was Priscilla's father's rival; he was the one who took over the *Herald*, actually. You don't want to hear this."

"I do. I knew nothing of any of this. Of course, everyone knew Frank had money the way he bought up land when he first came to town. He never talked about anything to do with his life in San Francisco."

"Probably didn't want to remember it. The old man was always so disgusted with the both of us. It's probably why we both left. I went sooner."

"I see." She saw nothing. Frank left someone named Priscilla and a possible position in any of his father's businesses, not the least of which was an apparently prestigious newspaper, to come west, stake out a ranch, and run a small town newspaper whose circulation probably equaled the number on staff of the newspaper his father owned.

"The soup," Reese announced, with some degree of satisfaction in his voice.

The soup. She wasn't hungry, but she felt a little less wary of Reese because of his candid revelations. She picked up her spoon and lifted the fragrant hot liquid to her lips.

They ate in silence through the entrée, the usual hotel fare: a choice of beef, chicken, and lamb, with vegetables, gravies, fried potatoes, olives, relishes, and biscuits.

Over dessert, a creamy lemon custard, apple pie, and coffee, Reese said, "This dinner was really quite tolerable. You know Maggie, I wouldn't mind moving here if my presence at the flat really bothers you."

His sudden offer disarmed her. Wouldn't it be easy if she were the one to make the decision. And what did he hope to gain by making the offer? His expression was open, all good natured and full of good humor, as though there were a conspiracy between them now to shut out his mother.

He was really very likable, she thought, even as she shook her head. "No, that's between you and your mother, Reese. I'm afraid I'm going to be very busy in the coming weeks and it really makes no difference to me."

"I wish it did," Reese said regretfully.

"But I have no time for anything else except the newspaper now," Maggie responded, smiling to soften the harshness of her words. He wasn't intimating anything more personal than this anyway, she told herself. She wondered if she had the backbone to ask him exactly what he planned to do in Colville, since he seemed to be settling in so completely. "It's all I ever wanted to do," she added wistfully, more to herself than him, but he heard, and it told him volumes about her.

"And what keeps you so busy on the paper?" he asked offhandedly, even though he knew: his mother had told him every last detail.

"Everything," she said simply.

"Indispensible Maggie," he said with a heartwarming little grin. "No help at all?"

"Are you looking for a job?"

"It's not a bad idea. . . ."

"Well, it might be except that I'm really as fully staffed as I can afford to be right now. We have A.J. and Jean Vilroy, our job printer and artist, and Arch Warfield, our star reporter. And me. I edit and set type. I did it for my father and I never got it out of my system. A.J. handles everything else, and Jean does layouts and wedding announcements. I buy preprinted advertising supplements and newsprint from Denver, and we do four pages of local news on a two-part fold. The whole town subscribes, we have a couple of the older men delivering papers on a route that goes down to Denver, and we send out some weeklies by mail to surrounding communities. It's hardly a business or a life that could make you rich, Reese. I never did understand Frank's ardor, given his background. But I grew up here; I was practically raised in the newsroom by my father after my mother died and father had made a disaster out of a ranching venture. After that, we moved back to town and he bought into the paper. That's all I ever knew.

"But Frank—and you—your father must have groomed you to run an empire if what you tell me about him is true. And yet both of you wound up in Colville." She didn't finish the thought. It sounded nonsensical even as the words formed in her mind.

"I came to see Mother, of course," he said instantly, filling the space where she would have said the words. It made sense too, except that she knew what Mother Colleran had said: he had been sent for, and he might never have come of his own volition.

She let it pass, however. There was time enough to find out the hidden truths they were all concealing. She didn't have the energy for it tonight.

"Of course," she agreed quickly. "Well then, you must spend as much time with her as possible."

"I hope," he said guilessly, "to spend some time with you as well."

"We are spending time right now, and very delightful time, too, I might add. I don't know when I have felt more relaxed." Actually she felt nerveless, tired, drained. But he was neither bad nor so arrogant as she had thought initially. His smile was warm. It encompassed her as he toasted her with his coffee cup and said,

"Imagine if I had never come to visit Mother."

"But you would have, one time or another."

He didn't allow her to distract him. "I might never have met you, Maggie. And I think that would have been a damned shame."

"Nice to meet you, too." What else could she say? She had just spent two hours with him and she knew just as little about him as when she had sat down. No, she knew he could be charming and forthcoming to some extent. She felt less leery of him, but no less suspicious of his reasons for obeying his mother's summons. And she knew she could like him, every bit as much as she had liked Frank initially, and it scared her that she was that susceptible to both men of the Colleran family.

"Maggie . . ."

The odd note in his voice pulled her from her introspection. Her head tilted slightly as she looked up at him, and he noticed for the first time how really flawless her features were. Every angle flattered her, every component of her face finely modeled and in perfect alignment with every other feature. And when she smiled, her smile reached all the way to her unusual gray eyes. Her smile was perfection too.

He almost forgot what he was going to say, so struck was he by her unexpected beauty, a beauty that warred with the descriptions his mother had given him. He shook himself mentally and met her smile eagerly.

"Let's be friends, Maggie."

Her expression clouded for a moment. It was such a strange thing for him to say. "Of course we're friends," she said, and stretched her hand across the table. There was something about him, a vulnerability, perhaps, she didn't know. He was very likable, and he took her hand in a strong hard grip and squeezed it. The arrogance was gone altogether, and in its place was the same boyish appeal that had drawn her to Frank. But as he paid their bill and helped her out of her chair, she didn't stop to wonder what depth of flaws it hid. She ignored the issue completely as he escorted her back to the *Morning Call* offices, ignored the internal warning gong that sounded deep in her consciousness.

She was up early after a restless night grappling with all the surprises of the day before. Coffee, which she prepared on the office stove, calmed her, and as she listed the day's chores she felt more in control, more able to cope as long as she could take action. Everything else she shunted aside, because there was no point in worrying about things she couldn't change.

A.J. came in an hour later, carrying the brown-wrapped bundle of readyprint. "Think we've got enough advertising this week to add another page, Maggie. And Lord knows, Danforth's article will eat up a half page itself."

"Oh Lord, really? All right. Let me see what you've done with Warfield's copy."

He dropped the newsprint in the printing room and came back with a cup of coffee. "Here." He tossed her some pages and she scanned them quickly.

"All right. If he must have his say, he must."

"And he must, Miz Maggie. I do think Mr. Coutts settled it in the best way possible."

"I did not libel him. I never mentioned names."

"There's some as don't understand why you're quite so het up about the railroad coming anyway, Miz Maggie," he said, settling in opposite her. "Fact is, I heard an interesting new speculation yesterday."

"Really? And what would that be?"

"Well, there's folks that say you're raising all this opposition to drive up the price they'll offer on the land, seeing as how you stand to make out real well if you decide to sell."

"Oh, A.J.!" She was appalled. "*Who* said that?"

"Rumor said it, Miz Maggie; I wouldn't necessarily be attributing it to the one I heard it from."

"No, of course not." She bent her head for a long moment. This was really too much. Her resistance was a puny thing, if the reaction of Harold Danforth was anything to go by. It hardly counted for anything. No one was scared of Maggie Colleran. Offended, perhaps. Angered, most likely. But not scared. Nor did she command a particle of the influence Frank could have exerted were he alive and actively opposed to the encroaching trunk line.

She sighed. "Well, let's see. The survey team will probably be out this morning; they'll start just below Colville, to the point where they've already acquired land—Danforth land, right, A.J.? I wonder if I should . . ."

"Now, Miz Maggie . . ."

"Well, *someone* should. Just see what they're doing and where."

"You scared they're going to go across Colleran land?"

"I'm scared for all of us up along the basin. It's me and the Mapeses and Logan. As far as I know, Annie and Sean are holding on tight, but the ranch is a family business, and if either of them leaves or gets married, it's gone. I wonder if Denver North can wait that long."

"Oh, them big companies got a lot of resources we don't know anything about," A.J. said comfortably, but his words sent a chill through her.

"Especially money," Maggie added sarcastically. "Can't fight that money. Lord, I wish . . ."

"Now, Miz Maggie, we got work to do."

"I know. But I can't send Arch. I just can't. And I have to know, damn it. I think . . . A.J., I think I'm going to drive out there anyway."

"Oh, Miz Maggie, now you can't go gallivanting, you have to do the editorial today."

49

"I don't have to *do* anything," Maggie retorted. "I'm the boss, remember."

"No, ma'am. Everybody thinks I'm the boss."

"Nonsense. It's an open secret, A.J."

"I'll go."

"And what will you look for, A.J.? You know about boundaries and water holes and downed fences, covenants and titles?"

"Only in the Bible," he admitted with a trace of humor.

"So, you see . . ."

"Miz Maggie, I just reckon you ought not to go riding out there alone, given how high tempers are running about this whole thing."

"Are you suggesting that I wouldn't be welcome— alone—anywhere I chose to go, A.J.?"

"Oh no, ma'am, I wouldn't think of it," A.J. said, thunking his coffee cup down on her worktable as he got to his feet. "Though maybe Mr. Frank's brother might be available to escort you out this morning, Miz Maggie."

Maggie stared at him as he picked up his cup and ambled into the back room. "Humph," she muttered. "Mr. Frank's brother, indeed . . ."

"In word and deed, Maggie." A moment later, as if she had conjured him up by her mere thoughts, Reese appeared in the doorway, dressed to the teeth, a cracked coffee cup from the supply in the back room steaming in his hand.

No more coffee, she thought. "Good morning, Reese. How did you sleep?"

"Fitfully. Frank wasn't in love with comfortable beds."

"Oh, he had a bit of the martyr in him. Besides," she added cryptically, "he spent very little time there."

He let the comment pass, storing it for a time in the

future when he would be powerful enough to make Maggie reveal all her secrets.

She was really something so early in the morning. She wore practical calico in a dark blue pattern, unhooped, without a bustle, the kind of dress that wore dirt very well: the dust of a bustling small town main street, the invariable spot of ink that coated her fingers and sometimes her clothing, the printing inks that smeared generously over the thick leather apron that she wore to protect her clothes. But she wasn't wearing the apron now, and the slightly larger-than-fashionable buttons that fastened the bodice of her dress strained across the unexpectedly sensual dip between her breasts, which were accentuated by the tight fit of the dress. Her black hair was braided as usual, and curling strands that had not caught in the fastener tumbled around her cheeks. Even in the strong first light of day, she was as beautiful as she had seemed last night, more so, because he could see the creamy texture of her skin and the smooth firm line of her lips. Her eyes were bright and clear, and as she turned to hand something to A.J., he had a superb view of her straight, perfect profile.

All she needed, he thought, were the right clothes and the right surroundings. She would be a sensation in San Francisco society.

He could see why Frank had been taken with her. In the face of all that radiance, he would never have considered anything but her loveliness. He must have been shocked out of his wits when he discovered she was intelligent too.

"Tell me what Mr. Frank's brother can do for you today, Maggie."

So he had heard her. She slanted a look up at him. "Keep your mother busy and out of my business, if you please." She had hoped to startle him with her rudeness, but he took her comment with an equanimity that suggested he was well aware of his mother's propensity to be dictatorial.

Downright interfering, in fact.

"Mother is busy with church things this morning, Maggie. I really am at your disposal if you need me."

"Your mother? Church? Oh no, she doesn't go to church. Don't tell me she pulled the wool over your eyes."

"Maggie, you're trying to distract me."

"Yes, because you were eavesdropping and I don't like it."

"I promise never to do it again." He smiled at her winningly. "I thought we came to an understanding last night, Maggie."

"Really? I don't believe it included your poking your nose into my business as well."

He sloughed off this candor. "But I'm here; you must let me help you when I can."

He was so sincere. Her eyes swept over him assessingly. How much did he mean? How much like Frank was he after all? Her sleepless night was testament to her confusion. In the cold light of morning she still wasn't sure. But he met her gaze squarely, hiding nothing. His expression was concerned, soft; the lines around his eyes crinkled as he smiled ruefully.

"You don't trust me," he said, absolutely sure that this plain speaking would elicit the denial he wanted.

"Maybe I don't," she responded. He was surprised by her candor and her refusal to be backed into a corner.

"Tell me what I can do."

"I will," A.J. said, ambling back into the room. "You can take Miz Maggie out to the survey site so she can assure herself that the team isn't encroaching on her property or anyone else's up at the basin."

"No one is going to 'take' me anywhere," Maggie contradicted firmly, getting up from her worktable and sending A.J. a warning look. "I will go. By myself."

"Perhaps a friend might accompany you," Reese suggested, carefully choosing his words.

She relented. "Perhaps . . . a friend . . . might." She threw down her pen. "You win, A.J., but just this time, and only because Danforth's article is coming out this weekend."

"Yes, Miz Maggie," he said meekly.

"Tell Jean I'll be back by noon," she added from the hallway as she reached into the under-stairs closet for her well-worn cloak. "Come, Reese; let me show you the countryside in and around Colville."

What he saw was land, acres and acres of land, some of it free range, especially the farther away they traveled from town. Most of it was fenced in, claimed and now owned by a generation of first-comers who had ventured into the wilderness, or bought by the enterprising speculator who saw beyond the moment and the desolation.

The land was thick with forestation and creased by rutty roads that veered off in all directions. They followed one that led past several neat ranch houses that were visible from the road, and headed north toward Gully Basin, a small lake that was the point of the triangular meeting of the boundaries of the Colleran and Mapes acreages.

"Frank snapped it up before Sean could blink," Maggie said reflectively as they jounced down the dirt track that led to the rough clapboard cabin that was euphemistically called the Colleran ranch. "He should have had first shot at it. We spent our first year here, Frank and I," she added as the house, a rectangular cabin that could not have been more than one room deep, came into view.

"Appalling," Reese murmured, pulling on the reins to slow the pace of their wagon. But he saw immediately what Maggie could not have known: Frank wanted the land and, for some reason, Maggie herself, and with his usual cunning, he had gotten both.

"Oh, I don't know. We had a spirit of adventure when we first moved in. You can see—it's quite obvious— there is only one room, one side with the bedstead and the other with the stove and a table and some chairs. Quite luxurious by pioneering standards, of course. *They* had dirt floors and sod roofs and an open fireplace only if they were lucky and there were stones enough to build one."

"What did you do? What did Frank do?" Reese could not even envision it, given what he knew Frank had been used to. And yet he had done it.

"We ran cattle. Or we tried to. I will say Frank had thought I ought to be in the kitchen churning butter all the time, and I was adamant about riding with the herd. But we made out. After, when he died, Sean Mapes or Logan Ramsey took what was left to winter pasture and to market. I think there's still a few dozen head of calves between them. I did love riding out," she added pensively, "almost as much as I love working at the paper."

The morning was bright with a sun that picked out every wart and crevice on the surface of the walls of the rude house. Reese couldn't get over it. Frank *here,* and Maggie!

"This land," she went on, "is geographically dead in the middle of the course that Denver North wants to lay up to Cheyenne. Now, they didn't buy near town except for what they needed to build the station, but this beyond

54

here is all free range, where drovers winter over on the way to Cheyenne. They've bought the rights to lay track there. But they'll have to go wide around Gully Basin if the three families here won't sell up, and Sean and Logan aren't about to because they're still running cattle on the land."

"And the money is no inducement?" Reese asked curiously. He couldn't understand her; the ranch and the acreage were useless to her unless she intended to ranch, and it didn't in the least look like she cared about that.

"I'll tell you what is no inducement," she said suddenly, passionately. "Cheap housing for the track workers, camp kitchens that could burn down the forest, cheap entertainments that will set up shop in town and bring in gamblers and prostitutes . . ."

"And money—"

"And upset the balance of things. The people coming in won't be builders, they'll be transients. They'll take the money all right, and maybe they'll become indebted to the corporation or some gaming house, or they'll get someone in deep trouble and they'll just walk out and leave the town with the problems. They won't care about options and freedom, just about the money, how much stake they can get from day to day until they can make it big anywhere from here to Cheyenne. And this town will have to clean up the mess. But the progress will look great in the company's report to the Denver North shareholders, and they won't have to be accountable to anyone, least of all to the towns along the way that they wreck."

Her passion silenced him. Maybe this was what Frank had seen in her, but everything she said smacked of the kind of meddling Frank never would have tolerated.

"I grew up here," she added after a while as they sat staring at the Colleran ranch house. "I'll still be here when Denver North has gone."

She stopped abruptly as she listened to the bitterness in her words. She was saying too much and he was too skillful a listener. She bit her lip. It was so easy to sermonize when the fact remained that the town of Colville stood to gain enormously from the presence of the line north. No one, except she and perhaps Sean and Logan ever saw past that, and everyone always raised the exact same point as Reese: money.

It always came down to money and who stood to gain most and the hell with the consequences. It was Harold Danforth and his cronies' attitude, and it was so blatantly self-serving that it was painful.

"Well," she said finally, "now you've seen the homestead. It's time to rout out those railroad men."

With some difficulty, Reese turned the team around and the wagon bounced back to the road. From there Maggie directed him east, toward the most likely place the team might be.

"It's so beautiful here," she murmured at one point. And then again, after another three quarters of an hour: "This is Ramsey land now, and that adjoins leased acreage and the Danforth property." She kept her eyes resolutely on the road, praying they wouldn't see Logan. She felt ill-prepared to deal with him at the moment.

The sun was behind them now, warming her back and her chilled thoughts. Beside her, Reese was silent, companionable, making no judgments and asking no further questions.

She didn't think it odd, either. Reese had been in town a day and had learned her side first. No doubt he'd hear the rest in the course of the next several days, at the hotel restaurant or around the stove at Bodey's store or over the front desk at the *Morning Call* if he stayed in town long enough.

"I suppose now," she said at length, "it could be said

we're trespassing. This used to be Danforth land." She pointed to a turn in the road. "They may be down there."

Reese marveled. She knew her town and her territory like no one else. They could just see the big white tent and men moving around as they approached—and someone else.

"Damn, that looks like that Ramsey fella," Reese growled.

"Yes it is," Maggie said, her voice neutral and her heart filled with a sudden shot of resentment. What *was* he doing here, at this hour, and why did she feel as if his presence here took something away from her?

Reese drew the wagon up beside him, looking for all the world as if he would have liked to trample him. Logan came to Maggie.

"Mornin', Maggie. They've set up shop here already."

"So I see. You remember Reese?" Maggie asked pointedly.

"So I do," Logan said laconically, but he kept his sky-blue gaze on Maggie. "They've plotted out a way to get around the basin, Maggie; I just went over it with them."

"Sounds like you ought to hire this go-getter as a reporter," Reese said ungraciously. He was just a little suspicious of Logan's appearance on the scene so early, a little wary of how much information he had already acquired.

"Oh no, not me. I'm just a range-roving cowboy." A faint smile quirked across his lips. "Want to come see, Maggie?"

"Sure, lead the way."

"No, this is not accessible by wagon. We have to ride. I'll take you up, and when we're done, I'll take you back to town."

Maggie looked into his eyes. She had known him forever and had always felt secure with him. And yet, for that moment she hesitated, hesitated because of what he

57

had said, because of his kiss, because she would have to abandon Reese. But the lure of seeing the course was greater than any of her concerns, and she turned regretfully to Reese. "I'm going to do that."

"If you must," Reese muttered. Then, jacking himself up to appear enthusiastic, he added, "Of course you must. I can find my way back. It was a pretty direct route."

"Right, just back along the track here and onto the road in the opposite direction. Take the turnoff to Colville; it's clearly marked."

"He'll be all right," Logan said. Swinging himself onto his big white stallion, he leaned over to give Maggie his hand, and hoisted her easily onto the saddle in front of him.

She mounted, Reese thought enviously, as though she had done it a hundred times just like that, with him.

But he couldn't know the hundreds of little darting feelings that assaulted her as she sat before Logan on horseback for the first time in ten years.

Everything was different now, she thought, as they waited for Reese to turn the wagon and head off in the other direction.

"I do have you exactly where I want you," Logan murmured in her ear, confirming her dread.

"I don't know what you're talking about," she said primly.

"You could have at least asked where."

"Nonsense, I know where I am. Logan, stop talking in riddles and let's get started."

"Oh, sweetheart, would I ever love to get started with you."

"I think if you say one more word in this vein, Logan Ramsey, I will get off this horse and *walk* back to town."

"Yes, ma'am," Logan said meekly, hiding the smile he knew she could not see.

But she could hear it in his voice, and there was a sweetness in her in response to it that she hadn't expected to feel. No, she hadn't expected to feel anything: this was Logan, her childhood friend, dependable and secure.

This was not a *man* in whom she was interested, and yet, and yet . . . she was insanely aware of the long length of his torso behind her, solid as a rock. And of his words, what he had said, what he meant. His arms around her now, where no man's arms had been for the past two years or more.

"It sure is tough going here," Logan said. "Hang on." She wasn't sure if he were talking about her or the rocky range they were about to travel, but his hands tightened on the reins and around her and she leaned back against him almost involuntarily as his horse began a descent.

When they hit level ground again he loosened his grip and one arm moved slowly from her waist upward to hold her shoulders. Or was it her imagination that his forearm brushed against her breasts? He held her so tightly she couldn't be sure what he had done, and the heat of his body and the iron bar of his arm around her were like living things—pulsating with a life she was responding to in spite of herself.

This was crazy. Five words in the heat of a grueling day were going to change her life forever; she could never perceive Logan the same way again. "I'm going to win you . . . ," he had said, and now somehow, he had maneuvered her into his arms and for one moment she doubted that he even had anything legitimate to show her.

"They'll be clearing out through here after they grade that little hill, and they plan to go around the basin and through Big Gully. Did you know?"

"No, I didn't." Instantly she felt ashamed of herself for doubting him.

59

"It may not work out, of course, but this is the way for now." He nosed the horse through the back brush and along the free range that skirted his acreage. "They'll have to add a hundred miles of track to the route; it's the least direct—but you know that. I'm a little worried about how desperate the corporation feels about spending that money."

"We all should be," she said sourly. It wasn't a pretty route either. There were odd hillocks and drops, and forests that would require a lumber crew to come in to clear it away.

"If they go through Big Gully," Logan said, his voice close to her ear, "they'll be beyond the far hundred by five miles."

"But who is to say it still won't affect the grazing fields?" Maggie commented, keeping her eyes resolutely ahead. She felt like she was going crazy. She had felt the faintest flick of his tongue against her ear.

"Yes," he murmured, and his lips pressed ever so gently against her lobe. She pretended she did not feel a little jolt of incandescent sensation. "You're right." He reined in the horse as they passed into a copse of bushes. "Maggie . . ."

"Are they going to cut through here?" she asked doggedly, resisting the demand of the hand that had cupped her chin.

"Lean against me, Maggie."

"No, I don't want this." She knew she didn't want it, and she knew if she leaned against him she would feel the thrust of his desire, which had been nudging her for the past fifteen minutes. She wanted none of that . . . she thought . . . but his tongue tugged teasingly at her earlobe, and his insistent hand moved her mouth closer to his, and closer . . .

"Just a kiss, Maggie," he whispered, "let me taste you," as his tongue sought her lips, just to lick them, and thrust at the moment she least expected into the warm honey of her mouth again.

She wasn't prepared for him, for anything. Not Logan, not another man, not her hunger, nor her eager surrender to his forceful invasion of her mouth. Or his arms enfolding her in a way that rubbed against her breasts and cupped them, until his fingers found her hardening nipples with unerring accuracy even under the layers of material.

She held his hands and he held her captive with his kiss and his caress. Her body flooded with feminine heat, her mouth could not get enough of him. He was the first man to release this volcanic yearning in her.

Just when she thought that his stroking her nipples and his exploring, stroking tongue, would bring her to completion, she felt him pull away gently but abruptly. His hands slid down and away from her breasts to take the reins again.

She made a small sound in her throat.

"I love your kisses, Maggie," he murmured.

Not enough, she thought violently. Her whole body was stiff with arousal and she did not know what to do. She felt frantic and scared and tense with unfulfilled desire. And *he* wanted to talk!

"I dreamt of your kisses for five long, barren years, Maggie."

"I'm here now."

"But I want more than your kisses."

I want more too, she thought, but she couldn't say it. Her body was cooling down now, and she was utterly dismayed at what she was feeling, and what he had made her want.

"Logan, don't . . ."

"But I'm going to. I made you come alive, Maggie, for the first time in years. Who else do you think could do that?"

61

Anybody, she thought grimly. Any damned body, because she was more desperate and more greedy than even Frank had accused her of being. He had had a word for it, and she wasn't sure, at this moment when she felt like devouring Logan's mouth and stripping off her clothes to let him feel her naked body, she wasn't sure that Frank hadn't been absolutely right.

Chapter Four

They rode quietly back to town. Logan knew just when not to press a point and just when to keep silent. He knew, she thought trenchantly, exactly what she was feeling and what she was thinking. If it wasn't a surprise to him, it had been a catastrophic revelation to her.

He even knew where to put his hands so as not to touch her again, and that annoyed her most of all. His body was like a wall behind her, solid, with no feeling. There might never have been the intimacy between them. He knew just how to handle it and she did not.

No one gave them a second glance as Logan drew up in front of the *Morning Call* building, but Maggie had the distinct feeling her mother-in-law was at an upstairs window, spying on her. She couldn't wait to remove herself from the erotic heat of his body. She swung herself down from the saddle before Logan could lift a hand to help her, and turned a defiant face to him.

He spoke before she could think of what to say. "I'm coming for you now, Maggie. No one is going to get in my way."

She bridled. "I hope you don't think I'm just going to stand still and wait," she said tartly, swallowing her anger and the words that bubbled up in her throat. She was furious with herself and with him. Everything was changed now. Everything. Against her wishes, but not against her treacherous body, he had moved their friendship into a realm that went beyond anything she had felt with Frank. And she was angry that she had responded to him so flagrantly, scared that her hunger would scare him.

"Oh no," he murmured, looking at her as if he had never seen her before, "I expect you to run as far and as fast as you can, Maggie. I promise you won't get far."

"Maybe you won't," she retorted, and he smiled a wicked little smile that set her hackles up like nothing else he had done so far. She wheeled away before she could find words to counter his smug male assertion.

She stared after him, fuming, for at least five minutes. She didn't know this Logan Ramsey, she thought. Or she had never been aware of him while he had been lurking there all along, masquerading as her friend and wanting the same thing that all men want.

That was a laugh. Perhaps the truth was that Maggie Colleran's little devil had been lurking there all along, wanting the same thing that all *women* wanted.

Except, she didn't want it—not another marriage, another man in her life to tell her what to do and when to do it. No, she could do without that all right. She had had enough of that with Frank. The truth was that Maggie Colleran wanted the same thing that men wanted. What was unpalatable was just how much, and just how easily she could be aroused to reach for it.

A.J. met her at the door. "Oh, Miz Maggie, Harold Danforth is here, checking his article and having a fit."

She froze. "Send for Dennis; I can't negotiate with him. He'll deny he said any of it if I start arguing with him. But he can't get around my lawyer."

Here was the last thing she needed, but as she made her way to the back of the office, she saw that Danforth had indeed settled in at her worktable and was furiously scribbling away.

She sighed and said, "Harold."

He looked up, his square pudgy face compressed into one round frown. "Oh, there you are, Maggie. This is all wrong. All wrong."

She crossed her arms and leaned back against her desk. "I believe you and Dennis Coutts agreed on the terms and the wording. And I agreed to print whatever you wrote. I haven't reneged on *my* part of the agreement, Harold. But I see you are doing a fair job of pulling back on yours."

"No, no. Just a clarification. You didn't change anything?" he demanded suspiciously.

"You had a written copy to compare, Harold. *I* don't go back on my word. That's not . . ." she died a little as she said it, "how Frank operated this newspaper. Or me."

She stared him down, thinking he looked like nothing so much as a stuffed pig with his starched collar and bulging jowls. His suit was a size too tight, but he never would admit that he carried extra weight. The word was, he still rode out with his men, pretending to be the cowboy he never was. All he was, she thought, was lucky. He had bought some land in the right place and now it was the right time to sell up, take the money and run.

"All right, Harold," she said briskly. "Take your problems, if they are real, to Dennis. He will contact me if I need to do anything. I trust," she added ominously, "that I won't. What you don't have is the right to come in here and take over my office whenever you please. Excuse me now."

Reluctantly he gave over her chair, and in a huff, snatched up the paper on which he had been writing and made for the door. "This isn't the end of it, Maggie Colleran. Frank would have sold up, you know. He would have come in with the rest of us and allowed Denver

65

North up through the basin. They're threatening to scale down the payments now because they have to lay more track and grade down the land. You'll be sorry, Maggie. . . ." His words drifted back from the door, and she sank into her chair and put her head in her hands.

He was so right, she thought. It would be far easier to sell or even lease a right of way than to hold out the way she was. She would have money to invest in the paper or to buy herself a new dress or to do any of a hundred other things . . . including sending her mother-in-law to perdition. But why, first and foremost, a new dress?

She didn't like the way her thoughts were heading. She didn't like anything about this day so far. She felt as though five different people had invaded her privacy and she wanted none of them there. She hated herself for invoking Frank's name. Maybe she was distressed the most about that. It was too easy, and she was too prone to do it. And then, *they* wouldn't let him die. They wanted his spirit, still alive, to walk among them.

Damn him.

She had never been able to make *him* do what she wanted.

She wondered who, after all this time, she was really fighting.

What she loved to do most was spiking type, and late Friday afternoon, when the sun streamed heavily in the back room windows, she sat at her type boxes, printer's sticks in hand, and picked and laid the type one letter at a time, one line at a time, according to the layout. The office was closed. A.J. was at the books. Jean was laying out typefaces for the headlines. They worked quietly and well together, with a minimum of comment.

It occurred to her, in an edgy kind of way, that she and Jean had done this very chore every Friday afternoon for a year since Frank's death, and yet this was the first time she was aware of him as a man, the first time she wondered about his emotions in more than an abstract way.

He did everything with a thorough, graceful efficiency that was almost unobtrusive. His calm expression gave away nothing of what he was thinking. Nothing. And she had never thought to ask.

He stood beside her, tall and lean, pulling type, hardly ever saying a word, his practicality and common sense like a crutch to her, strong and stalwart, to be leaned on whenever she was in need. But what about him? What did he need? How did he make do? And what if, in the foreseeable future, he should want to leave Colville— leave *her*?

She felt a moment's pure terror sweep over her at how fragile the relationships were between her and Jean, and her and A.J.

And all because Logan Ramsey had kissed her.

She shook herself mentally. She was thinking utter nonsense. A.J. and Jean had stayed because they wanted to be in Colville, nothing more and nothing less. She was their boss. She didn't need to know motives and life histories to employ a man, she only needed to know he could do his job well, as well as she did hers. It was as simple as that. Nothing would interfere with that and the paper would go on as it always had, and if one of them left her, she would find someone to replace him.

But still—Jean was not bound to her with a contract. He was young, vibrant, talented. He could pick up and go at a moment's notice. Why hadn't he?

He slanted a look at her as he sensed her eyes on him, and she turned her head away abruptly. "You'll have to set the Danforth letter, Jean," she said brusquely, reaching for a well-used cloth that was smeared with a thousand wipings of her ink-stained fingers. "I do not have the stomach."

"As you wish," he said noncommittally, sliding onto her high stool as she moved across the room to examine and proof the first plates she had spiked.

"I'm tired of this railroad business," she said suddenly, and she realized she was. Her puny protestations made no dent in the progress of things. Life would go on after Denver North passed through.

"It will soon be over," Jean said comfortingly.

"No! What no one understands is, once they come through, it will never be over. Still . . ." She reversed several pieces of type on one long line, "everyone wants the bounty the railroad will bring."

"Except Maggie."

His stark comment startled her; she couldn't tell if he were being sarcastic or if he agreed with her. She darted a look at him and was surprised to see his whole body turned toward her in a posture she could not define. In another moment, he had swiveled around again to focus on his work, and she thought she had dreamed the anger she saw in him, and—impossibly—the desire.

They pulled the first issues of the paper late that night and on into the morning, until the first two hundred bifold pages were stacked, ready for distribution.

There was nothing that made this week different than any other, Maggie thought as she wearily climbed into bed, except that Reese Colleran slept in a bedroom down the hall from hers and two men whom she had considered friends suddenly wanted to be more. Nothing different.

Or was she different? Had she somehow changed with Frank's passing and a year's solitude?

On the surface nothing was different that morning either. Mother Colleran carped as usual as she made her way downstairs to let in the delivery crew. Maggie hadn't slept much, nor had she come to any conclusions while she tossed and turned. The whole day had been an aberration, something out of context, never to be repeated again because she had imagined the whole.

But she wasn't imagining the tall bulk of Logan Ramsey's body relaxing against the doorframe, waiting for her as if he had always been waiting for her.

Instantly she felt closed in, surrounded. His appearance made things complicated and lent credence to the things he had said, the things she didn't want to know.

There was only one way to handle that: she would have to keep as far away as possible from him so she didn't have to listen to his words or feel what he could make her feel.

"What do *you* want?" she asked briskly as she swept into the room and past him without looking at him.

"I won't say the obvious thing," he drawled, amused by her testy tone.

"Good." She knelt beside A.J., who was counting out and bundling papers on the floor, and took the first bundle up into her arms. "I'll take this over to Bodey's store."

Two male voices said simultaneously, "I'll help," and she looked up, startled, to see Reese standing in the stairwell door, and Logan's grim expression.

"Let's hire these ole boys on," A.J. said, heaving a bundle up into Reese's arms. "These can go by the express office and the stage stop if you don't mind. These to the hotel, Logan—" Another packet flew through the air toward Ramsey, "and I thank you kindly, gentlemen."

"Just a range-rovin' cowboy," Maggie murmured as Logan passed her as she held the door open for him and Reese.

"Nothing more, nothing less," he agreed, as he waited

for her to fall into step beside him. "But a man of many talents nonetheless. Don't you agree, Maggie?"

"You roped in a bundle of newspapers at ten paces. I'm mighty impressed," Maggie said lightly, utterly avoiding the question and wondering what passersby thought of the odd triumverate making its way down the plankboard walk. She felt like she was enclosed in a parenthesis. This early in the morning few stores were open except Arwin Bodey's general store and the hotel, which kept round-the-clock hours.

"Ah, Arwin," she said gratefully, hailing him as he poked his head out the door. "Reese, you can just dump those by the express office door. Someone will pick them up in about an hour. Logan, those go to the hotel desk, please. Excuse me, gentlemen," and she left them both standing nonplussed outside Bodey's door.

"Oh, Maggie, come on in and tell me all the news," Arwin said comfortably as she plunked her bundle down on his well-worn counter.

"The usual," she said noncommittally as she watched them slice through the cord with his pocket knife.

"Beg your pardon, Maggie, but isn't this issue Harold Danforth's moment in the sun?"

"Oh that, I believe so. Except I know there's a lot of people who agree with him, Arwin, and there's nothing I can say that will sway them."

"You're right. The really big news will be when you decide to sell up," Arwin said, scanning the tightly printed front page. "So, what can I do for you this morning, Maggie?"

"Mother Colleran has prepared her usual list, so I'd appreciate delivery on those items later on today. We'll need a sack of coffee for the office, and I guess that will do it." She handed Arwin the list, and thought again how much she liked him. He was kind, straightforward, and personable without being invasive. Except this morning.

"Hear tell Mother Colleran and you have a visitor," he said idly as he turned the page to read Danforth's letter.

She stiffened. "Then of course you've heard tell who it is."

"Staying with you and Mother Colleran?" Arwin pursued, rubbing his chin and staring at the printed page.

"If that's what you've heard."

"Now, Maggie . . ."

"Whose business is it?"

"But it's Frank's *brother*," Arwin said reasonably.

"I believe I made mention of it in the social notes," Maggie said stonily. So there it was, everyone knew and was aware Reese was living with her. Why did she care anyway?

Arwin sighed. "Well, Harold's letter will give them a load of fodder to chew on, Maggie. They won't jaw over you above an hour, rest assured."

"Oh, I'm sick of the whole thing."

"Which whole thing?" Arwin asked gently. "The railroad or the Collerans?"

"Both," she said with some asperity. "Both."

Arwin was too perceptive, she thought as she walked slowly back to the office. But what he didn't know was she was getting sick of the fight because there was no fight. No one, reading Harold Danforth's letter, would have less sympathy for him: he said all the right things, the things that business people and landowners wanted to hear: money was coming into the town and everyone would benefit. Everyone would profit. Colville would expand and Denver North would bring in more business and new people and Colville would grow. There was just no way for her to fight that logic.

She knew, in her heart of hearts, that she would have preferred to preserve Colville just as it was this very morning, quiet and warm with a spring promise of life and bursting energy. It was just the time of day she liked, too, with the early morning gray sky blending into bright blue as the sun rose, and the intermittent sounds of a horses' hooves or the rumbling of a wagon breaking the calm silence.

All that would change in the space of an hour. Saturday was come-to-town day in Colville, and most everyone gathered at either the newspaper office or Bodey's store. More than anything, they came to talk. Sometimes, for a rare treat, they took luncheon at the hotel; invariably they came away with an extra five-pound bag of flour and perhaps a changed opinion that they might unleash over the counter at the *Morning Call*.

She knew them all and they had no quarrel with her, at least not until the Denver North project had gotten started. Now, she knew, some of her friends and neighbors were not so sure. They saw dollar signs where she saw strangers coming into their midst and moving onto their property and into their lives. They saw quick profits and she saw long-lasting problems, and she only wanted to contain the moment so that it would never change. She knew inevitably it would.

She found herself standing before the dress shop window staring at the one mannikin on display in draped and ruffled finery. She backed away, horrified, and bumped into a terrifyingly broad body and two reassuring male hands that reached out and steadied her gently.

She knew it was Logan, but still the fact of his presence behind her unnerved her, and the touch of his hands made her skittish. She shook him off and began walking determinedly toward the office. She didn't have to talk to him, nor had she asked him to present himself this morning like some fool to whom she had given the merest encouragement.

It wasn't fair. The worst of it was, he kept up with her

with good humor and never said a word until they reached the door of the office. And then she whirled on him.

"Don't you have a cow to herd or something?"

"Nope. Just a cantankerous mare who needs corraling, but I know she'll come around in her own sweet time."

She felt like spitting. "Why are you doing this, Logan?"

"When was I to do this, Maggie? They'd have run me out of town if I'd come near Mrs. Frank before they'd well and truly buried Frank himself. I waited the proper time. No one can fault me there."

"I fault you for even talking this nonsense. We were friends."

"We're still friends."

She had no response for that. She didn't feel like he was a friend. Now he was her adversary who wanted to take something precious from her and give her something precious in return. She couldn't even define if it were a fair exchange, and she was sure he thought it was.

But this was Logan, with whom she had roamed the free range in and around Colville, whom she had leaned on when her mother died or her father went too deep into debt. The one in whom she had confided before she gave her soul to Frank and lost it forever. How could he want to change that?

Nothing, she thought, would ever be the same. She pushed open the door to a frenzy of voices, and Logan followed her into the room.

"Well, don't that Danforth got a point?"

"I just don't see, Maggie, how things is gonna become so all-fired different after all."

"Yeah, a stranger's dollar is just as good as a neighbor's, Maggie."

Maggie covered her ears. "Gentlemen, you sure got over here almighty early to tell me how wrong I am."

"Well, that's just it, Maggie. We ain't gonna let nothing happen in town. Harold's right: we gotta get on the bandwagon and make it happen, make it work for us and not the other way around."

"Under whose control? Whose rules? When will the town committee pass ordinances? After the damage is done? Please, gentlemen, take your money and run, but don't say I didn't tell you so."

"Aw now, Maggie . . ."

She looked around her affectionately. She thought of these men as her regulars, farmers and ranchers who stopped by like clockwork every Saturday to be first to get the news, chew it up, and work it over. She always had a pot of coffee on for them, and she always found A.J. most comfortably in their midst, as if this were really his element rather than the editorial desk.

Logan watched her maneuver among them with amusement. They really adored her, he thought. This was a notion that both pleased and disconcerted him. She was Maggie to them, not Mrs. Frank; she was one of them, home grown and part of the Colville soil. To them, her father had never relinquished ownership of the paper: she carried on in *his* stead, not Frank's. Because of that they respected her, even if they thought she were a mite wrong-minded about the railroad thing.

She handled all their comments good naturedly as she pushed her way past the counter and closeted herself behind it.

"Don't worry, Maggie. We'll take care of things. We'll watch 'em closely."

"We won't let Harold Danforth get too greedy, Maggie."

"You ever gonna sell up, Maggie? I still think you're crazy if you don't."

She shook her head despairingly and sent Logan an exasperated look, a conspirator's look, he thought, one

74

that delved into their long friendship and shared the moment. He wished he could capture the look and the feeling instantly in his hands so he could take it out and show her. Then perhaps she would understand what she needed and what he was feeling.

But the comradely expression in her eyes faded as she met the intensity in his, and she turned away abruptly.

He had a distinct sense of losing time as she moved away from him. Time was becoming precious. He had already lost five years, and now, when he should have been able to have the freedom to court her in a leisurely way, he felt instead as if he could not keep himself from taking her hostage and running away with her.

Time. There was a subtle pressure ballooning time all out of proportion, and he didn't understand what it was. It wasn't only Maggie's reluctance or her stress over Denver North. It was something else, something he couldn't define.

A moment later, three things happened simultaneously: Jean Vilroy approached her with something for her to look at, Dennis Coutts came in the front door, and Reese Colleran emerged from the back room.

And as she turned from one to the other, giving each an instant of her undivided attention, he saw clearly the thing that had him so disquieted, the thing he feared: all three men wanted her, and he knew right then he had no time at all. He would have to use drastic measures.

Chapter Five

For Maggie, it was as if time stood still at that point. She had allowed Harold Danforth to have his say and he had swayed the impecunious ranching town to his side with reasonable arguments, not soaring promises. No one would have known how well Harold Danforth had made out as he sold his golden grass for the promise of a glorious economic future.

Folks would talk about his letter for weeks, Maggie thought, and all she could do was become the voice of doom as each encroachment ate up Colville and revealed its darker side.

"Well, what did you expect?" Mother Colleran asked smugly. "Now you see, Frank never would have made that mistake. Whatever he thought, he would have gone right with popular opinion. That's why everyone loved him. I think you mishandled this terribly, Maggie, but that is water under the dam now, isn't it?"

Maggie closed her eyes and took a deep breath. There was no escaping Mother Colleran. She came up or she went down depending on where Maggie was at any one moment and what she felt she wanted to say in her gouging way. Maggie could not get away from the responsibility of her. Any suggestions she had ever made had fallen on deaf ears. Mother Colleran was in Colville to stay, mystically joined to the daughter-in-law she hated.

"I wish you would write your own letter to the paper," she said with deadly calm, "since you have no right to make an editorial opinion—at least no right that Frank's estate gives you."

"You—" the old woman began apopleptically, and Reese cut her off tactfully.

"I think Maggie did exactly what she should have done, and she did it honorably and fairly. Frank would have wanted it that way."

"Nonsense!" Mother Colleran snapped. "Frank didn't want her two feet near that newsroom and well she knew it. I don't know how she maneuvered things so that she was left everything, really I don't."

"But you don't have to know," Maggie pointed out, a fact that she had hammered home dozens of times to her in private. She resented having to do so now publicly, in front of Reese. "Things are the way they are, and your words, Mother Colleran, will not change them. But you certainly have the option of leaving if things here do not please you. Dennis has already said that—"

"I will not leave the place where Frank is buried."

Maggie had heard that before too, but Reese had heard none of it, and his head moved between them in lively curiosity as this conversation went on.

Maggie decided to change her tactics. "What about you, Reese?"

Her question startled him. "What about me?"

"Surely this visit has some kind of time limit on it? What do you think your mother should do when you plan to leave? Since she so continually expresses her dissatisfaction with the way I run things and how she must live. Perhaps she might be happier with you?"

She smiled at him, but she was interested to note that

78

her question totally discomfitted him. His pale blue eyes flashed once toward his mother, and then met hers with disarming frankness.

"Please, Maggie, I've only just arrived. How can I make long term decisions like that? Mother and I hadn't quite decided how long she wants me to stay, and quite honestly, I'm thinking that Denver North may bring some opportunities for me that I hadn't quite perceived before. Maybe," he added with a warm smile at his mother, "it might be time for me to settle down."

"Don't be stupid," his mother said instantly. "You're a wanderer, Reese Colleran, an adventurer, and you're talking a whole lot of nonsense. The point is—"

"The point is, as we've discussed endlessly, Frank left no specific instructions about the newspaper, and I plan to carry on in my own way. I think this topic of discussion is closed."

"It is not closed, Maggie; you know full well what Frank's intent always was, and that goes for the ranchland too. And now you have this golden opportunity—"

Maggie stood up from the dining table abruptly. "All of this is my business, Mother Colleran, and not yours. Reese, if you can accomplish one thing during your visit here, I hope it may be that you can convince your mother that Frank really intended for me to have control of the paper and control of the land, and that what your mother wants doesn't enter into things."

"Maggie—" he said, but it was futile. She moved away from the table and left by the back room stairwell. Reese turned to his mother in irritation. "Don't *do* that, Mother. You set up a family dinner and then you promptly go at her with a bullwhip about things that are obviously old arguments between you."

"That's right. Frank would turn over in his grave if he could hear her refusing the kind of money Denver North is offering."

"But they are not offering it to you," Reese said bluntly, and was gratified to see her small, squat body stiffen and her pursed mouth grasp for words that were not readily there.

"Well," she said at last, "Maggie has a duty to me, and to Frank, to see that everything is done just as he would have done it, and he would have taken the money. He might even have sold the paper, and we might have gone back to San Francisco."

Reese let that suggestion hang in the air for a moment. "Do you want that, Mother? I can take you back to San Francisco."

"No I don't," she said promptly, with a trace of a sob in her voice. "I wanted to go with Frank. What use would it be if I went with you?"

It was a stunning question, one that presupposed plans and schemes of which he was not aware, and a relationship between his mother and Frank that shared secrets and dreams. He thought for one instant that he did not want to know, and he let the question fall into the silence, unanswered, as his mother wiped away a tear.

He heard Maggie's footfall finally, softly, behind the closed door, and he knew she had been listening. He reached across the table and patted his mother's hand.

So Reese was on her side. She didn't know how comforting that thought should be, after all. Perhaps his usefulness would extend solely to controlling his mother, in which case Maggie felt he could have her undying gratitude.

For the rest, she didn't know. She felt an odd emptiness now in place of that zealous ardor that had compelled her all these months, and she couldn't see how to cope with it. Monday the routine would start all over again, and she felt she had nothing to fight for.

Or did her distraction stem from something else?

She didn't want to think about that either, but she could not ignore the uncomfortable fact that everything had changed today in indefinable ways. Her life, which she liked very well the way it was, had been substantially affected.

She was ready for a fight all right, but her enemy was amorphous, inhuman, and she had no weapons against the shifting winds of change.

The sense of it was even present in the back room as she entered and encountered Jean taking apart the galleys. It was the usual Saturday evening task, and yet the difference was there: she was aware of the tension in him and the secret desire lurking beneath his calm, efficient exterior.

Without a word, she took a type tray and joined him at the type case, but the air between them seemed strained, and she had all she could do to concentrate on removing the type and replacing it in the case. She almost felt as though she must say something, but she had no idea what to say.

The silence became unnerving, yet on the surface everything was the same. She and Jean never had much conversation as they performed this ritual postpublication chore, but today unspoken words swirled in the air, never to be uttered by the proud man who was only the employee of the fiercely independent lady publisher. That wall, she realized, would always be between them, that and her own tangible horror of change.

After an half hour during which they worked silently side by side, she sensed the tautness between them ease, and she thought she had imagined it all. He looked at her no differently than he usually did as he prepared to clean up and dismantle the press. He said no more or less than the usual commonplaces when they finally finished wiping down the machinery and he began his own cleanup at the backroom sink.

He left her with his customary goodnight bidding, and she felt mortified that she had thought such things about him at all.

It had to be because of Logan. She felt edgy, nervy, as if he were hovering in the shadows, ready to pop out at her to test the validity of her protestations. And if he did . . . Logan was a stranger now, she thought as she locked up behind Jean. She didn't know this Logan Ramsey at all, and already his challenge had colored how she looked at everything.

It wasn't fair.

She doused the lights in the main office before retiring to the printing room to pump up some water and tackle the cleaning of her own ink-stained hands.

And there he was, as if she had conjured him up, leaning against the soapstone sink, waiting for her, *sneaking* into her home and her life where she did not want him.

"Hello, Logan." She was amazed her voice sounded so even, so calm. "I would have thought you'd have gone home by now."

He gave her an amused look. "Now how could you think that, Maggie? I had a lot of business in town today. I even treated myself to dinner at the hotel."

"You're mighty busy for a man who hadn't been to town in six months or more," she said tartly. "And I don't recall you had any business *here.*"

"I disagree with you there, Maggie. My most important business is here."

She made a dismissive movement with her hand. "I won't listen to this, Logan. You can't just walk in here and change things around and expect me to fall down in gratitude."

"I hardly expected *that*, Maggie. I've had vast

experience with how all-fired stubborn you can be."

She pivoted away from him abruptly as the double-edged meaning of his words struck her and echoes of the past erupted in her memory. Oh yes, he knew.

Why on earth would you hang around that Frank Colleran, Maggie? He's no good. . . .

Don't let him buy out your father, Maggie; he's up to no good. I don't care how tired your father is. . . . Maggie, I'll help you run the damned thing, but don't sell out to Frank. . . .

Are you going to marry him? Are you sure? Why, Maggie, why?

She had been so sure about everything—then. She was sure of nothing now.

"Go back to your ranch, Logan," she said finally. "There's nothing for you here." But she didn't face him as she said the words; she wasn't even sure she wanted him to do that.

"Nonsense, Maggie. I plan to camp out in town until I have you where I want you."

He knew those words would do the trick; slowly she wheeled around to face him. "You'll never get me anywhere I don't want to be, Logan Ramsey."

"I wouldn't issue such challenges, Maggie. I can be pretty persuasive."

His words sent a shudder through her.

"Persuade someone else then. You want a ranch woman, Logan, not a town woman who's used to running her own life. You need someone to share your life, not fight it."

"Are you going to fight it?"

He asked the question so gently, and yet she sensed the steely resolution beneath his words. She felt as though he were rubbing her the wrong way deliberately, forcing her to retaliate to his provocative words.

"I'll fight it," she said at last, because he left her no

other choice, but she was disconcerted that her unequivocal response did not faze him in the least.

"Good," he said. "I expected nothing less."

"I expected more," she retorted, stung. She felt like throwing something at him. It struck her that it wasn't the first time in as many days she wanted to attack the threat he represented. And yet, her thrust was a goad, and in her heart of hearts she knew it.

Instantly, the light in his eyes deepened. "But you could have had more, Maggie," he said gently. "*You* chose Frank."

"And I still have to live with that, don't I?" she asked nastily. She couldn't leave herself open to him, she *couldn't*. And yet there was no defense; he started walking toward her and she felt like running, running from the lies and the truth both.

"No, Maggie. *I* had to live with that. I had five years of living with *that* and anything my imagination could conjure up, five years of hell imagining you with Frank, five years of hell fantasizing what it could have been like for you and me."

"That's absurd. There was no you and me."

"There would have been."

"You can't know that."

"I know it now."

"I don't. I don't want to know it. I don't want it, not now, not ever."

That stopped him cold. For one terrifying instant she saw the dark underside of his soul. She saw that he could not seriously consider the possibility. She wondered if his certainty had become an obsession, and the thought scared her.

"You do want it, Maggie," he said gently, turning away. "You just don't know it."

This abrupt release of tension confused her. She watched him walk slowly back into the printing room and she didn't understand. She had expected an adamant pursuit that could be just as adamantly rejected. It would have been so much easier.

But she couldn't let herself become afraid of him just because of the things he was saying. He was not in control of her desire, *she* was, and she wanted no entanglements, in spite of her shocking response to him.

She followed Logan slowly into the printing room. "Why don't you go home?"

"It's cold and lonely in my home, Maggie. I'd much rather be here with you."

"Fine. There's a nice leather desk chair in there that used to belong to Frank. Make yourself comfortable on it."

"Maggie . . ."

"Logan . . ." She brushed by him in exasperation and began pumping up some water into the sink. She felt like crying and she hated his persistence. He was the last person in the world she would have expected to say such things, to want such things.

And the irony was, she needed him. She needed him to be what he had always been, but his perception of what he had always been was far different from hers.

For one telling moment she felt overwhelmed with a sadness and frustration that vented itself in an emphatic *thump* of the pump handle, which sent water spraying all over her. She reached blindly for the soap and touched a warm intrusive hand.

"Let me," Logan said softly, catching her hands tightly in his own. "Let me."

"I don't want you to do anything."

"Of course you don't," he said soothingly, as he doused her hands with cold water. "You never did."

She wrenched her hands away and he pulled them right back. "Surely you weren't that oblivious, Maggie."

"I must have been," she said, unable to keep the surly

85

note out of her voice.

"Or I was too subtle." He reached for the soap and began rubbing it on her wet hands until they were coated with lather. He massaged the soap into her skin with slow mesmerizing motions that immobilized her with panic.

His hands on hers were warm, hypnotic, compelling— the last thing she wanted to feel, his fingers moving slowly and sensitively up and down the backs of her hands, her knuckles, her long slender fingers. Turning her hands palm side up, he felt, yes, felt, the tender skin of her palms, and caressed each finger with the slick soapiness of his hands.

She couldn't move. The slippery wet seduction of his expert massage was as stunning to her as his kiss. He did not look at her; he didn't need to. The bend of her body told him all he needed to know. He had all he could do to stop himself from telling her how he had dreamed of her hands touching him in just the way he touched her now.

But words weren't necessary now; he had said all he needed to say, and as he held her hands captive and captivated, he didn't let up his sensual exploration of them. He knew she felt it as deeply as if he were exploring the secrets of her body.

Not subtle now, she was thinking, as she watched with blinding intensity the movement of his fingers over her hands. She felt disembodied and connected at the same time. He was doing it to her and she was feeling it down to her toes. At the same time, she was watching and commenting on it in some nether region of her mind, wanting desperately to resist the sensual movement of his fingers.

She thought that if he moved his fingers up just a little, right to the veins at the base of her wrist—yes—and then suddenly found the hollow directly below her thumb— yes— and so gently around to her wristbone. . . . But how could it be that his fingers sliding the satiny wet soap all over her hands could arouse her to such a fever pitch that she felt wild to invite his kiss and to feel his hands on her body?

He sensed it. He felt the shift of tension in her. Then and only then did he lift his head and look into her eyes.

Her face was still, as if she were holding in all the emotion she was feeling and could only reveal it in the hunger of her eyes. It was all there, and it was all for him.

He pulled her toward him so that only the grip of his hands on hers separated them. Very gently his lips grazed hers, and then his mouth settled on hers insistently, tugging, demanding, his tongue licking her lips, tasting their texture.

"You knew," he murmured. "Every time you came out with me, every time you challenged me, every time you talked to me, Maggie, you knew. . . ."

"I didn't know," she whispered. "Don't tell me now."

"You have to know."

"Not now."

"*When,* Maggie?"

His question hung on the breath of air between them. If only she could tell him: she wanted everything and nothing. If he could possess her without conquering her; if he could love her without needing her always; if he could let her give rein to her wanton feelings without giving her a child; if only he would just kiss her. . . .

He didn't even need an answer from her. His mouth found hers unerringly and this time his own greed overcame his patience. This was Maggie, for whom he had yearned for so many years, butter in his hands, fluid against him with a reluctant need that she did not yet know he could assuage. No, she knew. She knew because she trusted *him* and no one else, and as he began his erotic exploration of her mouth she wound her arms around him and answered him as completely as if she had spoken the words.

She sought him with the same hot wet eagerness with which he wanted her, without fear of what he would think or the carnality of her nature. She held him for the moment, demanded his kiss just for the moment, and savored him as if she were going to die tomorrow. It was only Logan. She felt safe in his arms and secure in the notion he would never go beyond the boundaries that she set.

And yet she could not get enough of the voluptuous feelings he evoked. He knew just how to kiss her, just when to ease up and when to pursue her, when to tantalize her and how to arouse her. Her blood turned molten at the way he played with her, and she had to grasp him tightly, to pull him closer where she could feel the tumultuous desire in him that could fill the empty place in her.

She felt as though they were in a cocoon, alone together, joined, tense with the expectation of what was to come, what, above and beyond sanity, she wanted to come.

"Oh, Maggie . . ." She heard his voice, hoarse with feeling as his hands cupped her face and he rained neat little kisses all over her mouth. "Oh, God, Maggie . . ." His tongue dipped into her mouth and out again, leaving her bereft. Her fingers grasped his hair and pulled his mouth down on hers again.

She knew how to ask for what she wanted, and yet, just for a moment, she hesitated. What *would* he think, what would he do? How could she make him do her desire without telling, without showing? A sensual excitement possessed her at the thought of his response to her volatile emotions.

"Maggie . . ." His voice was a mere breath hanging over her.

"What?" She licked her lips and waited.

"Is it me, or is it memories?"

Oh my God, she thought; he understood, he understood everything. "Both," she whispered, her body flexing against him, just the faintest movement, an invitation to discover what she really meant.

He held *her* now, not her memories; he could wipe them away or he could alienate her forever. He felt violent again with the knowledge that her memories were with Frank and not with him. His mouth closed over hers again, to make new memories and evoke fresh desire, to awaken those voluptuous feelings that came solely from his touch, his mouth.

He never thought he would feel such anger when he finally had her in his arms. What she needed she had discovered with Frank. He knew her repressed need drove her, not any desire for him. Not yet. Not yet.

How odd that he resented this undreamed of sensuality in her that wanted to use him the way he would seek out a woman for hire if he were possessed by the same unslaked desire.

He had to build on that and not toss it away out of a jealous rage that had nothing to vent itself upon. Whatever Frank Colleran had taken that had been precious to him was unredeemable now. Maybe Frank's influence had made her what she was: a ferocious tigress devouring him with an irresistible voluptuous heat that was oh so tempting and yet that might shut the door to all of his dreams.

She felt the explosive tightness in him that signified his readiness for completion—any kind of the completion—the kind of completion that would leave her helpless and possibly with a child.

No! She twisted away from him abruptly. Oh no, no! Somehow, a shred of sanity got the upper hand over her desire. Immersed as she was in a sensual fog, she nonetheless knew the next step was not the one she wanted to take. She would live with the void and count her blessings; even he could understand that. But she couldn't look at him and she couldn't stop shaking with the force of her need.

But then, what were his luscious kisses but the foreshadow of the thing she now sought so desperately to avoid.

She couldn't avoid *him.* He still held her, and the tautness in him was every bit as galvanic as hers: release was one turbulent moment away, and he had to clamp down on his need and submerge himself in hers.

With every ounce of self control he possessed, he let her go.

She didn't move. Her body fought the same war as his, she wanted him the same way he wanted her, with the force of the moment and the burgeoning allure between them, born of something old and something disturbingly new, the thing that would disrupt her life and put her in a place she did not want to be.

She couldn't give in to it. Her whole posture told him clearly that she was fighting it but that her common sense and her memories would win.

He had to find the thing that might bind her to him again. He didn't care how or why or whose reasons were pure and whose were not. He needed her any way he could have her, and her indecision gave him a blessed respite to seduce her need.

"There are other ways, Maggie," he said softly, so gently, so . . . *urgently* . . . that her head snapped up.

"No, there is only one way, and that way will allow you to walk away and me to become dependent forever. I can't allow that. I apologize for losing control and letting you . . ." She couldn't finish beyond that; she felt close to tears with the knowledge that she had to send him away altogether and that she would never again experience the things he made her feel, the things she had denied and buried when Frank had finally abandoned her for a woman more submissive and less imaginative. No, those were old wounds she had no right resurrecting, particularly with someone like Logan. He would want so much and she could give so little.

"There are other ways," he reiterated insistently. "Maggie, let me show you." He reached out and touched her cheek.

"No."

His hand slid downward, from her jaw to her neck and she shuddered. "Let me love you, Maggie."

"I can't."

"Why not?" His fingers slipped around the prim neckline of her dress, beneath her hair to the base of her neck where they rubbed her aching flesh gently, reassuringly, and in a way that was so arousing that she wondered whether he could touch her anywhere that would not electrify her whole body.

"Logan . . ." She stopped as his fingers began playing with her hair and he drew closer to her and closer. He was going to kiss her again and she drowned in the feeling.

"Yes?" He was winning and he knew it. The least little pressure of his fingers pushed her to yield. He felt her body give in to her feelings even as she warred with her ambivalence over her need.

"Don't kiss me."

"I won't." His lips touched hers again and he heard the faint moan at the back of her throat. "I won't make love to you. I won't show you anything you don't want me to. I won't. . . ." Oh, and now, as his whispered words penetrated and he positioned her mouth exactly beneath his, she sighed, "Don't," and opened her mouth willingly to receive his kiss. He murmured, "I won't, I won't, I *won't*," against the softness of her lips, her tongue, the sweetness of her taste. "Trust me, Maggie," he whispered to the willingness of her body as he held her now; he felt her fingers dig into his shoulders ferociously.

His tongue seduced her all over again, and this time she let no reservations about the course she would take deter her from feeling the ineffable desire that he aroused in her.

Other ways intrigued her. She knew nothing of other ways, and yet he was willing to contain his ardor to ensure hers with *other ways. . . .*

She felt as though she were steaming out of control, and yet she didn't care. What would he do? What "other ways?" *What* could subdue the fierce hunger in her that wouldn't leave her feeling fragile and exploited?

When he set her away from him she felt as though she had fallen off a cliff. But he still held her close, and his expression as he looked at her was soft and beguiling. She had known him forever, but this expression she had seen on his face in a time and a circumstance she could not recall.

She touched his mouth wonderingly and felt his sweet smile.

"You knew, Maggie."

His words were soft, noncensuring, and still she felt stupid that she hadn't known, hadn't been perceptive enough to realize, not before and surely not after. But then Frank had become a part of her past and she didn't want to know anything of any other men.

The thought of Frank cooled her fervor. There would always be Frank, she thought. Not even Logan could make him go away. Not even death could wipe his memory from her soul.

She knew that the fire in her was damped down for tonight. It was enough that she had allowed herself to feel this much, to give this much. She needed time to examine what she felt and how he aroused her. She needed to

92

come to terms with it, to allow herself to let him show her "other ways" and to discover somehow a way to allay the guilt that would surely follow if she used him this way.

Logan let her go as he sensed her moving away from him in her mind and in her heart. He had time now, and her own nature and her overriding curiosity on his side. No one else had touched her in quite the same way. He had this in his favor as well.

He tilted her face up to his and marveled at how lovely she was, and how sensual. "Tomorrow," he murmured, not even sure if he wanted to give her that much time.

"Yes."

She watched him go. It was late by then, and she wiped her hands and thought about the way he had touched her. She wondered how she would ever get through the day until tomorrow.

Chapter Six

She slept. It was as if something had been released within her, some tentative decision made. She had thought she wouldn't sleep at all. The next day was Sunday, a day when she had plenty of leisure time to consider things she did not want to think about at all.

Sunday the office was closed. The town went to church and then those who had spare time afterward congregated at Arwin Bodey's store. Sometimes Maggie walked over, sometimes she stayed in the office.

This morning she was torn. Mother Colleran, whose expression was suspiciously benign, pronounced herself pleased with Frank's memorial service, so much so she was thinking of going to church this Sunday. Reese looked bemused as she added, "Of course, *you* will accompany me. Maggie hasn't been to church, apart from this week, since she and Frank were married. You would think she would feel she could use some heavenly guidance. By the way," she added with malice as she rose from the breakfast table, "what was that Logan Ramsey doing here so late last night?"

Maggie froze. "Visiting," she said shortly, pushing back her chair. "I will clean up, Mother Colleran, if you and Reese are ready to go."

Her mother-in-law nodded and went to get a hat and Reese sent her a helpless look. "I'm damn well not ready to go sit in church all morning," he hissed as Maggie removed his plate.

"Neither am I," Maggie said calmly. "I suggest you find someone to bring her home and escape as early as you can."

"I thought churchgoing was women's work."

"Not this woman," Maggie corrected, removing herself to the kitchen as Mother Colleran appeared duly swathed in black and impatient to leave.

"Will you be here, if I can get back?" he whispered as he passed her on the way out.

She shrugged. "Probably." But she truthfully did not know what she wanted to do with her freedom this day. She watched them emerge from the apartment door at the back of the building, where a horse and buggy awaited them on Mother Colleran's instructions. She saw Reese look up at the windows, almost as if he could see her there and knew she would be watching.

She let the curtain drop. Reese couldn't possibly see her. She didn't want to be seen. She wanted to be alone today to think about Logan and the evening before.

Her body reacted instantly as she remembered his kisses and his words, and the things he wanted—the things she wanted. No, impossible things. How could she even have let him kiss her when she could offer nothing in return? All that could happen was that he would find out exactly what kind of woman she was. What kind of woman Frank had thought she was.

She thought that woman was gone forever, carefully hidden where no one could see.

And still Logan had found her.

Or he had always known she was there.

The thought was overwhelming. Could any man see the hunger in her and know what she was? Could Reese?

If he had said the same words, and had kissed her the same way, would she have been as ready to fall into his arms?

All she could think about was her willingness in Logan's arms the previous night. The memory excited her and blotted out everything else. *Everything*. All these years she had closed up inside her this desire seemed like a useless wasteland of deprivation to her now. One kiss, one touch, the right words, and she had come alive like some fairytale princess from a spell. All that hard-won composure and denial had been just a lie she had told herself.

Whatever Frank had felt those three years ago about her and burning ardor, he had not denied himself the thing he refused her. But it was always so with men, she thought. They could have everything and allow their women nothing.

So Logan would come and he would hold her and kiss her and talk of other ways and her need would be assuaged for the moment, and perhaps, she thought, that was all there had to be.

He would never hurt her, she thought, and it reassured her to know that as she wandered from the back of the apartment into the parlor that overlooked the street and looked out of the window there.

It was quieter than it had been the day before, with only an intermittent wagon or lone horse cantering its way along the plank boardwalk. There were no pedestrians—a lone cowboy perhaps on his way to Arwin's store, but everyone punctiliously attended church on Sunday.

From the window where she stood, she thought Colville looked like a small peaceful town that had been blessed by God, a place that could never be touched by commercial greed.

She decided to go to Arwin's store and face the derision

97

of the congregants there. Without a doubt, public sentiment was not running in her favor.

It was already crowding up when she arrived, but Arwin at least was happy to see her. The jibes were good-natured as she made her way to the back of the store.

"So what do you think, Arwin?"

"Have a cup of coffee, Maggie."

"That doesn't require a lot of thought," she said, smiling, taking the cup he offered her.

"How's that Reese fella?"

"He's off to church with Mother Colleran, and not too happy about it."

"Well, he's here on a visit, ain't he? Come to see the old lady? What else has he got to do?"

"You're right; I never thought of that. She's so busy deifying Frank, she probably hasn't even noticed who took her to church today to begin with."

Arwin clucked at her. "That was nasty, Maggie."

"Well, was it?" she asked reasonably. "Every damn body in town thinks it's his duty to theorize that the coming of Denver North is exactly what Frank would have wanted. Why, as far as they're concerned he would have sold the ranch to facilitate matters for them. Frank must have been some seer. I never saw that in him, but maybe everyone else did."

"He was a regular magician, Maggie, full of hocus-pocus."

"That's about it," she agreed caustically.

"Well, you'd probably better lay off a bit then. If everyone's so convinced, they'll resent you even more for selling it down so consistently. They'll think you can't see both sides, they'll think—maybe—you were doing Frank dirty by opposing the things he wanted, which, by definition, are the things they want."

"Oh, please, is it that bad?"

"Worse. There's a group that have made a passel of

money selling off land, and they're going to build closer in to town and be right there when that line comes steaming through. They're going to travel up to Cheyenne and take the line whichever way the wind is blowing at the moment, Maggie, because they ain't never been two miles down the road from the center of town in their whole lives. You watch out for them; they're powerful and ignorant."

"I'm still going to fight, Arwin."

"Who?" he asked cynically.

"Frank," she retorted, setting down her cup.

"What if I told you Melinda Sable is looking to buy and build along the far side of town?" Arwin asked confidentially, drawing her slightly aside and turning so that their backs were to the assembling crowd.

"How?"

"Danged if I know. I heard a breath of it the other day, couldn't believe it. Don't know where she'd get the money, but I'm damned sure that whoever loaned it to her is looking to make a big profit."

"Well, it wasn't Frank," Maggie said acerbically. "Damn, that's bad news."

"Supposed to be secret news, but nothing's secret in this town."

"Or this store."

"It's the only thing that keeps me going, Maggie."

"Me too," she said satirically.

"Don't go off the deep end about it," Arwin cautioned. "It's just rumor."

"I know. I'll have a field day with the engineers when they come and try to figure out how to grade the track around Big Gully."

"They mayn't have to in the end, Maggie. I'm willing to bet they're going to have cases full of money to offer Sean and Annie, and maybe even Logan."

"Maybe," she sighed.

"And maybe they got the payoff reserved for you, Maggie," Arwin added carefully, slanting a birdlike look at her.

"I heard that too," she said. "It's crazy."

"You ain't running cattle; you refuse to live there and build it up, Maggie. What do you expect people to say?"

"Possibly that I mean what I say. But . . . oh . . . there's Reese." She waved to him as he stood uncertainly in the doorway looking around. She wondered how he had gotten away from his mother so quickly. Services were not over till noon and it was only eleven o'clock. "Reese, this is Arwin Bodey. I believe you two nodded to each other yesterday morning. Arwin, this is, of course, Frank's brother, Reese Colleran."

The men shook hands cordially and everyone watched covertly as the buzz of conversation continued around them.

"And where is Mother Colleran?" Maggie asked sweetly.

"In excellent hands," Reese said firmly, in a tone that brooked no questions. He had found a place for her and a ride, and he had been amused to see his mother welcomed into the fold of the church ladies who revered her for being Frank Colleran's mother. For the moment, for the morning, it was enough, and it left him with the free hour or so to find Maggie and share that fleeting time with her. "Are you finished here?"

Maggie leveled a humorous look at Arwin. "I expect I am. Arwin has filled me in on all the gossip and I can now go back to the office and write the locals column. Isn't that right, Arwin?"

"Don't tease, Maggie."

"I wouldn't dream of it." She allowed Reese to precede her as they walked out of the store, and she could hear the muted whispers around them: "That's Frank's brother." "Oh, you can see he's a Colleran." "Don't he

100

have the look of Frank about him?" "They say he's living with Maggie and the mother. . . ."

The last was the worst, and they made the door before Maggie could hear the anonymous response to it.

"Well now," Maggie said as they stood outside in the brisk spring sunshine. "I take it you have something in mind?"

"Nothing much really. We've done the hotel dinner, I've seen you run the paper, we've scouted the surrounding area for railroad spies, and you've shown me what's left of the Colleran ranch and property. I don't believe there's much else except your own fine company, Maggie."

She shook her head. "That's really too much, Reese. This is my day of rest, too. I don't generally do much more than trade words with your mother for hours on end about how unfairly I treat her or how unfairly Frank's will treated her."

"Let's walk then, and you can tell me about that."

"Oh, but surely you've gotten an earful of my crimes."

"I refuse to let her vilify you."

"Nonetheless," Maggie said, carefully watching his expression, "she threatened me with *you.*"

He looked shocked. "How can that be?"

"Apparently things are going to change somehow now that you've come."

"Truly, Maggie, it's an old, disappointed woman's rantings. What could possibly change?"

"I couldn't figure that out myself. After all, Frank's will was lawfully probated, and I've complied with all the terms to the letter of the law—which includes, by the way, responsibility for your mother and a stipend for her, which she refuses to take. I've undertaken running the newspaper, and by the terms of the will, I'm to keep the Colleran ranch intact except for certain circumstances that Mother Colleran has interpreted as meaning lucrative offers. Neither she nor you were left anything by Frank, and I think your mother somehow thinks I engineered that, even though Frank and I were not close at the time he died. This is a will made by a man who loved his wife and was confident of her abilities. I don't know why he did not change it. It wasn't changed to reflect the status of our marriage at the time he died."

"I see."

"I wonder if you do. Your mother was adamantly against Frank's marrying me, and now, since you've told me about—Priscilla, was that her name?—I can perhaps understand that. But she never accepted the marriage, even after Frank assured her over and over that it was exactly what he wanted to do, and she has resented me for all these years."

"Of course Frank loved you. You are a beautiful and vital woman."

Maggie ignored that. "Yet your mother insists on staying with me and fighting with me as if somehow she were defending Frank against me. It makes no sense to me whatsoever."

"She loved Frank too much," Reese said soberly.

"Yes, she did. And she's very anxious to keep the town myth about him perpetuated."

"Perhaps he really was an extraordinary man."

"Do you believe that?"

"No."

Maggie smiled. "He was an extraordinary salesman, and he knew how to sell himself."

They walked in silence a few moments more. Reese marveled at her all over again, her perception and her strength. He was willing to bet that no one in Colville saw Frank Colleran in quite the same light as Maggie, and though it was possible her candor was tinged with the faintest odor of the scorned wife, she was also a woman who seemed to see things with unclouded clarity. She

102

couldn't have been in love with Frank at the end. Possibly she was even grateful to Melinda Sable for becoming his convenience.

However, he also knew she would never confess any of this to him. All he could hope to do was make her understand that she had an allure and a seductiveness for him as well. But he was already aware that fine words and easy phrases would never convince her of his sincerity.

"Most men in business know how to sell themselves, Maggie," he said suddenly, as the thought occurred to him as well as a way to approach her.

She stopped and turned to look at him. "Is that true? Do *you?*" She had to shield her eyes from the sun at that moment; she had to see his face clearly.

"I hope to sell myself to you, Maggie," he murmured intimately. He wasn't surprised when she turned away from him; he had the feeling that her reaction was that those words had come too easily to him and that they had made her suspicious. He took her arm and pushed her to continue walking. "Sounds glib, doesn't it?" he said, just a little ruefully.

"It sounds rehearsed," she said succinctly, "and not worth your effort. You've known me all of three or four days, and you couldn't possibly know that yet."

"I'm not delighted that you think I don't know my own mind," Reese retorted sharply, and then he pulled back. He could not push a woman like Maggie and he knew it. "I hope you'll give me time to prove that to you."

"As long as you like," she said sardonically, because she knew she could never allow herself to be taken by Frank's brother. Like to like, she thought, but he didn't have to know that. When his pursuit proved futile, he would leave, and she was going to do her utmost to see that it was soon.

Nonetheless, his declaration distracted her and made it impossible for her to enjoy their walk. Now she had to

103

look for hidden meanings in his conversation, and to be aware of personal references creeping into the most mundane exchanges between them. She was very sure she didn't like him at all just this minute.

"I wish," she said pointedly, "you hadn't done that."

"Excuse me, Maggie; when should I have done *that?* Or do you think I'm not aware that others have feelings for you too. My dear girl, I refuse to sit back and let someone else get the upper hand when I know very well that you and I understand each other. I took a chance. You shot me down—for now. Nothing has changed, Maggie. I will try to prove to you I mean what I say."

"I expect you will," she murmured, put out with him. Others have feelings indeed, she thought angrily. All of a sudden, in just one day! When had she become so desirable? she wondered caustically. She surely presented the most unfeminine of pictures, with her inky hands, unruly hair and plain cotton dresses, and her bossy manner. Men never saw her as being attractive and captivating, and they never had. Not even Frank.

Reese laughed. "You're like a porcupine, Maggie, thrusting out your spikes so everyone will keep hands off. A smart man can see through those tactics. You don't scare me one bit."

His smug answer made her bristle, and she had to force herself not to make a stinging reply. "Good," she said lightly; she didn't want him to think that anything he said was meaningful to her. "I believe we have no place else to go," she added, as they reached what was nominally considered the end of Main Street, a place where the plank boardwalk dwindled into stones and finally the rough track that led to the Denver road.

"I wish we could go further," Reese said regretfully. "But this is enough for today." He offered her his arm and they turned around and walked back into town in silence.

"Do you have any plans for this week?" Maggie asked idly after a while.

He looked at her speculatively. "I'd like to help you out this week, Maggie."

She didn't answer him. She didn't know quite what to make of this seemingly helpful request. As they drew up before the office door, she said finally, "We'll see," and was saved from elaborating on that by the arrival of a buggy bearing Mother Colleran and driven by Dennis Coutts.

"Maggie!" he hailed her. "What luck. I was hoping, when I offered to drive Mother Colleran home, that I would run into you. Do you have time to come for a ride with me now?"

Maggie looked at Mother Colleran and then at Reese, who was glaring at Dennis. "I'd like that very much," she said sweetly, and waited for Reese to help her into the buggy.

She was thankful Dennis didn't say much as they drove away. He was heading out of town in the opposite direction, toward the ranch land and the free range, and she supposed there might be a reason for it, or then again, there might not. She knew that she did not need to make idle talk with Dennis. If he had something on his mind, he would air it soon enough.

Meantime, the air was sweet and the sun was warm. The buggy whipped by the town landmarks: the express station, Arwin's store, the turnoff to the ridge that led to the church, the hotel, the trickle of homes that edged that end of town along the main street.

"So where do you suppose Melinda Sable is going to build this new house I hear about?" Maggie wondered aloud, after they had cleared the main street and had veered off onto the west road.

"Oh, you heard about that, did you?"

"Do you know?"

"I would think on the other side of town, Maggie, near where they're going to build the depot. She wants to run a boarding house; she sees real opportunity there."

"Oh, I bet she does," Maggie murmured ironically.

"Now Maggie, maybe she does."

"Now Dennis, you know what kind of opportunity she sees: men and money and luxury accommodations for a half hour, and it doesn't include home-cooked meals."

She was gratified that he looked shocked.

"Maggie, that's really—you can't go around saying those things."

"Truly? Excuse me, *my* husband was the one who abandoned his wife for the town whore. I'll say exactly what I want to and what everyone knows, and I don't care one whit that she was supposedly faithful to him. It wouldn't surprise me, Dennis, if she had consoled herself with every man in town, including *you.*"

He had the grace to look slightly uncomfortable. "I don't think we came for a ride to talk about Melinda Sable, Maggie."

"Oh. Then what did we come out for, Dennis? Do you want to chastise me yet again for something I've done that Frank would not have liked?"

She was a witch, he thought, as he drew the buggy to a halt so he could properly deal with her stinging tongue.

"Let's just say the Reverend Minister had much to say about this edition of the paper, Maggie. Let's just say the church is squarely behind Harold Danforth's philosophy of expansion, growth, and profit for everyone."

"Including Melinda Sable," Maggie put in sarcastically.

"Even Melinda," Dennis agreed resignedly. "I just wonder, Maggie, if it isn't time for us to start looking for an editor whose views are more in tune with the town managers and the majority of the landholders."

She wasn't shocked; she had known it would come one

day, especially because Dennis was the most conservative manager she had ever known. The wonder was he had let her have her head so long, and had freely interpreted Frank's wishes to suit *her* purposes.

Nonetheless, she was silent for so long that Dennis thought she might be crying. Or maybe he hoped she would be crying because it would be much easier to approach her and make her see things his way.

But when he leaned over and touched her, he saw that she was only staring out into the distance, her face grim and her mouth set. She was the same old Maggie, and she was girding for a fight.

He rushed in immediately to make his point. "We always said that someday . . . I mean, Maggie, this might be the ideal time. You could retire, you could . . . remarry. You wouldn't have all those responsibilities any more. Someone else could carry on and you would still reap the profits with none of the work."

She laughed. He hadn't expected that, and he could not for the life of him see what amused her so.

"Maggie, I'm *serious.*"

"I know you are. I'm waiting to hear the rest. Who would take over? Who, for God's sake, would I marry? Tell me, Dennis. Tell me how you're going to order my life now just as Frank would have wished."

"He said—"

"I know exactly what the will says, Dennis."

"Well, Arch Warfield could take over . . . or Reese," he added as he saw the militant look in her eye. "You could sell the ranch, go to San Francisco. You could stay here, live comfortably at the hotel if you wanted. Or remarry. Marry *me,* for instance."

Now there was dead silence between them. She wasn't ready to speak; she wasn't sure she could. A thousand thoughts swirled around her brain, including the notion that Dennis and her mother-in-law had conspired to bring Reese to Colville expressly to wrest control of the paper away from her. It was unspeakable. She didn't even hear the rest.

"*Maggie!*"

"I hear you, Dennis." But she wouldn't look at him. "Maggie."

"This is absurd. I'm not giving up the paper and I'm not interested in marrying and that's the end of it. I will promise you one thing: I'll pull back on opposition to the rail line. There's nothing I can do about it anyway, but I reserve the right to comment on how its intrusion changes Colville. Does *that* serve the letter of the intent of the will, Dennis?"

"It doesn't serve my intent," he muttered, taking up the reins again. "I can enforce your ouster, Maggie, if you don't . . ."

"But you won't do that, Dennis. Too many people see me as the beleaguered widow, and believe me, I can play that part to the hilt, including making everyone believe I'm doing exactly what Frank wanted. It's a powerful phrase, Dennis, and I'm sure you know it."

"I believe he would have wanted me to take care of you, Maggie. Why can't you see that?"

"You are taking care of me, Dennis, as much as I need taking care of. Unfortunately, Frank died before he could write another will; we don't know a lot about what he really wanted."

"Or he was killed before he got to write that will, Maggie."

"We've talked that all out, Dennis. We don't know, and if you're looking to make me the scapegoat, fine. We'll be enemies instead of—"

"Possibly lovers," he broke in violently and then curbed his words. "Damn, I never meant to say that, not yet. Forgive me, Maggie."

He waited a moment, but she said nothing, which

108

piqued his anger still more. She never did anything another woman would have done. She might have fainted at his suggestion, so bold and lewd did it seem to him, having been said in broad daylight and at a time when she was unchaperoned and he was feeling the heat of other men's interest in her. It was a suggestion that he felt only he had the right to follow, one given him by virtue of the terms of Frank's will, and he still could not get her to see it that way.

"There's nothing to forgive," she said finally, as she sensed his antagonism. "I know exactly how you feel about me, Dennis. You don't need to say anything else."

"I don't like hearing that, Maggie. I had supposed, after a decent interval, that you might be receptive to what I had to say."

"What is a decent interval?" she asked whimsically.

"When Frank was finally really dead and gone for you."

"But he's been that for at least two years, Dennis. Surely you understood that."

"I was thinking of you."

"As you always do, and I do appreciate it, but I'm telling you that the last thing I want to think about is either giving up the newspaper or remarrying, and you will just have to live with that."

"I'll change your mind, Maggie. Now that I know . . ."

She took a deep breath. Why was it that when another man said the same words he had the ability to excite her, to make her think of the possibilities, when someone like Dennis could only produce distaste within her at the thought?

"Dennis, I cannot listen to this."

"You're not ready."

"No, I'm not, and I won't ever be. I do not want to give my life over to a man ever again, Dennis, and I wonder if you can understand that. Already you have me giving up the paper, selling my property, traveling like some genteel schoolmarm, marrying—and marrying you so you can take still further command of what I can or cannot do."

"Yes, and it's because I think this Denver North business is so totally outside the realm of your understanding, Maggie, that it warrants my taking some steps to rectify it."

"Outside the—!" She was totally nonplussed by this attack, and could hardly keep down the harsh words that rose to her lips. "I don't think it's too hard for any simpleton to understand that while the line can be an economic boon to Colville, it can also be a disaster. Perhaps this town needs a woman's perception to make it understand what it's letting itself in for. Perhaps the greedy business*men* of the town don't—"

"Maggie, Maggie!" Dennis held up his hands in defeat. "I didn't mean it like that."

"Oh, you meant it exactly like that, Dennis, and that is exactly how it would be if I encouraged you to think you could find a place in my heart. I think our business is finished now. You can take me back to the office."

"Maggie, don't close the door on me."

"Nonsense, Dennis, I would never do that. You are a dear and valued friend, one whose advice is always welcomed."

"I want you, Maggie."

"You want to conquer me, Dennis. You want to do what even Frank couldn't do. How could I allow that?"

"Perhaps," he said ominously, snapping the reins so that the buggy jerked forward and caught her off balance, "that is one decision that won't be in your hands."

"So, Miz Maggie, you thought you were so smart with your fancy words and fine ideas, and everyone's talking

110

about Harold Danforth anyway." Arch Warfield, laying in wait for her when she returned with Dennis, waved a copy of the *Morning Call* in her face.

"I expect we'll see which of us history proves right," Maggie said with a calm she was far from feeling. Dennis had let her down without a word and let her face Warfield without so much as a goodbye. She had watched him drive off with mixed emotions before she turned to answer Warfield, who rudely hopped off the boardwalk and stalked away in the direction of Bodey's store.

It was midafternoon by then, and Bodey closed at two on Sundays. Arch wouldn't find much of an audience, she reflected as she let herself into the office. Maybe it was enough that he had castigated her today.

The office was an oasis of quiet. She could hear Mother Colleran clumping around above her, and a lighter, firmer step that had to be Reese. Just as well that she stayed down here. She felt drained from her battle of wits with Dennis.

It was that damned perfidious will, she thought, easing herself into her desk chair with her back to the door and her elbows propped on her worktable. It kept rising like a spectre to haunt her, and she and Dennis kept beating at it like it was some kind of burning bush they had to extinguish. Dennis always wanted one thing, and she the other, and he nearly always gave in to her.

She had always theorized that Frank had written the will directly after their marriage, and that in spite of her obsession with working at the paper he had forgotten to change it. It just wasn't possible that he saw her as the proper manager and editor and that he had really wanted her to carry on after his death. But then, he hadn't expected to die.

And now, somehow, Dennis was trying to interpret its terms to mean that Frank would have blessed a marriage between them!

111

It was so outrageous a thought it defied belief. And yet he obviously believed it.

She didn't know quite where to go from there. He was the executor and the man to whom she was bound by the terms of the will to turn to for advice and money, which was allocated to her at his discretion.

She wondered what his discretion would be after this rejection of his advances. He wasn't a man to take such a rebuff lightly. He took his duty to Frank—and to her—very seriously.

He *could* make her step down from the paper.

No, he could fight her to take control of the paper, and she would go down battling with every ounce of strength.

He wouldn't do that.

He was a decorous man who was proud of his standing in Colville and of his service to Frank while he was alive and to his widow after his death. He would never censure her publicly. He would never do anything that would reflect badly on him.

What *could* he do?

She supposed, in a blinding moment of insight, she ought to reread the terms of the will; she thought she knew them by heart, but possibly there *was* something there that he could use against her.

Unless . . . unless he was content to bide his time and wait her out or doggedly pursue her in spite of her protestations. Yes, that would be just like him. He might very well pretend that he had shocked her by his proposals, that he hadn't waited long enough, or phrased things delicately enough so that she could consider them completely.

He was powerless, she thought, unless he became vindictive. And then he would be a formidable enemy. But she refused to consider that. She could win him over somehow. The events of the day were explosive enough without her mulling over just how vicious an opponent

Dennis Coutts might make. It didn't warrant the effort. Things weren't that bad.

They weren't . . .

"Well, Miss . . . you took long enough."

"Long enough for what, Mother Colleran?" she asked, looking up blindly, never having heard her mother-in-law's approach.

"You know what," Mother Colleran snapped. "And with that Dennis Coutts! Honestly, Maggie, you think someone didn't see you or that the whole town won't be talking about you tomorrow?"

"Well, fine," Maggie retorted. "It will replace Reese's living with *us* as the topic of conversation around Bodey's store."

Her mother-in-law looked horrified. "But Reese is *family*, not some upstart who wants to seize an opportunity."

"What opportunity is that, Mother Colleran?"

Her mother-in-law sent her a smug look. "Everyone knows that Dennis Coutts has had his eye on you ever since Frank was laid to rest. You're not that simple, Maggie. Surely you could see that?"

"Why no. Dennis is a good friend and trusted advisor, Mother Colleran, who somehow read into the terms of Frank's will that Frank's indigent mother should have a home and a stipend. I believe we owe him a great deal of gratitude for his sensitivity."

"He's a rotten advisor and friend," Mother Colleran hissed, "if he didn't convince Frank to change his will before he died."

"But we all have to live with that, Mother Colleran, including me."

"I don't see where *you've* come off so badly, my girl. I would go so far as to say it looks very suspicious."

"You have said it before, Mother Colleran. I am now waiting to see how Reese is going to prove it."

She caught her; she caught the old witch, and it was gratifying to watch her sputter to find words that would deny the charge that both of them knew to be true. Maybe the thing the old crow hadn't counted on was Reese liking her so much. Good. She liked him too, and if he had other plans she could learn to dislike him very fast.

"Nonsense," Mother Colleran said sharply, finally regaining a sense of what she should say, "Reese is here to visit me, nothing more, nothing less."

"That's fine, Mother Colleran. I'm glad. I'm glad you were able to hunt him down, and I'm glad he was able to come at your request. But over and above that, I'm glad you understand that his presence here makes no difference to me whatsoever."

She was stunned to see that complacent look settle on her mother-in-law's thick features.

"Maybe it will, maybe it won't," she said placidly, as if the implicit threat meant nothing to her at all. "We'll see, my dear Maggie, we'll see."

Chapter Seven

—

It became, finally, a day she wished were well over by the time her mother-in-law left her alone. Instead the thought occurred to her that she had yet to see Logan this day as he had promised, and she was wary of seeing him at all.

No, she didn't want to see him. She had had enough of men and their wants and wishes today. Logan had very definite wants and wishes, and she did not have the stamina to cope with another dictatorial man.

But as the afternoon wore into evening, she began to feel petulant about the fact that he did not come. Instead, she ate a solitary dinner in the apartment while Reese and her mother-in-law dined at the hotel after she declined to join them.

She made her mind utterly blank, pushing away thoughts of the afternoon and what Reese had said, and Dennis Coutts, and Mother Colleran; all of it she relegated to a little waste basket in the back of her head and concentrated instead on the coming week's work, on where she wanted to go and the things she wanted to know, and how much or little she ought to dog the steps of the engineers as they laid out the plan for the track. How much or little she ought to let Reese help, if he really were sincere in his offer to help—and what kind of help he could give her that she would willingly accept.

And so she came back to Reese and Dennis and the magic of Logan's presence the previous night, and what she had felt, and . . . what she wanted to feel again.

So . . .

She made the admission. In spite of exigencies of the day, *and* her feelings about Reese and Dennis, she wanted to see Logan. She just wanted to *see* him. She had had the feeling the morning of Frank's memorial service—she needed to see Logan.

It was crazy.

Reese and Mother Colleran returned and roundly castigated her for passing up a good meal and the unexpected and welcome company at the table: friends of Mother Colleran's, at which Maggie looked askance, who had wanted to meet Reese, were so happy to meet Reese, and would have loved to see Maggie, even if they did disagree with her railroad politics. Yes, they had wanted to tell her so, too.

And Dennis was there, and that Logan Ramsey, Mother Colleran was not loath to tell her. All her friends except the Mapes, and everyone knew they couldn't afford the luxury of having a hotel dinner anyway.

Logan was in town. Her heartbeat accelerated with alarming speed. But he hadn't come, and there was nothing to say he might come later. Maybe later? Maybe the same time as the night before?

She was going crazy. She didn't want to see him after all. He had nothing to offer her except the very same words she had heard from Reese and Dennis; he wanted the very same thing, and he had no compunction about being blunt about it either.

All his fine talk about "other ways" . . .

Her body stiffened instantly at the thought, and she almost felt as though her mother-in-law could see it and

116

knew exactly what was on her mind.

She could not allow Logan to do this to her, yet she couldn't stop thinking about his words and his kisses. . . .

The discouraging thing was Mother Colleran's self-satisfied expression as she sat and listened and did a bit of knitting that she kept by her parlor chair. It was an elegant device, the knitting; she never got beyond the first ten rows or so, and yet her preoccupation with it gave her an air of concentrated intelligence that she did not really possess. Maggie was sure she ripped out half the rows she made every night.

It was a sweet family scene, with the kerosene lamps shedding a soft warm light over the room and a fire crackling in the fireplace and sending out a wispy, smoky heat that did not warm the air at all. Reese somehow took on the stance of the man of the house, deferring to his elderly mother, playing to the pretty lady who sat in a side chair by the fire—the woman of the house in the steel engraving. It was perfect—and specious.

They had to go to bed sometime, she thought, and she waited them out until Mother Colleran's head began drooping and her gnarled fingers dropped the knitting into her lap.

Only then did Reese stop talking. With a conspiratorial smile at Maggie he took charge of waking his mother and seeing her comfortably to bed.

And after . . . "Maggie?"

"I'm wide awake, Reese. Don't let me stop you though."

"I'll keep you company for a while." He sounded eager, too eager, and she curled up inside in resignation. It wasn't that he wasn't an entertaining talker. He had a hundred stories, both amusing and hair-raising, about his travels, and he took gentle swipes periodically at the family situation that had sent him from the bosom of his family when the Collerans were one of the pillars of San

117

Francisco society.

Maggie listened to them and did not hear them. Eventually, she thought, he had to become tired of the sound of his own voice. Or perhaps he was testing her, or waiting for some kind of invitation he must know would never come.

And what if Logan were waiting for her?

Let him wait.

She almost couldn't bear the thought of it. It was as if the events of the day were telescoped in her mind to something minuscule and meaningless in comparison to the fevered excitement of the thought of being with Logan.

Except of course he apparently did not want to be with her. He hadn't come, and she had only the drone of Reese's pleasant voice to keep her company.

"I believe I am getting tired," she said finally.

"All right then. But I must tell you, Maggie, I could really warm up to this familial feeling you exude very easily. I am very much at home here, and I hope you don't mind my telling you, in spite of what we said this morning."

"No, I don't mind," she said, but the thought crossed her mind that he would be comfortable around anyone who was willing to listen to him for as many hours as she had.

She touched his shoulder as she passed him on her way to her room. He was still so likable and harmless—so far. His candor sat well with her, and she even thought she felt a little affection for him, especially after he had defended her to his mother.

She sank onto her bed wearily, feeling the weight of a massive disappointment sink into her bones as she listened for the tell-tale thump of Reese's boots that would indicate he was on his way to bed.

But his footsteps receded instead, and moments later,

she heard their measured tread down the outside stairs. She ran to the window in time to see him emerge from the apartment door, and head down the boardwalk, back in the direction of the hotel.

She felt an irrational fury that he had the freedom to go and come back like that while she was tied to her room by the rules of propriety. She almost thought she should run after him and seek Logan out herself, but that, she thought, would make her no better than Melinda Sable, who by virtue of her reputation had the latitude to do the things that she, Maggie, yearned to do.

God, it was so unfair.

She could run a newspaper and support her mother-in-law, but she couldn't walk abroad at night, couldn't make love with impunity and without consequences, couldn't eat alone at the hotel as Reese was no doubt doing now: having a midnight tidbit along with his whiskey, damn him.

All she could do was wait, and it seemed to her, as she stared into the blackness of the night, that a woman's life was compounded of so many small moments of waiting. She did not know how it was possible to endure the uncertainty.

The only way was not to place her reliance on anyone but herself; it was the only way. Anything else led to disaster. Look at her braying at the window, wishing for something with Logan that she knew she could not have.

It was better that he had not come, better for her. After tonight she would never be caught waiting again.

And then a dark shadow moved and her heart felt like it would shatter. She knew if she made her way down the inner stairs to the office that she would find Logan at the door.

Without making a sound, she slipped down to the

printing room and lit a lamp. A moment later he knocked at the door and she opened it with trembling hands to let him in.

And then she didn't know what to do.

But Logan knew what to do. He took her right into his arms and held her tightly. She felt all the tension drain out of her body, then he released her, picked up the lamp, took her hand and said, "Come into the office. We'll talk."

He set the lamp down at the far end of the room and put her in her desk chair while he grabbed a plain wooden chair, turned it around, and settled himself opposite her with his arms braced on the chair rail.

She couldn't say anything for a long while. She couldn't find a single word to bridge that gap between the events of the day and his arrival at her door. She just stared at him, and his eyes kindled, brighter than the lamplight.

"What are you thinking, Maggie?" he asked finally, with a smile in his voice.

She didn't know what she was thinking, but she felt that she couldn't let him believe that she had been *waiting* for him. "I was thinking how fortuitous it was that I just happened to be down here when you arrived." Well, the lie tripped neatly from her tongue, but she saw she didn't fool him at all.

"*Are* we going to play those kinds of games, Maggie?" he murmured, extending one hand to touch her face.

"That is all I have been doing all day," she snapped, rearing back, away from his dangerous, dangerous caress.

"Everyone wants your head," he said sympathetically, removing his hand immediately.

"And me," she added testily, this time without considering the effect of her words.

He stiffened imperceptibly and the atmosphere between them altered. He didn't need any elaboration; he knew exactly what she meant.

"I see," he said slowly, "but you weren't waiting for me."

"I am rather worn out by men with unrealistic expectations today," Maggie said tightly, and then she wondered why she was trying to scare him off when her feelings about him were so contradictory.

He smiled. It was an endearing little smile that lifted one corner of his mouth in a conspiratorial salute to her distress. "I can assure you, Maggie, that *I* have no unrealistic expectations whatsoever."

"I was sure of it," she said tartly, hating his smile and the companionable warmth in his voice.

"Of course, they haven't known you as long as I have."

"That might be a distinct advantage," Maggie said heatedly. She hated his smugness and her growing feeling he knew exactly why she was so irritated.

He shrugged. "It might well be actually. No one else will ever get to see you in a fit of ill humor. You surely don't put on your best face for me. On the other hand, I want you in spite of all that, so maybe that's a distinct advantage to you."

Oh, and didn't he turn that around neatly, she thought. But what had she expected him to say? Or was she angry because he had not tried to touch her, or kiss her, or seduce her?

"And I was so sure you would rethink that notion."

"Which one, the advantage or the fact that I want you?"

"*Both.*"

He shook his head. "No, Maggie. That's too easy—for you."

"I beg to differ. It's too easy for you, and impossibly hard for me."

The expression in his eyes flickered and softened. "I

121

told you, it doesn't have to be."

"With you."

"Only with me, Maggie," he said, examining her tired face. "But you know that. You especially know it today."

She turned her head away. How perceptive of him. How distressingly clever. She had wanted to hear that, and she hadn't, and the split in her desire tore her two ways. If he were so astute he would not press her, he wouldn't touch her, he would never speak of some kind of connection between them.

And if he didn't, she would brand him a liar and no better than any other man of her acquaintance.

She liked that; her impossible need put him right in a corner where he had to make the right decision—only she could define what it was.

"Do I?" she murmured.

"Don't evade me, Maggie; you can't do it."

"Oh, I guess I can't, since you know me so well."

"And I know why I'm here, too, Maggie. Do you want to deny that?"

"I could."

"I'd leave."

That abrupt rejoinder made her raise her eyes to his. Implicit in the two words was the no-nonsense warning— *I won't come back.* Men like Logan didn't play coy games; they were straightforward and real, and she believed that his feeling for her was genuine. But it had been born out of a common past and his subsequent loss of her to Frank. Now she was not the same Maggie Lynch he thought he knew.

All he knew was that he had the power to arouse her deepest secret yearnings. Her only decision was whether she wanted to explore those feelings or put Logan out of her life altogether.

"Yes, you would," she said slowly as the light went out of his eyes and his expression closed up. She waited for him to say something else, but he watched her guardedly and did not say another word.

He was not going to pressure her, she realized; it would be her decision, and she wondered what she had thought he might do.

She knew what, in the darkest place in her heart, she thought she wanted him to do, and she knew what she had to say.

"I don't want you to leave."

The tension eased from his body and his face. "What *do* you want, Maggie?"

"I don't know," she whispered. "You'll have to tell me."

He shook his head again. "I can only tell you what I want, Maggie. I can tell you about my dreams and my fears, and the things I thought about and couldn't share with you, and everything I imagined could happen between us, and a lot that was just plain daydreams that got crazy out of hand from pain and maybe loneliness. I could tell you about long, long nights trailing cows up to Cheyenne and all the forbidden things I thought about, and I could tell you about aching nights in my own bed. But then, you see, there was never a chance that my wants would be satisfied."

"And now?" she murmured, spellbound by his voice and the heated images his words conjured up.

"And now there's a chance," he said gently.

Yes, she thought, and there was more than a chance if she could only let herself acknowledge that she wanted to hear everything he had to tell her.

"We have time, Maggie," he added softly, as he read indecision in her eyes. "We don't have to do anything but talk."

She almost said, I don't want to talk, but then she thought that perhaps she did. "What would we talk about?"

And she saw she didn't fool him one bit with that question.

"You," he said pointedly.

She visibly shied away from him. Not her. There was nothing about her he did not know anyway. Not now. "What about you?" she evaded.

"I'll tell you anything you want to know."

Her eyes widened at that blatant male forthrightness. It was nothing more than a brazen challenge, even though there was not a nuance of provocation in his tone. She had to take it up. She had to. Even the thought of asking a question made her insides churn with a kind of forbidden excitement, as if this were something she should not want, should not even test. But he made her feel that way, and his words evoked an unbearable tension in her because she knew now the weight of her own privation.

And yet, to demand to hear these things was almost unthinkable; a woman could not command the knowledge of a man's innermost thoughts and feelings. She had no right to make him reveal anything to her, she who had not recognized the depth of feeling within him to begin with. She had no claims here, and yet he was handing her everything in the hope that together somehow they could nuture something out of the remnants of a broken past.

What would she want to know? She knew he wanted her and that he was intent on pursuing her, perhaps he even wanted to marry her, though he had said nothing of that. She knew what he made her feel, and she knew there was a passion in her that had been doused like fire, but that still lived in a faint smoldering ember in the center of her womanhood. He didn't have to tell her any of this. She knew the things she wanted to know were the things he had dreamed on those long empty nights that he had been alone and she had been in Frank Colleran's arms.

She had the feeling he knew it too, and that he wanted to wipe all those memories from her mind and her heart, and that he would do it with words before he did it with his kisses.

He waited for her to ask, and she could not quite bring herself to do it.

"What should I want to know?" she asked finally.

A faint smile played across his mouth. "You're a damned incurious woman, Maggie. I can't believe that you don't have a single question."

"Not one," she said stoutly. After all, neither of them had had a life before this moment when any words she uttered would create a new one.

His smile deepened. Stubborn woman, he thought, seeing all the questions in her eyes. "I thought we weren't going to play games, Maggie."

"I'm hard pressed to find a reason to pry into your private life," she retorted.

But oh so curious, he thought, admiring her backbone, admiring *her*. "I'll answer your questions, Maggie; you don't even have to ask them."

"But you don't—"

"I do. And I'll tell you exactly what you want to know. All the dreams, because I knew I could never touch you again after you chose Frank. All those nights of wanting you in my arms when I knew I could not have you. And all the things I wanted to do if I could only have another chance. All the things I imagined when nothing was possible ever again."

She swallowed against the tightness in her throat. She wanted to speak, she wanted to ask him what forbidden things he had imagined, and her throat closed up so she couldn't say a word.

"But you know what I imagined, Maggie," he murmured, almost as if he could read her mind. "I

125

imagined just kissing you for hours at a time. I envisioned what it would be like to undress you every night, and I carried you naked to my bed and made love to you there. I made love to you everywhere; in the fields, in the house, in this office, on that table where I knew did your writing—everywhere. I saw you in your thick leather apron and you were naked underneath, ready for me. I saw you dressed to work in this office with the knowledge that what was underneath you wore solely for me. I imagined you sitting in that chair at your desk dressed only in a silken robe, waiting for me. I had you sitting in my lap, fully dressed, and letting me feel you everywhere, letting me touch, letting me kiss . . . is it enough, Maggie? Do you want to know more?"

She reached out her hand blindly, whether to negate his question or encourage him he did not know, and he took it into his firm grip and held it tightly. "I conjured a hundred different ways to make love to you in a hundred different places. I have you now, Maggie, and I'm not going to let go."

He tugged on her hand to draw her forward. "Maggie!" He felt her resistance, and he pulled again gently until he felt her give and her body move forward, until she was directly opposite him, face to face, her eyes shuttered and her expression faintly wary.

He relinquished her hand to touch her face. "That's all you have to know, Maggie. The rest I'll show you, not tonight, maybe not for a while, but soon sometime, you will let me love you and we'll explore those hundred ways."

She found her voice then, after feeling utterly overwhelmed by his raw emotion, because she knew it didn't matter what he wanted. What mattered was the end result, the cost to her if she were careless and allowed herself to be entranced by his wanton words.

"And then what?" she asked, and her voice was hoarse with some other kind of passion.

He knew what it was and what she wanted to hear. "Maggie, I would marry you in a minute, but you don't love me and you don't want to be married right now. You've said it and I believe it. You think it leads to constraints that won't allow you the freedom you have now. Fine. You don't want a child. Fine. But you need me and I sure as hell want you, and that is just how we will be until you decide otherwise."

"That is too much to ask of you," she threw at him, because she needed to find distance from those heated words that had painted forbidden pictures for her. She saw herself everywhere, with him, just as he wanted. She wanted to do it, all of it, and she wanted to run away from her desire.

"Damn it, Maggie, it was too much to ask for me to accept your marriage to Frank. Nothing is too damned much after that. Maggie—if I touch you, you'll know. If I kiss you again, you want me to kiss you again, you want all of that . . ." his voice deepened as he gauged her response, "and I want you."

She felt helpless and torn. He understood so much and she comprehended so little. "How—where?" Already the complications intruded, dancing around in her mind tormentingly. Even if she wanted to she had Mother Colleran to contend with, and Reese, and *he* was so far away to begin with.

"Here, whenever I can get away. You'll know, Maggie."

Yes, she thought, I will know. She saw no reason to say no; she couldn't see how it could work. And that, she thought, would damp down his desire faster than anything else.

He left without touching her, and she felt an angry

127

disappointment that he had not at least kissed her. She had wanted him to kiss her, and now she would have to wait—for everything. She wondered if it had been deliberate, if he had known that she would spend the long night hours thinking of the carnal images he had evoked and the desire he had aroused in her, and she wondered how long he would taunt her by staying away.

Chapter Eight

In the morning everything was the same—and nothing was the same. She dressed for business as usual and was down in the office at six o'clock as was her habit. A.J. joined her shortly thereafter and they talked over the coming week's events and how to pitch their coverage of the railroad story from then on. They talked about the events Arch Warfield should cover and whether Maggie herself should follow the progress of the engineers or whether A.J. should do it. They prepared their newsprint order and checked back over the business ads they had printed the week before to make sure to solicit new ads this week. They checked the print case to be sure that the typefaces were clean and unbroken.

They did all the small chores they normally did the weekday following publication, and yet Maggie felt the difference and the underlying excitement that something cataclysmic was going to happen, something that appealed to her deepest sense of her womanly self. Not knowing when it would happen heightened her expectation and her tension. And the waiting, she discovered, made her want it more.

Her hands trembled as she wrote down the day's schedule and she thought about his seductive words. She bit her lips and remembered his kisses. She felt her body strain to the memory of his touch.

He didn't come, and her restless night was fraught with sensual visions of what might have happened and what didn't. How could his fancies have captivated her so completely when she had resisted them so ardently?

He did not come, and she felt, the next day, that that was fine and just as it should be. She was not Melinda Sable, to be had at any man's whim for whatever price she cared to claim. Logan was no different from any other man: if his ploy didn't work, he would seek solace elsewhere, and no doubt he had done that. And it was just as well. She didn't want the entanglement, she didn't need the tension of the emotion.

She felt frenetic at the end of the day. Her body was telling her a totally different story, and she hated having no control over her desire. It crept up on her willy-nilly, at times when she needed her full faculties for the job at hand. She would sit staring, thinking wanton thoughts that had nothing to do with the work on her desk.

How had he done this to her? No, she was doing it to herself. She had let him talk and now she couldn't forget a word he had said.

He did not come.

She went out in the streets the next day in Reese's company, stayed a half hour in Bodey's store, stopped by the stage depot to hear news of any new arrivals in town, had lunch with Reese at the hotel, and listened for gossip, and all the while the thrumming excitement pulsed through her veins. And there was the waiting—the waiting that was the lot of women like her.

She felt taut as a bowstring, ready to snap.

Reese found her curiously preoccupied and not a little distracted.

"Well, I hardly have the same means of seeking relief as a man does," she said waspishly, and realized after she said it that he could interpret it more than one way. God, her unruly mouth.

"Oh now Maggie, surely there's a decanter of whiskey in some sideboard in that apartment. You don't need company to drink, for heaven's sake."

She sent him a skeptical look. "I don't drink anyway."

"Of course you don't," he said comfortingly.

And then back at the office there was Jean, looking at her with a hectic expression in his eyes as she entered with Reese.

On her desk was a stack of handwritten notes. More words, she thought, sinking down into her chair resignedly. Just not the right ones.

His note was on the bottom. *Tonight, same time.*

She crumpled it up, started to toss it away and then thought the better of it and slipped it into her pocket of her apron.

Tonight.

She felt feverish all over again. She couldn't for the life of her imagine tonight. Tonight felt like it was a thousand hours away. Tonight he would . . . come. How could she envision anything past that, when she felt such betrayal that she had had to wait.

Mother Colleran got in her way. Dennis sent his own note, reminding her to remember her promise about her treatment of the railroad. Jean seemed everywhere around her, hovering in a way that made her extraordinarily uncomfortable.

Everything felt out of shape and moving in the slowest possible motion. Mother Colleran ate dinner and Reese went out. Maggie ate at her desk in the company of Jean, who had decided to work late.

Tonight, same time. Would Jean never leave?

He finally left. She went upstairs to spend an hour or so with Mother Colleran, whose everlasting complaint was that no one paid any attention to her, and even though Reese was here he seemed to have found a set of friends to keep him away at night, and anyway, the whole thing was Maggie's fault. Maggie wasn't nice enough to Reese. Maggie wouldn't let him help with the newspaper. Maggie, Maggie, Maggie . . .

She went downstairs finally to escape the carping. The woman was mad. She couldn't possibly have thought Maggie would let Reese anywhere near the paper.

It didn't matter. Nothing mattered but the slow ticking of the clock and her growing anticipation as the night sounds around her melted into silence and a rhythmic beating that mirrored the pounding of her own heart.

Much later, as she listened, she heard Reese come back and then go out again. She decided she would not light a lamp tonight, in case Reese should return and come to investigate. She would do nothing but remain by the door until she heard Logan's signal. She would let him in of her own free will and then she would bear the consequences.

Later still, there was a soft knock at the rear door in the printing room. She opened the door and felt his solid male presence as he entered and closed the door silently behind him.

He reached for her unerringly in the dark, and she knew this was the ineffable moment for which she had waited. She felt the touch of his hands first, drawing her tightly against the length of his body. Then there was the shock of his hands moving up her arms to her shoulders and neck and upward to cup her face to center it, in the dark, in that breathless instant before his lips touched hers. And then there was just the pure hot sensation of penetration and the luscious taste of him seeking the essence of her.

What was the essence but the giving, the surrendering of that part of her sensual soul to his demand of that

132

moment? She yielded it willingly.

Here, in the dark, there were no questions that could not be answered; there was only the sense that this capitulation was foreordained, not because of her hunger but because of his constancy and his desire to change and reorder the past.

"There's no light," she whispered against his lips at one point.

"We don't need one," he murmured, touching her lips with his fingers, feeling their softness and texture, feeling them quiver as he stroked the tender inner side of the lower lip before nipping at it lightly.

No, she thought, they didn't need one. The darkness illuminated everything for her. The forbidden became admissable, because she knew he would do nothing she did not want him to do.

And she wanted his kisses. If she had nothing else but tonight her ordeal of waiting would have been worth it. She adored how he kissed her, the way he slowly and voluptuously fit his mouth against hers in just such a way that she could do nothing but part her lips to admit his questing tongue. Her arms wound around him to pull him even deeper within her, and she allowed herself the kind of wanton response she had never experienced with Frank.

He lost himself in it. Never had he thought that she would give herself to him so completely so soon. There was no submerged anger in her tonight. Her need for what he offered was real: he could taste her fierce demand. Her glittering sensuality was totally untapped, he thought, and he was going to be the one to unleash the storm within her. Oh, but slowly, ever so slowly. He knew she thought she would be using him, that *he* was to be her convenience. And why not, as long as he wanted it this much? But she didn't know the rest. She didn't know she could love him, she didn't know he was going to seduce her until she was conscious only of the need to join with him, and *only* him. Then she would know where her destiny lay.

Even so, her passionate kisses made his head reel, made him almost lose command of his senses, made him want to reach for her and couple with her in the most primitive and elemental way. It was that terrible craving for her that he had to learn to control.

But if he touched her anywhere he might explode. She might explode. He never dreamed that her kisses could be so incendiary, or that the press of her body against his would arouse him to a fever to possess her that was almost impossible to subdue. He wanted everything— tonight, and he knew nothing was possible but the lush possession of her mouth and his firm hold of her pulsating body.

It was enough for tonight to feel her yearning and stroke her desire.

"Maggie . . ."

"Don't stop."

"Shhh . . ." He touched her lips. "Come inside . . ."

"Yes—" She took his hand and carefully led him into the office. Yes, here there would be even more privacy, in the dark, with the door closed and the magic of him to light her way. She found her chair and he settled into it and pulled her down on his lap.

The feeling of taking her body against his was so natural. Every movement of her torso as she twisted to find a comfortable position sounded a chord in him that demanded to be answered.

A sensual heat arose between them as she became aware of his pounding heart and powerful scent and the thick, pulsating length of him beneath her.

She licked her lips, thinking of what that meant to her—that she was here with him willingly, that she wanted his kisses, that she wanted him to hold her, and

134

more, that she wanted him to touch her anywhere he wanted to.

She drew her breath in with a little hiss as her imagination envisioned the torrid caresses that he had yet to initiate. Only the avid thrust of his rock-hard manhood against her bottom told her that his desire was growing every bit as volcanic as hers.

He was holding back as he had promised, and yet he had her in his arms in a way that would allow him to feel her and arouse her just as he had dreamed of doing. Just the way she wanted him to.

And so it happened: *she* had crossed the line into a fevered erotic yearning that was rushing headlong into pure greediness, a greed to experience the lush sensations she knew he could excite in her.

But he had said, and she remembered, that he would not do anything she did not want him to.

She wanted him to.

When had she come to that?

Her hands moved of their own volition around his neck to pull his mouth down against hers.

"I need your kisses," she whispered, and gratifyingly, his mouth crushed down over hers as though he had been waiting for this bold invitation.

"Tell me more, Maggie," he murmured between his sultry kisses and the heated thrust of his tongue as he expertly explored every inch of her mouth.

"I want more," she sighed, opening her mouth to him again, reveling in the feel of his hands in her hair, holding her again in that precise way as if he were drinking nectar from her lips.

She moved her own hands to touch his face, downward to feel the movement of his mouth on hers as he plunged voraciously into her mouth, seeking, dueling, playing, tasting, easing away to lick her lips, to rim them with the wet heat of his tongue.

Everything he did in this carnal probing aroused her beyond anything in her experience. She didn't want him to stop, and she wanted, she wanted . . .

. . . she didn't want to want . . .

. . . she felt him sucking her tongue so very gently . . .

. . . she felt him elongating under her as if that part of him were some separate entity seducing her as well . . .

. . . she wanted . . .

His sucking became intense, overtly sensual, bewitching her with the ravishing motion of his lips pulling against her tongue just . . . lusciously . . . so . . .

She moved with this erotic provocation because she could not help it; her body wanted the movement that the gorgeous motion of his lips foretold. She remembered, oh how she remembered . . . and there for the taking was the powerful essence, the potent maleness, the culmination of what she really wanted.

Her hips ground against his towering sex in a timeless mating dance. Timeless, the whole was timeless, and they would come to it, she knew now they would come to it, as her body felt the living heat of his manhood through the layers of clothes and the hot naked kisses of his mouth, kisses that made her want to strip away her clothes and bare herself to him totally.

His mouth moved away from hers, hovering a mere breath away as his sensitive fingers touched her swollen lips. She was shaking with excitement and arousal. He wanted to move his hands, he wanted to feel her pulsating body that he had incited into such an erotic heat, and all he could do was wait.

"Maggie . . ."

"Oh God . . ."

"I'll stay here all night kissing you."

"Yes, kiss me, kiss me again just the same way; I love how you kiss me," and a moment later, his tongue sought hers and his lips closed around it and began the same

136

rhythmic caress, while he felt the one part of her body that she could not deny him—her beautiful face and neck and the insatiable motion of her wanton tongue.

And then it all became one, a fusion of her body rocking against his ramrod manhood, arching upward as if she were demanding his caress, and the firm enticing thrust of her tongue in concert with his mouth, and the darkness, and the fiery response of her, and the smooth texture of her skin, and his explosive need of her. His one hand reached for her, sliding down her chest to meet the straining tip of her breast. The buttons, the hell-be-damned buttons . . . He gripped the buttons and ripped them away, stripping the impeding material from her body until he could feel the naked lushness of her breast in his hand.

He wouldn't let her break the kiss. He held her and he kissed her until her faint tremor turned into yearning once more. Only then did he begin his exquisite exploration of her luscious breast. He felt her arch toward him so he could hold her more fully; he felt her body squirm tantalizingly against his tumescence as he touched her nipple and caressed and gently squeezed its voluptuous tip.

Her hips jolted against him at the first wild feeling of his fingers. She had been waiting for this, she thought somewhere in the cataclysmic fog where she floated in a sensual haze. She loved how he played with her nipple, rubbing his fingers over it, sliding his hand all over the roundness of her breast and then back again to the lush tip, holding it between his fingers so gently she could just barely tell they were there.

The knowing and the not knowing incited her to a tumultuous arousal. Her body responded to his hot kisses and his fondling of her nipple; white-hot moistness drenched her. Her body rippled, ready for anything, wanting everything, as his fingers surrounded her nipple and made her firmly aware of his possession.

Her body melted against him and her mouth went wild with urgent kisses. Her hips undulated erotically against the iron length of him in rhythm with the hot pulling of his lips against her tongue and the lush stroking of his fingers on her pebble-hard nipple.

Heat gushed through her, streaming through her veins, spiraling downward in a smoldering paroxysm of sensation that resonated into a crystalline feeling that hovered for one long moment somewhere in the deepest feminine part of her before it shattered into a huge glistening point of light.

She tore her mouth away from his and wrenched his hand away from her body, feeling him shudder just as she collapsed against him. He wrapped his arms around her as tightly as he could, and his lips brushed her hair.

"You are wonderful," he murmured against her ear.

That was wonderful, she wanted to say. She felt her nakedness now, and she was glad of the darkness, and yet the time in his arms seemed so short before he had to be going. She started thinking about the nature of what they had done in the dark and how she wanted to do it again—soon.

"When?" she finally brought herself to ask him.

He felt himself stiffen again at the thought of when. He wished he could carry her off to the ranch and make love to her all night, all day, all the time.

"Tomorrow," he promised, even though he did not know whether it could be tomorrow, or even whether he could bear to let her go tonight.

"Tomorrow," she murmured, nestling against him for the few more moments they had left of this night.

His body reacted and she knew it. His desire spurted to life again and they both felt it.

She trembled at the thought of it, and she remembered what he had done. She almost thought of begging him to

138

stay. . . . Oh, but stay where?

He knew she was moments away from full, wanton arousal. He ached to caress her all over again. But the time . . . he felt the full impact of the fleeting time and the knowledge that this would be their only meeting place until she decided she wanted something more.

There was no time to be leisurely, no time for second kisses and caresses lest they lead elsewhere, and no time for completion after that. God, he hated it. He wanted her again and all he could do was prepare to leave her. His only consolation was that she was as unhappy about it as he was.

Tomorrow . . . the talisman; they would have time all over again tomorrow. It shouldn't take her long to see that all they had was endless tomorrows with no future, he thought. In the end she would want their union just as much as he.

Tomorrow was Thursday already, and with one part of her mind she dealt with the complexities of pulling the paper together, handling Arch Warfield and his militant pro-railroad articles with some diplomacy. And with the other, she damped down the hot memories of the previous night and tried to pretend it had not happened.

She was in the buggy with Reese, following the survey team to check its progress, when it occurred to her that it might make things easier if Logan had a key so he could let himself in to wait for her.

She was in the back room with Jean doing local advertising layout when she thought of not wearing underclothing when she dressed for him tonight.

She was at her worktable, penciling out the more fulsome phrases in Arch Warfield's articles when she remembered his succulent kisses. Her body vibrated instantly with yearning.

She had her usual consultations with A.J., and although she thought she sounded coherent she wasn't sure since she was remembering the feeling of Logan caressing her breast.

How could she stand to wait until tonight? *Late* tonight.

"Well, let's see," she murmured, as A.J. plunked himself down next to her so they could go over the order of the newsworthy articles. "Nothing new on Denver North. The survey will be completed this week, and then I suppose the circus will begin. All right. No especially important visitors in town. The usual aunt from Denver and cousin from Texas, I believe. Now, I understand we have some new advertising, so maybe that should be more prominent than inside the backfold page. I'm running a shorter editorial this week. My heart's not in it for some reason, or maybe I'm just suspicious that Denver North is being so amenable to spending thousands of extra dollars to circle Gully Basin. But I guess we'll find out about that soon enough. Anything else, A.J.?"

"Well, we're thinking about listing property assessments and sales; the clerk requested we consider it so it'll be made public without him having to do so much work."

Maggie grimaced. "All right."

"We got some new babies. This was one quiet week, I'll tell you; I wonder if we shouldn't think about tacking in some Denver news."

Maggie shook her head. "No, then they'll expect it every week, and I'm not sure we can get hold of a Denver paper that frequently. This is enough. We'll dig out some filler. You can publish the property sales too, and the assessments. The new menu for the hotel dining room, if there is one. Reese's comings and goings, if you can figure them out. Mother Colleran's new interest in church social clubs. I'm babbling. Sorry, A.J."

"No problem, Miz Maggie. Maybe you should buy yourself a new dress. I heard the dress lady got a whole raft of them in the express today, ready-made."

"A.J.," she chided, dismissing him by turning her attention back to Warfield's convoluted prose.

The notion stuck. A new dress. One that perhaps would not have to be supported by stays. One that didn't have so many buttons, buttons that were irreplaceable, buttons she had crawled on the floor that very morning to retrieve. A simple dress. One he could remove with . . .

She caught her breath. She was thinking that far ahead already. And even farther ahead than that. She wanted him to undress her. She wanted him—*right now*.

Maggie threw down her pencil and walked to the front door, then turned around to look back into the room. It was so different in daylight. There was no scent of lust in this room in the daylight. No sense of the sensual darkness that had enfolded her in its torrid embrace. In the darkness, she thought, she could be as brazen as a queen.

She felt the heat creep into her cheeks. She couldn't keep thinking these thoughts. Her mind should be on business. Her mind was on Logan.

What if she should see him today? Could she look him in the eye after begging for his kisses and succumbing to his wanton caresses? Or did she only want him now in the dark, where the sole link between them was her desire for things erotic and forbidden?

What could she wear tonight to dress for him?

Why was she thinking this way?

Why was Jean looking at her so strangely from across the room?

She shook her head to clear away her dangerous thoughts and went outside, just for a moment, to let the clear oncoming spring air warm her.

She was a danger to herself, she thought, and she had not even known it. For the five years she had been courted and had been married to Frank, estranged from him, and finally widowed by him, she had never known the depth of hunger within her. And now it was unleashed. She saw that she could become a slave to it—or that Logan could make her one.

Nonetheless, even that sobering thought could not deter her from thinking about the night ahead. She would slake her thirst, she thought; she would fill the bottomless craving with sensual experiences that she could store against the day when he would demand more.

It made so much sense. He knew her limits and *he* was willing to abide by the boundaries that she had delineated. She couldn't see any reason why, in the cool light of the afternoon, she should not take advantage of what he was offering.

In the distance she saw Dennis Coutts on horseback, cantering down the main street, looking businesslike and determined. He was the last person she wanted to see today, but she knew he had seen her, so she stayed where she was until he reined his horse in and dismounted.

"I was thinking of you just as I got into town," he said in his same old companionable way.

"How nice to hear that. Any news for me?"

"I think not. I have a feeling your regular stringers would have scooped me anyway. No, things are quiet. Harold is busy counting his money and Denver North seems satisfied, for the moment. I trust you've held good to your word—you're not going after them this week?"

"No, not this week at any rate. Not that Arch has toned down his moralistic prose about the matter. I wish it were possible, but maybe you can tell me if it *is* possible, Dennis. Warfield is adamant that he and Frank had some kind of contract. I know I've asked you about it before, but it seems to me that whenever I find cause to get rid of him he brings it up, as if I'm supposed to honor it in spite of the circumstances. I know you've said you know nothing about it, but . . ."

He put up a temporizing hand. "I'll check it out again, Maggie. If he disturbs you that much, there must be a way to terminate him."

"Thanks, Dennis. Anything else?"

There was a brief pause before he answered her. "Nothing you'd care to listen to."

His tone was so bitter that she felt a pang. It would have worked out so wonderfully for him if he could have stepped into Frank's shoes, she thought, as she looked away from him to avoid the pain in his eyes. But she never could have given herself to him, not with the abandon with which she had welcomed Logan's desire— not Dennis, not ever. She couldn't picture herself begging for his kisses and wanting to feel his hands on her.

When she looked at him she saw that the hot look in his eyes was still intense, still hopeful. "Don't put that between us," she said, reaching out her hand to touch his arm.

He pulled away from her pettishly. "You don't have to console me, Maggie. I understand the situation clearly. All I want you to do is give me a chance to change your mind—when you're ready."

"How can I promise that?"

"Yes, well, we do go around in circles on this particular subject. Let's just say a pleasant good afternoon then," he muttered testily, and he mounted and left her standing there utterly nonplussed.

He hadn't believed her, obviously. What had she told him? She didn't want to give her life over to a man. . . . The irony of it. She had given one night to Logan Ramsey and look at how he controlled her thoughts already. She could concentrate on nothing else but the thought of

143

what was to come tonight.

Night fell finally. She was upstairs in her room trying to decide what to wear. Even the notion of taking this time to lay out a wardrobe that would give him the easiest access to her body amused her. She ought to be doing everything she could to obstruct his hands. But still, it was easy to dispense with the bothersome drawers and stockings and just wear the low-heeled kid boots as usual. A skirt . . . She had an old one that did not require the fasionable draping over a frame that was so impossible on the frontier. And she had a shirtwaist to go with it, but that seemed like too much. How daring did she think she could be?

How daring had he been?

She looked down at the plain cotton camisole she wore in place of the little corset he had destroyed last night. The remnants of her dress hung in her closet to remind her of everything exciting and forbidden. In truth, she needed to wear nothing more than this, and as she decided that she felt her body stiffen and her nipples peak against the soft, much washed material of the camisole.

She licked her lips uncertainly. She was making a statement by the way she dressed, she thought, and she had to be careful that it didn't lead anywhere but the path *she* wanted to follow.

Nevertheless, as she donned a jacket over the camisole in preparation for the evening's after dinner hour with Mother Colleran, she felt the edgy excitement possess her at the knowledge she was naked under those clothes and that very soon, she would be encouraging Logan to discover it too.

She was so aware of her nakedness as she sat with Mother Colleran. With every movement she made she could feel the hardness of her nipples against the camisole and the mounding wetness of her femininity. Her desire flared like a living thing. She wondered that her mother-in-law could not read her salacious thoughts as she sat so decorously across the room from her and reveled in sensual anticipation.

Any moment, any moment . . . Mother Colleran went to bed. Reese had been long gone. She went to her room and removed her jacket. Ten minutes later, she slipped down the stairs and awaited Logan's signal.

It came instantly, softly, impatiently, as though he had been waiting a long time. "Hurry," she breathed, throwing herself into his arms so that the weight of them together eased the door closed. His lips were on hers before he was wholly in the room. His tongue entered her mouth with a long taut thrust, and she opened herself to receive him. A hot wanton wetness possessed her tongue, and she gave herself to it with total sensual abandon. He avidly tasted her all over again, as if he hadn't spent hours exploring her mouth the night before.

She heard words somewhere in between his luscious kisses; she answered him, hardly breathing the words as his lips hovered above hers, seeking her lips even before she had finished speaking.

"Ah," she murmured at each firm foray of his tongue between her lips. "I couldn't wait . . . I couldn't wait . . ." Her tongue sought his. "I couldn't wait. Kiss me again. Don't talk . . ." He didn't talk. He kissed her and he kissed her, his tongue sliding all over her lips and into her mouth, reaching endlessly for the arousing lushness of her, easing away to murmur against her lips, nipping at her lips, her words inciting him with brazen sensuality as she demanded his kisses.

"Oh yes," she breathed now and again, "yes—kiss the way you kissed me last night. . . ." He took her tongue between his lips and sucked it just the way he had the night before, arousing them both with the hot lush

145

pulling motion.

He gave in to the sensual sucking, and it was a long, long time before he eased his mouth away from hers; then she knew what he wanted and she wordlessly led him into the privacy of the office and locked that door, while he seated himself at her desk and waited for her to come to him.

Everything now moved in a slow, rhythmic motion. She came to him slowly and slid boldly onto his lap, pressing herself blatantly against his rigid erection, writhing against it, provoking him every way she could think of with her insolent movements. She wanted yesterday, she thought hazily, as she felt the granite length of him even more fully. Consciously or not, she had hiked her skirt up so that she was sitting naked on his lap. She wanted everything that had happened yesterday, and more. . . .

He felt the difference instantly; it was her naked bottom wriggling so provokingly against his straining hardness. His hands went to her hips, settling her nakedness tightly against his thick length. "Do you feel me?" he murmured, seeking her lips again.

"I feel you," she whispered, thrilled by the inflexible massiveness of him. "Do you feel me?" she added boldly.

His tongue flicked her lips. "Do you want me to feel you?"

She caught her breath at this potent question. "I want you to feel me," she whispered.

"Everywhere?"

She could hardly breathe. His whispered words aroused her to a fevered pitch. He knew she was naked beneath her clothes, and he was letting her decide. But what was there to decide when all she could think of was the memory of his hot kisses and caressing fingers arousing her nipple. She wanted that and more. She wanted the feeling of his stiff, virile maleness taut against her bare buttocks, exciting her beyond words.

"Anywhere," she whispered, enthralled by the potent sex of him. "Everywhere. Just . . . feel me, now," and she waited for the caressing touch of his fingers.

His lips hovered over hers. "I know you're naked under your clothes," he murmured, and took a long delving kiss inside her mouth.

"I dressed for you," she whispered. As his tongue sought her sweet taste once more, she felt his hand move from her hip down her leg to the point where he could pull up her skirt and feel the bare flesh of her trembling thigh. She melted against him as his hand contacted skin and began a slow descent toward her foot.

She felt him pull her boot away and his fingers caressing the shape of her foot, feeling each toe, sliding up to her ankle and then upward still until he was holding her naked buttocks in his hand, pressing her more tightly against him, mouth to mouth, body to body. Then she felt both hands under her buttocks feeling the pert round-ness of them, exploring every inch of them upward and downward, then settling her nakedness back down hard against his throbbing male member.

He never broke the kiss. Her whole sensation became the caress of his tongue and the feeling of his fingers exploring her feet, her legs, her thighs. Somehow he turned her body so she was facing forward. Her legs were propped up on either side of his and her skirt was pushed all the way back so he had the freedom to feel every inch of her. In turn, she could feel the voluptuous movement of her naked buttocks against his powerful hardness.

She was all open to him, and he leisurely explored all of her that he could feel, sliding both hands all over her, around her body, skimming past the velvet heat of her femininity, grazing the lush tuft that crowned its entry, teasing it, cupping the thrusting mound without enter-ing, and then leaving it, sliding his hands up to her breasts to cover them and to feel her stiff peaked nipples against the flat of his palms.

She went wild in his hands as he pulled away the thin bodice of her camisole and gently took each nipple between his thumb and forefinger just so she could feel the erotic contact. She never wanted to stop feeling his hands on her. From the lush caress of her nipples, his hands sleeked back down her body to her feet and stroked them gently. Then they returned to her thighs and between her legs. Then his concentrated seduction began.

He had possessed her mouth and tongue and now he would possess her entirely. Slowly and expertly he stroked and caressed her silky skin, moving closer and closer to his lush conquest.

She was caught in the hot wet world of his languorous kisses and the slow shimmering heat of his knowledge-able caresses as he shifted unerringly to the velvet center of her with a sure touch. His hands knew just what she wanted him to do. Her hips churned wildly against the hard penetration of his fingers, then every sensation converged on the single driving feeling of him exploring her provocative femininity.

It was too much, it was not enough. Her supple body clamored for more, rippling with the fierce urge to a union that she could not complete. There was only the glimmering sense of it as she strained against him and everything liquefied into the one relentless need to reach the luminous culmination.

She felt one hand, then two, and then herself, open and centered, pliant and bearing down on that one exquisite feeling that was coming . . . coming . . . in all its opulent release.

And it came, crackling and cascading all over her, an avalanche of unbearable feeling that threatened to swallow her whole. It pulsed all over her body and eddied away to leave her only with the tantalizing memory of it and the sense of his hands still within, still ready to urge her to further heights.

She didn't see how she could when her body felt so sated, and she gripped his hands and pulled them away, pushing her skirt down almost protectively before she curled up against him to savor his lovemaking.

Such other ways, she thought wonderingly, as she lifted her mouth to his again. Who could have imagined such possibilities, such fathomless enchantment?

He could.

The words came at her so clearly it was almost like they were written on a sign someplace in her mind.

He could, and he had. He had told her the words, she had given him his vision, and he had given her . . . rapture.

She knew that while she felt calm about it now, by tomorrow she would be possessed by the insensate yearning to feel his hands on her again.

"When again?" she murmured between the slow leisurely kisses she still demanded from him. "Kiss me first, then tell me," and he kissed her for a long, long time, while he thought about when and how the next moment could not be too soon.

"Sunday, it should be Sunday, after you've gone to press, Maggie."

"Oh God, Sunday?" she groaned. How would she stand it until Sunday? she wondered fretfully. She felt as if he were gone already, even though he was delivering light little kisses all over her mouth, murmuring reassurances and massaging her shoulders and back comfortingly.

She moved away from him for a moment and suddenly became conscious that her breasts were still bare. In the darkness he could not see, but she knew he had been aware of their thrusting softness against his body. She pulled up her camisole, and reached into her pocket and pressed something into his hand.

"A key?"

"I don't want you waiting; I don't want to wait. I want you to be here."

"I want to be here."

"Then take the key—and be here Sunday."

"I'll be here," he whispered, and closed his mouth over hers one more time.

Chapter Nine

It was a singularly uninspiring issue of the newspaper and even her regulars knew it.

"You didn't go after no one this week, Maggie?"

"What's the matter, lady, you gettin' mellow?"

"Now boys, what do you think I employ Arch for?" she asked teasingly.

"It sure sounds like nothin's happenin' in this here town. I thought we was a lot more lively than that. Maybe we gotta get a gang together and shoot up the ole Range Rider Saloon. Whaddya say, boys?"

"Now, now, I think we gotta give ole Maggie here another week to get the dirt together. She'll find that fly in the molasses, you'll see."

"Maybe Denver North is laying low," Maggie suggested in a chilling tone of voice. "Maybe they're moving in mysterious ways, behind the scenes, and we're only going to see the results years from now."

"Oh, Maggie, there ain't nothing they can do that we ain't gonna see outright sooner or later."

"Isn't that the truth?" she murmured, passing through the crowd into the office.

"Maggie, you're just born to be a cynic," a new voice added. She looked up to see Reese following her in through the front door.

"And isn't it a lucky thing," she said lightly. "How are you doing today, Reese?"

"Much better now that I've seen you. You've been damned busy, Maggie," he said, settling himself down in the chair next to her desk and picking up the copy of the current issue that lay on her worktable. "Hmmm, well, your star reporter is predicting big happenings in town once the building crew comes in. What do you think, Maggie?"

"I think I'll reserve comment until after the fact."

"You are the diplomat, Maggie," he said smiling, but she saw the smile didn't quite reach his eyes. She almost thought there was an underlying double meaning to his response.

"I think I am, actually," she said, sinking down into her chair, thinking that it held no sensual connotation for her in a room full of noisy people. "Tell me what you've been doing these past few days. I don't think we've hardly seen you."

"And that's the bossy newspaper lady in you," he evaded, still with the faint smile on his lips. "I'm finding the company in Colville extremely congenial. I wasn't particularly counting on you to entertain me, Maggie."

"Especially after I made it clear I wasn't going to?" she asked sweetly. "Ah, Reese, let's not spar with words. Your mother thinks I'm treating you as shabbily as an outdoor cat. You really have to assure her that you are not cut out to be the lackey of a lady boss."

"I could think of worse fates," he said cheerfully, and then brushed off the statement with a negating wave. "I'm not after the paper, Maggie, you should know that. I want to help you, certainly, but that's not the same as wanting to horn in and take over."

"No it isn't," she agreed, trying to keep the sharp edge out of her voice. "But I really dislike being held responsible for the way she thinks you should be occupying your time."

"I don't blame you, but I hope you have noticed that since I came she's become increasingly involved with the ladies' church society. And I hope you feel some proper gratitude at my cleverness."

"I don't think she needed that much of a push; this town thinks of Frank as some kind of icon, and after the memorial service, when that was brought very convincingly home to her, I'm sure she relished the thought of being Frank's mother publicly—wherever and whenever she could."

"Very astute, Maggie. So I'm not such a clever son after all."

"I wager you're clever enough, Reese. And you're damned likable."

"And I think, on that warming thought, I'll leave." He got up with an easy grace and made his way to the backroom staircase. Maggie watched him for a moment before her eyes swung to Jean, who was staring after Reese with the most enigmatic expression on his face.

That was Saturday, with Sunday yet to come, and already a keening restlessness possessed her that was very hard to disguise from the knowledgeable eyes of A.J. and Jean, both of whom had worked the cleanup detail with her Saturday evening. When Jean suggested they might take dinner at the hotel, she felt distinctly uncomfortable and begged off with not much of an excuse.

He shrugged it off. "You are probably right. The gossips have enough to speculate about with Reese's presence here. I would never want to embarrass you, Maggie."

"Of course not. No, I wasn't even thinking about that.

The hotel is expensive."

"But it is a rare treat for me, and just a suggestion only. Perhaps some other time."

"Perhaps," she said noncommittally, but she was rather astonished at the offer. There was no more than the usual emotion in the tone of his voice, and yet she had the impression that there was a great deal of emotion behind his reason for asking. She hadn't the faintest idea how to cope with that.

It was really getting to be too much. There was a flaring awareness in Jean's eyes, and she felt that moment of attenuated awareness between them that had no comparison with what she felt about Logan.

She wanted to tell him to just go away and never come back, but that wasn't possible. He was irreplaceable, and she had the grim feeling that he knew it.

Eventually he had no choice but to leave. He did so with his usual good manners, manners that effectively masked whatever lay below the surface.

And then finally Sunday came, and a leisurely morning alone as Reese once again escorted Mother Colleran to church and left her to her own devices.

How had she ever survived a week without Reese as the buffer between herself and her mother-in-law?

She had time to luxuriate in the anticipation of what was to happen tonight. She had time to remember all the delicious things Logan had done to her, and the glorious culmination at his hands. Her body went all molten thinking about it and the possibilities of the evening ahead. She decided how she would dress for him and was both amazed and aroused by her own daring.

It did require some planning, but by the time she was ready to slip downstairs she was dressed and ready for him. Praying that he was there, already waiting for her.

Downstairs in the back room, she locked the door and called to him in the office, her voice husky with

154

excitement. He was there, in the dark, waiting, just as she hoped, and she felt a frisson of nervousness before she stepped out of her boots and shucked the thin robe she had worn to cover her leather apron. Underneath this she was naked, and she felt her way carefully into the room until she came to him. He knew she was there by her fragrance and by her breathing and the scent of sensual excitement that permeated the air.

She climbed onto his lap, straddling his legs this time, so that the whole of her provocative femininity was centered over him. His hands reached for her, and she heard him groan as he realized what she was wearing and what she had done; his hands settled on her hips and pushed her nakedness down tightly against him. He was already hard for her and she felt a luscious throbbing spurt of elongation as she gyrated her hips to find the most form-fitting position. His hands guided her until, with a sigh, she finally settled down against his massive hot length.

They needed no words. Their lips met hungrily, openmouthed in a succulent kiss, and she moved with it, bearing down on his rock-hard manhood with groans of delight in the feel of him against her nakedness and the heat of his kisses as he plundered her mouth greedily.

She loved the sense of the rough material against her breasts and the feeling of nakedness behind. The angle of her body as she wantonly rotated against him thrust her bottom outward. Her smoldering movements invited his caresses. His hands moved to stroke her back down to the lush curve of her hips, and there he stayed, feeling the frenzied movement of her tantalizing his member, waiting for her further invitation to explore everywhere.

"Maggie."

"Was it hard waiting?" she whispered against his lips.

"It's hard now."

"Don't stop."

"Tell me what to do then."

She writhed against him as his words sent tantalizing pictures spiraling in her mind. "Touch me—touch me everywhere," she breathed, and settled her mouth against his ecstatically as she felt his hands move downward, finally, to the sweet, firm lushness of her buttocks, to begin his sensual probing of all her secrets.

Their kisses grew longer, more languid, and his hands moved more slowly as they explored her intimately from behind. She lifted herself and settled against his questing fingers until finally they slipped with luscious expertise into the exact place she wanted them. There he rested as he made love to her mouth and tongue with sumptuous thoroughness.

She surrendered utterly to every sensation. White-hot tendrils curled through her and he sensed her readiness for his sultry thrusts into her moist satin heat. Slowly at first he plunged into her, savoring her rapturous response and her sensuous shifts to give him pure unfettered entry to her most intimate place.

And then her body went wild with all the separate feelings melting into one voluptuous urge. She wanted him, she wanted him, and her kisses became voracious with that ravenous need. And she wanted more than that, more, and she didn't know what more was; her hands boldly roamed all over him not knowing what she wanted to feel until they came into contact with his pulsating hardness. That, that; she pulled at his clothes frantically as he thrust into her, and with one lovely tear, she freed the towering evidence of his male virility into her hungry hands.

He hadn't expected that. He almost lost control feeling her fingers sliding up and down the forceful ramrod length of him. And then she sat back so she could revel in the feeling of his hands possessing her in the same way.

And then suddenly she moved and he moved and her

hands moved brazenly all over his potent maleness. He thrust into her with ferocious little surging movements and heard her moans and felt her hands stroking him in long, torrid motions. It was as if he were deep within her and they were one. They came to the shattering crowning point simultaneously.

And then the thump of footsteps, unexpected and startling.

"Reese!" Maggie whispered frantically, totally jolted out of the magic of the moment. Her heart accelerated again. "Oh, Lord . . ." her hands cupped Logan's face and she dropped a hard kiss on his lips. "Logan . . ."

But he was calm, even in the face of the stunning climax they had shared. "Shhh. Go into the backroom and get on a light. Close the door. Did you have a robe?"

"Yes," she whispered, backing off of his lap, and wiping her sticky fingers on his shirttails. "Oh damn. Logan . . ."

"I'm up to winter pasture this week, Maggie. We're bringing the herd down. I won't see you till Friday. Hurry. I hear him calling you."

That was the worst, Reese seeking her for some unfathomable reason in the deep of the night. She made her way cautiously out of the office and closed the door carefully behind her. Logan had the key, he would be fine.

She groped for her robe, not at all pleased that she might have to face Reese in that skimpy garment. She shucked her apron, shoved her feet into her boots and tied the sash haphazardly around her waist.

A light . . . The light was easier; she knew her way around the back room like a blind person. It took another moment, accompanied by the clump of footsteps down the inner stairs, for her to light the lamp, unlock the door and thrust her apron back onto its hook.

A moment later Reese poked his head through the door.

"For God's sake, Maggie, you scared me half to death."

"Why is that, Reese?" she asked calmly from her seat at the type case, where her shaking fingers were arranging letters into a jumbled commentary on her feelings. The bastard hadn't even allowed her a moment to savor what had happened.

She looked up at Reese.

"What the hell are you doing here?"

"What are you?" she countered, evading the question. M-I-N-E, she had spelled. She wanted to brand the word on Logan's flanks. She hated Reese at that moment.

"Well, hell," he growled, and she knew he had had just a bit too much to drink; moreover, his eyes were raking the thin material of her robe and the outline of her nipples pushing hard against the fabric. "I thought . . . I thought . . . ." he seemed distracted for a moment as his eyes rested on her taut-nippled breasts. She felt naked as his greedy gaze devoured the sight of her, naked and distinctly unclean.

"God, you're beautiful in the dead of night, Maggie. What the devil are you doing down here alone at this hour dressed like that?"

"I, I thought I heard a noise," she lied. "What are *you* doing down here in the dead of night?"

He tried to gauge her expression. He wasn't so far gone he couldn't tell a lie from the truth. In Maggie's case, he wasn't sure. The long sleek lines of her body got in the way of his thinking, and he wondered about her self-imposed celibacy. That was a body made to be loved, and he was damned tempted to force the issue then and there. There was even a little part of him that had the passing thought that this little hide-and-seek game was deliberate, and that she was goading him to take the step he would love to take.

In fact during these last two weeks he had been looking for some little sign that she didn't really mean what she

158

had told him. But this was the first time he had seen her in anything but her prim dark dresses and that godawful leather apron.

"I thought you'd like to know . . ." he said with a self-satisfied tone in his voice.

"Yes?" She slid off the stool and reached for the lamp, a signal that she wanted to hear the whole of it and quick.

He was transfixed again, this time by the whole of her practically naked in front of him and the incongruous touch of the heavy boots she usually wore around the office. Almost a scene for seduction, he thought, his rampant imagination easing up just a bit. Frank was a fool; he decided to wait for another concretely seductive gesture.

"I thought you should be the first to know. The word is over at the hotel that the lawyer from Denver North is going to be setting up shop in one of the suites come next Thursday, Maggie. He's here to do business, and I don't wonder that he might be after you."

The worst news. She schooled her face into a calm expression as she picked up the lamp. "I'm not scared," she said finally, handing him the light, and preceding him to the door. "I'll meet with him, and I'll tell him no to his face." She mounted the stairs.

"Well, you might want to reconsider, after all," he said, as he followed her, holding the lamp high so he could have a clear view of the movement of her buttocks as she climbed the stairs.

Was she wiggling that way purposely? Her boots made the most desire-damping sound he had ever heard, but he could feast on the tempting contour of her bottom for the whole minute it took to make it up the stairs, savoring it because her flimsy robe hid absolutely nothing. It was as if she were naked just for him.

She was terribly aware of the nature of his thoughts, since she was still breathless from the excitement of lovemaking and the thrilling scare of near-discovery. But he wouldn't know that it was someone else who brought that particular light to her eyes. He would think it was her response—albeit an unwilling one—to his allure. He might even think she hadn't meant a word of what she said.

Damn and damn. What a coil. It *had* looked as if she had been playing some coquettish game with him, especially the way she was dressed.

He was still looking at her in that knowing way, and she needed to get out of the parlor in thirty seconds unless she wanted him to be sure that what he was thinking might be true.

"Thanks, Reese," she said finally. "I'll look into it tomorrow."

She knew his hot eyes followed her as she made her way down the hallway to her bedroom and closed the door emphatically behind her.

The lawyer, she thought, sinking onto her bed, was the least of her problems. The very worst thing was having to shunt Logan's cataclysmic lovemaking to the back of her thoughts because something terrifying had just occurred to her.

Their dark haven was safe no longer.

And there was nowhere else they could go.

"I heard you were running around half naked last night, Maggie. I swear I don't know what's come over you. Supposing someone heard about it. Supposing someone thought you were trying to seduce Reese. Were you, Maggie? *Were* you? I won't have it. I won't have it in my house."

"It's *my* house, Mother Colleran, and the last thing in the world I want to do is lead Reese into temptation. I believe I have told him so as well."

"Well, miss, what you tell and what you show are two different things. When you run around after intruders with nothing on under your robe, you can be sure a man will get a different message."

"Oh really? How would you know, Mother Colleran? Did someone seduce you sometime when you were naked under your robe?"

The idea was ludicrous, Maggie thought, taking in her mother-in-law's sputtering indignation. That squat old crow. It was hard to imagine that she had ever been young and beautiful and loved. Hers had probably been an arranged marriage of San Francisco dynasties, and her sons were probably to have been heirs to something or the other. She had probably seen herself as some kind of queen bee, instead, she had wound up a drone, and Maggie barely heard her words as she prepared to go down to Bodey's store and hear the whole story of the coming of the lawyer.

"And how *do* you know this anyway?" she finally asked.

"Well, Reese just didn't think it was highly likely anyone would break into the office, and he wondered whether anything like this had ever happened before. I told him no. I tell you, Maggie, your story sounds suspicious."

"Well then, perhaps I was meeting my other lover," she said facetiously from the door, pushed just that little step further into melding the truth and the lie.

And was that a mistake. The self-satisfied look on Mother Colleran's face told her that it was just the kind of answer her mother-in-law hoped to goad out of her. Indeed, the old lady looked as if she could very well believe it.

So she had accomplished what she had come for, Maggie thought disgustedly as she made her way to Bodey's store. She got the rise and she got a nice tidbit to repeat to Reese.

"Maggie!" Arwin Bodey hailed her.

She thought again how much she liked him. He was a plain man with a no-nonsense manner and he always said what was on his mind. And he had a prescience that was very unsettling.

"You hear about that lawyer now, Maggie?"

"I heard," she said bluntly.

"Yep, I heard Reese was in a tearing hurry to tell you the news. Wonder why?"

"Is there anything you *don't* hear?" she asked good-humoredly. "Or are you the one hanging over the bar next to Reese every night?"

"Oh now, Reese can hold his liquor, same as Frank could. No, Lilah don't cotton to men and their drinking over the counter. They just all come by in the morning for some headache remedies and I see no point to hushing them up when they're telling me their sad histories."

"Amazing. I could swear I thought you read minds."

"Well, I wish I could read someone's mind. This here lawyer, they're settin' him up in the luxury suite in the hotel with an office in one room and a parlor and a bedroom. It sounds like he's here to do big business, Maggie, and I don't feel that bodes well for Colville."

She shook her head. "Sure, he'll buy a few thousand more acres here and there and patch together the line and that will be the end of it."

"No, Maggie, you don't understand. I think he's here for you and Logan and the Mapes, but primarily for you."

"That's absurd. The Colleran ranchland couldn't be all that vital."

"Maggie, you've looked at the map. You know if you draw a straight line from Danforth down to Gully Basin, the line to Cheyenne goes right through Logan and you. You don't think they want it? Or that the cost to them

162

would still be less than grading down the gully and retracking for however many miles they'll have to down that long quarter of rangeland. Oh, Maggie, be careful. Too many people want the rail line, and you're in the definite minority of those who don't."

"I just can't see it being that critical."

"You're being naive."

She was shocked. Arwin was a good friend, and never once had he ever hauled her down as harshly as he did just now.

"I'll protect myself," she said finally.

"Oh, but Maggie, how you going to tell the sharks from the whales?"

"Yes, and who will gobble up the town faster. Maybe I'll throw them some bait, and we'll see who gets bloodied first."

"And maybe," Arwin added somberly, "they'll all take a damned big bite out of *you*."

After that, she thought she didn't want to see Arwin again for a month. Every visit ended with a prophesy of gloom. She felt as though she were a branch of a tree caught in a turbulent storm, where it would take only a crack of lightning or a strong wind to destroy her altogether.

She couldn't fight lawyers and railroad directors. She could barely keep her own end up with her mother-in-law. And she had allowed herself, even knowing the consequences, to pitch headlong into something with Logan that could never lead to anything concrete—ever.

She had needed only one night, one incident, to bring it home forcibly to her. It had been sheer folly to encourage him, to allow herself to wallow in his unleashed desire.

That was the thing that gnawed at her this morning,

not lawyers and mothers-in-law, or what Reese might have been led to think last night. She cared about none of them; she cared about Logan, and she knew there was nowhere to go with him, nowhere that wasn't a dark office, a hideaway, a room somewhere where no one knew them, but there was nowhere like that in Colville, or his ranch, assuming she could travel at night with impunity, which of course she could not. There was no hope, none.

And she knew too that things could only escalate from last night. She already felt the driving need for completion, to have him within her. And it would happen. She knew it would happen the first night she crept down the stairs to meet him.

And if it happened . . . she could have joined with him last night, so urgently did she feel the force of her feminine response to him . . . if it had happened . . .

She took a deep breath. There was no going back. There might be a child. He would want her to marry him. She would have to live at the ranch that was his livelihood. He wouldn't live in town. No, she didn't know whether or not he would live in town, but it seemed likely he would not want to. And she didn't want a child now, she didn't want constraints. The decision had to be that she had stored up enough memories and could not chance another near-discovery and the drenching fear that utterly decimated her passion.

She could live without that now; she knew it in a way that she had never felt it with Frank. She could even have a wrenching regret that Logan had not been the one to court her first, but she couldn't go back. She couldn't go forward either, and she damned the fates and blocked out all the words they had said and all the things he made her feel.

She never should have allowed him to seduce her.

She had been a partner to it all because in the dark

words were easy and the molten sensations all seemed part of something not real, something that would never reach beyond that room and that passion-fraught darkness.

But it had gone outside the room, and now she was in danger—from her feelings and from external forces that sought to control her as completely as her passions. She didn't even know which was the worse threat.

She found out on Thursday, when A.J. picked up the readyprint from the express station. He returned with something more: a handbill that was being placed all around town publicizing construction jobs on the railroad, with good pay and accommodations. And on the inner page of the supplement, a small ad announced the news: "Come one, come all, ready money and good jobs for everyone on the Colville line."

"Well, the lawyer's name is Mr. Brown," Dennis told her, "and he wants to see you at your convenience."

"I don't trust lawyers named Mr. Brown, and I'm sure we have nothing to discuss," Maggie said plainly, sifting through the papers on her worktable in order to give Dennis the impression she was inundated with work so that he would not bother her any further with this lawyer nonsense.

"You should at least give him a chance to speak with you," Dennis said.

"Why?"

He looked uncertain for a moment. "Because he contacted me, as the executor for Frank's estate, to see whether there is some way, under the terms of the will, around your adamant refusal to hear their offer."

"And you told him there was none of course and that we had nothing to talk about."

"I'm not sure that's true, Maggie."

"I see. You've gone through the clauses with a magnifying glass and you've found something that could be *construed*, but doesn't *say* in as many words, that . . ."

"Maggie!" He was at the end of his tether at her sarcasm.

"All *right*. So I meet with Mr. Anonymous Brown and he offers me many thousands of dollars to sell up and I say no and that is the end of it. Is that what you want?"

"I want you to listen very carefully to what he has to say, Maggie, and make an *informed* decision, always remembering your duty to Frank's mother, and your own monetary need, especially concerning the paper, which isn't going to run at a profit any time soon."

"Fine. Now we know whose side you are on."

"I am on your side, Maggie. The land is useless to you and the money is not."

"That is one way of looking at it."

"And what is the other? That in twenty or thirty years you'll retire and want to be bucolic in your old age and run cattle? Please Maggie. You are really being quite irrational about this. Believe me, the cost of buying the land is less than rerouting, and they will dig deep in the corporation's pockets to find a sum that you will find very attractive."

"I suppose you might have some idea of what it could be?"

"I don't. But you will tell me, Maggie, and we will discuss it, and then we both will come to an informed decision as to what you should do."

More pressure. Pressure from all sides: Arch Warfield's smug assurance that Maggie now had to let him have a free hand with his coverage of the railroad's progress since she had let them advertise in the paper. Pressure because of the fact that Logan was returning the next day and she would have to deal with him sometime on the weekend. And now Mr. Brown, the mysterious, glad-handing, high-rolling Mr. Brown, with his dollars falling out of his pockets as he walked, paving the dusty streets of Colville with promises.

"Going to see Mr. Brown are you?" Mother Colleran said as she found Maggie rummaging through her closet for her most severe dress.

"Oh, did Dennis incite you to put pressure on me as well, Mother Colleran? I hope you know that your comfort is not my first concern," Maggie said edgily as she discarded one dress after another, finally settling on the one she had worn to Frank's memorial service even though she would swelter in it on this warm day.

"I think all you have to remember is that Frank would have sold that land in a trice, Maggie. He was forever regretting even having started the ranch in the first place. It's not hallowed ground or anything."

"Oh my heavens, it *isn't?* You mean there is one place that Frank touched that isn't consecrated by his mere presence?"

"Don't blaspheme, you shameless girl. I always knew you hated Frank anyway."

"No one would believe you if they were told, Mother Colleran. I would deny it, and everyone knows how valiantly Mrs. Frank has carried on, shouldering the burden of her indigent mother-in-law. Have you never heard them say that?"

Mother Colleran shook her head. "Poor Maggie. You live in a dream world, and your lies will drive you mad someday. And then I will take over everything."

That statement was stunning. "Oooh?" Maggie murmured consideringly. "Is that the plan? The wonder is you've waited so long."

"You're right about that," Mother Colleran snapped, and she turned on her heel and left the room.

For the first time Maggie felt a real fear. Was that her plan? *And* Reese's purpose in having come to Colville?

Dear God, she thought, but the old hag never would have come right out and said it if that were her intention. It was stupid. It was a warning.

Yes, it was a warning, and Maggie felt it deeply as she was ushered into the elegantly appointed hotel office of Mr. Brown, whose offer to her could fend off every threat.

"Maggie Colleran." He had the deep rumbling voice of an actor. His hands swallowed her and he pressed them with sincere welcome and motioned her to a delicate chair.

"Mr. Brown," she murmured with irony; such a nondescript name for such a flamboyant presence.

"We have business to discuss."

"You have business to discuss. I'm just not sure whether it is with me," Maggie said pointedly, not allowing him to obscure his purpose with a lot of fancy words.

He looked nonplussed, then he smiled and she thought he was the oiliest man she had ever met. "We'll cut to the core, Maggie Colleran. We need the land, and my sources tell me you could be in need of money."

"Or they could be wrong."

"Twenty thousand dollars."

"I'd call that cutting through to the core all right, Mr. Brown, except that the apples in your barrel are all rotten. Your offer is unacceptable, and before you say anything else, I will tell you that any offer is unacceptable. *My* lawyer must have told you I don't want to sell. I haven't changed my mind."

Mr. Brown shrugged. "I suppose that's the way it will have to be then, Maggie Colleran. I'm sorry we can't do business."

"Oh, but I know you *will* be doing business, Mr. Brown, and I'm sure you will spend your money very wisely."

"It would give me great pleasure to spend it on you," Mr. Brown said evenly. "Perhaps there will even come a day you might change your mind. But until then, I bid you good afternoon."

"So nice to meet you, Mr. Brown," she said, and was politely escorted out of his presence.

That couldn't be the end of it, she thought; although she had not expected him to raise his offer at all, she had anticipated a great deal more harrassment. Mr. Brown's abruptness dismayed her. She felt wary and pressured from a source she could not identify. It wasn't Mr. Brown. It was something in the air, something unidentifiable, something that surrounded her.

Which, as she came into broad daylight on this balmy March afternoon, seemed like a horror story that she herself made up; looking for threats around every corner, and enemies where there were none.

It made Mother Colleran's prediction all the more chilling. She had the brief sensation that she was indeed going mad and that nothing around her was really what it seemed.

Chapter Ten

When she returned to the office she went after the railroad full bore, ordering A.J. to strike everything from the editorial page while she rewrote her column, removed Warfield's sodden prose to the back page, and added an additional article about the coming of Mr. Brown and what the motive of the railroad directors could possibly be in sending him as their emissary.

"This is too harsh, Miz Maggie," A.J. cautioned her.

"I don't like being bribed. And I will wager you the offer will go up within the week, especially after this edition appears."

"This is asking for trouble," Jean said, reading her copy over her shoulder. She looked up at him to see his troubled dark eyes.

"Am I going crazy? Is everyone suddenly convinced that we should not hold Denver North accountable for anything?" she demanded.

"Now, now, Miz Maggie, we just don't want no libel actions on our hands. You'd have to sell out to fight the damn company in court," A.J. said with a trace of humor. "And you've cause not to be too objective about what you're putting in that box of copy. You'd be very prudent, Miz Maggie, if you'd just let me . . ."

"All right, all right," she said abruptly, thrusting the page at him. "You tone it down. I'm ready to spit ems. We have to shift the layout on those two pages, Jean. Damn, I wish I could black out that ad. Why *can't* I black out that ad?" And that, she thought, as she paced the room, was the one thing that blighted the whole. Because of her contract with the printing company, she was forced to run the supplement just as it was, and by damn, she was going to rewrite that contract tomorrow.

"Maggie."

She stopped pacing. "Yes, Jean?"

"I do not like to see you so agitated."

"I don't like it myself. I don't like it when someone else has control of what goes in these pages. I just never thought . . . it has to be deliberate . . . it has to be. Did you see those handbills? They're all over the place, and when I left that lawyer's hotel office today there was a line of people queuing up outside his door. Damn it, he'll be paying them a portion of the money he offered me, and they'll take it."

"That's right, Miz Maggie, because the town's economics ain't exactly what you'd call well-to-do," A.J. put in, returning her page of copy to her, and she could see already there were neat slashes through the best of her excoriating phrases.

She thrust it into Jean's hands. "You take it. I don't want to see what he's done to it. What else for tonight, A.J.?"

"We're ready to go, Miz Maggie, as soon as Jean lays out the back page."

Later there was silence as she and Jean worked side by side at the type desk. Jean set her article and laid it onto the plate, and they each took two pages and set them while A.J. inked the press and laid out the newsprint.

The rhythmic sorting of the type calmed her somewhat. The silence was peaceful, and she had the usual sense of their work relationship running like a well-oiled machine; everything was done automatically and with precision.

This meticulousness was a pure pleasure to her, especially because she saw in it what she liked most about Jean and A.J. both. Jean had come from nowhere, and everywhere, and with his exactness and delicacy he had made a place here, while A.J. had run from the minefields when his luck ran out, and somehow Frank had seen his potential and had given him a home.

She was lucky to have them, lucky that the whole had not slipped away from her after Frank's death. She was an elf fighting giants, she thought, and nothing magical would turn the tide. The only thing magical in her life she had to wave her wand and turn back to dust.

Colville would go on in spite of her, in spite of Denver North, and maybe even because of it. *That* was the epilogue to the story and nothing else.

"Well, Maggie, you say one thing and then you do another. How is one to know that you mean what you say? I hear tell there's a Denver North ad right in this very week's edition of the paper. Is that true?" Mother Colleran again, up early, too early, Maggie thought, and following her downstairs as she prepared to help A.J. bundle the papers.

"It's true. It came from Denver and I had no say in whether it went in the paper or not, Mother Colleran. Does that answer your question?"

"Well, they just are not going to understand how you can take their money for your paper and not take their money for the land."

"I understand it perfectly, and I have no quarrel with myself."

"It doesn't sound rational, Maggie. I really would

173

think about it, if I were you."

Maggie froze. There was that insinuation again. The old bitch was going to spread it around, point it out, make sure everyone read it and knew that Maggie had been offered money by Denver North and turned it down. Was that sane? That was exactly how the old she-witch would put it, too.

Her fears were well-founded. There wasn't one of her regulars who did not comment on the incongruity, and not without malice. She had been painted into a corner and the floor was still wet; her footprint would seal her guilt.

She almost did not want to leave the office that morning, but she knew she had to be seen and she could not be cowed by an incident that had to be a deliberate set up.

She walked Main Street briskly and bore the brunt of the derisive comments. The only thing that counted, she found out that morning, was the fact that the ad appeared. Nothing else mattered: she was compromised through no doing of her own.

She was exhausted by the time she returned. The crowd outside the counter had grown larger, and the voices deeper with disappointment in her.

"Maggie, how could you—and then write the things you did?"

"Yeah, Maggie, we heard they was offering you big money. You just tryin' to up the ante now, givin' and takin' at the same time?"

"We always said there was somethin' in it for her. Goes to show, now don't it, if she's puttin' their advertisin' right in the middle of her paper? I tell you, Frank wouldn't have pussyfooted around at all. He'd've been right in the forefront of bringin' the railroad to town and would've advertised 'em for free."

She felt an intense pain at how easily those she

174

considered friends turned on her and immediately set Frank up as god again. Damned Philistines, bowing willingly to the golden calf of a locomotive engine.

She brushed by them briskly and closeted herself in the backroom. A.J. brought her coffee. "It's real bad, Miz Maggie."

"I know. We might just as well have put the damned thing on the front page. I don't think anyone has read anything else."

"That's for sure. And there's nothing to say you won't find the damned thing right in the supplement again next week either."

"No, we have to do something about that today. We can . . ."

"No, you ain't thinking straight, Miz Maggie. They're not going to refuse a Denver ad in Denver. They're just not going to care about the politics of a railroad invading this town. They've got a hundred subscribers or more, they can't run two hundred copies just for us minus Denver North. You understand?"

"I don't want to understand," Maggie said stormily. "We can't do without it either. We need the newsprint. I hate this. I hate being tied up so I can't move, hate having someone else in control."

A.J. shook his head. "They're doing it, Miz Maggie, and they probably are doing it purposely, just like you think. But it's also good business. They'll get a stock of workers just like me who want to run from the minefields to something easier and quicker. Some people like the idea—couple of weeks work, get a paycheck, they're on the road again looking for the next best dollar."

"I know, I know. It will kill the town, and it's going to kill us because no one understands that we didn't take that ad."

"So we just keep on going, Miz Maggie, best as we can, and only you can decide whether we're going to tussle

175

them down to the wire or whether we'll let up and see what happens."

"I don't know," she groaned, "I just don't know."

"Well, I'll tell you something, Miz Maggie. Neither would Mr. Frank have either. He wouldn't have known which way was the best road not taken, so don't you fret about that."

"No, A.J., you're wrong. Frank would have gone exactly the opposite way from me. He was a salesman, A.J. He would have given the people just what they wanted."

But even knowing that was no consolation. Frank's name was invoked so often that day she was sure he had been canonized.

And then there was Dennis. "Maggie, are you insane?"

And that word again.

"I beg your pardon, Dennis?" Polite, she had to be polite, and she had to make everyone understand that she was taking nothing, that the ads were not hers, that she was as opposed as ever to Denver North, and that there was no amount of money that would make her give in.

But she knew: his copy of the *Morning Call* was open to the insert, where he had encircled the Denver North ad with a bold black pencil.

"*And* you turned down their offer!" He was incredulous.

"Say it louder, Dennis. Everyone thinks I'm about to sell out to them because my supplier accepted their lousy little ad."

"Let's go upstairs."

"I do not want to go anywhere. I'm tired of defending this. It is and it will be and I can't do anything about it."

"Then you'll do the right thing and curb your criticism before we get hauled up before a magistrate for defamation or some other such charges."

"God, you're all so afraid of what Denver North can do. Obviously they'll railroad me and get what they want anyway, am I right?"

"You're too flippant, Maggie. You don't wield the same kind of power as . . ." His voice trailed off, and she finished in a clipped voice, ". . . as Frank would have, if he were still alive."

"I didn't mean to say it quite so baldly, but yes, you don't."

"Then tie me to the tracks, Dennis, and let them run right over me."

"Look, Maggie, it doesn't have to be so black and white."

"But this is a newspaper, Dennis. Of course everything is black and white."

"Maggie . . ."

"Dennis, I can't listen to much more."

"Fine, I'll end it, but I don't want you to think that that ad has pushed everything else out of the limelight. *I* read what you wrote about Mr. Brown and his offers, and I swear Maggie, it is just short of libelous."

"Or right on target with the truth," she countered.

"Only if the majority agrees with you, which they don't, and it's a sure thing that Denver North is going to put a lot of money into promoting the positive aspects of their building here."

"I see," she said slowly. *"That's* Mr. Brown's purpose."

"No, Maggie. Mr. Brown's purpose is to buy land, short and simple. Your land first, the Mapes' and Logan's land if he can get it. That is it. And I think you're losing your mind if you see ulterior motives where there are none, and if you refuse to see the advantage in selling your property. *I* think that is as much as I have to say about it today."

177

"And it is more than enough, thank you, Dennis," she said so dismissively that he turned on his heel and marched out the front door. He didn't want to take care of her today, she thought broodingly. He looked ready to strangle her for being so obtuse.

She felt a thickness in her throat, almost as though there were hands around her neck, slowly slowly choking the life out of her. But it was almost the same. She could really begin to think she had enemies everywhere.

With all that, she was not thinking of Logan at all, and she was hardly in the mood for Reese's company either when he joined her in the back room late that evening.

"Hiding again, Maggie?"

"No, repositioning type. Want to help?"

He waved her suggestion away, but he thought he might have stayed if she had been dressed the way she had been the previous night. "You're very good at it."

"I've been doing it since I can remember. My father taught me, you know. I can't tell you how many hours I spent in this room. I love it."

"Yes," he agreed, "no one will run you out, Maggie."

"No, I don't think so,"

"I'm on your side, Maggie. I hope you know that."

"That's nice to hear," she said noncommittally, without looking at him. "What about your mother?"

"I have a feeling she always takes the line of least resistance. She wants everything to be easy for her and she never counts the cost for anyone else."

"I suppose that's true. She certainly has a fine old time haunting me with all her rude and suggestive comments. I have never heard a word of gratitude that I didn't throw her out into the streets after Frank died. Believe me, she was impossible enough to live with then."

"Maggie, you have to understand, she's had such

178

disappointments in her life."

"Me too," Maggie said shortly.

"All right. I'll talk to her again. I will, Maggie. Between us, we'll get *her* to understand."

"I think that's too much to ask, Reese. I'm not sure she has the mental capacity for understanding."

"Maggie, she *is* my mother." His voice took on the faintest tone of censure.

"Of course, Reese. To you she must be heart-warmingly lovable."

"You *are* in a mood, Maggie."

"It's been a gut-wrenching day, if you don't mind."

"It must be wrenching to turn down twenty thousand dollars."

Her hands stopped their constant motion for a fraction of a second. "Ah, I see. Well, I'll tell you, Reese, when they offer you an equivalent sum for your property, I'm sure you will snap it up faster than you can toss a drink down your gullet. And quite rightly too."

"Sorry, Maggie. It's just so crazy."

Another pause of her fingers. There wasn't a thing she could say that wouldn't sound like an agreement or a defense. "Are you on your way out, Reese?"

He looked startled. "I guess I was."

She looked at him without a word. He grimaced and left her without any further comment.

At least her oldest friends did not desert her. The next day, she saw the Mapes' wagon hitched up in front of Bodey's store as she walked up for her usual Sunday morning visit.

The minute she entered the door, Annie Mapes launched herself at her. "Maggie, Maggie, how awful, how can you stand it? Is everyone being perfectly horrible? *We* don't care, Sean and I, we . . ." She

179

grabbed Maggie, and waltzed her down the main aisle of the store and almost smack into Arwin's stove.

"Hi, Maggie." This was Sean, in his usual measured tone, with his usual care and concern. She didn't need to see them every day or even once a month to know they loved her. She always knew they were there, unwavering in their loyalty to her, as she was to them.

"Hi, Sean, Arwin."

"How you feeling, Maggie?"

"Wrung out. How are you doing, Arwin? Getting a lot of business around the stove these two days?"

"I'd say, I'd say."

"Well, we don't care what anybody says, do we, Sean? We know Maggie's got everybody's best interests at heart and she always has."

Artless Annie, Maggie thought, feeling a hundred years older than her childhood friend. "Thanks, Annie. What about you two? Everything going all right? Any rumbles about buying you out? Did you hear about my debacle with the Denver North lawyer?"

Sean answered her this time and Annie looked faintly abashed. "We're doing all right, Maggie, but in our usual straits. I can't say that money wouldn't look attractive to us right now. . . ."

"Sean—" Annie protested.

"There are days," he said slowly, "when I do wish that someone would make it easy for us to walk away."

"I don't want to hear that," Annie protested. "I don't. He won't do it, Maggie. I don't want to leave Colville and neither does he."

She was so earnest, just on the point of tears almost, and she was the sweetest thing, with her silken yellow hair and pale complexion that no amount of outdoor work ever turned brown. Sean was her counterpart in looks if not temperament, with the same flawless

180

features and skin. They were often taken for twins, or for husband and wife.

She wondered whether to tell them the dollar figure of her offer, but she knew they would hear soon enough. "They offered me twenty thousand dollars, Sean."

He was astounded, and so was Arwin.

"I was so sure you had heard," she said to Arwin.

"Maggie . . ." he growled at her, shaking her head. He didn't know what to think.

"My God," Sean said finally. "I wouldn't turn that kind of money down, Maggie, really I wouldn't."

"I understand," she said, because she knew how tightly against the line of utter poverty they lived.

"We, I, would go to Denver . . . in fact, I was even thinking about taking one of those jobs they're offering."

Annie looked stricken, as if this were the first time she had heard such a thing. "No, he wouldn't. He wouldn't."

"He would be crazy not to," Maggie said. She didn't know why none of this surprised her.

Sean smiled at her wanly. "Thanks, Maggie."

"No disloyalty to you," Annie said caustically. "Everyone knows we're such good friends."

"It's all right, Annie."

"That damned railroad is tearing everything apart, just as you've been saying, Maggie. How soon before it comes between us, too?"

"It won't."

"But Sean . . ."

"That's your business, not mine," Maggie said, and she felt very strongly she had better leave right then before Annie's distress escalated and something was said that could never be retracted later.

She hugged Annie tightly, and Sean with just a bit more reserve, and left the store. Still and all, she thought, the Mapes could be bought by Denver North. She

181

wondered how much less their price might be.

She felt like a character in a play, walking in and out of scenes with people, all of whom were telling her things she did not want to hear.

Soon it would be Logan's turn, and she was rather grateful that her malaise over the insert and her articles had preoccupied her to the point where thoughts of him could not intrude. She was in no mood for reliving their lovemaking. She could only remember the mechanics of it, and the compelling need. Anything else she did not want to recall, because it would lead to the extravagant yearning that had propelled her into his arms in the first place.

Perfectly right. Last Sunday was it, that he had possessed her in that erotic way? No more of that. He needed a proper mate who would put no boundaries and conditions on his feelings and her own. She even had a candidate, she thought, as the idea flashed into her mind. Just as she had told him: a farm woman, someone accustomed to his way of life, willing to bear all the children he could give her with all the ecstasy his heat could generate. And who would be so perfect for him but Annie Mapes?

It would solve all her problems. Sean could go off and seek some life he thought might be better, and Annie's loyalties would remain intact, while Logan would acquire the kind of wife he deserved.

Logan and Annie. They had known each other forever. It made such perfect sense. As she thought about it, she couldn't understand why he hadn't perceived Annie's perfect qualities and sought her out himself. But there was an answer for that. He had had an impossible dream about an imperfect Maggie whom he glorified all out of proportion to reality. She thought it would be easy to

182

point out the truth, especially when it was so blindingly clear to her.

Logan and Annie. Yes. Annie would work with him side by side, just as he had a right to expect, and just as she would never be able to do. Annie would want children. Annie hardly ever wanted to come to town.

And she never wanted to be anywhere else but *in* town.

But it would never work that way.

Sunday again, with blessed peace in the morning and Mother Colleran's voice ringing in her ears as she left for church, "I'll pray for you, Maggie."

I hope they crucify you, Maggie thought hostilely, and watched from the window as Reese solicitously helped his mother into her carriage and climbed into the driver's seat to take her to church like a dutiful son.

She could not understand Reese. Reese had become a visitor who had somehow removed himself from his mother and Maggie except when he was home to tend to necessities. They did not know what he did during the day, except when he volunteered to drive Maggie where she might want to go or took Mother Colleran to church. They knew he spent every evening at the hotel, but for what purpose other than to drink, they could not conjecture. It wasn't as if there were contacts to be made in the elegant confines of the hotel.

Nor could Maggie understand why he insisted on staying. He struck her as a man who was restless and got bored easily, yet he endured evenings in his mother's company, telling the same stories with different embellishments, and had somehow found congenial company in a farm and ranching town a hundred miles from nowhere.

It didn't seem to be an ideal situation for a man like Reese Colleran, and he didn't seem to be on his way anywhere with any great hurry.

He even sat through church services.

And when he was in her presence, she reflected, he hardly ever took his eyes off of her. She had the lurking feeling that he was always looking at her breasts, always remembering that one revealing evening when he could see them as clearly as if she had been naked.

She just didn't understand the reason he had come and the reason he remained. She wished she could kick him out of the apartment and straight over to the hotel where he spent most of his time anyway.

She would suggest it to him.

Maybe she would go live there herself.

Imagine what might be possible if she lived there.

Privacy.

Visitors.

Overnight visitors, visitors who would not have to slink out into the middle of the night like criminals, because no one would ever ever interrupt her in her own room.

Lovely.

But not a solution. She knew what she was doing: she was looking for a way to continue with Logan, and yet she knew that even if she were alone and in complete privacy, there was still no way to avoid their union with all its tempestuous consequences.

Even the thought of it was arousing. She knew, she knew, and she could not let herself keep thinking about it, about what it would mean. There was such a temptation to discount the aftermath for the sake of those moments of pure, glistening pleasure.

She did not want to be lost in a sensual reverie on a Sunday afternoon. It was deliciously quiet, a time she did not have to do anything, feel anything, go anywhere, see anyone.

And yet she was consumed with a reckless restlessness because nothing was settled, nothing.

She wandered down to the office. The emptiness of it

was not peaceful to her. *She* felt empty, and she swiped at the papers on her worktable futilely. The papers fluttered and scattered and several fell to the floor. She stooped and picked them up, cursorily glancing at each. At one. Logan's firm handwriting: Come to *me*.

Her breath caught in her throat. Come to him? Come to *him?* Just hitch up a buckboard and drive out to him bold as brass, as if no one would be watching, as if his hands wouldn't be around to see?

To him?

She could go to him, and she could tell him the conclusion she had come to; that was a reasonable excuse for a visit. Damn, who would see her or question her anyway?

There was no one in her house, no one to whom she had to answer anyway ... she wanted to go to him. She was overwhelmed by how urgent the feeling was.

A half hour later, as she barreled down the track toward his spread, she was shaking with perturbation. She wasn't sure things would go exactly the way she planned. Perhaps he would take her appearance as sending a totally different message than the one she intended.

Another fifteen minutes and she had driven her team into his dooryard. She saw him waiting for her on the porch.

She hadn't been there in years. She remembered a rough-hewn building there, the equivalent of what Frank had built on his ranchland, and here she saw a fully completed ranch house that looked large and commodious.

He came out to meet her without a word, unhitched the team, and sent them out to the pasture. After he had pulled the wagon to the side, near the barn, she thought: it looked like any other wagon. It looked like something he might have in his barn.

185

She felt his hand at her elbow and a firm push toward the house.

"You've never been here."

"Never."

They stepped up onto the porch and she turned, momentarily, to look at the view. It faced the long drive that separated verdant grazing fields. Towering trees in the distance marked the boundary of the property. To the right was the barn and more grassland, to her left, a garden, and beyond that outbuildings concealed by a giant hedge.

He opened the door and she preceded him inside, into a large square room with a fireplace and a sofa and some chairs. The walls were covered with hand-loomed rugs and animal skins, as was the floor. At the far end there were several doors leading from the room, and a narrow staircase winding upward.

There was a curious silence in the air. She looked back to see him leaning against the door, watching her, his eyes scorching her with his need that she knew was reflected in her own eyes.

And now she knew the lie. She had not come to assuage her conscience, she had come for him, and she had to struggle against it as hard as possible.

When she didn't move toward him, he walked slowly into the room. "Let's see the rest of the house." His voice was flat, even-toned. Whatever she was feeling, he was sure she still wanted him and he was willing to wait.

He showed her the separate kitchen, with its immense cooking fireplace, iron stove, and oven. He showed her his bedroom on the first floor, off of the parlor. It too had its own fireplace, and a large comfortable looking bed, a dresser, and a hooked rug on the floor. He led her upstairs to show her the two bedrooms in the eaves of the house, and then down to the root cellar, where wooden boxes contained neatly labeled jars of fruit and vegetables.

"The wife of one of the men cooks for me," he said, although she had not asked for explanations. She was thinking how very self-sufficient he was. Such a comfortable home, built, she was sure, over the last five or six years since his parents had died. He needed nothing more than someone to keep house and make sure there were stores and that he was well fed, that and occasional surcease for his desires. And that, she thought acidly, was easily found in town. For a price.

He hardly needed her.

In a corner of the parlor, close by the kitchen door, there was a plain oak table and chairs. She chose to draw one of these out and sit in it rather than make herself at home on the sofa. His expression wavered between amusement and gravity as he joined her.

"You definitely have something on your mind, Maggie, and I get the feeling it is not our mutual enjoyment."

"You're a perceptive man, Logan."

"Was it an easy trip here?"

"Forty-five minutes from town, as you well know."

He nodded. "A pleasant trip, Maggie."

"Except perhaps in the winter," she retorted as his direction became evident.

"Winter days and nights can be very pleasant in front of a fireplace—with the right company."

She swallowed hard and plunged ahead. "I don't doubt it. But not this company, Logan."

"Oh no? How so?"

"For all the reasons you know, and for some that have become evident just in the brief time since . . ."

"Is there something you want that we haven't explored yet, Maggie?"

Crystal clear images of his explorations drifted into her mind, behind her eyes, insistent, as real as real. *"We were almost caught the last time,"* she reminded him tartly.

"We don't have to put ourselves in that position, Maggie. You know that."

"No, I thought about it, Logan. There is no way possible to keep up what we're doing that is sane and makes sense to both of us."

"You came to tell me that?"

"Face to face."

"Brave Maggie. There is a very sane way and you know it."

"I live in town. I work in town. I am not ready for a family. I'm surely not ready to consider marriage again. What sane way, Logan? Mother Colleran snoops, and Reese thinks I arranged myself downstairs that night just for him. He keeps waiting for some concrete invitation and I feel like a fraud."

"But you're very real, Maggie. That is why you are here right now. You want what we have, Maggie, just as much as I do. I don't even care what you call it. It doesn't matter. And you want a sane, sensible, comfortable way to continue it."

How right he was, she thought, girding herself. How much she would have given if the end result did not have to be a marital vow. How lucky men were that they could take that sensual pleasure freely wherever it was offered and never had to count the cost even when they paid for it.

"I thought of a sensible solution," she said firmly.

He gave her a skeptical look. "I'm waiting to hear."

"You find someone else," she said succinctly, cutting to the heart of it. When he did not respond she went on, "Someone who is free to fall in love and perhaps to get married. Someone who is used to the kind of life you lead.

188

Someone who wants a family. . . ."

"I see," he said flatly. "And who is this paragon?"

She looked away from him. "Annie Mapes."

He made a strangled sound. "Annie? You're telling me that you want me to give you up and court Annie instead? You want me to make love to *Annie Mapes* the way I make love to you? You want me to—"

"You do not have to paint in the details, Logan."

"I think I do."

"She's perfect for you, and a lot more compliant than I am."

"That's for sure," he muttered. "Of all the goddamned things. *Annie Mapes* . . . She's got as much gut in her as the fence post outside. You remember her as a kid? You tried everything and she cried about everything. Hell, Maggie, that's not even a compliment."

"It makes sense to me. There is just no way that . . ." She started to get up. She would tangle herself up in her words if she kept on trying to make sense of it to him when it already made so much sense to her. She was not available; Annie was; and Logan needed someone. Simple.

"Leaving?" he asked lazily.

"I think I've made my point."

"I've yet to make mine."

"There can't be any discussion about this, Logan."

"Not if you don't want there to be."

"I guess I don't. I can't see where it could lead because we're both so strong-willed. You would want your way and I most certainly would want mine."

"Oh, I definitely want my way, Maggie."

"That's settled then." She turned to the door, aware that he shoved his chair out and was preparing to follow her. She kept her back to him as she made for the door, but she could not close out his words.

"Nothing's settled, Maggie, when you want to hand me

189

over to Annie Mapes and tell me you want me to transfer all the feelings I have for you to her. You sure you want that, Maggie? All those feelings? All those things we did? What kind of lover do you think she will be? Willing? Scared? Do you think she will touch me the same way you touched me? Do you think she'll let me know her naked body the same way I know yours?''

She kept going, knowing that if she stopped there would be no end. She reached for the doorknob and threw open the door.

"Do you think . . ." his voice followed her, "do you think her kisses will taste so luscious to me, do you think . . ."

He followed her out the door. He had one last chance, one desperate gamble.

"Do you think," he called to her, "I would really let you walk away?"

She heard the words the same moment she felt the thick rough rope circle her hand and land emphatically around her shoulders. He pulled and the lariat tightened around her arms. She didn't try to fight it. He was stronger and she was immobilized, and she did not know how she felt about it.

He pulled her gently back to him and wound the rope around her one more time. Without a word, he hoisted her up on his shoulder and carried her back into the house.

"What are you doing? What are you going to do with me? Logan! Logan . . ." But she knew; there could only be one destination. He dumped her on his bed and kicked the door closed.

"Just what I expected," she muttered, yanking at the rope. "Your solution is to hog tie me and then try to seduce me."

"Nothing of the sort, Maggie." He sat down next to her and began loosening her bonds. "Let's just say the situation called for drastic measures."

"And the door is locked, of course."

"A precaution." He looked amused.

"And you think all you have to do is kiss me and I'll capitulate."

"Never, Maggie. I certainly think it will take a lot more than one kiss. However, I promise you I'm not going to kiss you."

"So you'll touch me first; you know just where I am vulnerable."

He shook his head. "Maggie, Maggie, Maggie. I won't lay a hand on you, now that I know you're willing to have another woman submit to my caresses."

She snapped her teeth together. "I don't understand it. What is the point of this?"

He smiled at her conspiratorally. "I don't want to let you go."

"You are crazy. How long am I to be kept here?"

"As long as it takes, Maggie."

"And you're not going to . . ." Did she feel the faintest pang of disappointment when he shook his head. "What *are* you going to do, Logan?"

"Why, I think I'll get comfortable, Maggie."

It was the last thing she expected him to say. "It sounds like you intend to keep me here for a long long time," she said grumpily, and then she bolted upright. "What are you *doing?*"

He was taking off his clothes. She watched wide-eyed as he shucked them all, one by one, and tossed them across the room until he was buck naked.

She stared at him in fascination. Daylight became him; the sun streaming in through the window played on all the male angles of his body. His legs were long and muscular to the juncture of his thighs, where his potent masculinity rose, long and angular, utterly entrancing. His hips and stomach were flat and lean, and his chest broad and muscular, with a mat of hair that crept deliciously downward. When he bent over to retrieve his clothing from the floor she had a clear view of the long line up his back that sloped down to his hips and bottom and his firm male buttocks.

He sat down at the foot of the bed opposite her, one leg angled up and the other braced on the bedrail. His one arm rested along the footboard, the other balanced on his knee. He did not say one word.

She knew why; he had thought to shock her, to arouse her, to make her capitulate. She kept her eyes steadily on his, resentful of the little smile she could just see playing around the corners of his mouth. It became a challenge for her not to look at him, one she was determined to win because he had so flagrantly presented himself to her for just that purpose.

She would not let him get away with it. A male body was a male body, whether it was dressed or not. It was a simple matter of just not looking at him.

The silence stretched out between them. The air thickened, becoming hot with her determination. She was losing. After a long long time she understood she was losing. It didn't matter if he were dressed or naked now; she was filled with the wanton awareness of him and his erotic prowess, and she only wanted to give in to it. She did not need to feast her eyes on him—the image of him was in her consciousness as clearly as if she were staring at him.

The atmosphere became electric with possibilities. He did not move, he did not say a word. He waited.

She felt the awareness of his nakedness arousing her like nothing else before. The sense of him waiting for her excited her unbearably. Oh, he wasn't going to seduce her, she thought, just a little provoked by his tactics. He was just going to sit there naked, blatantly male, and drive every sane thought out of her mind as she imagined

192

things she could do, things she would feel if only she made a move toward him.

What would he do? He would take her into his arms and pull her tightly against him and she would feel gorgeous manhood hard against her body. She would hold him, she would kiss him, she would run her hands all over his nakedness, she would grasp the essence of him and explore what it could mean to her. She would love the contrast between his being naked and her being clothed, and yet, it wouldn't be enough just to have the freedom to feel his body. She would want the melting sensation of it next to her skin. She would want . . .

She shook her head violently. She knew what she would want, what the vision of that wondrous living heat of him would arouse in her.

She felt her body expanding for him, her femininity yearning for him. She was made for him, and his ramrod member made her achingly aware of the emptiness in her.

But she could have him, she thought. She could just reach over and . . . She swallowed convulsively at the idea of taking the whole of his towering manhood into her hands. Her eyes changed, flickered with a lambent light of arousal.

"Maggie, come kiss me." His voice was sensual, commanding, as he sensed her readiness. She sent him a provocative little look and then allowed herself to rest her sultry gaze on the rampant maleness brazenly revealed to her. Then she inched her way toward him, never moving her eyes from his nakedness until she felt his hands reach out for her and haul her up against his bare chest.

It became all one sensation—his mouth crushing down on hers, open, seeking, his arms closing around her and his legs wrapping her in a sensual embrace so that the whole of his nakedness was aligned with her body and she could feel every long hard thrusting inch of him against her.

His kisses were long and slow and thorough, and she gave herself to them as his tongue explored every exquisite inch of her mouth. Slowly and slower still, he rolled her over so that they were laying side to side with his arms and legs still surrounding her in their erotic embrace.

But now her hands were free to explore his nakedness, and she reveled in the sensation of touching him wherever she wanted to. Her wanton hands roamed all over him; there was not an inch of him she did not caress and feel and stroke.

He was totally at her command. He kissed her just the way she wanted him to, he moved with her just the way she wanted him to, and he whispered love words to her as she grasped him and began the ageless drive to completion, totally in control of his desire.

And when he lay spent in her arms, she wanted him still more.

But there was time, there was time. He had said there were other ways, and other ways there were, but her need for him now was so intense she thought she would explode with it.

She wanted to arouse him again to the same pulsating peak, but she didn't know what to do. She held him lightly in the same sensual way and kissed him urgently, trying to tell him with the movements of her body and her lips and tongue that she wanted him.

He felt her driving need and wanted to prolong it, to make her so wild with wanting him that she would seek the only culmination possible. He wanted to arouse her to the same fever pitch as he had felt for her. He wanted her hands all over him again with the same erotic desire to feel his nakedness. He invited her to play with him with his langorous motions. He covered her mouth with deep carnal kisses and felt the spurt of renewed desire.

She felt it in her hands, the lusty surge of him. Her kisses grew frantic with urgency. His hands reached for her, and she blindly remembered she was still dressed. She couldn't wait for him to strip her. She wanted to take off her clothes for *him*. She eased herself away from him and his hot demanding kisses, away from his pulsating body.

Now she could see he was becoming aroused again. He lay there propped on one elbow, waiting to see what she was going to do.

She unbuttoned her dress and slid it off her arms, letting it fall to the floor. Then she unhooked her corset and tossed it across the room. She touched her stiff peaked breasts under the shroud of the thin camisole she wore, then slid the neckline down so that her breasts were naked for him to see. She sat down on the bed to slide off her cotton stockings, uncovering her legs with slow, seductive grace.

Finally she stood up and slid off all over her underthings so that she was totally naked and ready for him.

And he was ready for her. Every erotic movement she had made aroused him still more. She knelt on the edge of the bed, wanting him, her body vibrated with need of him. He reached for her at that moment and pulled her naked body against his.

The ecstasy of bare skin against bare skin was almost overwhelming. He knew just what she wanted: the hot touch of his tongue against her mouth, the slide of his fingers against her nipple, the touch of his hand sliding down her writhing buttocks as she thrust herself closer and closer to his nakedness.

She was all honey, ready for him, grinding her hips against his hard heat in primitive invitation. Her mouth was all honey, as open to his carnal caress as the rest of her shimmering body. He rolled her on top of him so that

195

she lay directly over his hard staff. He wanted her melting for him, demanding nothing less from him than the fullness of his manhood. Her body writhed with pleasure as he aroused her still more with his torrid caresses.

"Maggie." He whispered as his hands explored her inch by inch. "Tell me what you want."

She felt his hands sleeking down her buttocks. She felt the thrusts of his elongated male member. She thought of how it had become hard again just for her. She felt his caress of the taut nub of her nipple. She moved her legs and straddled his hips so that she could rub herself against that towering staff. "I want you," she breathed. "I want you."

She felt him cover her mouth again, then his hands slowly stroked her body downward, toward her velvet center. He caressed her there until she moaned with wanton need. And then, and only then, did he position himself over her and with one long thick lush stroke enter her welcoming fold.

The sensation of him filling her was indescribable. He was there, so thick and so hard and long that there seemed no end to him and no beginning to her.

She angled her legs outward so that she was totally open to him, and they lay this way for a long tantalizing time. He kissed her over and over, caressing her with his tongue. When he felt the tension in her escalate he moved, and she thought she would explode with joy.

This was what she needed, his thick, hard length driving into her, on and on and on. She loved the feeling of his male essence contained within her, enfolded by her, pleasuring her with each virile thrust, loved the knowledge that she was the one who had aroused him. She rocked against him, rotating her hips against him, enticing him into the mystery of her fathomless femininity.

"You were made for me," he whispered into her mouth, into her soul. "You are mine," and the words resonated in her heart.

He was perfect for her. The hard luscious length of him fit her exquisitely. The flatness of his hips aligned with hers flawlessly so that the intimate core of her was centered exactly on him. She could touch him everywhere, with her hands, with her feet, and she could look into his eyes and see the same sensation she was feeling mirrored there, stunning in its shared intensity.

She was a wild willing temptress, sleek as a cat beneath him, melting into him, unquenchable in her demand. Her long luscious legs surrounded him, held him, felt him, spread for him to give herself to him with a torrid sensuality that left him gasping.

At the thought of her honey moist haven wide and wanton for him he felt all his power gathering suddenly. His body constricted, and he drove himself into her forcefully with long lusty strokes over and over, to the litany of the ecstatic moans deep in her throat.

And then the creamy sensations began, swelling upward, pluming outward, opulent, thick, billowing out from a hard nub of voluptuous feeling that was hot gold, spiraling and melting deep within her into a cataclysmic release.

He wanted to hold her, caress her, tell her she was wonderful, and he couldn't wait. He needed completion with her, and in four hard, potent strokes he unleashed his drenching climax deep within her quivering core.

Chapter Eleven

"Where have *you* been?

The voice was Reese's and the tone jolted her right back to reality. She had been counting the minutes, reaffirming her initial impression of how long it had taken her to get to Logan's ranch, and she looked at Reese through unfocused eyes.

"Excuse me?" she said blankly as she descended from the buckboard onto the plank walk where he was standing directly in front of the office.

"I've been damned worried about you. Why didn't you leave a note or something?"

She still had no idea what he was talking about. "A note to whom, Reese?"

He looked offended. "Me."

"Why?" She didn't look at him as she efficiently hitched the wagon to the post. "I didn't know I had to clear my whereabouts with you."

He got it finally. He followed her into the office. "I was worried, Maggie. Mother says she can't recall when you've ever gone off someplace no one knew."

"Well, this is the first time."

He perched on the edge of her desk as she sank into her chair.

"But where were you?"

"And it may not be the last either," she added, flashing him an enigmatic smile.

It was a secret smile, one that shut him out and made him want to know what lay behind it. Already her attention was centered somewhere else, and he was jangling with curiosity.

"Let me take you and mother out to dinner tonight," he offered.

"Thank you, no."

"What excuse, Maggie? You have no excuse except that you don't want to be seen in my company. You would be a lot more honest if you had said that," he said angrily, sliding away from her.

"Reese, you are acting like a child. Is it so important that I go to dinner with you?"

"I *thought* we had decided we were to be friends."

"We are." But even she wasn't sure of that. She wanted to placate him so that she would have time to savor the wild sweet hours she had spent with Logan. If she argued with him, she would have that to contend with instead, and what was a dinner after all? Two hours of her time, if that. "Fine, I accept your invitation."

He looked pleased. "Honestly, Maggie, we have hardly had any time in the last week to talk. This whole thing with the Denver North recruiting ads, for instance . . . I know how upset you are. I can at least share the burden if you won't let me help any other way."

She smiled at him uncertainly. She wasn't sure that was a worry she really wanted to share with him.

Worse, Mother Colleran declined to join them for dinner, and that removed her excuse for ending the evening early.

The hotel dining room was crowded. As they entered, she saw a number of familiar faces, including Mr. Brown, who sat in an unobtrusive corner by himself.

They made desultory small talk until the waiter had passed them the menus. After they ordered, Reese brought up the notices in the supplement again. "What are you going to do, Maggie?"

"There is nothing I can do about that advertising. You know as well as I do that it comes from Denver and I have no control over what goes into it."

"But how can you justify . . ."

"I shouldn't have to justify, Reese. Everyone knows my position, I haven't changed it, and whenever I feel there's something to be said, I will say it. A disclaimer will take care of the rest."

He looked at her admiringly. "That's damned clever, Maggie."

"Yes, I thought of it today." Today, during the long, daydreaming wagon ride back to town. No, not long. Forty-five minutes. Not onerous. Thinking time. Time to luxuriate in feelings and experiences she had thought to deny herself forever. There *was* a way, she thought, just as Logan had said.

She wished he were sitting across the table from her, admiring her cleverness.

"It might be a little too late," Reese said with a sudden casualness that brought her immediately to attention.

"How so?"

He shrugged. "Because of the talk. You heard the talk, Maggie. An explanation after the fact might not hold water."

"But I'll hold to it nonetheless. People will believe whatever they want to, I suppose," Maggie said, wanting to add that this was to be her last word on the subject. She was saved from that by the arrival of their dinner—a reasonable excuse not to talk for a while.

But after, with coffee and dessert, Reese wanted to tackle the problem of how she could save face.

"There is no way, Reese. The supplements will come in

every week, and every week I will wager you there will be a hiring notice displayed prominently on the first page. I think Denver North has done it on purpose, and I'm not going to worry about it sullying my reputation."

"All right, fine. You can't relinquish your revenues from running the supplement—"

"Nor can they specially print a supplement for this region."

"All right, then . . ."

"We charge into the fray and say the hell with . . ."

"Maggie Colleran."

She froze. She knew that voice and she was not happy that he had chosen to come straight across the room deliberately to seek her out in the view of everyone dining there this evening.

"Mr. Brown."

"A fine hotel," he said. "Delightful food."

"We in Colville like it," she said shortly.

"Many in Colville are looking to better their positions," Mr. Brown said. "They would give a great deal to be in a position to dine here whenever they would, to buy the carriage that would bring them here, to rent rooms here by the month and be perfectly comfortable and have their every whim attended to. I must say, I'm enjoying it immensely. Good night, Maggie Colleran."

She stared at him as he stalked away. "Good Lord, what was *that* about?" And then she felt as though she were being watched, and she turned slowly and looked around the room.

Everyone's eyes were on her, reflecting accusation and betrayal.

She carried on. She curled the voluptuous memory of her afternoon with Logan close to her heart and went about her business as if nothing had happened.

But everything had happened and everything was changed. Sometime in the middle of the week she had the distinct feeling that Logan was deliberately leaving her alone so she could sort out her feelings.

But for the first time, she had no conflict. She knew why. Logan accepted what she was, or at least on the surface he did. He let her be what she was. He was on the ranch, she was in her office, and sometime in the week they would come together again. She wasn't worried when, or how. She was too in love with the sensations and the freedom she felt to be concerned with the future.

Only at night did the exquisite yearning almost overpower her, and then she wanted him desperately in her arms and in her bed.

"Well, they're hiring on," Arch Warfield announced the following Thursday. "You ought to see the line, Maggie. They got so many applicants I don't know where they're going to put them."

She went to see the line and it was not encouraging. The money was good—too good, and the men on the line were not all men of Colville and surrounding counties.

"Write the story," she told Warfield, knowing exactly what kind of story he would write. She would balance it somehow. There had to be some way.

She couldn't allow herself a single distraction: Logan's sensual temptation was the furthest thing from her mind as she set type Friday night. A.J. was at the press and Jean was inking the type. The disclaimer was written and set prominently on the front page. She didn't like how it looked, but that was how it would go.

And in the midst of this, Logan walked in.

She was startled to see him. Her mind flashed on the vision of him on his bed the previous Sunday afternoon. She shook it away and greeted him briskly.

"I'll help," he offered, and A.J. immediately set him to work inserting the supplements into the ink-dried first press of the paper.

They worked for four hours beyond that, which was not unusual, and it struck Maggie that there was a faint petulance in Jean's manner, almost as if he resented Logan's intrusion into their ritual. Not that it mattered, of course, but there was a certain rhythm that had shifted, and she knew it was due to her constant awareness of him across the room.

A.J. and Jean left her reluctantly, even after she assured them that she was very happy to see Logan, and when she was sure they had gone she locked all the doors and turned down the lights and allowed herself the luxury of feasting her eyes on him.

"I want you, Maggie—right now."

"How? Not here."

"Here. It's been hell this week, Maggie. Turn off the lights and come to me here."

Every other consideration flew out of her head. She did as he said and groped her way back to him inside the darkened back room, melting into his waiting arms. "It's been hell for me, too," she whispered, as he rained light nipping little kisses on her mouth. She wondered how she had borne it when this was all she had wanted, in her heart of hearts, all week.

His kiss deepened and she gave herself to it in the dark, trusting him implicitly to know what she wanted and how to give it to her.

She felt a renewed excitement and wound her arms around him, pressing her body against him. She felt him hardening as he molded her body to his and thrilled to the feeling of how she aroused him with her kisses and her touch.

From the thick honey of his kisses, she felt him pulling up her skirt, and easing her against the wall so that it would brace her and he would be free to do all the things she desired. His hands slid knowingly over her thighs, seeking the opening that would expose her velvet cleft to his touch. A moment later, his fingers slipped deftly into the textured heat of her, and she shifted against him to ease his way.

He caressed her there and felt the tempestuous arousal that told him that she needed more than his caresses. And he was ready for her.

She felt the long, thick hard slide of his potency into her satin sheath and it was wondrous. She was clothed, supported by a wall, beguiled by his hot kisses and filled with his virile manhood. Behind, she felt his one hand grasp her buttocks, and she thrilled to the feel of his hand guiding her as they coupled in this new way.

Her hips writhed under his masterful hand as he shifted within her.

"Don't move," she sighed. "No, move . . ." She didn't know. She loved his hard fullness inside her; she wanted to savor it and she needed him driving her to culmination.

They remained in this erotic embrace for a long while as they kissed each other with slow, languid wet kisses, wishing they could be private and naked.

He moved, slowly at first; he had to move. Her moans and sighs and her volatile whispers told him how much she loved the feel of him thick inside her. Her open-mouthed kisses almost sent him spiraling to completion.

He wanted her with him. He wanted her. His whole body tightened as he thrust forcefully into her sweet heat; he was all taut and tight and hard and driving, driving, centering her as he guided and caressed her buttocks to the rhythm of his thrusts, feeling her know just what to do, how to move with him, how to do everything just as he needed her to do it, feeling her explode finally into a frenzy of wild gyrations, grinding against him as an avalanche of sensation cascaded like a waterfall all through her body.

He couldn't contain himself after that. He tore his mouth from hers to moan her name before his final penetrating lunge propelled him over the edge.

She loved knowing the perfume of their union would still be with her when she awakened.

"Sunday," he had said when he left her. "Come to me Sunday." She couldn't wait for Sunday. She didn't care about the paper; she only cared that there was still one more day until she could be with him again.

And with no second thoughts, she reflected, as she made her Saturday delivery rounds.

"Now Maggie," Arwin said like some Greek chorus, "this excuse on the front page is useless. Everyone saw you talking so sweetly to Mr. Brown at dinner the other night."

"Did they?" she murmured. She should have followed her first instinct, to either slap his face or leave the room—or both.

Too late now. She was getting in deeper and deeper—so deep it could not be a coincidence. It scared her a little. A little body of negative opinion was mounting against her for reasons she couldn't yet discern.

"Isn't it interesting that this is what people are saying?" she asked Reese later. He looked appalled. "It's a small town, Reese. Every action has its consequences."

But somehow she was not thinking about consequences with Logan. There was an unrequited hunger in her that only wanted the sensation of the moment. Everytime she thought about him her anticipation rose to a fever pitch. She marveled that she had been so stupid as to think she could use Logan and then hand him over to Annie Mapes.

She was a mile from his ranch the next morning when she realized she had spent the whole trip thinking about

206

their carnal togetherness. Her body was already stiff with the awareness of what awaited her, and her excitement was all the more stimulating because she had deliberately worn garments she knew were easy to remove and no underclothing.

He was all she wanted, everything from him and no one else, and it seemed to her that her journey to him carried its own reward. She loved seeing him waiting for her in the dooryard, looking tall and lean and gorgeously male. Expecting *her*. Wanting *her*.

He reached for her the moment she reined in the horses and she braced her hands on his muscular shoulders. He lifted her and held her close so that her body slid down the length of his until he could fit his mouth to hers in a hot urgent kiss. He held her at her waist and around her buttocks, and her legs wrapped around his.

He knew she was naked, and the sensations of her movements against him were overwhelmingly tempting. He wanted to take her right there, wanton and willing as she so clearly seemed to be.

Slowly he lowered her to the ground, to force her to release her legs, release him. He eased his mouth away reluctantly and moved his hands from her bottom to cup her face.

"I can't get enough of you," he murmured.

"Start now," she whispered, licking her lips to invite his kiss again. He took the invitation and she opened her mouth to him and met his kiss ferociously.

He kissed her just the way she wanted to be kissed, with deep, wet, voluptuous kisses that incited them both.

"Maggie, this is insane."

"Don't stop."

He didn't stop. He went on kissing her, deeper and deeper, and his hands moved this time because his need to feel her body's response was too great. He cupped her breasts. They were so soft, so warm, so unfettered. He could feel the stiff peak of her nipples under the material, thrusting against his fingers.

He began unbuttoning her shirt and she helped him, shrugging it off her shoulders before he had pulled it from the waistband of her skirt, baring her breasts for him and arching her back to entice his caresses.

He held each luscious breast in each hand as he gazed into her sparkling gray eyes. His fingers moved then to center on each taut nipple so that she knew he was there, just there, and she drew in her breath, her heart pounding with the excitement of waiting for the feeling of him touching each rigid tip. The intensity of the waiting was sensual, arousing. Her mouth went dry, her tongue wet her lips again, and in that instant his fingers constricted, lightly squeezing against her hard nipples. The sensation shot through her like quicksilver.

He held her like that, each pebble-hard nipple compressed between his fingers, and his mouth settled on hers. All she felt in the next lush moments was the slide of his tongue seeking her and the exquisite pressure of his fingers caressing each taut nipple.

She was fragrant with wanting him, honey-warm and ready for him. As the seductive touch of his fingers played with her luscious nipples, she moved her hips enticingly up against him and begged for his love in the most primitive female way.

He could not resist her thrusting wanton movements. One of his hands reached for her skirt and ripped it away, then he lifted her up against him and carried her to the back of her wagon. Tossing the skirt down first, he lowered her naked body onto it gently and fell into another succulent kiss.

Now she was all his, naked and willing, and his hands explored her everywhere as he delved into her mouth with those slow, luscious kisses she loved so much.

She began feeling him under his clothing. His hips were just level with her as she sat, and she had perfect access to the hard throbbing length of him. She was not shy about caressing him thoroughly through the thickness of his pants. Her legs straddled his thighs so that she could get closer to him.

He helped her. He wanted her hands on him while he felt every part of her. In a moment, he pulled away the waistband of his pants and then he was in her hands, hard and hot, eager for her touch.

He returned to the lushness of her mouth as her hands teased and tormented him, and then he began his seduction.

She was so ready for him, so open, moaning with the erotic sense of his maleness hard in her hands. She tore her mouth away from his to kiss it, to feel its luscious rigidity with her lips and tongue, to suck the tip lightly, until he was almost gone.

Slowly she looked up at him. Reading the heat of his desire in his eyes, she shifted her body slightly so that she could position him exactly at the most intimate part of her, the place where, with one sultry thrust, he could enter and possess her.

She was at the perfect angle to see everything. She braced herself with one hand and with the other she moved him to the point of her desire and angled her thighs to give him perfect access. She knew she would never forget the sight and sensation of him taking her in just that way. He came into her gradually, in unhurried movements so that she could feel him, inch by hard long inch, and see him and understand the full nature of his carnal possession.

He lowered his mouth to hers for a long erotic kiss to let her feel the full thick thrusting length of him deep inside her.

He loved this positioning of her body, and he lengthened the kiss to keep her tightly connected to him for as long as possible. Even her hands, playing with his firm buttocks, pressed him closer, as if he were not deeply enough within her.

And then he moved her downward so that she was lying on the wagon bed, and he caressed her body as he moved away from her so that he could remove her boots and position her legs on his shoulders.

From his upright position, he could see everything now, every emotion on her face, her luscious nipples taut with excitement, her churning hips seeking the sensation of his motion, the long swooping length of her legs, everything, and he moved, finally, to begin his primitive rhythm.

It was like nothing she had ever felt before. At this angle, with him standing just at the juncture of her thighs and her on her back, she was totally open to him, knowing he could watch and see everything. The thought of that was thrilling, provocative.

She felt herself going wild with fantasies about what he could see, and her body reacted intensely. Her hands thrashed around for something to hold onto. She found the edge of a rusted ring that was used as a tie-down, and she grasped it.

Her arching body and thrusting breasts excited him still more. His hands massaged the long length of her legs as he drove into her again and again. His hands slid under her to lift her upward more tightly against him, still plunging into her with a wild possession. Her hips gyrated provocatively with every thrust, her urgency growing. He loved watching her naked body writhe for him, loved the knowledge that it was his virile manhood that drove her to this ecstatic response. He heard her moaning with every hard thrust, and he loved it that his possession of her brought her to this.

She was all sensual feeling and motion motion motion.

The center of her being bore down on the thick hardness of him. Her quivering body tensed, and he took her to a shattering culmination that rocketed through her like a firecracker and exploded into a thousand sizzling fingers of light all over her.

And there he rested in union with her for one long perfect moment.

When she opened her eyes and lifted herself on her elbows so that she could savor the sight of their connected bodies, her insolent look invited his final savage surrender. With one torrid surge he drove deep into her feminine core.

Later, they lay on his bed, naked, satiated, exchanging languid kisses, not moving, barely speaking. She had the brief fleeting thought that she wasn't even thinking. But it didn't matter. *This* mattered, this afternoon, this man, this kiss, this touch. He hadn't even chided her for her ridiculous notion of leaving him. He had done nothing but make love to her and tell her how wonderful she was.

It was almost possible, in the golden aftermath, to believe there could be some kind of life with Logan. It might even be possible to have this much life with him, if he were willing. But she rather thought he would not be. He was giving her her head and waiting to see how far she ran. And she had run straight back into his arms, demanding his kisses.

She wondered how he had known she would want him so intensely. It wasn't love, it was a trust, a bond from their past, and a nature within her that knew no sensual bounds. She had tried to deny this nature, but everything else paled in comparison to this release and this freedom. Now she was willing to pay the price to have him. She wondered when, or if, he would broach the subject of a future.

211

She turned to look at him and was awed by her response to his face in repose. His whole body was quiescent, relaxed. She just loved looking at him. She remembered the day—was it a month ago—that she had ached for the sight of him, just to know he was there.

He was so very *there*. She hadn't even had time to examine the brief, fleeting feeling of what would have happened if . . . There was no regret. She could make a case that she would not have been ready for him had she not married Frank first, but that was absurd. Frank had been what he was and his nature could not have been changed any more than hers.

Logan had brought in her clothing, and she reached for her shirt to slip it over her shoulders, unaware that he watched her through hooded eyes.

He felt a tenuous link to her now, he thought, as he admired the way the soft fabric of the shirt draped over the curve of her breasts. She had capitulated to him faster than he ever could have imagined in his dreams. It made him wonder about her relationship with Frank, but he knew it was something he could never ask her.

It didn't matter. Frank could never have elicited that incredibly intense response from her. She was all his now, and he was never going to let her get away.

"Why are you getting dressed?" he asked lazily, as he became aware that she was buttoning the shirt.

She came and sat on the bed next to him, lifting her legs onto the mattress beside him. "I think," she murmured provocatively as she placed her bare foot on his hip and slid it downward along the side of his naked leg, "because I want you to undress me again."

She was gratified to see that the sensual motion of her foot and her husky words had acted on him visibly, and that he was turning toward her with that lambent light in his eyes.

"Maybe I don't even have to undress you," he said

impudently, sliding his hand over her hip and under the shirt to stroke her breast and the budding nipple.

She pushed him away. "No, I most definitely want you to undress me." She shifted her body and swung her legs over the edge of the bed. "Where is my skirt?"

And then she felt him grab her around the waist and haul her back to him. She struggled against his hard grip, her naked bottom undulating wildly against his ever lengthening tumescence, until he pushed her face down onto the mattress and covered her with his erotic weight.

"Maggie, Maggie, Maggie . . ." he whispered in her ear, as his hands held her wriggling buttocks firmly.

"You're not going to undress me," she said with a pout in her voice.

"You can't arouse a man like that and then expect him to wait while you get dressed so he can undress you," he chided. "I can't wait, Maggie. I'm ready for you."

"Let me see."

"I'll let you touch." He thrust himself into her hands and she felt him, sliding her hands avidly from the hard, ridged tip to the firm root of him and below, between his straddled legs, to cup the taut sacs there that loved to feel her touch.

"Let me see," she asked again. It was like a game, a thrilling game where now she could only imagine his nakedness, his hard long length, and what he might do to her.

"Think about it," he murmured. But she heard the note in his voice and felt the firm caress of his hands sliding all over her thighs and buttocks and the small of her back.

"I'm thinking about it," she breathed, as she felt him slide his arm under her and lift her upward onto her knees. Now she was butted right up against his hard shaft. It nudged her, almost like a reminder, and rubbed against her suggestively. "I'm imagining it." Her voice grew husky. "I want it. I want *you*."

"How convenient you're so deliciously naked," he murmured. "Now, Maggie—"

"I *do*." She felt agitation now. He was on his knees behind her, and the whole hard length of him caressed her buttocks. The feel of it was pure arousal to her, heightened by the fact that she could not see him, could not touch him. She had only the sense of him behind her, hot, wanting her, and her own compelling desire to feel him within her once again.

It was exactly the opposite sensation engendered by their earlier union. She was totally in *his* hands, and they were all over her, caressing her boldly to prepare her for his intimate possession.

It came quickly, in one virile penetrating thrust, and he was deep within from this wholly new position. She felt him writhe against her to place himself in exact alignment with her, and she loved the sense of being outside of him while still totally filled with his manhood.

For him, the motion and the goal were all the same. For her, everything was different, enthralling; the feeling of him within her from behind, the sense of freedom, the provocative sensation of being connected to him in just this one way, the way her imagination ran riot, the way his hands had the freedom to explore her—all of it, different, arousing, utterly exciting. . . .

"Oh, Maggie—" The throaty note in his voice lured her into turning her head to look at him. Again, the fire in her look incited him. The movement, which he had been withholding for the pure pleasure of feeling himself inside her in this way, the movement began almost of its own volition. With the first surging plunge, she threw her head back, and he heard her sweet satisfying moan from deep in her throat. The sound was like a seductive perfume to him.

He wanted her, and he poured his desire into each

214

torrid thrust, showing her, telling her with his lunging potent manhood what he had yet to say with words: she was his, in this way, in every way, she didn't have to know it, he knew it, and as she rolled her torso with him and in opposition to his movements, he thought that she knew it too.

She reveled in the feeling of him behind her, his large hot hands guiding her, feeling her, taking every motion of her hips, adding to it, moving with her, exciting her with his touch, everywhere. She felt a glimmer of possibilities suddenly, a white-hot tendril of feeling attacking her vitals—she gasped at the sensation of it. She heard herself cry out as the tendrils unfurled, slowly at first, gossamer, until the first molten feeling slithered downward, downward. Then her hips began a wild fluid gyration as she sought the radiant center of all that feeling. It came closer, closer with each forceful thrust of his towering sex. Closer. She moaned as he felt her urgency and met it with his own.

She was utterly wanton in his hands as he drove her to the final glittering moment—the point, the center, the incandescent heat that expanded into a paroxysm of groans that kept rhythm with insensate feeling that totally possessed her.

Oh yes, oh yes, he heard her words on and on and on, *oh yes,* and it was for him, *oh yes,* as he poured his living heat into her in a gorgeous spuming ending of utter complete perfection.

It was enough, it had to be enough, but even as she prepared to leave him later that afternoon, she felt as if it could never be enough. There was still more that she wanted, more he would give.

But he knew not to touch her and not to ask the thousand questions and make the dozens of comments

215

that he knew she would not want to hear. He had to let her go this time, and it was the hardest thing in the world to watch the wagon recede in the distance and know her mind was already turned to business in town.

But she *was* thinking about him, *and* her, and it was a problem with no solution. Nothing had changed except that he had come after her as he promised and that she had succumbed to his artful masculinity.

It was easy to think that she didn't have to make any decisions tomorrow. She didn't have to deal with her feelings, she could just shunt this wondrous aspect of her life to one side while she took care of business. But she knew it was not that simple. Her need for him was escalating with each searing encounter.

She didn't know what to do about it, and speculating on all the possibilities kept her occupied until she pulled up on Main Street once again.

It was strangely deserted, even for a late Sunday afternoon. She let herself into the office, to that unnerving quiet, and went upstairs to the apartment. It too was empty, and this was not usual. She felt a jangling sense of something out of place.

Or maybe it was she who was out of place.

"Well, Maggie my dear, I suppose you were smart to get out of town today."

"Mother Colleran," she said resignedly, as her mother-in-law slithered into the parlor from her bedroom. She shot the old woman a resentful glance. "I'm very sure I was smart to get away from *here.*"

"You're not so smart, Maggie. You know, Frank would not have had any of these problems."

"But he's not here," Maggie pointed out for about the hundredth time. And where could *she* go to escape the viper's tongue?

"They're up in arms again, Maggie. You should've heard the talk about you around Bodey's store today."

216

"I'm glad I didn't," she muttered, feeling all the magic of the day evaporate.

"You could remedy things . . ."

"I don't know of anything that needs a remedy, Mother Colleran."

"They are saying that you want to take the livelihood out of the hands of men who want to *work*, Maggie. Not smart, my dear. There are a lot of working men around here."

"Now I understand," Maggie murmured. Her article about transient workers. Another nail in the box they were building around her.

"Mr. Brown is so mad . . ."

"Mr. Brown?" Maggie asked softly, her interest piqued.

"Arwin said."

"Mr. Brown hangs out around Arwin's store?"

"Came in to talk about credit for the men, Maggie. Don't be stupid. And he's very unhappy that in addition to impeding the right of way for the line you're trying to turn the town against workers who will spend money in town and maybe even settle down here. Even Arwin could see the sense of that, and everyone knows he's on your side. Maybe he's switched now, Maggie. You'd better be careful. I don't think you've got three friends left in this town, unless you count Reese and those two deadbeats that help you run things into the ground down there."

"I see," Maggie said, but Mother Colleran wasn't finished.

"Colville men are applying for those construction jobs you know. Your former friend Sean Mapes was the first in line this morning; I saw him when we went to church. Mr. Brown never made him an offer, you know. I don't think he wants the Mapes property as dearly as he wants yours, Maggie. So Sean has to go begging."

217

Poor Annie. It was the first thought that occurred to her.

"You should have taken Mr. Brown's offer, Maggie. People say they saw him talking to you the other night. They think maybe you're ready to back down in spite of what you write and what you say. No one knows where you stand any more, you know. This never would have happened to Frank. I almost hate to go to church now; they look at me strangely and they don't have to say it, I see it in their eyes: Frank would have been for the railroad. They know the money would be pouring in by now. I'm mortified, Maggie. I can hardly bear to sleep here."

"Please don't. I'll be glad to have Dennis pay your bill at the hotel.

"And how would *that* look? Everyone would say I deserted you. Don't be stupid, Maggie," and she turned and flounced out of the room.

Maggie buried her head in her hands. There was no talking to her in any rational way. She never knew how much of the nonsense she spewed was real and how much was her speaking her thoughts as they occurred to her.

But once she exited the room Mother Colleran became irrelevant; Maggie often thought she was a figment of her imagination anyway. But some of the things she had said today rang true: Sean's defection, Arwin's reservations, along with the powerful influence of whatever Mr. Brown might have to offer him.

So what had happened? Suspicions had been raised about whether her concerns were legitimate or just a ruse to force up the price on her land. The offer had been made and she had rejected it, yet when she was seen in polite conversation with Mr. Brown, speculation began again as to what she had to gain. She had written a negative article and advertising had appeared that she could not reject, and now speculation was that she was

218

going to sell out altogether.

It was fascinating: they wanted her to maintain a morality about the situation while they waited for her to succumb to its lure.

And there was more to come. Tuesday the building of worker accommodations began down the line. Reese drove her out there two days later, and it was worse than she envisioned: a half dozen shacks had been thrown up along the survey site, haphazardly nailed together, rudely constructed with tarpaper roofs and paper windows. Inside each was a crude plank floor and a small pot-bellied stove. The worker provided the rest, on credit from the company, and when the first section of track had been laid, the worker dismantled the house and toted it to the next site.

So when Warfield wrote in glowing terms of the superior housing the company would be providing its workers, she felt like she was living in a dream where her perceptions were totally out of kilter with everyone else's.

"How may I get rid of him?" she demanded of Dennis as she showed him the article.

"There's nothing about a contract," Dennis assured her, his worried gaze roaming her face. She was angry, yes, he thought, but there was something else about her now, an impatience, a sense of her mind being occupied elsewhere.

"On the other hand, when I tell him he's relieved of his duties, he adamantly refuses to go."

Dennis shook his head sympathetically. "Send him to me. You should have done that weeks ago anyway, Maggie. I know why you haven't, and it's just as I said— you're letting my feelings for you get in the way."

She took a deep breath. How could she tell him? She had forgotten all about that. "I'll send him to you," she promised.

"But be careful now, Maggie. There's a great deal of tension in town right now. No one wants to know what you are planning to tell them this issue."

"I won't tone it down, Dennis. That would be bending over too far the other way anyway."

"Maybe you've got a very bad conflict of interest, Maggie, and you can't have reader support until you resolve it."

It was something she had never thought of, and she looked at him appraisingly. "That's very interesting; all I have been hearing is how I am trying to get a better price on the property."

"Better than was offered?"

"The gossips say so."

"Why wouldn't you sell then?"

She threw up her hands. "How can you offer me insight in one breath and enmity in the next?"

"Maggie, it's so simple: selling off the land would resolve the conflict."

"How? It's like tacitly agreeing to everything that will follow if I give them the right of way they need."

"Sell it to someone else."

"Who will then make a fat profit?"

Now Dennis threw up his hands. "You win, Maggie. It's unresolvable unless you turn over the editor's chair to someone who can be totally objective. I'm not sure you are, and I'm certain Arch Warfield isn't, and you're going to be backed into a very tight corner as long as you keep writing and the railroad keeps coming. And it will."

"That sounds like a threat, Dennis."

"It was a caution, Maggie, and a reminder that I'm here when you need me." But he saw her slough that off with a shrug that roiled him with an internal anger she would never see. Everything was perfectly obvious to him: Maggie should accept his proposal and turn the newspaper operation over to Reese, who seemed very fair minded. She would never have to worry about anything again.

"I'm grateful for that," she said, three beats after his reminder, and she saw the displeasure flash across his face. Well, there was no help for it. She knew the things he would not say now, but still, beneath his words, the beat of his desire to take care of her thrummed like a living thing. He was still determined to maneuver her somehow into a place where she could not refuse him.

She was glad to see him leave, as always, and it was not a pleasant realization.

Later, when she had finished her article, she handed it to A.J. for his objective evaluation. "Dennis thinks I have absolutely no check on my emotions."

"I'll assure him, Miz Maggie, you got me."

Somehow she felt assured. A.J. had a no-nonsense practicality about him and an eye for cutting through the verbal trappings of a phony. She sensed his real affection for her and she respected him because, in spite of his background, he was a real gentleman.

"Yep, Miz Maggie, you have the right of it here. I seen that kind of shack all over the mining community, and it wasn't long before there was fires and deaths, and the next man came along and settled right over the ashes."

"Thank you, A.J.," she said gravely, and she meant it with all her heart.

And Arch Warfield knew enough not to show up the rest of the week because it was inevitable that A.J. would cut his stories.

And Maggie knew enough not to yearn for what was not possible any time during the week.

On Saturday morning she allowed herself the luxury of sitting and thinking about Logan in the half hour or so before she expected A.J. Coffee cup in hand, she walked from window to window in the office and then into the back room, where she settled down at the type case and stared at the empty spaces.

A whole week had gone by and she had not seen him, she had hardly thought about him, she had not wanted him. And now, as she remembered her long afternoon with him, her yearning flooded back, poignant and almost unbearable in its intensity, unresolvable in its finality.

With that conclusion, she heard the scrape of A.J.'s key in the door and got up to go out into the office to greet him.

As she crossed the threshold, she heard two shots ring out, and A.J. crumpled into the office right before her eyes.

When she bent over him, she saw the shattered skull and endless blood pouring out of a hole in his back that had torn out his heart.

Chapter Twelve

They got Doc Shields, they got the paper out, and then Maggie cried—in Jean Vilroy's arms. Reese took her away and made her lay down, and Jean stoically finished their usual Saturday chores and ignored Reese when he returned and tried to help.

They were A.J.'s only family, and even while Mother Colleran grumbled about the expense, Maggie and Dennis arranged the funeral and the service at the church. They bought the burial plot and were, with Logan and Arwin Bodey, the ones in attendance when A.J. Lloyd was laid to rest.

Logan had come because Arwin had thought to send a message to him. This little thoughtfulness overwhelmed Maggie, and Reese insisted she must rest after the services or she might break down altogether.

His proprietary attitude dared anyone to oppose him, particularly Logan. He didn't like Logan at all, or the mysterious way he appeared in time for the funeral, or the fact that Maggie was so glad to see him, even awash in her tears.

Logan took a room at the hotel and waited.

Monday morning, Reese sat down in the editor's chair of the *Morning Call*.

Maggie didn't know it. Maggie had fallen into a laudanum-induced sleep that she dearly needed, Mother Colleran told everybody. She was positively devastated by A.J.'s death. She discovered the body, you know, she told her cronies. The whole back of his head shot away, just like that. And they got him in the heart. Mother Colleran was a heroine again. Everyone, she found out, had truly liked A.J.

Well, she didn't understand it, and she was sure everyone would adore Reese, if only Maggie would see the sense of allowing him to help her run the paper.

But Maggie didn't see the sense of it at all. She was flaming angry when she finally awakened late Tuesday afternoon and found she had lost a day and a half.

"But don't worry," Mother Colleran said placatingly, "Reese stepped in and everything is going just the way you would have wished."

"Reese?"

"Maggie, my dear, you were overwrought. Someone had to."

"I was *asleep!*"

"Well of course you were; how else could you rest and regain your strength? Really, Maggie, I think you should go down there and thank Reese for volunteering to run things. Any other man would have . . ."

"Done the same," Maggie growled, feeling cornered again.

"That was rude, Maggie. You should be grateful. Everything is fine. Reese is very good at managing, you know. Maybe he'll prove his worth to you now that A.J. is gone."

The words chilled her. As artlessly as Mother Colleran said them, they still seemed to have meaning all their own. Now that A.J. was gone, there might be a place for Reese. Murder. But it was murder, and if the sheriff had questioned anyone, she did not know it.

"Well, we told the sheriff you had a breakdown, Maggie, and Reese and I were sound asleep up here. You actually were the only one awake at the time, and he was right there by the door when it happened. Well, we told the sheriff that, and he hunted around for clues and bullets and the like. They were sure he was shot from behind, though, Maggie. I wouldn't think you are a suspect. Unless you were outside."

Her head started pounding. Complications upon complications. She didn't know what any of it meant.

Finally she went downstairs to confront Reese, and she confronted a workroom that hummed with activity. The regulars crowded as usual around the front counter, but there was no A.J. to commiserate with them. Instead, they were bemoaning his loss to whoever would listen. Arch Warfield was industriously scribbling away at a desk, while Reese himself was going through copy with an unnervingly experienced eye.

He sensed her presence. "Maggie! How wonderful you're up and feeling better. Come look at this. Tell me what you think."

And it went downhill from there.

When she tried to tell him, he waved her off. "Look, Maggie, A.J.'s loss is a big blow to you. You have to let me help. If it means anything to you, I'm younger, stronger, I have some experience, stronger legs, and a more congenial disposition. Besides which, it would be nice to work side by side."

His audacity crowded all her sorrow about A.J. out of her mind.

"I appreciate that, Reese, really I do. I think if you just let me get a sense of what has to be done, I could find a way to use you the most effectively."

"I can think of one way, Maggie."

"And if you mention that again, I'll fire you before I even hire you."

"All right, Maggie. Let me tell you what has been going on."

A.J.'s death was the big news and the whole of the front page was devoted to it. Maggie went directly to the sheriff's office before she even looked at Reese's copy, and she gave her testimony and heard his theory, which was not much different from the one that Mother Colleran had told her. She returned to the office with his admonition that she was not free from suspicion until his investigation had been completed.

But she knew this sheriff. In his mind, A.J. was expendable if no suitable suspects were in the offing. Nor could he prove that Maggie wasn't where she had said she was. He might not ever follow up another clue if it required too much effort. He was damned lucky she wasn't going anywhere.

Then again, maybe she would. She felt like Reese was crowding her out with his cheerful assurances that he had everything under control.

Worse, his article was damned accurate and she had no reason to cut a word. The only thing she could do was demand he give her back her chair, and he did that with easy grace. He was laughing at her, she thought, mocking her tight hold on the one thing that was hers.

But A.J.'s death scared her. If someone thought he had to murder A.J., that someone wanted something very badly. Colville was not a town renowned for its lawlessness. The worst thing that every happened was when somebody shot out the chandeliers in the barroom or someone's cattle got rustled or a boundary dispute turned hostile.

What possible reason could anyone have for wanting A.J.'s death?

She didn't like the one answer that occurred to her.

She shut it away, certain that there was another explanation. She felt disoriented. She had the sinking feeling she was walking around in the worst of her nightmares and that she might soon awake to find that none of this was real.

It was real. And the best real thing that followed on all this was that Logan came. She remembered hazily that he had been at the funeral and then had suddenly disappeared.

"Are you all right?"

"I don't know. I'm feeling dislocated, like something is missing. Something *is* missing." The tears welled up in her eyes. "Oh, damn it."

"Listen, Maggie, the old she witch up there has been telling everyone you're prostrate with a case of nerves, totally unhinged by A.J.'s death."

"I don't doubt it. Reese was sitting in my chair when I came down this afternoon. I can't tell you, I *won't* tell you, but . . ."

"I'll tell you, Maggie. I've been at the hotel for the past two days, and gossip is running wild about A.J."

"Why shouldn't it? When was the last time someone was killed in Colville?" she demanded, feeling a faint slither of pleasure that he had elected to stay in town, and presumably for *her*.

"I'm sure I can't remember, but this, this is so odd, so unanswerable; it makes no sense at all. And I'll tell you, Maggie, there are some that want to pin the blame on you." He watched her haggard face as he said it. He had made a different connection with this information, one she hadn't thought of. He was curious to see if she would sort it out.

"But I adored A.J.," she began, and then stopped. "That doesn't matter, does it?" she said flatly as an idea occurred to her. She saw by the expression in his sky-blue eyes that he had thought of that too. "Oh my Lord."

227

He took her hands into his own and squeezed them, hard, as if to impress upon her that he was the only support she needed. She gazed wonderingly into his eyes. This was the man who had held her shimmering nakedness in his hands only two days ago, the man who knew he did not have to do one thing more but continue his sensual odyssey with her. The man who had known her for most of her life was now pledging to stand by her. This man loved her, she thought, and she felt a violent resistance to the realization, and a faint welling of joy that it was so.

"Do you see?" he demanded.

"Yes," she whispered. She saw, she saw more; she saw the next nail being laid into the box where she envisioned herself. She saw forebodingly that it looked just like a cage, and that the jailer who wielded the hammer looked just like Frank.

"What good is that Logan Ramsey going to do you?" Mother Colleran demanded. "He can't run a newspaper, he can't take A.J.'s place. I don't understand why you won't let Reese help you."

"I have decided just what he can do," Maggie said, but she already knew: nothing. She didn't want him near the place and she could not define why.

"You are not well enough to take over both A.J.'s duties and your own," Mother Colleran went on. "I heard you crying last night."

"Nonsense, Mother Colleran."

"Please, I know what I heard. You never grieved for Frank like that."

"Indeed. It was hard to mourn someone who chose the town whore over his wife. But heavens, why talk about that? Frank's propensities in the marital area, my dear mother-in-law, left much to be desired, and he found someone who could accept the very little he had to give.

There was nothing to mourn. There was nothing solid down there at all. I'm thankful that someone took him off of my hands," she added for good measure, some part of her loving this vicious attack. It had the added benefit of turning the thrust of the conversation away from Reese's desire to sit in her editorial chair.

But the thought of that made her think of her nights there with Logan, and a sudden jolt of desire stemmed her words and left her breathless for a moment. She wondered what she was doing here, defending her decisions to this sour old woman who still witlessly worshiped a son who was dead and who had ultimately proved to be worthless.

"He was your husband," Mother Colleran retorted. "It didn't matter what he did, he deserved better than he got from you. And didn't I tell him that, over and over. He never did listen, Maggie, but later he told me I had been right, and his marrying you was a big mistake."

"He should have married Melinda Sable instead, Mother Colleran? A malleable whore? I guess he should have. He had the makings of a whore himself."

Mother Colleran smacked her. "Frank was a saint!" she shouted, and wheeled away blindly, overcome by a murderous feeling of wanting to choke away Maggie's surety. She ran for her room, her only safe haven in the home of the woman who hated her. *Hated her.* She had told Frank again and again, and now Reese, and still Maggie was here and in control and she, their mother, had nothing.

Maggie stared after her in shock. She had never, in all their verbal battles, goaded her mother-in-law to physical violence.

Reese found her there, in the parlor, sitting tightly on the edge of a chair, rubbing her cheek periodically in disbelief. He was utterly nonplussed that his mother had struck her.

"Mother's the gentlest soul alive," he protested, and

Maggie looked at him as if he had come from another world. "You must have provoked her terribly."

"I believe we were discussing you."

"Well you see, Mother is a lioness protecting her cubs."

"Or a madame, selling his services," Maggie muttered so low that he couldn't quite catch her words. No wonder she had always characterized the old witch as Madame Mother, she thought.

"The mark is fading," he assured her cheerfully. "Now tell me what I can do for you, Maggie. We have a newspaper to get out."

She wanted to tell him exactly what to do. Instead, they drove out to monitor the progress of the building crew and the first tie-in of track that was due to reach Junction City, just below Fort Fremont about thirty miles away, in approximately two weeks. The crew rode out every morning now, clearing and posting the land to the south, toward the fort. A mile at a time, a dollar a day, with unlimited credit for whatever were a man's needs.

She saw Sean Mapes on the work gang and she felt like crying. And then she thought that perhaps when the crew had reached the boundary of the Danforth land, Sean would be offered the opportunity to sell out. It wouldn't happen for two months or more yet, but he would have been working all that time, laboring to earn the money to keep the ranch going another day, another hour. He might be very glad to leave the burden behind. He had as much as said so.

Reese didn't miss the lean frame of Sean Mapes either, nor did he comment on it. He knew that Maggie would perceive all the permutations from Sean's decision to take the money. And he knew what the final outcome would be. So, he thought, reading her expression as she watched Sean, did she.

"But how can you comment about that?" he argued as

they returned to the office. "You would have to put yourself in Sean's position, see things through Sean's eyes. You are just not equipped to be objective about that story."

"Probably not," she agreed reluctantly, but privately she had decided she would write it anyway, one way or another.

But once they were back at the office again, Reese hovered. "I know what I can do for you, Maggie," he said teasingly, but when she looked up at him inquiringly, she saw that his pale eyes were deadly serious and that the undertone she had heard was really what he meant. And then he added lightly, "I can be your conscience."

"You serve me better by keeping your mother out of the way," she said astringently.

"Maggie, you and Warfield can't do it all, and you're taxing Jean to the limit as well, since you can't handle all of the things you used to help *him* with. You have a resource here. Use it. Use *me*." Again she heard that sensual double meaning, and she hated herself because she really could see the logic of his argument, while her intuition firmly resisted it.

"All right," she said finally. "Why don't you do the article—if you're man enough to let me edit it."

The challenge was enough. She could almost feel Mother Colleran smiling. She felt as if she were being drawn into some kind of trap. She had given in to him, hadn't she? Or maybe, she thought, she was precipitating some kind of climax.

"It is good that you permitted Reese to take some of the burden, Maggie."

"I suppose I had no choice," Maggie said from her position at the type case. She was setting type alone, and Jean was performing all of A.J.'s duties as they prepared

231

to print this week's edition of the paper. She felt a brief rush of anger again. The whole week she had been sure A.J. was going to walk right through that door, and now she was left to cope because something was missing.

There was a different atmosphere in the office now, a kind of brisk efficiency. Reese didn't encourage spectators or visitors, and he claimed the regulars distracted him when he was trying to write. Out the door they went, but because he had his fair share of the Colleran charm, none of them resented it. Maggie was agog with amazement.

But the sense of comraderie was gone as well. They shifted into a functional team who worked well, especially because Reese handled Arch Warfield.

Maggie wasn't sure just how it had happened. Warfield came in with his usual snide remarks, and Reese jumped in immediately and deflected him. Now, suddenly, Warfield was Reese's project and not her own.

"I think it's time Warfield found another job," she said to him after Warfield left the office.

"He's a good reporter, Maggie. He finds things out in fine detail. It's a valuable talent."

"His attitude isn't. He acts like I owe him something for some reason."

"He's probably resentful of the fact he's stuck in Colville."

"He can take the first stage out to Denver as far as I'm concerned," Maggie said, and Reese smiled at her indulgently.

"Don't let personalities get in the way of keeping good workers," he said chidingly.

Because of that, Maggie had not seen Warfield's article until the very moment she began typesetting it. The headline screamed at her: *Sheriff Hedges on Guilt of Only Murder Suspect.*

It could only mean *her.*

She looked up at Jean. "I'm beginning to think it is not

good. Come look at this."

He stood by her shoulder and she pushed the article directly into the light. They both read:

"A murder unsolved," was how Sheriff Wade Edson characterized the death of A.J. Lloyd last Sunday. Lloyd, the nominal editor of this publication, was shot twice last Sunday early in the morning. There were no witnesses except Mrs. Frank Colleran, who was in the office at the time and has given her statement to the sheriff's office. According to Sheriff Edson, Mrs. Colleran saw no one; she heard Mr. Lloyd's key in the door of the front office and subsequently the sound of two shots. When she ran into the office, she found Mr. Lloyd's body lying on the threshold, the door pushed open by the force of his body, the back of his head shattered by a bullet, and another lodged in his body. Sheriff Edson has not been able to find evidence linking anyone to the murder. It was well known, that Mrs. Colleran worked very closely with Mr. Lloyd, but the sheriff claims there is nothing to suggest that Mrs. Colleran could be guilty of the murder. "The only thing we know," he said, "is the fact that Mrs. Colleran was alone in that office that morning, for which we have only her word. But we have no way to prove that she could have gone around out the back way and shot Mr. Lloyd from behind and returned inside so that she could discover the body, and no suggestion that she even had a motive for wanting Mr. Lloyd's death." The investigation is continuing.

"He misuses the words," Jean said quietly.

"Indeed he does," she agreed, her indignation rising. "I wonder how he thought I would miss this." But she knew; he had thought that Jean would be typesetting tonight and that it was so automatic that he never read the words. She took a pencil and began rewriting, cutting the phrase with the possible scenario and connecting the paragraph at the point where it read, "for which we have only her word," and adding, "and we have absolutely no evidence at all that she even had a motive for wanting Mr. Lloyd's death."

"That's better," she said out loud. "Let him invent all he wants. He won't get in *my* paper."

Logan came that night, as if he had read her thoughts. It was late and she was standing helplessly in the middle of the room with stacks of papers at her feet all sorted and folded with inserts. She didn't know whether to begin bundling or just sit down and cry for the sorrow of how much she missed A.J.

And then he was there, leading her to the place where he would comfort her, away from the light and the turmoil of her work.

She nestled into his lap as he settled into her chair and just let him hold her for a long, long time. He felt so good, so strong; she felt surrounded by him, suffused with his musky male scent and the desire in him that was never far from the surface.

He did not need to do a thing to arouse her; just the closeness of his long strong body awakened her senses. He could feel her need grow in response to his masculinity. Her breathing altered, slowing down, become deeper, thickening as the thought of everything they had done together swirled through her mind.

They were alone there, although this time there was a small dimmed lamp in the back room that sent a long slender finger of illumination into the office.

And there was his hard throbbing manhood reaching

for her, thrilling her with his need.

She settled herself tightly against him and let herself feel his arousal, let him know by her sensuous little movements how much she enjoyed feeling it in that way.

"Is this a night for kisses, Maggie?" he murmured in her ear.

"I would love your kisses," she whispered.

"You know what might happen," he cautioned her huskily.

She licked her lips breathlessly. "Hurry up and kiss me," she sighed, and took him into her mouth before she had finished the last word.

His kisses were gorgeous, voluptuous, all she wanted just at that moment. He sucked at her tongue, he kissed it, he played with it, and she knew she had needed him tonight just for this.

He didn't touch her anywhere else. He cupped her face and held it immobile so he could delve into her mouth as deeply as possible. It was the most sensual of all kisses, penetrating her as fully as if he were making love to her.

His hard driving possession of her mouth sent little spirals of sensual hunger coiling around her vitals, and the culmination of each lush kiss made her beg for still more. He whispered to her in the dark, erotic words that made her moan with excitement and undulate wildly against his body. He heard her whisper, "I need you," and he answered her need with a husky growl, "Tell me," before their mouths melted together once more in a swirling intense kiss.

"Would you . . ."

"Anything . . ."

Another kiss, deep, enveloping, and her body arched upward against his powerful erection. His hands felt the curve of her thighs and buttocks as she strained against him, telling him with the bold movements of her body and her brazen kisses.

"Show me," he whispered, and she moaned, "yes," and kissed him again hungrily as if she could not bear to leave his erotic seat. And then she slid off his lap and leaned against the table so that her back was facing him.

She knew that he was more than ready for her, and she pulled up her skirt in overt invitation. He came up behind her and she felt the heat of his hands grasping her and the nudge of his hard sex against her buttocks, then the massive thrust of him possessing her.

"Oh yes," she whispered, "oh yes," as each separate sensation thrilled her—the feeling of him behind her, deep and hard within her, her buttocks thrust against his hips, the feeling of being clothed and naked all at once, the exciting knowledge of what was to come, and the driving sense of his surging hot manhood within her, explosive with need—her need.

"Don't move," she murmured, her voice throaty with desire. "Just let me feel you," and he held himself still until he heard her enchanted command: "*Now.*"

Then he began a series of tight thrusting little movements that kept him deep inside her, thrilling her to the core with the way his hands guided her, encouraged her, caressed her, and played all over her writhing buttocks as she enticed him to deep strokes that made her shimmy against him in shameless abandon.

He drove into the velvet core of her, making her cry out as she met his every thrust.

He could feel the building of tension in her with every wild wanton twist of her buttocks, and he held her tightly there to feel every voluptuous movement, meeting her demand with long thick strokes until her body stiffened and curved into his, and he surged into her, once, twice, three times. Finally he pulled himself almost all the way out of her and drove again with one last thrust that sent her into a spasm of pure explosive rapture.

It was almost too much for him. His hands flexed

against her as he held himself tightly to give her time to savor her release. But she wanted him, she wanted more, and she turned to look at him with a flaring invitation in her eyes.

She loved the sight of them together like that, and she moved against him, angling her body to give him the erotic invitation that he needed to begin his torrential drive toward release.

She didn't expect his urgent thrusting to awaken her again, but her breathing became thick and she wet her lips as she felt the cascade of feeling building and building. She drove herself against him frantically, seeking his heat and the hard hot sense of him joining with her. It was too much, too much. They plunged simultaneously into climax in one stunning moment of union that left them utterly satiated.

And then she couldn't bear for him to move. Not yet, not yet, and he leaned over her and held her for a precious moment.

Someone entered the back room and stopped abruptly as he heard the soft slithery sound of a presence in the office beyond.

He heard voices, and he pressed himself against the wall lest he be revealed by his shadow. And he listened.

He heard Maggie first, uttering a soft sensual sigh, and then the damning words: "I love that, that was *wonderful,*" and then Logan's voice murmuring her name, and in such a way that he had to forcibly restrain himself from barging into the room.

Slowly Reese edged his way along the wall until he could just see into the office. What he saw made him freeze.

Maggie didn't need a savior: she needed salvation. There was only one conclusion he could draw from the scene that met his eyes: the coarse cowboy had had his way with the revered, pristine, touch-me-not Mrs.

Frank—and damn her bitchy soul to hell.

And how he had had her. It didn't leave much to the imagination, as he watched Logan's hands slowly and familiarly slide over the fabric of her skirt, caressing her bottom as she just stood there, leaning against the desk, enjoying the feel of his hands on her. *Damn her, damn her, damn her!* Who would have guessed from those dark spinster dresses and thick leather apron she wore that she was really a bitch ready to roll with the first man who got to her. Oh, hadn't he been wrong about Maggie. All her fine words about him not approaching her, and look at who she had chosen in his stead.

Damn her. She didn't want to be dependent on anyone, did she, he thought resentfully. The evidence before him suggested she was a slave to the greatest need of all.

His imagination ran riot, thinking about all the things Maggie must have done in the dark of the room, wallowing in the hands of that cowboy.

The aloof, reserved, ascetic, *chaste* Maggie Colleran. Damn her. Damn her. But now he knew. Oh, he knew what Maggie Colleran was all about, and it had nothing to do with business at all.

She had the soul of a whore, and he felt a malicious vindication that his instinct about her that night when he had found her alone, nearly naked in the office, had been correct. Oh, more than correct. If only he had even had a glimmering of what lay beneath the surface of her cool disdain he would have acted on that instinct and shown her what a man felt like.

Yes. He slithered away into the shadows, his mind consumed with images of Maggie naked and willing. She was a rutting bitch, and she needed to be handled like the whore she was. Next time—and there would be a next time, he vowed viciously—it would be with him, and he knew just how to put her into his power.

Chapter Thirteen

The first sight that greeted his eyes the following morning was Maggie bent over a stack of papers that she was bundling for distribution.

Immediately his mind filled with the image of her as he had seen her the night before, and his pendulous organ stiffened to attention as his lustful thoughts crowded out any coherent conversation for several long lascivious moments.

"Good morning, Maggie." Amazing his voice sounded so normal. He had lain awake all night imagining Maggie with the cowboy, her exquisite moaning and writhing in ecstasy. All these weeks she had slept down the hallway from him, and he could have taken her in spite of her protests if only he had known what a whore she was.

"Reese—just in time. I was going to deliver by myself."

He could make her deliver, he thought, taking a paper from the top of the pile just to scan the contents.

Damn. Damn her! The whoring bitch, to cut his story like that. That he would make her pay for. That and everything else since he had arrived in town, including her virginal touch-me-not attitude.

"Looks good," he said, keeping his voice even. "Tell

me what to do." Oh yes, tell me, he thought viciously, tell me just like you told the cowboy what to do.

He lifted the bundle and followed her out the back door to the buckboard. Even as he imagined himself throwing her onto the wagon bed and taking her there, they loaded the bundles onto the wagon. "That's fine." Maggie said. "Now, there's four more bundles inside that will be picked up later for distribution to the outlying ranches. And after that, there's nothing else except breaking up the type trays so we can start again. Thanks, Reese."

He helped her up onto the driver's perch and murmured, "My pleasure." My pleasure it will be, he thought, watching her snap the reins.

He couldn't get her out of his mind: he kept envisioning her hot and seductive, waiting for *him*, smiling at *him* with a wanton invitation. How could he not have seen what kind of bitch she was? Damn, and he had treated her with the respect that only his brother's wife deserved. He became obsessed with catching her together with Logan just one more time . . .

The argument raged all around the pot-bellied stove in Bodey's store: What mattered most? The money, the railroad, the town, the consequences? Even Maggie could not have forseen such a rabid debate about it. It was like watching a storm brew. All the components were there: rumbling, expanding, heating up . . . At some point lightning would strike, and Maggie's ominous feeling would take on some definitive shape.

Meantime, she watched men squandering outrageous salaries daily on the streets of Colville. They got drunk, they went looking for a lady for hire, they bought things from Arwin to send back home, and when they were bored, they tore up the town, just as she had predicted.

"Oh, Maggie, you're making too much of it."

Or not enough, she thought. God, she missed A.J. It had been two weeks now. Logan was running cattle, Reese was in the office even as she tried to get him to go away, the work of setting up every week was becoming more and more burdensome, and she didn't understand the cause. It was like Reese was all over her, never leaving her alone, demanding her help, evading her objections, and making himself uselessly helpful.

But for once Mother Colleran wasn't griping and things were running somewhat smoothly. She didn't have the sense something awful was about to happen.

Except that she would not see Logan until this Sunday, and she could not even think that far ahead for how voraciously she wanted him.

"Ah, Maggie, you can see the railroad business isn't such an intrusion after all," Reese said one afternoon.

"Excuse me? My friend Annie Mapes' brother is driving her to distraction with his drinking and gambling, and every night someone comes in and shoots up the street. But no, it's no intrusion. Just the boys having some fun, right?"

Just one boy wanting to have some fun, he amended in his mind. He knew all the things he wanted to say to her, too, and he used any excuse to try to touch her now. He had decided he was not going to have her until he had caught her with Logan one more time. The waiting was hard. The vision of her that night had magnified into the notion that she had been aware that someone was watching, and that it was him, and that her cold indifference was merely an attitude designed to tease him into begging *her.*

What if he had begged her the night he found her downstairs alone, practically naked? Had she been waiting for Logan or him? Did it matter which man?

"It's damned hard work, Maggie, you know that. A man has to have some release." This man needs some release, Maggie. Let me give it to you just the way you want it.

She felt tired of him, of the whole argument. Money was flowing into Colville. It was the only god anyone answered to.

"Fine. I'll have to find some new antagonist; this one has obviously poled right over me. As have you," she added tartly.

I'd like to pole right into you, Reese thought. The time was coming, the time was almost right. He had got his mother shut up so that Maggie would feel gratitude to him, and he was making himself as helpful as possible to her, but something was different, something was off slightly.

He knew part of it had to do with the fact that A.J.'s murderer was still at large, and part of it was that things had seemed to slow down to an almost manageable pace. The inevitable was happening, and Maggie's fierce struggle had been a useless waste of her time and talent. It was almost like she was beaten down by it, had given up because there was just nothing more to fight.

But she kept on. The houses were a fire hazard, the men were a hazard to themselves, their salaries were going toward credit, many men had left town already, discouraged by the working conditions and the work, there were new single women arriving in town every day, painted ladies who were renting every available room in town. They sashayed up and down the streets at night; they enticed the men by day, coming out to the building sites in wagons that offered the space to take a sensual respite; and they raked in the money the men were so willing to spend. There had been two fights over favorites.

If Maggie had been among them, he thought lustfully, someone would have been killed. They would have all wanted her if they had even a notion of her whorish nature or the fact that a mere cowboy was servicing her over her damned desk in the dark of the night.

He adored the contradiction of it, and the fact that only he knew.

He couldn't wait for Logan's return.

She watched the track coming closer day after day and thought the day would come when it would run right over her.

In a week where a day seemed like a lifetime, finally there was only another day to be gotten through before she would see Logan. She had pushed out the paper for another week, with all her concerns headlining the front page. She knew already the church women were up in arms about the prostitutes, but they were a minority. She didn't know how far to push, and thought that far probably wasn't far enough. Meanwhile, the excitement of Logan's lovemaking had receded into a distant memory, and she hated that. Only at night could she resurrect the intensity of it, and after a while she stopped doing that because her yearning was too overpowering.

If she were living at the ranch, she thought the forbidden thought, she could have seen him every night. He would have come home to her, tired from his day's work, hot, sweaty, rigid with a clamoring desire which could only be slaked by her; and she would have been waiting for him every night, ripe, seductive, excited by the scent of him and his throbbing need to possess her.

She needed him just like that, but she needed this too, she thought, as she sat alone in the remnants of the week's work, without the stamina to rise up and finish the chores that had to be done.

Jean came to her rescue this time, offering to return in the evening and help her clean up. She did not know if there were enough money in Frank's legacy to pay him for his loyalty to her.

Once again they worked side by side dismantling type

243

frames and cleaning the press. They worked for the most part without speaking, and she felt grateful to him.

But then she looked at him for one unguarded moment and caught the passion flaring in his eyes. She turned away, straight into the outstretched hands of Reese, who had come downstairs when he heard noises. She knew he had seen the same unchecked desire and that he was intensely displeased.

"You shouldn't encourage him," he said sharply when Jean had finally left. *You should encourage me,* he thought savagely. *Me.*

"I haven't," she protested, pacing edgily around the backroom. She supposed he had to say what he was going to say for Frank's sake, because no one would be pleased that she had had a moment's weakness for an itinerant artist. Nonetheless, Reese didn't really have the right to chastise her like that.

"You didn't see his eyes." *Did you see mine? They're hungry for the sight of you naked, Maggie.*

"I saw."

"You're an amazingly seductive woman, Maggie," he said daringly. *Oh yes, oh yes. Now.*

"Me?"

And look at her playing sweet innocent when she knew exactly what she did with that sweaty, cow-smelling cowboy with his hands all over her.

"I think it's the idea of you in this position of power. Men want to conquer you." *I want to seize you and throw you under me, take you by force.*

"Nonsense," she said testily. But Dennis had said the exact same thing. "Men would love to step on me and push me out of the way and I won't let them do it. Look at you."

He drew in his breath in an angry hiss. *I would love to step on you and push you, Maggie. Let me do it to you; I*

244

know how to do it just how you like it.

"I thought I was helping you," he said stiffly. "I am not trying to trample you, Maggie. I do have feelings about you, if you don't remember." *Feelings, oh God, do I have feelings. If I told you my feelings would you present yourself to me and let me do anything I wanted to you? Oh Maggie, I just dream of doing it to you.*

"I do remember."

I'd like to give you something else to remember, Maggie. "I'm glad Maggie. We said we'd be friends. I was hoping that after these two weeks we worked together you'd feel that we became a little closer." *A lot closer, like you were that night with the cowboy. Could you get that close to me, right now? I'm engorged with feelings for you, Maggie. I'd just love to show you how solid they are.*

"I think you've settled in nicely, actually," she temporized.

"I do too." *But I haven't settled in nearly as hard as I want to, Maggie. And you'll feel it when I do, every inch of it.*

"Jean wishes I would poke my nose somewhere else." *And I wish I could poke something else in you.*

"We need his talents, Reese."

And I need your talents, you whore. Just like the cowboy. How did he seduce you, or did you beg him dammit? "Don't fall for him, Maggie; women always fall for men like him. Don't be kind. Let him know as only you can that he can't have you." *Only me, only me.*

"You're assuming so much, Reese. He has affection for me. I know that. Maybe he feels a little more."

You preening whore, He'd love to feel a little more. "You cannot let it go beyond that. He is merely an assistant at work." *Who'd love to work his way into you, bitch, and you know it.* "I won't say anything more. Maybe it isn't my business."

"Maybe it isn't," she shrugged. "And maybe I like your consideration."

Then consider me, Maggie.

"I'm tired," she added, and he looked for the signal, the beckoning, but there was none, unless he counted her inviting little yawn and the way she opened her mouth, or the enticing sway of her hips as she made her way up the stairs. He raged that he hadn't taken her that other night, on the stairs, with her taut nipples and naked body already there for him, without her whore's games and bitch's denials.

He watched her primping and readying herself to meet Logan. She was going to the hotel to have lunch with Logan.

"Oh, what a coincidence," he murmured. "It happens I'll be there myself. Mother and I . . ."

It was so late, it was well after church, well after her patience had nearly ground down to the breaking point.

"Walk with us," Reese suggested, and she couldn't think of a way to excuse herself.

They made an odd threesome. Reese held Maggie possessively by one arm, all the while bending a courteous ear to his mother, who was shooting black looks in his direction that he refused to heed.

"It doesn't hurt to let him wait a little while," Reese said.

"You know he's an old friend," Maggie said. She didn't quite know what to think about this public display or Reese's vacillating humor. Today he seemed absorbed, faintly aloof.

She would have run a mile, he thought, if she knew he were planning to follow her all day. They stepped up into the hotel entrance and were taken immediately to the dining room.

Logan was waiting, and the sight of him took Maggie's breath away.

When had she ever seen him dressed like a gentleman?

246

His eyes met hers, clear as the sky, and he smiled gently at her.

"Maggie. Reese. Mrs. Colleran."

Oh, he was so damned polite, a cowboy dressed up in a man's clothes, Reese thought snidely. "Ramsey. Well, Mother and I have a table waiting. Excuse us."

Maggie watched them walk away and then the waiter seated her. "Why here, Logan? I wanted to come to you."

"And I wanted to come to you," he said softly, his eyes roaming her tired face, noting that the sparkle had gone from her eyes. "This is for you, Maggie. I believe there is more to *us* than just our lovemaking."

"But I wanted . . ." But how could she say what she wanted in the midst of an afternoon crowd of people, some of whom she had known all her life.

"I do too."

"Where? When?"

"There's time."

"Oh God, I feel like there's never been time."

"No," he said consideringly, "not like this there isn't."

"I know. I thought about it."

"So did I." Her eyes rested on his hands and she caught her breath. Thinking was nothing; wanting and completion were everything. Desire spumed in her like a living thing.

"How can I eat?" she demanded.

He smiled, because he was feeling exactly the same. "I'd take you on the table if I could, Maggie."

She opened her mouth to say something provocative and then closed it again as she met Reese's heated gaze from across the room.

Reese looked away. What was she saying to him, the lusty bitch? She was probably negotiating with him, maybe even teasing him by telling him she couldn't do that anymore. Yes, he could imagine such a conversation very nicely, but that vision was superseded by the image of them together the previous night, and his rage that Logan had had her grew in proportion to his own desire.

They wouldn't leave yet, he thought, licking his lips with anticipation. It would look exactly like what it was: an assignation with only one purpose.

They ate sparingly and his throat thickened; he would be stuck with his mother while the cowboy was taking his pleasure from her willing body. He had to get rid of his mother. He glanced around hastily and saw that there were people in the room with whom his mother was acquainted.

He ate as quickly as good manners and his rampaging desire would allow, and then pointedly suggested to his mother that there were friends in the room trying to catch her eye, and that if she didn't mind, he wouldn't wait.

A few minutes later, Maggie and Logan left, and after a moment's interval, Reese covertly followed them out of the door.

There was nowhere for them to go, he thought, but the apartment. Perhaps they even thought that he would be so busy with his mother that he wouldn't notice they had gone. He let himself into the back room by the same rear entrance. Everything was quiet; he was quiet. He heard a step on the stairs, and he heard her groan and the end of a long lingering kiss.

He slipped off his boots and hid them carefully behind the door to the stairwell, which was slightly ajar. He positioned himself carefully to hear everything.

"I hate this," she murmured. "Where do we find privacy?"

"You tell me, Maggie."

"I don't want to think about it now."

"Then this is what we will have."

"Does it matter to you?"

"You matter. I told you, Maggie, I was going to come

after you and I swore I would give you all the time you wanted. If this is what you think we have to do, then we'll do it."

"What do you think?" she asked in a melting voice.

"I think I want you, Maggie," he whispered, "right here, right now."

"How?"

"Like this."

There was a brief pause and then that erotic sound she made at the back of her throat, then her husky whisper, "Oh yes."

Oh yes, oh yes—the words reverberated through Reese like a gunshot. Oh yes, he could imagine it, the two of them in that narrow confined space, Maggie with her wriggling backside on the step, her dress thrown up, her legs long and enfolding, wrapped around him tightly as he entered her and began his relentless quest to conquer her.

And the whispers, the low moans of pleasure—he could hear them clearly and he was desperate to see. No, he didn't need to see, he knew what Maggie was like now. She had never been the woman Frank Colleran had thought he had married. She had always been no better than the whore Frank had chosen over her, and the goddamned fool had probably never known it. He had never been aware of what he had missed.

But he, Reese, would not miss.

The question of privacy haunted Maggie. She almost felt as though Logan had maneuvered her into this sensual thrall in order to make her choose. She was violently unhappy about the nature of the alternatives, and there were only two. Either she could settle for Sunday afternoons with him at the ranch, where at least he had control over who was around to see them, or be satisfied with that wrenching coupling on the stairs or in the office, or a hotel if they were desperate.

And on top of that, she was trying to balance the worrisome fear of conceiving against the loss of the cataclysmic pleasure of Logan's pursuit.

A.J.'s death preyed on her mind. It almost seemed as if the sheriff were doing nothing, and that at some appropriate time, he would storm the door and arrest *her* for murder on the very premises that Arch Warfield had outlined in his article.

And then the two things she dreaded would happen: Reese would take over running the paper and Dennis would need a power of attorney to allot the money for him to keep publishing. The thought of that made her wonder whether the two of them didn't have more decisive motives for murdering A.J. than the killer.

But that was fanciful. On the other hand, both had indicated they were ready to be more to her than just friends. Neither of them had been happy about her refusal to consider it. And Reese was almost jealously preoccupied by the fact that Jean wanted her.

God, if they knew about Logan ... What had Reese really thought about that lunch at the hotel? What else could he have done? Where else could they have gone?

And she was back to *that* question again.

There was no answer to anything, just the pervasive feeling that she was like a fish, swimming unaware into a net, and that sometime, somewhere, someone was going to pull it tightly around her and she would never know who and she would never know why.

"Well now, here's today's news," Reese said, coming in the front door that Wednesday. "Melinda Sable has contracted to build her house finally."

"The wonder is she could find anyone with the way Denver North has been snapping everyone up," Maggie murmured in a moderate tone. She really had no quarrel with Melinda Sable. Melinda was really very discreet—look at how she handled Frank. She had a selected clientele, and when a man was loyal to her, she repaid that loyalty a thousandfold.

But this news meant that she was going up against the ladies of the trade with a vengeance. And she wouldn't be tawdry or shoddy about it either.

"Oh, I expect Melinda has some sweet convincing ways," Reese said with a faintly arch note in his voice. "I bet she could make anyone do anything she wanted him to." I bet, he thought, she'd hire you in an instant, o Maggie of the prostitute's soul. You'd be the star of her show and you couldn't turn anyone down if you wanted to.

"I *know* she can," Maggie said, discomfitted by the way Reese seemed to know all about Melinda. But everyone knew about Melinda. She had wondered all these years what Melinda knew about *her*. "Where do you suppose her money is coming from?"

"Dear Maggie, she must have money."

"Or someone or something might be financing her," Maggie contradicted.

"There is no one rich enough in town to do that," Reese said emphatically, and then could have bitten his tongue. He understood what Maggie was getting at. He didn't like her assumption one bit and he said so.

"I think it's a reasonable supposition. A clean house, clean fun for the working man, more or less, a classy place where he can let off . . . steam. It sounds like a good investment to me."

"Maggie, you are not supposed to know about these things anyway," Reese protested, felt he had to protest, but he knew that Maggie knew all about them. He was steaming for her with her suggestive scenario about Melinda's place.

"I know all kinds of things," Maggie said lightly. "We'll keep an eye on Melinda, rest assured."

251

"That's a man's job, Maggie," he said, with emphasis, watching to see how she responded to that.

"I wouldn't be too sure," she retorted, and he thought there was a faintly provocative note in her voice.

He turned away. She was too damned provoking, given what he knew about her. He was finding it harder and harder to work side by side with her and his ever-rising desire. He wanted to test her again, to see whether the invitation he sought would finally be forthcoming.

"Are we driving out to the track site this week?" he asked offhandedly. He had been so good with her, alone in the carriage. But that was before he had caught her whoring with a cowboy.

"I believe we should. I think they're coming up close near Danforth land now. I'm thinking I'd like to talk to one of the prostitutes, too."

Oh, would you? he almost murmured out loud. To get some tips?

"All right," he said, reining himself in. "I'll check with the sheriff again see how he's getting on."

"He's not getting on," Maggie said crisply. "I saw him yesterday."

"Then we'll go . . . soon?"

"We'll go now," Maggie said decisively.

"I'll meet you out front."

"Fine. I can check how Jean's doing with those church notices he's printing up."

Jean looked at her soulfully. "That one is getting very possessive—of you and the things he sees here."

His perception made Maggie uncomfortable. "And you, Jean?" she asked quietly.

"I? I am hopeless," he said, and turned back to his work.

He had admitted nothing and very cleverly, Maggie thought later as she and Reese approached the track site. "Busy here," she commented. "They may be closer than we think. Is Denver North in some kind of hurry? I

252

thought this was a six-month project."

"I don't know."

They pulled in to the day-gang camp. Things were as usual. There was a crew down the line working with the men going up north. There was a supply wagon heading out that way with food and a fresh supply of tools. A one-horse dump cart was rumbling out in the other direction, toward Gully Basin for the initial grading operation. On site, a gang of men were either lined up at the chuck wagon, clearing brush, or laying out posts and string as far as the eye could see. Some wagons were parked away in the distance, and there was movement unrelated to the work of the moment; pastel colors coupled with rough denim, but never anywhere near the sight of a supervisor or a gang foreman.

"The word came down," the supervisor said, shading his eyes to try to see the wagons and his men. "They want it done—and fast."

"Do they want it done right?" Maggie asked, and Reese shot her look.

"They got a subsidy from the government, Miss Maggie; they'll take on all the men they need to finish it right."

"They're after the summer beef," Maggie said, making a note on a pad she had brought with her.

"I suppose they reckon by the time them drovers get 'em up toward Denver, they'll be past Colville and coming on to Cheyenne. And by the time the train gets to Colville, they'll have met up with that ole Union Pacific," the supervisor said.

"I thank you," Maggie said. "Reese?"

He climbed back into the buggy. "What's next, Miss Maggie?"

"I'm not sure. I don't think I want to interrupt those good ladies from their appointed rounds."

Reese snapped the reins and they moved forward. "Did you ever wonder," he mused, "what it would be like to

253

choose a life like that?" Did you, Maggie? Did you? You must have.

She gave it some thought—or pretended to give it some thought. "I suppose every woman wonders," she said finally. Hadn't she? *Hadn't she*—when Frank was suddenly gone all those long hours at night. Hadn't she visualized it, the allure, the mystery, the smoky sex of it. Hadn't she wondered why Frank had run toward it instead of exploring all that she had offered him; hadn't he berated her for being the very thing he sought in another woman's arms, a woman who was the whore that he called *her?* She was surprised she had answered him so dispassionately when she flamed with resentment everytime she thought of it.

"And what *do* women wonder?" Reese asked offhandedly, leading her, guiding her to the point of no return. His first question had agitated her. Why? Because she pretended to be what she was not. She was a good woman, the respected wife and widow of his beloved older brother. How could Mrs. Frank be a stoked up bitch, mating with a cowdog every chance she got?

"Women wonder why," she said finally.

"Why what?" he pursued it.

"Why men choose not to see what they have and try to find it someplace else," she said reluctantly. "I really don't feel like talking about this, Reese."

"You should write about it, from a woman's point of view," he suggested. He was desperate to know her real thoughts. "How ladies are sitting home thinking their men are out there earning good pay and not knowing what they are squandering on a quick roll in the fields."

"Or elsewhere," she added bitterly.

"Oh, Maggie, you sound so sad."

"Nonsense. It was just the thought."

"Well, tell me then, have you thought about me?" Reese asked softly, jumping in, not because the moment was right but because he saw that she was vulnerable and there was an opening.

"How do you mean?"

Damned obtuse bitch . . . He felt his hackles rise. Her answer as good as meant *not much*. He calmed himself so he could proceed slowly and carefully. "We're friends, Maggie, but you know I wanted more than that. I just want you to know I still feel the same way."

She was silent for so long he thought he might throttle her. "I don't need a man, Reese. I thought I made that clear."

Oh God, you out and out bitching liar—he almost said out loud. She didn't need a man, for God's sake; right, she needed a man's anatomy, the right part in the right place. And not his, she was telling him. Damn her to hell . . . if she only knew . . .

"You need a man, Maggie." A *man*, bitch, not a cowdog.

"Reese, don't . . ."

"How can I not, Maggie?"

"You don't need to. I'm doing very well."

"You're in agony, Maggie, over the paper, over your life, over the sale of the land, over those whores you saw parading around that work crew . . ." He stopped, biting back the words, the real things he was thinking, about her needs and how maybe she envied them their freedom to go after the thing they couldn't live without. "Over all the damned things you can't change, including A.J.'s death. You need a man, Maggie, not to take care of you . . ." no, just to take *care* of you . . . "only to love you." He looked away from her to let his words sink in, the kind of words that would appeal to a whore who wouldn't admit she was a whore.

She felt a chill of recognition. Reese, of all people, had defined the thing that she hadn't wanted to admit to herself. And more than that, she thought, she wanted a man to love. *She had a man she could love.*

Only she didn't want the attachments that went along

with it.

"That's very perceptive, Reese."

"I care about you, Maggie."

"I appreciate that."

Appreciate it more, he thought while his lips said, "Give me a chance to love you," and his engorged manhood reached for her.

Now he had said it, and at least she didn't snap out an immediate rejection. He felt a rush of hope. When she finally looked as if she were about to speak, he held up his slightly shaking hand. "Don't say anything now, Maggie."

"I can't let you . . ."

"Let me," he rasped.

"Reese, it won't—"

"It *could*." His frustration level was rising now. How could it matter to her who was giving it to her? *How?* She couldn't have feelings for that cowdog, damn her. He wouldn't *let* her.

"I can't talk to you."

He wouldn't beg her again, he thought. Now he would tell her. "I'm taking my chance, Maggie."

"Fine."

That was too cavalier, as if it didn't matter. She was really something, he thought. He really did admire her disdain. He would have believed it if he didn't *know* different. He felt a distinct urge to show her, right there, right then, and make her beg for him. An image of her that night blasted through his mind: her intimate sigh . . . he couldn't get the moment out of his mind, didn't want to, because he meant to repeat it sometime in the future with her, oh yes, her. . . .

Chapter Fourteen

Sheriff Edson was waiting for her when she and Reese returned.

A feeling of foreboding settled in her gut. She felt the net pulling in around her, fractionally tighter, enough to scare her.

"Sheriff? What can I do for you?"

"Like to talk to you again, Maggie."

"Fine. What would you like to know? Sit down."

He sat where she indicated, by her worktable, and she sat opposite him and waited. Maybe it was better, she thought, not to have to respond to Reese's heated looks and sulky manner right now. He was acting as though the sheriff had come by expressly to spoil the afternoon for *him*.

"Well, we gotta go over this again, Maggie. We can't find a particle of a clue to lead us to A.J.'s murderer. I have to consider other theories that could fit the facts of what we do know."

"And all you do know has come from me," Maggie finished for him. She didn't know what to think, what to do. And Reese was *hovering*, damn him.

"That's right, Maggie." He sounded regretful, and she felt a pang of gratitude for that. He wasn't a stranger to her, although he had come to town well after Maggie's father had taken over the *Morning Call*. He didn't want to accuse her of anything. He just needed to see the sense of her story, to understand where she was, what she was doing, and *if* she could have been anywhere else but where she had told him. "I hope you don't mind going through it again."

She shook her head. "Maybe it would help if you understood that A.J. used to come in every day practically at the crack of dawn, and that my schedule pretty well met his. That is, usually he would be here before me, and I would come down from the apartment at about six o'clock. There would be coffee—sometimes I would make it, but most times A.J. did—and we would start our day's work before anyone arrived. That Saturday I was down earlier, and I was in the back room when I heard the key being inserted in the lock. And then I heard two shots, and I'm sure I was running in there before the second one was fired. It took me seconds to get in there—too late. He must have just opened the door because he was lying on the threshold as if the bullet had pushed him against it. There was blood everywhere. His head . . . well, you know."

"I'd appreciate it if you'd show me exactly where you were sitting that morning, Maggie."

She took him into the back room to show him the type case and the tall stool on which she had daydreamed the morning away.

The sheriff sat in her chair. "About six in the morning, you say?"

She nodded.

"Came down early to . . . ?"

"Think." How could she tell him about what.

"Think. All right. So you are sitting here, you are having coffee? Having coffee and you are thinking." He sat himself down on the stool as he considered her actions, almost as if he were trying to put himself in her place, to imagine it as she had told it to him. "And then . . . ?"

"I heard A.J.'s key."

"Ah, the key. Yes. Now Maggie, would you very much mind going out to the front door and inserting your key?"

"No, not at all." She stalked through the front office, telling everyone to be quiet, and she went outside, closed and locked the door, and then inserted her key and opened it. She did that twice and then she returned to the sheriff.

He looked doubtful. "I'm not sure I heard that, Maggie."

"Well, of course it's a lot noisier on the street now," she pointed out, feeling a chill at his words.

"Who cleaned up the blood?"

"Dennis took care of it."

"All right. You heard this key, you heard the shots, you ran with the first shot—let me time it. You run, Maggie."

She took his place on the stool, and when he clapped his hands, she bolted off of it and dashed into the front room and stopped as if she could still see the body.

"Ten seconds, Maggie," the sheriff said behind her. "Maybe."

"He was shot from behind," she said stiffly.

"Early in the morning, Maggie. *Early* in the morning."

"Not by me. I don't even own a gun."

"Not even for protection? Dennis never insisted?"

"Never. I think he thought *he* would protect me."

Edson allowed himself a faint smile. "Well, now, there's this other explanation . . ."

"I know it. I supposedly hear him coming and run around front from the back door there, shoot him, and then duck back in here and pretend to discover the body."

"That's the one. Care to try it, Maggie?"

"Fine," she said shortly, taking her place on the stool again. He clapped, and she ran across the room, out the door, around the short side of the building, timed her acted shots, and ran back into the building, angry and out of breath. Insane and impossible. "And besides," she added for good measure, "someone could have seen me."

"Thirty seconds, Maggie, more or less. Not much time. Time for someone to forget he had seen you actually."

"Only if you are determined to make me the prime suspect. Where is the gun then, Sheriff?"

"You tell me, Maggie."

"There is no gun. I had no reason to want to kill A.J. I just loved him."

"Frank's man, Maggie. Maybe he's a little resentful of Frank leaving him nothing and you getting everything. Maybe he's pushing you a little too much . . ."

"A.J.?" she said incredulously. "You can't twist the reality to fit the facts, Sheriff. A.J. loved it here. I loved him, I did not kill him, and if he had wanted *anything*, I would have given it to him, including a lot more money."

"You say now," the sheriff said complacently. "All right, Maggie. I have no more questions."

"That's good." She escorted him to the door, a stormy expression on her face. "You can't believe I would do anything to hurt A.J. after all these years."

The sheriff saluted her grimly. "Someone did, Maggie. Someone did."

By the time she dragged herself upstairs to go to bed she was exhausted. Reese had gone ahead of her, only after much importuning on her part, and she had had the feeling after he left that he had wanted her to coax him like that.

260

She did not need the burden of Reese's touchy little demands right now. She didn't want to have to prove that she recognized he had feelings for her. It was too wearing; it was like catering to the petulance of a child.

The net had been pulled tighter tonight. It seemed to her that the sheriff wanted to convince himself that only she could have fired the shots that killed A.J. It was appalling to her that he had made her reenact his fictitious version of events, and positively shocking how little time it would have taken to commit the murder.

. . . So little time that someone else had gotten away with it.

But why A.J.? *Why?*

It was the question that accompanied her dreams every night. And sometimes she almost thought she would find the answer in her dreams too.

Logan pervaded her dreams too, always lamenting the lack of time, demanding to know if she didn't mind that people were watching. Those dreams took place in a strange world where the passion only escalated no matter where they were and what they did, and in those dreams she never cared who was watching as long as she could have Logan's caresses:

Come to the ranch, the Logan of her dreams this night said, and everyone around her clapped and agreed she should go to the ranch.

But then they can't watch us, she protested, as if that were the most important of the things between them. I must have them watching us. Anywhere we want to go, anything we want to do, we have the freedom now. I can't lose my freedom. I can't lose the thing that drives me. I can't lose you. I want *everything.*

The watchers began clapping rhythmically in a corner behind her. You have to make a choice. You have to make a choice.

Another burden pulling her down weighting her,

Logan's weight, so welcome, so hot for her, and then gone. She clutched the darkness in this dream. I'll make a choice, she swore. When I find A.J.'s murderer, I'll make a choice . . . I'll make a choice . . . .

A crashing thump. A voice this time frantic: *"MAGGIE!"* followed by a jarring, smashing, splintering noise. She jolted awake to the smell of smoke and a fierce heat and Reese in her room, reaching blindly for her, grasping her hand as she choked on the smoke and reached for her robe. "Don't take anything, Maggie. We've got to get out of here, *now!*"

She moved, pulling the robe behind her, following him by hanging onto his hand to the parlor, to the door to the outside stairs. She heard the crackle of flames below, felt the heat of the floor under her feet, heard the rush of the fire as it ate through the wood. "Oh my God," she moaned, "the office . . ."

"Maggie!" he hissed urgently, throwing open the door. She ran to him and out the door onto the cold wooden staircase. "It could go any minute. Mother got out. Get down there now!"

"Oh my God, oh my God . . ." She scrambled down the stairs and onto the street. There was a crowd watching and a bell clanging somewhere in the distance, summoning the haphazard crew of fire volunteers.

They would be too late, she thought. The fire was suddenly everywhere, licking merrily through the windows and flaming up the wood. The office was burning, all the paper . . . Frank's desk. Lord! Frank's desk, the painting, the files, the worktables . . . She heaved a huge sigh and then became aware that onlookers were watching her.

In the glow of the fire she looked down at herself in her thin cotton gown and bare feet. The watchers! She became aware suddenly that she was clutching her robe. She threw it around her hastily, but their eyes watched

262

her. They knew who she was, and it was just like her dreams.

Reese came to her finally and watched it to the end with her, as the bucket brigade threw ineffectual little buckets of water anywhere they could and beat at the flames.

"It's gone, Maggie," he said finally, slipping his arm around her shoulders. She didn't protest, and for a moment it was perfect. She was in her gown and her thin robe and she was totally his, needing him, needing a man just at that moment. "We'll go to the hotel, Maggie. I already sent someone to make arrangements."

She nodded, she couldn't keep her eyes from that fearsome blaze, or bear to look at the watchers all around her.

"I can't believe this," she murmured. "My father bought the building and restructured it for the newspaper. And Frank . . ."

"Frank's gone, the *Morning Call* is gone. Only we are here, Maggie, you and I."

"I . . ." she started to say and stopped short. The sheriff was watching her and watching the building burn; she felt that chill again as he began walking toward her.

"Well now, Maggie."

"Sheriff," she whispered.

"Mighty convenient fire," he said conversationally.

"What do you mean?"

"You know what I mean, Maggie. I'm hot on your tail and suddenly the building burns down? Evidence gone, things I hadn't even thought to look for yet? Think about it, Maggie. It's a mighty timely fire, wouldn't you say?"

In the morning Dennis came to their suite of rooms, which consisted of a sitting room and three bedrooms all interconnected. He didn't look pleased, and Maggie wasn't too happy either.

"Who is paying for this, and for how long, Maggie?" he asked her briskly, sitting himself at the table with a briefcase and a scad of legal papers. She sat across from him in her robe and nightgown, feeling acutely uncomfortable because she felt as though he were scolding a child.

"I have no clothes, Dennis," she said stonily. "*They* have no clothes. They don't have income. I do."

"It's not bottomless."

"I grant you we don't need a suite, but I assure you it helped a little in terms of getting us through the ordeal."

"Fine. Just remember the cost. Management loved Frank but they never gave anyone a break, especially in times of distress. Have all the bills sent to me. And you sign that so that I have discretionary power to pay them."

Maggie glanced at the paper. "I think not, Dennis. I'd rather tote up the totals myself."

"Wouldn't you rather be occupied with starting up again?" he asked, incredulous.

"I'm not sure, Dennis. The damned thing only burned down about twelve hours ago, I swear, I don't know just *how* I feel."

"All right. I'll send over the dress lady, whatever her name is. We'll get you some clothes and we'll talk to the management. We'll see what happens."

"Thank you, Dennis. Could you order up some breakfast, too?"

"Anything you want, Maggie. I'm only your obedient servant, after all."

That sounded bitter, she thought later as she drank her coffee sitting across from Reese. His mother was prostrate, he reported; they might even have to call in a doctor.

"Fine," Maggie said. She thought she would rather say fine to anything today than having to make any decisions

264

but the most vital ones—like what to have for breakfast.

She felt as though everything had been wiped away. She had nothing, but she was not without resources. It was just that the thing that mattered the most was gone. She was exhausted and empty. She had nothing to do with her hands.

There wasn't even a piece of paper or a pencil in the whole of this expensive suite.

"How is it that *you* have something to wear?" she asked Reese, suddenly aware that he was dressed in pants and a soft cotton shirt.

"I hadn't undressed when I smelled the smoke," he said briefly, picking up his cup of coffee and bringing it to his lips. He did like sitting across a table from Maggie this way, just as he had envisioned. The thin material of her nightclothes clung to her and her hair was a tumble of touchable curls, disheveled from a very restless sleep. "Don't worry about the sheriff, Maggie. He just had to say that. It's not an accusation. He's fishing, and he doesn't have a lick of bait."

"Well, he isn't baiting *you*," Maggie said tartly, "so I'm afraid I can't get too comfortable with your assurances. However, I do want to go back to the office sometime today with you."

Take *that*, cowboy, Reese thought. He was willing to wager that Logan didn't even know about the fire, and so who did she need more, and who was here for her, he demanded of his worst adversary.

"You sure?" he asked solicitously.

"I have to."

"Did Dennis arrange for clothes?"

"Yes. He's not happy."

"It's not his money he's spending," Reese pointed out.

"Or mine," Maggie said tiredly.

* * *

The building was gutted; only the skeleton of a frame and the charred metal of the printing press and the type pieces all over the floor remained. It was so ugly she wanted to cry. She couldn't even save anything, except perhaps the press. Perhaps. She picked through the ruins, looking for anything that could have survived the fire.

The smoky smell of the charred wood almost overcame her, that and the sickly scent of kerosene from the broken lamps whose shards were buried in the timber.

"I could arrange to have this cleared away," Dennis said slowly, "but it would be costly, unless you were planning to rebuild. But the only way you could do that, Maggie, is to find a lot of cash. The estate can't run to that kind of expense *and* preserve the capital to support you and Mother Colleran."

"I could sell shares in the proposed new venture," she said humorlessly.

"Or you could sell something else," he reminded her with asperity. He knew it wasn't what she wanted to hear, but he had to make her think about it.

She opened her mouth to tell him a flat out no, and then closed it. She could not shut that door now, she thought. She didn't know what this disaster would do to her finances. She looked down at her plain divided riding skirt and its matching jacket. The cost of that alone multiplied by what it would take to outfit just her and Mother Colleran was staggering. And the nasty old witch was insisting that everything had to be the very best that could be gotten in town. What is more, *everything* had to be replaced. The old crow was in for a shock, she thought, with a kind of grim satisfaction. Let Reese outfit her if he could, *and* provide for her. Why the devil should Frank's estate do it?

"Frank would never have quibbled over the cost of this," Mother Colleran protested violently, when Maggie and Dennis had returned. She was showing Maggie the first of the five dresses she had purchased from the dress shop.

"Send them back," Maggie repeated adamantly. "There is no money for this kind of extravagance."

"That's Dennis's business. Dennis will figure out how to pay for them. I must have the things I need."

"And I say send them back, Mother Colleran. You may have whatever necessities you need, and two plain dresses, ready-made, for the moment. I trust I make myself clear."

"Frank would not have wanted you to treat me like this," Mother Colleran grumbled.

"Frank isn't here," Maggie said, yet again.

"Frank's business never would have burned down," the old woman lashed out as her parting shot.

"She's an old terror," Dennis commented.

"I hope she doesn't get too comfortable," Maggie said. "Either she or Reese."

Dennis motioned her to sit down. "Don't worry about that part, Maggie. I negotiated a rate to lease this suite for a month. I think by then you could make some decisions."

"That's awfully precipitous, Dennis."

He looked at her oddly. "I hope that was an attempt at humor."

"An attempt."

"All right. Well, let me lay a few things out for you, Maggie. I think you are probably liable to clear away the debris from the fire, so I'm going to have to allot money for that, *and* for your living expenses here. Now, you know that income from subscriptions, local ads and job printing covered about three quarters of the cost of running the paper, and that Frank's estate paid the rest, in accordance with his wishes. Now that there's no paper, there's no office upkeep or salaries. You have to decide one of three things: whether you are going to rebuild and start over, or just start over somewhere else with the paper, which still means startup costs for equipment, which could be offset by your selling the building property; or whether to sell everything, or just the ranch land, either of which decision gives you further options: you could live elsewhere, travel, even allowing for the support of your mother-in-law; or you could stay here, build yourself a house right on the newspaper building property, or somewhere just outside of town, something more grand, and imposing. You could get married . . ."

"Dennis," she said warningly.

"It's an option," he said flatly, "and I don't know why you won't even *listen*."

"I see. You're putting everything on the table for me, including *your* offer."

"That's it, Maggie," he agreed stiffly. "You know I've always believed that Frank put you in my hands because he intended that we should make a life together."

"I don't want to hear about that again. Neither you nor I know *what* Frank intended, except that probably, had he lived, he would have left me. He did not intend to 'hand' me over to anybody."

"I'm shocked, Maggie."

"Where was he when he died, Dennis?"

"He had business with one of Melinda Sable's boarders," Dennis said staunchly.

"He had bigger business with her," Maggie threw back. "All right. I know what the choices are, and I thank you for being concise and unemotional about the whole thing."

"We'll talk," he said, gathering up his things as he prepared to leave her.

"*I'll* talk," she murmured, as he closed the door.

* * *

268

Reese hovered. It was the only word for what he was doing. She knew if she criticized him he would only protest that he was concerned about her, that she looked drained, tired, uncertain. That he only wanted to help. He would squeeze her arm or her shoulder and suggest sympathetically that she should get out of her hot, heavy clothes and make herself more comfortable. Perhaps take a nap. She looked as if she hadn't slept in days.

She decided to ignore him, because if she didn't she would feel as if she were a stranger in her own hotel suite, which *she* was paying for. Besides which, it was insanely inconsiderate of him to coop the three of them up in this relatively small space for the coming month. The last thing she wanted to do was share a common room with them, as well as bed down in a room that was between theirs, *and* the smallest of the three bedrooms to boot.

She was tired, she was feeling constricted, and she decided that perhaps this once Reese's advice had some merit. A nap would refresh her. She thought there was a loose fitting pinafore among the things the dressmaker had brought to her this morning.

It was so easy to slip out of her clothes and into her thin robe and lie down and forget.

"Maggie, supper!"

The knocking at the door propelled her bolt upright, and for a confused moment she thought it was the night of the fire. But then Reese's voice penetrated and she shook her head to clear the fog. "I have to get dressed."

"Why do you? Why did we rent a suite if you can't go around informally in your own apartment?" he asked reasonably through the door. "Put on a robe, come out and have dinner with us, and then go back to sleep, Maggie. You obviously need the rest."

It sounded lovely, this kind of privacy. The kind she would love to have with Logan. And where was he, she wondered, groping for something to put on her feet. But there were carpets on the floor, she thought, and it was hardly worth the effort of looking for shoes to wear just to sit in the dining area of the sitting room to eat supper. She got up slowly and groped her way to the door. It had to be late; it was so dark.

Reese and her mother-in-law were already at the table when she flung open the door, and Reese drew in a thick heavy breath and swallowed convulsively at the sight of her. This was the Maggie he had been dreaming of, luscious with sleep, her hair in a frenzied disarray, her lips pouting and her eyes half-closed as if someone had just kissed her. Her robe was tied tightly around her so that the form-fitting material draped over her hips, and her hard pointed nipples were clearly visible through the fabric.

As she licked her lips lightly and walked forward he could just see a glimpse of her long bare leg as her robe parted with each long stride.

His protruberant member hungered now while he feasted his eyes on her nipples and on the V between her breasts, which had parted slightly as she bent forward. He allowed his mother to talk because he couldn't.

She raged over Maggie's parsimony. "Two dresses aren't nearly enough, Maggie. I can't just have one for everyday and one for church, and the *same* one every week! I'm Frank's mother. What will everyone think?"

"They'll think we had an unfortunate accident and you're brave and strong for continuing with your usual routine," Maggie said facetiously, wiping away a crumb from the corner of her mouth.

"Well, tell me why you're dressed in fine lace just to take a nap, and I have to make do with plain cotton."

"Because I'm Frank's wife," Maggie retorted.

Mother Colleran huffed and got up from the table, stamped to her room, and slammed the door.

"One to you, Maggie," Reese murmured.

"I told you to keep the old witch occupied, Reese. I don't even think she knows what she is saying half the time. Everything seems to run a straight line from her thoughts right out of her mouth. It is almost possible to feel sorry for her, because she has no descretion whatsoever, but then you get the feeling that sometimes she knows very well what she is saying and that she intends to gouge as hard as possible. It doesn't matter. No matter what she says or does, she still must come back to the fact that I control the money and that Frank left nothing to her."

It was the only thing she could have said that could cool his ardor, but he hardly heard any of it because his eyes were devouring the line of her breasts and their thrusting peaks. He was envisioning what would happen if he just reached over and brushed his fingers against one luscious nipple. He knew what would happen because she had dressed this way deliberately to entice him. He could just reach over and cup her soft breast, and rub his thumb over that tempting, pebble-hard nipple, and she would moan, *oh yes*, and rip off her robe and nestle in his lap and rub herself against his engorged male member. He would know just what to do with her then.

"Reese? Reese?"

"Yes, Maggie," he murmured. He could almost feel the stiff seductive pleasure point against his thumb. How the hell had Frank walked out on her? If she stood up, he could reach out and embrace her thighs and bring her closer to him so that he could insert his hand beneath her robe and find the pleasure that awaited him there.

She spoke, and he imagined that she asked, *would you like to touch me?*

"Reese, this is too much for me."

"Excuse me?" He came back to reality again as she repeated what she had said. She was pushing her plate over toward him.

271

"This is really too much food, Reese. Let's not order so much next time."

"Maggie . . ."

"I don't like the look in your eyes, Reese."

"I'm mesmerized by your voluptuous nipples, Maggie. Let me see them naked," he whispered.

"Don't talk to me like that."

Oh God, why not? he thought savagely. "Maggie, I need my chance with you. And when you walk out here practically naked, what else am I to think except that you're ready to hear my words?"

"I'm not ready. What I'm wearing is for my comfort, *not* yours. But I won't make that mistake again."

"Maggie, you need a man."

"*I don't need anyone.*" She rose majestically from her chair like some naiad out of the sea, and he thought he would die for a taste of her naked nipples. "Don't touch me, Reese. Don't come near me. We'll talk in the morning, and you had better spend the night thinking about whether you want to continue in this way or not, and whether you want the benefits of what Frank's estate can give you, or an invitation to leave."

"Maggie, you are a beautiful and desirable woman, and I would be less than human if I ignored what you chose to present at the dinner table this evening. Look at you. You might just as well be naked. I can see the shape of your nipples. I can see the curve of your bottom, Maggie. If you move your legs, I can see a whole lot more. Are you telling me you didn't intend to arouse me, Maggie, just so you could say no again?" He liked that, going on the attack and putting the blame for his lust squarely on her shoulders—where it belonged.

And it got to her.

"Fine, Reese, you win that one. I was stupid to think that in my own 'home' I could actually have the benefit of privacy. There is no privacy, obviously, but I'm beginning to think I might pay very dearly to get some."

She turned on her heel and stalked into her room.

The next morning it was as if nothing had happened. Reese had ordered in breakfast and it was waiting for her when she joined him. His attitude was faintly patronizing, as if he wanted to still hammer home the point that he considered his lapse of the night before her fault.

"What are you going to do today, Maggie?" he asked with a show of solicitousness.

"I don't know." She decided to pretend that last night had not happened, and that his question was sincerely meant.

"Yes, it's strange to have no place to go," Reese said, heartfelt words because he had experienced the same situation himself. He could feel a little sympathy for her, but he would have liked it just a little more if she had begged for his help this morning rather than sitting there with such cool self-possession. He had nothing to do, suddenly.

But then, neither did she.

She liked the fact that he understood that, but it hardly mitigated his presumptuousness of the night before. How much, she wondered, would she forgive him when she knew now that he was going to try to get to her any way he could. She wondered whether she should even remain with him and his mother in the suite. More than that, she wondered why she was spending her money on them and not herself. All these things she had to think about this morning, and she was not ready to think about anything. She had not seen Logan, and the frustration of that gnawed away at her.

If she were at the ranch, she thought errantly, someone would have come to tell her about the conflagration. Logan would have comforted her, he

273

would have come to town with her and been by her side through all of this, and the incident with Reese never would have happened.

God, she missed him. She needed him right now. She had never felt the onus of their separate lives more.

There had to be changes, she thought. There *had* to be. She felt rootless, not knowing which way to reach to dig in to find some substance.

She thought she might go back to the ruins of the office to see whether just being there would give her clues as to what she should do next.

And Jean, she had to find Jean . . .

But in the end, Jean found her. Reese admitted him to the sitting room, and his agitation was palpable.

"Maggie, Maggie . . ." He was almost incoherent, and he held something in his hands which he spread out on the table.

"Oh my God," Maggie breathed, and shot a stunned look at Reese, who was peering over Jean's shoulder.

"The *Colville Clarion*," Reese read slowly from the masthead. "Editor: Arch Warfield. Publisher: Harold Danforth."

They all looked at each other, and Reese went on: "Premier issue, March 27, 1870. The story of the fire, Maggie, is right on the front page."

Chapter Fifteen

From blocks away she could see there were curious observers milling around the desolation of the burned building. She wondered virulently what they were seeking, what they hoped to find in the midst of all that destruction. She imagined they all held copies of the new paper and that they were all looking to find pieces of her soul in the charred remains of the one thing that had been its living representation.

She walked slowly toward what was left of the building. For some reason, she had not considered that people in town would consider it some kind of spectacle that required an audience. But then, there were a lot of people who might have thought that, on the whole, it was a good thing for her to have been forced to shut down. The notion skirted around the edges of her mind. She had been burned out, and someone new had stepped into her place with a forum that was blatantly pro business. *Pro railroad,* she thought grimly. It wasn't something that shouted out of the pages of the bifold paper; it was there between the lines. It was all Arch Warfield, all the things she had never let him say in the pages of the *Morning Call.*

The bastard.

She took a deep breath before the anger took hold of her again. It just all seemed too coincidental, almost like a conspiracy. She felt the net tightening around her, gently, gently, just to let her know she was trapped but she still had a chance to fight.

What chance, she wondered bitterly, when everything else was gone?

The wreckage, coming on the heels of the publication of what would have been her competition, seemed doubly horrendous. She didn't have the strength to resurrect her paper, or herself.

"Hello, Maggie Colleran."

She jumped at the sound of that voice, the ubiquitous Mr. Brown. How fortuitous he should turn up on the morning of her worst defeat and in full view of anyone who cared to misconstrue just why she might be talking with him.

"Mr. Brown," she said coolly, without breaking stride. He immediately fell into step beside her.

"My deepest sympathy," he said after a moment.

"On what?" she snapped.

He waved his hand. "Your loss."

"Your gain," she rapped out, not knowing why she felt that. It had bubbled up from somewhere. Maybe the notion had been simmering deep down inside her since she had met him, she didn't know, but she was amazed to see she had shocked him.

"Mrs. Colleran! I have no idea what you mean."

"From the ashes rises a fledgling gazette, editorially excited about the coming expansion of Colville because of the railroad. How fortuitous. How . . . simultaneous, wouldn't you say, Mr. Brown?"

"I wouldn't say, Mrs. Colleran. I don't know what you're talking about."

"No, you don't, of course. Did you want to speak with me, Mr. Brown?"

"No, Mrs. Colleran, I think you have said more than enough," he said stiffly. "Excuse me."

She wondered what he had wanted as she continued on her way toward the ravaged building. He had said he wasn't making her any more offers on the ranch. He couldn't possibly want the remnants of the *Morning Call* building. Or could he?

The thought arrested her and she stopped in her tracks. Another decision, another damned decision, if it were true. If . . . ? Of course it was true. More, it made sense; it was like the piece of a puzzle she could not fit in its place. There was something about it that made sense.

She began walking again, and now, as she came into view of the passersby who were staring at the wreckage, she found herself accepting their sympathetic acknowledgement of her loss, consoling handshakes, solicitous nods.

"Oh, Maggie, I'm gonna miss the old place," mourned Gus, one of her regulars. He was an old man, grizzled with years on the Colorado frontier, who had lived in Colville for twenty years at least. She had known him for a long time, and he had hung out at the *Morning Call* office ever since her father had been editor of the paper.

"I know, Gus," she murmured. "Me too."

It didn't look any better up close. The night wind had blown through the charred timbers and alleviated some of the smoky smell. But nothing could diminish the stunning desolation that the fire had wrought.

And maybe there was nothing else to do other than hand it over on a platter to the rapacious Mr. Brown.

She stood staring at it for a long, long time, and nothing she saw gave her any clue as to what she wanted to do about it. She either had to find the money to begin again or she had to give it up, just as Dennis had made painstakingly clear to her. There was no middle ground.

But one thing seemed appallingly plain: whichever choice she made, she would probably wind up selling out to Denver North—if her supposition of Mr. Brown's interest were valid.

She was absolutely sure it was.

She felt a jarring sense of having been manipulated, but she wasn't quite certain how. The fire was an accident, except that the sheriff thought she had set it deliberately to destroy some amorphous evidence that even he didn't know where to find. And Dennis thought it was an ideal opportunity to try to take over her life again. And Reese saw it as an opportunity to . . .

What would Logan see it as? she wondered. Or she, ultimately?

And then she turned away, and Logan was there, as if her mere thought of him magically gave him substance, a sweet, tentative smile hovering around his lips and his sky-blue eyes telling her all the things he could not say to her out loud in public.

But everything suddenly took second place to the sweet savage rush of desire that spurted through her veins. He had come as she had known he would, as he always did, and just when she needed him, at the moment of crisis. Nothing mattered but that he was with her, walking toward her, and that his face mirrored the dismay she felt when she had first seen the devastation yesterday morning.

"Let's walk," he said. She didn't need to punish herself, he thought. He had watched her the whole time she stood staring at the destruction. It was Saturday, the day of publication. There was nothing for her here and he knew it, and even he felt the push to walk away from the scene of the devastation.

"There's more," she told him quietly.

"That's enough, Maggie. I'm sorry, I didn't know."

278

"Oh, but you knew; you came."

He shook his head. "I'm not a mind reader, Maggie. I came in as usual, and I was on my way to see you. I heard about it before I got past the outskirts of town."

"There's another newspaper," she said abruptly.

His reaction was instantaneous. "Hell. And what vulture came in and picked your carcass?"

"Arch Warfield. With Danforth's money. It's called the *Colville Clarion*, and it scooped us with the story of the fire right on the front page."

"Jesus, Maggie . . ."

"I'm numb. I don't even feel anything. I don't know *what* to feel."

"I know." And he did know; it was like someone had murdered something precious. She was reacting just like she did when her baby died: calm, collected, almost apathetic. The pain went very deep, almost to a place where she could not allow herself to feel it.

And no one would let her forget it either. Every second person they passed made a comment, or waved to her, or grabbed her hand.

"Sorry, Maggie," they said, or "Can we help?" or "Miss the paper today, Maggie," which sounded to him almost like a kindness.

"I want to go to Bodey's store," she said suddenly.

"Oh Maggie, it will be the worst there."

"I know. But I have to know." She would have him with her, which would make all the difference to her.

Arwin was emphatic. "This rag! This piece of cow dung. Damn it, Maggie, it's not fair."

"And they're giving it away, you say."

"Got men on the street hawking it. Got bundles going out on the express to all them faraway places, Maggie. Stuffing it in anybody's door who'll open up just out of curiosity. And got the biggest news of all on their damned front page. It makes a sane man wonder."

Maggie looked at Logan. He was leaning against the counter, his arms across his chest, his body in that peculiar stance of his when he was listening intently. He didn't say a word. He didn't volunteer an opinion. He listened, and he watched Maggie very carefully, and he wondered what to do.

He knew what he wanted to do. He wanted to carry her right off to the ranch and keep her there forever, but it was one of those ill-formulated things that would send her instantly in the opposite direction. He wanted to marry her, but how did he press his proposal on top of this disaster? He wanted to find someplace and just spend the next week holding her. He wanted luxurious privacy so that he could listen and encourage her to talk her heart out. He wanted . . .

God, he wanted. And Maggie didn't have the faintest idea at the moment what she wanted. She got some sense of the outrage the town was feeling, but it wasn't enough to shore her up to begin again. He could not see what she was going to do, and any of his wants would only add to the burden of any decision she had to make. God, she made it damned hard.

"You're at the hotel, I assume?" he asked her when they finally left Bodey's store.

She grimaced. "Yes, Reese kindly rented a suite of rooms where he and Mother Colleran can keep their eye on me constantly."

Mother Colleran took one look at Logan as he walked in the door with Maggie and said, point blank, "Get out, you." and to Maggie, "I won't have that man in my house."

"It's my house," Maggie said wearily. "Ignore her, Logan."

"I want him out of here. Maggie, this man runs a ranch, with cows and horses and *smells*. He has nothing to offer you. You need to sit down with Reese and figure things out. You don't need a roughneck cowboy who can't *do* anything for you."

Logan had had enough. The scent of the old bat's fear was tangible in the room; she was the kind of witch who could scent something that was a detriment to her a mile away. She knew he was trouble even if she didn't know why, could sense that if he walked into the picture she would be pushed out.

"Beg your pardon, ma'am," he said in his politest drawl. "I reckon there is something I can do for Maggie. I can marry her." He turned to Maggie, who looked utterly discomfited, and he boldly asked her, "*Will* you marry me, Maggie?"

"That was rotten."

"You didn't answer."

"I'm not going to either."

"You were just going to let the old bat stand there and tell you how much you didn't need me."

"I would have handled her."

"Hell, I handled her."

"She almost had a heart attack."

"She can lean on Reese, then. There's no damned reason she needs to have you around except she likes to spend your money and then castigate you because Frank left it to you in the first place. Maggie, we need to talk."

"We're talking."

"In whispers? Outside your expensive suite of rooms? That you're paying for?"

"It's a little inconvenient, I'll admit."

"Hell, Maggie, you're dead tired and you are ready to collapse on top of that. I wish you would come back to the ranch with me."

"How can I do that?"

"Get in the damned wagon. Who the hell would miss

you? Who of those animals would care?"

"Mother Colleran would call in Sheriff Edson if I turned up missing, and damn it, Logan, I've got enough problems with him already. If I disappeared, he'd charge me with murder."

"What?" He touched her lips. "Don't tell me . . . yet. I have an idea."

He pulled her after him and they went to the hotel lobby and the registration desk. "Hey, Logan," the clerk hailed him.

"Miles. I need a room tonight. Something came up. Anything available."

"Jeez, Logan . . . I . . . let me see here. Yeah. Room 306. Back room, though."

"I'm not looking for scenery, Miles. Thanks."

Miles tossed him a key and flashed a curious look over at Maggie. "Miz Colleran. Somethin' I can do for you?"

She jumped. "No, everything is fine."

Logan winked at her, tossed the key in the air, and left her standing in the lobby. She looked at Miles, he looked at her, and she thought for sure he knew that she was going to follow Logan up to the third floor.

It was hard doing it too, bold as brass, walking up the main staircase and hoping no one saw her. Everyone knew she was staying there with Reese, and she was absolutely sure that everyone knew their suite was on the second floor.

No one even questioned her presence on the third floor. Logan's room was way down a long corridor on the opposite side of the building from hers.

She rapped briskly on the door and he let her in.

It wasn't a large room. There was one big window that overlooked the back of the hotel, the carriage house, and stables. There was lots of wall space and it had been crammed with furniture, almost as if the room were a dumping place for that which was unserviceable or out of style. There was a bed that was spread with a quilt and heaped with pillows. There were two rocking chairs, a washstand with a basin and pitcher, a walnut bureau with three drawers and white rings decorating the top as if someone had often set a glass down there. There was a large, plain walnut wardrobe with panel doors and two drawers across the bottom. On the floor there was a hooked rug that was almost room-sized. And beside the bed there was a night stand with a kerosene lamp on it.

But now daylight streamed through the window and Maggie suddenly felt inordinately tired.

"Lie down," Logan ordered her, and there was nothing sensuous in his command. She lay down and burrowed her head into the mountain of pillows and just let a moment's peace seep into her bones.

"You're so smart," she murmured.

"Sometimes," he growled.

"I miss you."

"I went crazy thinking about you."

"I know. There has to be some changes."

"I suggested one, Maggie."

"No."

"No? Just outright no?"

"No, I don't mean it that way, I don't."

"What *do* you mean?"

"I don't know. I can't bear all this."

"Tell me about all this," Logan said gently, drawing up one of the rocking chairs to the side of the bed. "Tell me about the sheriff," he added, because he saw she was about to protest there was too much to tell.

"He came the other day, asking questions about the morning A.J. died. He had a theory—it was to have been in Arch Warfield's article in *my* paper last week but I cut it. He had this theory that it was possible that I had ducked out the back door, shot A.J., and then dashed back in and pretended to discover him. He asked me to reenact the scene; he timed it. He suggested it was the first and best explanation he had. And then after the fire, he was right on the spot to imply that I could have set the fire to destroy evidence, that his earlier visit and insinuation had scared me."

"All right. What else?"

"The end result of the fire is that I have been put in a position where I have to sell if I want to raise money to start up again. Or I can sell the property if I don't. And it's beginning to look like the only offer I'm going to get for either property is from Denver North."

"All right. Anything else?"

"I had a whiff of a feeling someone set the fire just to put me out of business to make way for the *Clarion*. And let's not forget that Dennis proposed to me again, and Reese has been making noises about wanting to . . . take over where Frank left off."

"And don't forget me," Logan reminded her grimly.

She didn't say anything for a moment, and then she nodded. "Yes. And you. You did ask me to marry you."

"Anything is possible," Logan said stoically.

"All right. And then I had this notion that A.J. might have been killed for one of two reasons: so somebody else could step into his place or so that I would be set up for murder. If I were convicted, someone else could move in and take control."

"I had that thought myself," Logan said.

"I remember."

"Is that everything?"

"Isn't that enough?"

He was quiet for a long time. "It's a lot," he said at last, but he didn't say what he was really thinking, that it was Maggie herself who seemed to be the focus of all these incidents. It scared him. He didn't want to ask if she were scared; he wasn't sure she recognized the danger. He didn't even know how to define it. "There is one easy answer."

"I know what it is, too. You want me to marry you," she said, and a faint note of resentment crept into her voice. She didn't want him to pursue it. She didn't want to think about it, because then she would have to make a decision about it, and she was in no fit state to decide anything.

"I was going to say you could walk away from the whole thing," he said mildly. "You don't have to marry anybody if you don't want to."

"You mean disappear?"

"More or less."

"And leave Dennis with all Frank's money sitting in limbo? Don't be silly, Logan."

"It was just a thought, Maggie."

"I suppose *your* limbo would be to immure me at the ranch?"

"It could have been," he said regretfully. "You do what you want to, Maggie. You always have."

"You just want to force me to say yes to your proposal," she accused him.

"Not hardly. I don't want to force you into anything. But you will be forced to deal with these circumstances, including the fact I want you and I want to marry you, and the fact that our lovemaking may produce still another complication in your life. I don't think I'm going to touch you again, Maggie. I think you have too much to handle now."

She was shocked by his abrupt attack. "That's fine," she said coolly. "Then you know what my answer to your proposal would be."

"I've always known it, Maggie. You never would back down. Or notice that I'm in town almost as often as if I lived here. You wouldn't be 'immured' anywhere, Maggie, but if you admitted that, then you would have no reason not to make up your mind, and you know we can't have that. I think we know where we both stand. Why don't you rest before you go back to your mother-in-law and Reese? It's probably the only peace you will get from now on."

He got up and kicked the rocker back behind him. It thumped into the wall noisily, and the slam of the door emphasized his departure.

But what about her other needs? What about her sinking sense of abandonment? Never touch her again, oh God. And he didn't care about the rest. He was like everybody else. He had the answer, he could only see that one solution.

And she couldn't see any at all.

It was just one more thing she was not going to think about—for a while at least. There was no rush. Dennis had given her a month. Logan had sloughed her off altogether, and Reese was impatient and conciliatory by turns.

"You ought to try and get a job on that new paper," Maggie told him inflexibly. "I just can't think about what to do right now."

"Just keep away from that cowboy," Mother Colleran warned.

"It sounds like a threat," Maggie said.

"Just some advice."

"It fell on deaf ears," Maggie told her.

She rode out to the Colleran ranch just to be sure nothing had changed. Nothing was different.

Another day she went to visit Annie Mapes, and Annie was different. Sean was a worriment; Sean had made more money in the last few months than the ranch had made in a year. He was being seduced, completely and utterly.

"Are *you* seeing any of it?" Maggie wanted to know.

Somehow it seemed easier to deal with Annie's problems than her own.

"A little," Annie said reluctantly. "Enough. I'm sorry about the fire, Maggie."

"Me too."

"What are you going to do?"

"I don't know. What about you?"

"I think Sean's going to want to sell up, Maggie, I have to warn you. I think he's rolling into debt and that unctuous Mr. Brown is going to use it to lever us off the land. Sean's been gambling too. There's a red room upstairs at the saloon."

"I understand," Maggie said.

"And I'll wind up boarding at Melinda Sable's new house," Annie said mournfully.

"Annie! What are you saying?"

"Well, you tell me, Maggie. What else will there be left for me? I haven't got a man somewhere waiting to marry me. I don't expect to get away from Colville, even after the extension line comes in. I won't have any money. And the only man I ever loved doesn't know I'm alive."

"Who?" Maggie whispered. "Who is the only man you ever loved?"

"Don't be stupid, Maggie. I always wanted Logan, from the time we were growing up. I thought you knew that."

Her heart plummeted. "No, I didn't know that."

"You were the only lucky one, Maggie. You got Frank Colleran, and everyone was green about it. And Logan—well, he just never looked at me at all."

"I'm so sorry, Annie."

"Can't make a man love where he doesn't want to, Maggie. But there is a place to get it when you need it. It works both ways in that respect, you know? It doesn't scare me. When a man needs enough, he doesn't care what his woman looks like. And when she wants enough, she doesn't have to be in love."

"No," Maggie whispered, "she doesn't."

"So I'll be all right, Maggie. I hope you'll be all right too."

She swallowed hard. " I will."

But how was she going to be all right now that she knew Annie's secret, and when she recalled that she had been blithely planning to hand Logan over to her, giving Annie her heart's desire.

She rode out to the construction site where the supervisor welcomed her cordially. "Sorry to hear the news, ma'am, even if you was down on the train coming through."

"I appreciate it. Where are they grading out now?"

"They're down near the Mapes' property line, ma'am. I'm hoping he'll sell out; we can bypass a lot of work if we could go straight on through. But I expect you know that."

"I know all about it," she said dully. So the Mapes would go, and next was Logan, whose outlying pasture was flat, perfect. And then her, or that pie-in-the-sky detour they had mapped out around Gully Basin.

The work went on, as relentless as an oncoming locomotive. She saw Warfield in the distance, and someone beside him, sketching. She saw the women of the fields, flirting with this man and that. She saw Logan walking away from her, leaving her to the mercy of all of it. She remembered suddenly she had no business here; she had no forum for her observations.

She had instead Mother Colleran and Reese demanding an accounting for every move. "This is insanity, Reese," she exploded at one point. "I might just as well . . ." she almost said, be married to you, but his expression was so hopeful.

"When are you going to be leaving?" she asked abruptly.

"What?" He was thrown off balance by her sudden

reversal. "Maggie, how can I leave you in such straits? I certainly won't think of going before you're settled somehow. I owe that much to Frank."

She turned away.

The net, the net tightening so subtly . . .

Arch Warfield accosted her, triumphantly. "So you see, Miss Maggie Bitch, someone else thought what I was writing was worth printing."

"And snapped up your mythical contract, I take it? Is he paying you as much as was Frank, under the table?" she flung out words again from someplace simmering inside her. And was that the crux of it, what Warfield had been hinting all that time?

His snide expression faded and he turned away from her as if he wanted to run.

She couldn't get away from anything, from anyone.

She watched, some mornings, as a construction crew removed the debris from the fire. It was heartwrenching.

There was no sign of Logan and no blinding flash from the heavens to reveal to her what her next move ought to be.

The second edition of the *Clarion* came out, heralding the Denver North approach to Colville, track being laid so many miles a day to reach Colville by the end of the week.

Maggie couldn't look at it, let alone read it, though Reese brought it in to show her.

She was a woman without a purpose, she thought. She just sat in those stuffy rooms or she made brief forays outside to walk, to think, to try to feel some inner pulse. But there was nothing; there was a blank.

The thing that hurt the most, she thought, was Logan's defection. It was an ultimatum he had given her. Marry him or else. She had a fantastical notion that he could have started the fire for the very same reason: to force her to make a decision; to destroy her livelihood so completely that she would have to turn to him.

Something in her protested that he couldn't be like that. But even she didn't know what men could be like. Look at how Frank had changed so radically in the second year they were married. Maybe Logan resented her working as much as Frank had. Maybe it was desperation. Maybe it was possible she was misreading everything.

But even these thoughts could not blot out the memories of his lovemaking. She missed it. She wanted it. She almost didn't care what he thought or wanted as long as he came to her.

And that made her as desperate as Annie Mapes, she thought. She had been a captive all the time she had thought she was free.

Dennis arrived. "I have an offer for the property, Maggie."

"Which property is that, Dennis?"

"Don't be difficult. The town property, let's call it."

"I haven't said yet that I wanted to sell."

"Nonetheless, there has been a lot of interest in it. I think you should at least listen."

"I'll listen."

"Ten thousand dollars."

Even her eyebrows went up. "My, my. Let me guess—Mr. Brown."

His eyebrows arched in surprise.

"No one else is throwing around that kind of money, Dennis. Don't be obtuse."

"So?"

"You must let me think about it."

"You can't take too long to think about it, Maggie."

"Why is that? Is there some other fire-razed property

on Main Street they want to bid on?"

"Let's just say there are other properties."

"Whose buildings they will have to raze, isn't that so?"

He was getting uncomfortable. She knew too damned much for a woman. "It's possible."

"And they might offer as much if the location were as good as mine, but they still would have the expense of tearing down a building, am I not correct?"

"It is possible," he conceded again.

"I need time to think about it."

"Maggie," he began, exasperated with her altogether.

"Dennis, this is Denver North; you didn't expect I was going to leap at the offer."

"I expected you were going to leap at the chance to replenish your finances, frankly."

"Oh?" Now she was a little taken aback by his bald pronouncement. "What do you mean, Dennis?"

"I mean, you have been eating into capital with large bites, Maggie, and you have to consider selling to offset your expenses."

"Such as?"

"The hotel, the clothes, your meals, and the removal of rubble from the building site," he enumerated. "You really can't keep on this way, Maggie, supporting your mother-in-law and Reese and yourself and expect the money to keep coming."

"I see." Pressure. She felt more pressure. And the thought that if she didn't have to take care of the ever ungrateful Madame Mother, *and* Reese, who in all his mystery had taken to disappearing everyday, she could live quite comfortably off the income from Frank's estate all by her blessed self.

"I still have to think about it, Dennis. Give me a day."

He looked doubtful. "Whatever you say, Maggie."

She looked at him curiously. "Are you afraid of

Mr. Brown?"

"No, no, no. I just want to do what's best for you, Maggie."

"With my consent."

"I think you would be wise. What on earth would you do with that property? Even if you wanted to build a house, you surely wouldn't want to be right in the center of town."

"Probably not," she agreed. "I'll think about it."

"I'll tell him."

"Yes," she said, "you tell him."

Pressure. Denver North was going to win one way or another. If they couldn't have one thing, they would take another, but somehow they were going to get Maggie Colleran.

But why would anyone want to "get" Maggie Colleran?

Or was someone after something else and she just got in the way?

She went again, as if she were drawn to it by some invisible rope, to the *Morning Call* building site. Ten thousand dollars . . .

From the opposite direction, she saw another figure walking along briskly toward the same destination and her step faltered. Melinda Sable. She had never said a word to Melinda Sable in all these years. She knew what the woman was, and what she had been to Frank, and she had never been able to forgive it.

She watched curiously as Melinda stepped across the street and stared at the vacant building site, almost as if she were trying to make up her mind about something.

She walked slowly toward the woman, loath to turn away, feeling as possessive of the land as she had about the building, not wanting Melinda Sable to go near it, to even look at it, and she needed to know why Melinda was there.

"Hello, Maggie." Melinda was the bold one, with her soft voice and golden curls and knowing eyes. She knew a secret that Maggie did not.

"Melinda." She could hardly bring herself to say the woman's name. She couldn't believe she was standing side by side with her looking at the end of Frank's ambition.

"The thought occurred to me," Melinda said suddenly, "that this would make a much better location for me than where I am building now."

"That's nice," Maggie said. "What do you expect me to do about it?"

It was rude, but she knew nothing would faze Melinda; it was one of the reasons for her success. That and her voluptuous body and her little-girl voice.

"Sell it to me," she suggested huskily.

Maggie laughed. It was outrageous that this woman could have enough money to make an offer. "I'd rather pitch a tent and live here myself," she said finally.

"Oh, Maggie. Don't waste time over fruitless emotions. Don't you think Frank would have loved the irony of me winding up on the ruins of his biggest enterprise and worst failure."

Maggie's eyes flickered at the latent hostility in Melinda's words.

"Frank didn't love anything," she said carefully, "not even you. He loved power and he gave it all to me, Melinda. I think he would have adored the fact that you must come begging to me, and that you still get into bed with whoever pays the highest price, man or corporation."

"Ooooh, little cat. How forthright you are, Maggie. I hope you understand after all this time that it was the one thing that Frank could not stand about you."

"I know it; he had to buy submissiveness, didn't he, Melinda. He bought me and then he bought you."

"Yes, and which one of us do you think was the better bargain? Which do you think he needed more—the newspaper or a soft, pliant woman?"

Maggie's whole body went hot, as though Melinda had suggested something that had lurked deep within her for years and defined it. She felt a hazy comprehension and wanted to strike out at Melinda because she had known what Maggie had not: that Frank had married her to get control of the newspaper.

"Maggie, Maggie, Maggie," Melinda said chidingly in her soft girlish voice. "You never did understand that a man adores a woman who enjoys his sensual favors, but the one thing he doesn't adore is for her to tell him what she wants. He wants to discover it, he wants to persuade her, he wants to coax her to do things that seem forbidden. And if he can do that, Maggie, he comes back—again and again and again, to see if he can beg her to go a little further and little further yet."

Her heart was pounding painfully. So that was the secret: Maggie was the whore and Melinda was the good girl. Nothing else had mattered except his utter possession of the one and his total power over the other. And they could have gone on that way for years, she thought, but someone had killed him and they never knew who.

Like A.J., she thought, suddenly, blindingly.

"A man wants to be the only one to initiate a woman into those sexual secrets, Maggie. He gets very upset when he sees all that passion coming from within, without his tutelage. You would have been so much smarter to lay back and make him show you what to do. But you were so young then, and he did need a woman who knew how to be feminine and pliant all at once."

"Yes," Maggie said, "he was just like that."

"So it would be delicious revenge if you would consider selling me the land, Maggie. Or we could be business partners. You do have a talent for it. And you have a nature, by the way, that a certain kind of man would pay dearly to explore and test over and over again. Wouldn't Frank love the idea of that? You could get everything you ever needed from such an arrangement, and you would never have to commit to anything but a certain amount of time per day. You could be so exclusive, Maggie. And you would be wealthy and free. Just like me, Maggie. Think about it. We never were enemies, you know. We both knew exactly what Frank was like, and we both gave him precisely what he needed."

Oh yes, Maggie thought, she had it exactly right. They had both known. She pulled him one way and Melinda the other, and he had loved it. That was Frank. He had loved denying her, and he had reveled in giving it to the baby-voiced Melinda, who knew just how to manipulate him. The bastard had never known it either, she thought. Melinda was the smart one and she was the fool. She even felt a moment's temptation at what Melinda was offering her: all the sensual gratification she could handle—and autonomy.

The proposition had a certain delicious appeal, she thought; she could even understand why Annie Mapes might succumb to it. She even felt a momentary gratification then at the thought of striking back at the men who were even now trying to cage her. They could just pay their way and take only what she offered and nothing more. She would have the power then to give or deny, and when she was tired, she could just walk away.

It was a heady, seductive proposal, and she stood a long time staring at the building site thinking about it.

Chapter Sixteen

She had absolutely nothing to do, that was her
problem, that and the terrible decision of whether to sell
her property. Then there were all the things caving in on
her: Logan's defection, Melinda Sable's revelations, the
sheriff's covert surveillance of her, the feeling she was
being pressured, pushed, manipulated, the notion that
Frank was laughing at her.

And what was Reese doing?

"I'm waiting for you to come to your senses, Maggie. I
could make you happy. I know you weren't happy with
Frank."

"I'm not happy now either."

"Give me my chance then, Maggie."

She shook her head, but the errant thought occurred
to her that if he had come to her at Melinda's house, she
could not have refused him and would have had to do
whatever he had paid her for. He was so much like Frank
in so many ways, she wondered if he were like him that
way too.

"Let me help you rebuild."

"I don't know if I want to."

"Then let me take you away."

"I want to stay here."

Reese's frustration with her was intense. Anything he proposed she would negate. He pushed his mother out of the way and pursued her intently.

"Let's walk, Maggie."

"I'm tired."

"There's an architect newly arrived in town. He could draw up plans for a new office building."

"He's probably a Denver North employee, and he'd make them so grandiose I would have to sell up to afford to build."

"Maggie, you are being intractable."

"I am being pushed and pressured and I don't like it."

"Then let me love you."

"But you do already, Reese."

He drew in his breath at the precision of her perception. "But you won't let me touch you or kiss you."

"I don't love you."

The bitch. "Maggie, if you could just make up your mind about the ranch. If you sold it . . . Sean Mapes sold up, didn't he? If you sold it, think of what you could do."

"I don't know what I want to do."

"We could go to San Francisco. I would love to show you San Francisco. You could leave all of this behind, everything, including all the bad memories of Frank."

"That," she said, "does have some appeal. I can't, Reese. I don't know why. If I could find out why, maybe I could decide."

"Let me help you do that at least."

"I don't know where to begin," she said. "I just don't."

That last refusal almost sent him over the edge, and she knew it, and that, to him, was the worst.

He began watching her again. She had already discovered that the *Clarion* was being published out of Harold Danforth's office in town, and she scrupulously avoided going near that part of town.

New construction crews arrived every day. They had begun framing what was to be the railroad station down at the southern end of town, near where Melinda Sable's house was being built.

The thought of Melinda Sable tantalized Reese. He hadn't gone near her, but he knew she was aware of him, because everyone knew Frank's brother was in town. But every day, with Maggie's aloofness, he began to think about Melinda Sable and all the delights he could demand for the purchase price.

He had made it a point, however, to cultivate everyone. Frank's brother had a reputation to maintain. He had already heard all the gossip there was to know about Maggie, who had led a very chaste life. But Melinda was another story altogether. Everyone whispered about her, but never did he hear a word about her liaison with Frank.

It was most peculiar to him and inordinately discreet of Frank. But if Maggie had treated Frank with anywhere near the standoffishness that she did him, he could understand perfectly why he had preferred to pay for unbridled adoration. It was so much easier, so much less an emotional investment. But then Frank, he surmised, had never seen Maggie with the cowdog. . . . Everytime Reese thought about it he went crazy.

Somehow in the course of his conversations with the locals he heard exactly how and where to approach Melinda Sable.

And now, after Maggie's latest refusal, the thought of having a willing body desire *him,* someone's luscious breasts tempting *him,* a woman's throaty voice begging *him* aroused him ferociously.

She was the kind of woman who noticed it immediately. Her eyes rested knowingly on his before she even greeted him. She looked up at him and smiled archly, murmuring in her sweet little-girl voice, "Hello, Frank's brother. I've been waiting for you."

It felt good to have someone wanting to see him. She settled him on a sofa with his feet up and a drink in his hand. Her coaxing little hands brushed with seeming innocence all over his lower torso as she leaned forward to grant him her lips, once, twice, and then again. Sweet doelike kisses, he thought, wanting to prolong them and spread her beneath him at the same time. He loved the way she played with him, advancing and retreating girlishly, scared and bold.

She was dressed for an evening at home. She hadn't really expected visitors. And she hadn't expected him so soon. So she had donned the kind of gown she would wear for an intimate evening at home. Over it she wore a robe of silk that covered her nakedness but still enticed the hand to stroke the material and feel the body pulsating beneath. It draped invitingly over the curves of her body, displaying the thrust of her taut breasts beneath the sleek material.

It invited his touch as he convinced her how excited her kisses made him. He took her hand and rested it on his lap and loved how she whispered in an awed voice how hard he was. He wanted her to do more, and she protested that she couldn't, even though he knew she wanted to. He thrust his tongue in her mouth again and felt her respond to his hot kisses.

He told her he couldn't keep his eyes off her voluptuous breasts. And then she said "you can touch if you want to," in a husky little voice that was utterly beguiling, exactly the way he had hoped another woman would invite his caresses. He reached over and cupped one breast. He moved his thumb over her seductive nipple until she moaned breathlessly.

She shifted away from him with a sweetly knowing smile and slowly began removing the silken robe, a tantalizing little ritual that excited him still more. And when she lowered just one side of her transparent gown to reveal one delectable breast she knew she had incited him beyond provocation. He crushed her to him and devoured the lushness of her breast in one hungry groan, before she could even make a movement to invite his caresses.

He needed her, he needed *that*, and he lapped at her exposed breast voraciously, ignoring the uncomfortable squirming of her body as she tried, because she was so unprepared for it, to get away from his wet possession.

"It's too much, it's too much," she moaned. He had already undressed the whole of her upper torso and was fastening his greedy mouth to her other breast.

In the heat of his ardor he heard her coy protestations as he uncovered his own lunging sex and then felt for the lush heat of hers.

"Oh not yet, not yet," she whispered.

"Now," he growled, and she crooned, "tell me what you want" and he told her, and her reaction was just what he expected, which heightened his urgency still more.

"I can't do that," she protested huskily, in a tone of voice that told him otherwise.

"We'll do it together," he muttered thickly in her ear.

"Show me how to do that," she murmured with a hot sensuous note as she pretended to give in to him.

Her capitulation thrilled him. He would be allowed to explore the deepest of his fantasies with her, the things he was dreaming and imagining that another woman was experiencing with that cowdog, and it seemed to him that his manhood responded accordingly.

Her pliant body responded perfectly to the command of his shaking hands as he positioned her properly, raised her to her knees, pushed away her gown so he had a clear view of her delicious nakedness, and began his heated exploration of her secret center.

Her reaction was everything he could have wanted,

everything he had imagined with another woman: the gasps of pleasure, the moans and sighs as he touched those secret places that produced the most sensation, and her begging words: *more, more more; give me more, give me everything*.

With one forceful push he took her, heard her groan of pure animal lust, and began the ascent to ecstasy. It didn't matter who was beneath him tonight; the replication of his fantasy with a hot, willing woman was his whole desire. And this woman wanted *him*, and sought the most of his powerful thrust. She let him know with her squeals and moans that she had experienced something special with *him* tonight, and that at the end, she was deliciously sated.

She covered his mouth with sweet little kisses and whispered suggestive things to tell him the depth of her enjoyment. She had provided the ending to his sensual dream and he was the one who was grateful. He wished Maggie could have seen how a woman should act, how a woman should respond to a man's overtures.

And he knew he would come back to her again and again just for that.

What he didn't know was, she did too.

"Well, Maggie Colleran."

And here was Mr. Brown again, jovial, she thought, because he had almost taken over the town. "Mr. Brown."

"I've been expecting to hear from you," he said.

"I thought there was not to be another offer on my ranch land."

"Oh no, Mrs. Colleran, I wouldn't insult you by making you another offer. However, you never know; things can happen. You might regret that you didn't sell at such a high price when you had the chance."

"I beg your pardon? Was that a threat?" She couldn't believe her ears. What could possibly happen to several thousand acres of rank grazing land?

"Mrs. Colleran, I am really offended. No, I am referring to your town property. You must admit the offer Mr. Coutts tendered is extremely generous."

"I'm not in a mood to be extremely generous," Maggie said. "I can't possibly make a decision about it so quickly."

"My dear, you must. You know, have you read this week's *Clarion?* The sheriff has been making noises about how quickly the rubble was cleared away. It seems he never got a chance to shift through it . . ." He patted her shoulder patronizingly. "Well, Mrs. Colleran, it is your decision, after all, and, as Mr. Coutts probably pointed out, there are other properties. It's just it would be so nice not to have to tear down a building in order to construct one to our specifications."

"I do see your point," she said quietly.

"I thought you would. Have Mr. Coutts get in touch with me soon, one way or the other, will you Mrs. Colleran?"

She watched him walk away with a stormy expression in her eyes. Pressure. A.J., Frank, the mysterious unsolved murders . . . A threat, ingratiatingly issued, but a threat just the same. And the prod of that damned rag that Arch Warfield and Harold Danforth were publishing. It had been two weeks since the fire, and it felt like two years.

She charged into Dennis's office. "That man just threatened me."

"What man?" Dennis asked mildly.

"That Brown. That monster. He actually suggested I might regret not selling him the Colleran ranch land, Dennis."

"You call that a threat? Really, Maggie, you know what I think your problem is? Indecision. The absolutely

303

right thing for you to do is sell the land and the town property and marry me and settle down. And if you were waiting for someone to *tell* you, there it is."

"I did *not* come here to hear another proposal, Dennis."

"Well, you have it anyway, Maggie. You are uncontrollable. I even wonder why I think I want to marry you so much. You wouldn't be still for an instant. I wonder if you could ever be happy with anyone."

That sent her out to the street, fuming with rage. That pompous lackey. And whoever said he had to be her lawyer anyway? Surely there was something in those damned provisions that gave her the power to remove him if necessary.

Hadn't she had the passing thought she ought to reread the whole thing? Could Dennis bypass her wishes altogether? Could he make the final decision about whether to sell the land? Oh Lord, she had put that off way too long, especially in light of the way he had been insidiously pushing for it.

She cut across the street to the squat building that housed the Mercantile Bank, where she kept her strongbox and her copy of the will. She knew Dennis had a box here too, and she had a most officious urge to know what it contained.

The bankers knew her; they were always happy to oblige. They even provided a private little room where she could be alone, and she wondered silently, with grim humor, if it were available for other occasions. It had a high window and a lockable door and a large square table to spread things out.

She dumped the contents of the strongbox out on its commodious surface and began a quick inventory. Everything was here that she had saved pertaining to her father's ownership and subsequent sale of the newspaper to Frank. There were bills of sale for the equipment

Frank had brought in before their marriage. There were marriage certificates, both her parents' and her own. She found her birth registration and the bill of sale for the Lynch ranch. She found the Consummation of Agreement that her father and Frank had signed just before her marriage, in which her father had turned over the running of the paper to Frank.

She put it aside.

She found a cancelled bankbook and letters from her father to her mother, whom she barely remembered. It was like sifting through selected moments of her life to find the turning points. And she was absolutely sure that Frank's will was one of them.

She held the thick pages of the document in her shaking hands.

The words jumped out at her: ". . . bequeath to my wife, Maggie Lynch Colleran . . ."

Why had he never changed the terms of the will?

. . . bequeathed her all the interest in all of his investments, with the principal to be kept intact, and sole unquestioned use of the interest to go to her wholly and at her demand;

. . . bequeathed her the sole ownership of the building at lower Main Street known as the *Morning Call Building,* to dispose of at her discretion;

. . . bequeathed the parcel of land known as the Colleran Ranch to Maggie Lynch Colleran solely in her lifetime, for disposal at her discretion as she should see fit and with the counsel and advice of the executor of this deed.

And nowhere did it mention anything about Dennis's ability to assign those rights only to himself without *her* consent.

It made no sense.

She thought that if only she could know why Frank had never changed the will she would know what to do.

She leafed through the remainder of the pages. Yes, here was the clause delineating Dennis's authority. He was to act in the capacity of her advisor. He was to disperse monies she required at *her* demand. He was to handle all legalities pertaining to business, and Maggie was to have sole discretion as to whether to sell or lease the *Morning Call* to a capable editor. Nowhere did it say she had permission to run the paper herself, she thought; Dennis had read into that somehow to please her. Or for some other reason?

By every provision written into the will, he fully expected to live a good long time, because everything oriented to the business was left to her. He just never would have done that, she thought. Especially not after he began his clandestine assignations with Melinda Sable.

There was no mention of the possibility of an heir. Or a brother. Or his mother. Or his mistress.

It was the will of a man who was in love with his wife, and it was all the more crazy because Frank's desire for her had run its course long before the end of the first year.

She folded away the documents and picked up the Consummation of Agreement between Frank and her father. It was a standard piece of work: for the sum of one thousand dollars her father had given over his rights in the newspaper to his future son-in-law on the condition that he marry his daughter, Maggie Lynch, on the prearranged date of June 25, 1865.

It was interesting to her to read it again, because she had not looked at it since the day her father and Frank signed it. And now, five years later, it read disconcertingly like Melinda Sable had said: her father had sold her for one thousand dollars, and Frank Colleran had bought a newspaper, and somewhere in there between the time they married and the time he died, he had decided the whole of it should go right back to her.

They sat mouth to mouth on the sofa and talked in thick whispers punctuated by the thrust of his tongue into her mouth. "I enjoyed what we did so much," he told Melinda as he stroked her silk-clad body. "I couldn't wait to come back."

"I know," she whispered girlishly. "I never knew we could do such delightful things. You were so masterful and gentle at the same time." Her fingers brushed his thighs and his erection while her tongue sought his.

He loved her trace of modesty, her compliments. He felt the tremulous touch of her fingers, and he entered her mouth and released his aching manhood all in one motion. He reached for her hand and forced her to put it on his rigid member. He liked the fact that he had to show her just what to do.

"Was it delightful?" he whispered.

"It was a little shameful," Melinda whispered back. "But no one but us has to know, do they? You wouldn't tell anyone that I loved doing something so improper?" She would never tell him she was clamoring for him to do it again. She had to maneuver him into it, even if he wanted it as desperately as she did. She stretched languidly as she thought of how completely he had filled her, but she couldn't rush him into it, no matter how aroused she felt. He wanted to coax her and have her beg him to return. It was a silly little game, so easy to play.

She gave him her lips, her tongue, her breasts, her dripping little words of encouragement. Her reluctant hand caressed him until he was ready for her.

"Did it really feel good?" he whispered.

"I never could have imagined it would feel so good," she told him. "That's what made it so wicked. And so unladylike."

"And exciting," he whispered. "Didn't it excite you?"

She gave him a teasing little smile. "What do you think?"

"I think you want it. Tell me you want it."

"I don't know if I want it," she murmured; "It felt so immoral."

"But you told me afterwards you wanted it just that way again next time," he protested.

"Maybe I changed my mind," she whispered. "But then again, maybe I didn't. Do you think it excited me?"

"I know you want it," he growled. "And I want it, just the same way."

"You're so big and strong," she whispered. "Be big and strong for me. You know how to do it. Show me how you do it."

The teasing bitch, he thought; he turned her over roughly and shoved himself in her with one thick thrust. And then she was Maggie, all smooth sinuous movements under his hands, begging for every inch of him, the way he just knew she begged the cowdog every night in his fantasies and in his dreams.

He was sated but still not satisfied. It was not Maggie, and only his driving need pushed him there, when nights got hot, and Maggie lay untouchable in the room next door.

On a night of such sultry heat several days later they were awakened by the clang of the fire bell.

Everyone dashed down to the lobby to watch the volunteers scramble to the truck, but one one knew where to go.

Then Annie Mapes appeared in a loaded wagon on her way into town, coming sooner still sooner because the whole of the rangeland from her house on north to the Colleran's was burning.

Maggie raced upstairs to throw on some clothes. She had to get a horse, a wagon, she had to *see*; the bastards, the bastards! That was the unthinkable threat he had meant . . .

"I'll take you," Reese said urgently, and she agreed while Mother Colleran wailed at her stupidity in the background. "If only you had sold up, Maggie . . . if only . . . if only . . ."

A crowd of wagons raced them; everyone wanted to see. It was a glow on the horizon even before they cleared the edge of town, and as they came closer they could see it feeding with a white heat on everything in its path.

Everyone wanted to get closer. They edged in, murmuring, shouting over the roar of the fire as it consumed a tree, and spread outward, ever outward. Soon only Maggie and Reese were inching forward, and Arch Warfield with a malevolent smile, taking notes.

"God, Maggie . . ." Even Reese could not have envisioned the voracious power of the fire. It was like nothing he had ever seen, not even the night that the *Morning Call* building burned.

"It'll keep going," Maggie said tonelessly. "It will break at the road, and down by Gully Basin. It took the house, I'm sure, and probably the Mapes' place too. If we're lucky, it will burn itself out down at the forest. It was a good move, Reese. Now they don't have to clear the land. They just have to get it away from me."

From the opposite direction she saw someone coming by the light of the flames. She knew it was Logan, just as he knew she would be the one in the forefront of the spectators.

He dismounted immediately and jumped into the wagon. "I'm driving her, Reese. You take my horse. Go *on*. There's nothing you can do here."

Maggie sat like a statue, her eyes on the crackling flames. Logan pushed Reese, and he automatically responded even though he had fully intended to stay rooted just where he was. Damned cowdog, he thought viciously, as Logan climbed into the seat and whacked the reins down on the horses' backs. They reared, scared by the smoke and the flames. Logan snapped the reins again, and they took off almost uncontrollably in the direction from which he had come.

Damn him to hell, Reese swore violently as his mount reared up and almost unseated him. Damn, *damn;* he had no choice but to follow them, and he had been thinking of another assignation with the luscious Melinda. Damn the fire, damn them, damn the cowdog.

He pushed his horse, and wheeled him around in the direction from which Logan had come.

"You're *not* going back to Colville tonight," Logan said forcefully, as if he had to emphasize every word to get through to her.

"You know, that bastard warned me, and I couldn't think of a single thing he could threaten me with."

"Have some coffee." He shoved a cup in her hands.

"Logan . . ."

"Don't worry, I won't touch you. I just don't think you ought to go back tonight."

"Who would believe it?" she murmured, sipping the hot liquid. She felt it steam down inside her, nudging her to life.

"Who cares," he said roughly.

"You don't," she answered simply. "You don't think I'm going to fall into your arms now, do you?"

"Whose arms are you falling into these days, Maggie?"

"That is the most abominable thing anyone has ever said to me."

"I beg your pardon. You live in such close quarters these days, for a woman who wants room and space and freedom, it does make a man wonder."

"That is so unfair!"

"Isn't it? Hell, I'm only the one who's been waiting for you all these years. I shouldn't give a damn in hell whether or not Reese Colleran is creeping around your room, should I? He's a town man, Maggie, and so convenient when there's a fire to race out and view."

"*Reese?* That's despicable."

"No, it isn't. They do say history repeats itself, Maggie. He's so damned like Frank it hurts. Maybe he's even better. Maybe you make a lot of noise to throw up smokescreens. How the hell do I know?"

"Logan, I can't listen to this."

"I know, you can't, you can't, you can't. It's a regular theme with you these days. I guess your mother-in-law has the right of it: a cowboy can't do anything for you."

His bitterness was scorching, and something she had never seen in him.

"But you know damned well my father sold me to Frank," she lashed out, suddenly.

"Hell, you were drooling all over him, Maggie. He was God Almighty when he came to town. Everyone wanted him and you set your sights and twitched your hips and there he was. You were something when you were twenty, Maggie. You were just as innocent as the sky and you knew everything in the world."

"Well I didn't know Frank wanted the *Morning Call*, and I tell you, Logan, that was all he wanted."

"Good story, Maggie. That's why he handed it over to you on a platter and why you're supporting his damned family. And maybe it's why that damned Reese thinks he can take Frank's place."

There was no talking to him tonight, she thought tiredly. She had never seen this side of him, all this

311

acrimony that had been bottled up for years. She had never given a thought to what he might be feeling or what he thought he had lost when he had given her the choice. But nobody was happy for the simple reason that she didn't like the choices: marriage . . . or . . . ruination?

But she *was* ruined, and even now accepting his proposal was not a choice for her. Not yet.

"You know," she said, "you never asked about Frank and me."

"It wasn't time."

"Maybe it's time."

"You don't have to explain anything, Maggie."

"Frank wanted the control of the *Morning Call* and he married me to get it."

"I like that, Maggie. As if he couldn't have started up something on his own here."

"Why should he have? He had nothing to lose and he was getting the possibility of an heir in the bargain. My bloodlines are very good, Logan. I'm sure he looked into it."

The thought arrested her for a moment. *Looked into it*, she mused. Yes. There was something to that, she just didn't know what.

"And he found you utterly enchanting anyway," Logan said sarcastically. "Who wouldn't?"

"He hated me," she told him flatly. "After the first year, he hated me."

"Why?" he asked carefully.

"Because I wanted to *do* things. We spent the first six months out at the ranch, and I wouldn't stay in the house canning vegetables and baking bread. And then he gave up and took me to town. He hated it that I was always in the office and that I could sling type better than he could."

She looked away from him for a moment, because the next was even harder to tell. "And he hated how willing I was when we made love. He . . . he thought it was unladylike. He called me his, his home whore, and after a while he used me like one. Then he went out and found someone he could pay to do the same things I wanted to do. But that was different, because then he had control. And he brought in his mother to make sure I wasn't . . . I didn't . . ."

She swallowed convulsively. "The baby was . . . he didn't want a baby. We had a fight that night, a horrible fight; he was sure it wasn't his, that I was the worst kind of bitch, slut, wanton, filth, and that his mother had missed something along the way. The fight got physical, but you know he was so much bigger than me. He pushed me. He struck me. He walked out on me before he knew what had happened, and he went to her and paid her for her services that night."

"Maggie . . ." he said softly.

"No, you should know this," she whispered, wiping the tears that were welling up in her eyes. "He was a bastard through and through. He didn't even care, and I didn't care after that. I was glad he had that piece of trash to go to. I didn't want him any more. He didn't deserve me. When he died, he was leaving her house. He was shot in the back, just like A.J."

Yes, she had thought that before, she was sure. Just like A.J. He looked into it. She focused on the thoughts and not on the pain she had just recreated so painstakingly for Logan.

"The son of a bitch," he muttered.

She took another breath. "And then everything came to me. I didn't understand it then, I don't understand it now. I went over his papers the other day, and the only thing that read differently to me was the contract between my father and Frank. It literally said that my father would hand over his interest in the ownership of the paper for the sum of one thousand dollars when

313

Frank married me. So he married me."

"Jesus, Maggie."

"I wish you had gotten there first," she whispered.

"I wish I had too."

He settled her down on the sofa in front of the fireplace, and he stoked the flames. "It's a wonder I can look at a fire with equanimity," she said.

He sat down on the floor with his knees drawn up against his chest. "I'm wondering about that. It can't devalue the land for *them*. If anything it becomes a fortuitous accident."

"I had that thought too. I don't know." She put her head back and stared at the fire. It was friendly and warm now, radiating a faint heat that would expand with the hours. It felt like she felt, contained and secure now that Logan understood the things he hadn't known before.

She felt safe with him, not terrorized, not trapped. The net couldn't swallow her here. There was sanity here, and a sense that all the swirling things she was thinking would coalesce into some kind of coherent whole.

She wanted him. The magic of Logan, she thought, was the fact that nothing else mattered when she was with him. He made her whole again and she knew in that moment it was the reason she had always needed him.

And she, not he, had almost thrown that enchantment away. She wanted to recapture it; she wanted him.

And she knew he wanted her.

They sat in deep silence for a very long time. She didn't know what to do, but she knew she was the one who had to make the first move. It was just the way it was, and the way she wanted it.

She loved the long tense moments of trying to decide how she would approach him. In her mind she could say and do anything she wanted, everything she had

314

imagined in her dreams.

In reality there was a barrier between them, as thick as her stubborn streak and twice as wide. It was tangible and it emanated from him, and as the heat grew between them it became something that could not be ignored.

What was it? She knew what it was. She would leave him tomorrow, like he was a man for hire, and he wanted her with him always.

We'll come to that, she thought, stretching out her hand and touching his thick hair as he gazed pensively into the fireplace. I'm coming to that. I just need a little time. Just a little time.

Her hand told him that as she stroked his hair down to the edge of his collar. She inserted her fingers there and began sliding them around the base of his neck.

Her touch electrified him; he had loved her so long, how could he refuse her? He felt her deep breaths against his ear as her fingers inched their way downward to feel the play of muscle along his shoulders. He felt her lips as she grazed his ear and neck with kisses. And then he turned his head and he felt her tongue as she forced her way into his mouth.

And then his arms closed around her as she tumbled on top of him.

Outside, Reese Colleran watched. There was a window from the parlor that looked directly out onto the porch. It was pitch black. The only illumination was the fire within. He watched as the cowdog slowly undressed Maggie and felt every inch of her satiny flesh.

Never had he imagined her body so beautiful; never had he dreamed a woman could be so willing. He had never seen anything like the ferocity with which she enticed that man with her kisses and the way she wrapped herself around him with wanton abandon.

He couldn't bear to watch it through this time. He needed desperately to slake his own rising desire, and he knew just where to go. The image of Maggie's nakedness rode with him as he raced to town.

It was very late when he got there, but he pounded on Melinda Sable's door violently. By the time she opened it, he had withdrawn a hundred-dollar bill and his aching member.

Her heated gaze ate it up, and he knew she was ready. She gave him a knowing little smile and closed the door behind him.

She awoke beside him, naked, on the floor. "Logan!" she shook him urgently, and he woke up with a start.

"What's the matter, Maggie?"

"What if someone comes?"

"They'll knock on the door."

"This is nothing to laugh about."

"I'm not laughing," he said huskily, reaching for her. "Lie down with me, Maggie."

She nestled against him, back to front, and his arms surrounded her. She felt utterly enfolded by his heat and his scent and the enticing male essence of him.

She reached back and grasped his hard muscular thigh. She felt an immediate reaction. He threw his leg over her and she felt him nudging her and hardening deliciously against her.

"I want you," he whispered in her ear.

"I'm waiting," she murmured, raising her arms behind his neck so that she could both command his kisses and arch herself against him. His tongue immediately possessed her willing mouth and one arm wrapped tightly around her hips, while the other hand covered her breast, just covered it, and held it, with the peak of her nipple pressing hard into the palm of his hand.

"Perfect," she breathed against his lips.

"Almost perfect," he whispered, taking her kisses. "Wrap your leg around me, Maggie."

"Yes," she murmured, and slid her bare leg over his thigh just as he wanted.

There, when she was open to him, he slid gently into her welcoming fold and held her there to feel the pulsating heart of his desire. She was home to him, beside him, open to him, possessing him as thoroughly as he possessed her. It was an ineffable moment of discovery, a pure bonding that connected them into a new whole. He had never wanted her more and he was content to lie embedded within her, full and whole and perfect.

He did not move for a very long time, and his languid kisses only incited them both. She began thrusting against him with tight little movements that begged him for the full measure of his driving manhood.

"Now, Maggie?"

"I want you desperately," she whispered.

"Show me how much."

"You show me."

Even so, his movements were both limited and enhanced by the way he possessed her. She enfolded him totally and felt each short movement of him deep inside her. She loved how deeply he lay within her and how his hands had access to every inch of her body. She withheld nothing from him when he made love to her this way. Her kisses told him so. The luxurious writhing of her body against him excited him beyond anything he had felt before.

She was Eve, an innocent and temptress in one luscious body. She knew all the secrets of time, yet he found secrets to be discovered.

She gave him her breasts, and he discovered the mystery of her proud nipples. She gave him her feminine heat, and he found the source of her satiety. With each

317

virile stroke of his towering manhood he took her toward completion.

This stunning tribute to her voluptuous femininity resonated deep within her. She rode with *him*, only him; her body shimmied against him, her leg thrust against him, almost as if she were trying to get away from the intensity of his possession. Her kiss-swollen lips begged him for more, and he gave it to her.

He drove into hot velvet, his tongue caressed hot velvet, she smoldered against him with her sinuous movements, seeking the thing he most wanted to give her.

Slowly it came, from a golden, hot center, elusive and powerfully there, golden molten, dissolving through her veins in a shimmering, sumptuous conclusion to the splendor of his love.

He felt it coming, rippling through her, twisting through him, propelling him like a rock-hard piston to thrust and thrust and thrust until he felt her soaring and breaking down onto him, into the force of his shattering climax.

"I have to see it," she said, as he grimly prepared to take her back into Colville.

"You don't want to see it, Maggie."

"I do. I have to know."

He looked at her sharply. "I don't want you to go."

"I don't want to go. But I have to. I have to figure it out, Logan."

He didn't understand that cryptic statement, and he let it pass; the important thing was, she didn't want to leave him.

They drove in silence toward the Colleran land. There was still a smokiness in the air, and as they passed by the Mapes' they saw the heat of the devastation. The house was gone, the land was barren and naked. Charred trees, bushes, scorched grass were all the eye could see. There was nothing remaining of the cabin where Maggie had spent her first weeks of marriage to Frank. Everything was blackened, burned to the root.

She took a deep breath. "Maybe it's better."

"Don't give in, Maggie."

"Oh no. Not until I understand why Frank left it to me. I don't know where to go to find that out."

They were silent again as he guided the wagon toward town. She was deep in her thoughts and he wasn't sure if he wanted to interrupt her, until suddenly she gave a short laugh.

"I was thinking about Mother Colleran. She said things would change when Reese arrived." She turned her head back to look at the desolation one more time. "They did, didn't they?"

"He never said why he came?"

"She sent for him, or at least that was what she said."

He thought about that for a while. "After Reese came everything changed. How?"

"What we talked about: Denver North running that ad for construction workers in the readyprint supplement, gossip about my driving up the price of the land by refusing to sell. Dennis's proposal—Dennis asked me to marry him, remember? He thought Frank would have wanted it." She ignored his shudder. "A.J.'s death. The fire. *Two* fires. Is that enough? Haven't we had this conversation before?"

He grimaced. "It does sound a little familiar, but neither of us were thinking about these things that have happened in term of how they related to Reese's arrival."

She thought about it. "That's true. I'm not sure if they have any bearing at all."

"Or maybe they are the very reason why he came to Colville."

It was a startling idea. "He came to Colville to set all these things in motion? That's crazy; he didn't know anything about Frank's business or me or Denver North before he came."

"Or maybe he did," Logan said soberly.

That was worse, because she had thought that too. "I considered that. Sometimes it felt like he was aching to take control of the paper away from me. And then when A.J. died, I thought he was shot so that someone could step in and take over from *him*."

"All these feelings," Logan muttered.

"And one very suspicious sheriff who would just love to find a reason to hang A.J.'s murder on me. He's still sniffing around. Even that unctuous Mr. Brown mentioned it when I met him just after the fire."

"Ummm," Logan said thoughtfully as they reached the outskirts of town. "I think you're in danger, Maggie," he said abruptly.

"Not if I sell the burned acreage," she said. "Dennis has been pressuring me to do it. He claims my finances are sinking lower than a mine shaft these days with all the drain on my income. I could just sell up and be gone if I go crawling to Mr. Brown."

"What are you going to do, Maggie?"

"I surely don't know."

"God, I hate to leave you alone here, but we have to get the cattle out before they hunker down on the Mapes' land. I can get back in two or three days."

"I'll be all right."

"Go to Arwin if you need help."

"I will. Nothing is going to happen, though."

"Don't be too sure," he said ominously. "Now, do you think Reese had the sense to stable my horse in the hotel's barns?"

*   *   *

He had said it, she had answered it with a nonchalance that she was far from feeling, but as she walked into the hotel, Maggie had a pervasive sense that something was not right. She felt a supreme reluctance to return to the suite, and on an impulse she stopped by the desk where Miles was in attendance and asked if there were another free room.

Miles, the ultimate desk clerk, did not blink an eye. He scanned the booking list and finally said "No, ma'am. I'm sorry." She believed him because it would have meant more money from her pocket.

She had to go back to the suite, where Logan thought she was in danger.

She let herself in bravely. There was no one there. She breathed a sigh of relief and then wondered if they hadn't sent a search party for her. But why should they? Reese knew she was with Logan.

Reese didn't like the fact that she had gone with Logan.

She wondered where Reese was.

It was curiously stale and silent in the sitting room. She sat down tentatively on the little sofa, almost as if she expected to have to leap up and dash out.

Her oozing fear seemed radically misplaced in the face of the normalcy of the suite and the fact that both her mother-in-law and Reese were gone. She had expected a confrontation and had walked into blankness. She was exaggerating things in her mind; nothing could be as spooky as it seemed when she went over it in the silence and dark of night.

On the other hand, the man had issued a thinly disguised threat, and days later the something that *might* have happened did.

Except that Mr. Brown had made it very clear he wasn't going to make her another offer for that land.

Who, she wondered, would?

She ought to go to him and demand something

incredibly outrageous. He would say scorched earth wasn't worth it. He would try to break her, to pull down the price he initially offered her, she thought, and that was the why of it. She had been bad—she hadn't cooperated . . . odd word to use . . . and she had been punished.

But why would she think in terms of cooperation?

. . . *looked into it* . . . that phrase resurfaced unexpectedly. She was sure Frank had looked into it. Her. Her family. He was the type of man who did not do things impulsively. He checked things out. He must have checked her out.

He wouldn't have married her, a fresh-faced, innocent twenty year old with a newspaper dowry just out of hand. He hadn't come to Colville specifically looking for her.

He must have looked into it.

Why would she connect that to her thinking about cooperation?

Cooperation. Colville.

She didn't see any connection, but the notion of looking into it was so insistent in her mind.

He came from a prominent San Francisco family and he wound up in Colville. She remembered saying those very words to Reese.

"Maggie!"

She heard Reese's voice and looked up to see him standing in the doorway, so purposeful and vigorous.

. . . and he wound up in Colville too.

He must have looked into it.

And then the thing clicked that had been nagging at her since she said the words, and a whomp of fear hit her in the stomach like a brick.

She looked up and smiled at Reese. "Reese, I've been here for hours. Where have *you* been?"

*   *   *

322

Now she had to tread carefully. She had an inkling of what was going on, just an inkling, and she did not know where to look for the whole explanation. She needed Logan desperately now, and oh, where was he? Herding cows. What could a cowboy do for her indeed!

Reese was ready to court and coddle her, and that was almost unbearable. Mother Colleran came in and out, chiding Maggie for her indiscretion.

"Everybody saw you, Maggie; I could die from embarrassment that you actually went off with that man in front of a hundred people."

"He's an old friend, Mother Colleran. I felt faint. My land was burning up. I was grateful he could offer me a place to lie down." Tonelessly, she offered her mother-in-law all the palliatives she would need to placate her gossipy friends.

"And she's better now," Reese said. "We'll just have a nice dinner out in the hotel dining room and she will be fine."

"I won't be fine," she said to him later. "The grassland is burned to a cinder."

"That's too bad, Maggie."

"Yes it is, and I have been feeling as though the fates really have it in for me. What are the chances of two destructive fires happening in a single lifetime, let alone within weeks of each other, Reese?"

He looked startled. "I hadn't thought about it. Look, Maggie, some drifter camped on your land and was a bit too careless with a campfire. The other . . . I don't know."

"That would be a reasonable explanation *if* the other hadn't happened, and *if* Mr. Brown hadn't suggested that that land was ripe for disaster. It was so heavy-handed it is almost laughable."

"Mr. Brown never struck me as being obvious," Reese said.

"I would not have thought so either. I suppose now everyone thinks I'd be better off unloading the land, including our Mr. Brown. Including, perhaps, you?"

"Maggie, Maggie, Maggie, you do whatever you have to do. You've been so adamant about it, how could anyone fault any decision you make?"

"You tell me, Reese."

"I can't," he murmured, but he thought he would like to. He wanted to tell her other things, things she was missing by denying him. He was spending himself extravagantly at Melinda Sable's and somehow he wanted her to know it.

"What will you do then?" she asked suddenly.

"I like Colville," he said.

"But the estate is not limitless, Reese. I can't support you and Mother Colleran on it, and frankly I don't intend to. And if I don't sell my property, I'm going to be close to appropriating principal. By the terms of the will I can't do that, no matter what."

"I'm working on something," he said in a faintly resentful tone.

"Good," she said. "We have one more week of luxury in the suite, and then I'm afraid we'll all have to find other accommodations. I can't afford the hotel, either."

"That fire really scared you, didn't it?" he asked nastily.

"No, Dennis scared me. He's given me an either-or-choice. I don't like it, but there's nothing I can do about it. I don't have a business to offset the drain on my income, unfortunately. We don't have living quarters that we own. We have nothing, Reese, that isn't coming directly from Frank's estate, and frankly, I resent the expense."

"All right, Maggie. That's damned clear. Frank left everything to you, and by God, *you* are the only one who is going to benefit. You want it all. Fine. You'll get it all. I

324

can make other arrangements. I'm afraid you'll have my mother to contend with for a while yet. I can't take her where I will be going right now." He stood up abruptly and threw down some money. *Bitch, bitch bitch,* he was screaming inside, She would deny him everything, *everything.* The cowdog would get it all, every last cent that had been Frank's and should have been his and his mother's. Damn, damn, damn.

He stalked out of the dining room, looking tall and elegant and so much like Frank in his manner that people just stopped and stared.

Maggie looked down at her plate. On it was a hundred-dollar bill.

"Arwin, do you know precisely when Denver North came scouting around here looking for a route to join up in Cheyenne?"

"Well now, Maggie, let me think. Hmmm. Do you know, I think it was a few years before Frank came, yes I do. They sent a party of boss types up here along with a survey team and they all rubbed their chins, and said, yep, it looks okay, and then they went away and nobody came for a while."

"Thanks, Arwin."

"Why did you want to know?"

"I'm not sure, isn't it strange? I mean, just after Frank died was when we got the first notice that they were coming in and buying up land and going to survey. They had permits and government rights of way and whatever other kind of paper they always have. I was just wondering . . ."

But she didn't know what she was wondering.

Did Frank know Denver North was going to be coming and buying up every piece of land in sight?

There, she had phrased the question and it sent a chill

down her spine. What if she asked Arwin? What would he say?

"Wondering what, Maggie?"

"Whether it has any bearing on why someone fired my land last night," she said slowly.

"Reese said it was a drifter."

"Reese was here?"

"Bright and early this morning."

Spreading the story, she thought grimly.

She walked slowly back to the hotel, thinking. She had her amazement that Frank had settled in Colville, and her astonishment that Reese had followed him here. She had everything that had happened since Reese had arrived, including the pressure being put on her to sell the ranch land. And she had the fact that Frank had left her everything to dispose of as she would. What did it all add up to?

She had Logan.

He would come tomorrow, she knew he would. She only had to get through one more night, a much easier task since she had asked Reese to leave the suite.

She had to remember to ask Miles to locate a room for Mother Colleran and herself, preferably far apart, for the rest of the time they would spend in the hotel.

Dennis was waiting for her when she returned to the hotel.

"Out early?"

"Taking a walk."

"I have to remind you, Maggie, your month of deliberation is almost up."

"I'm aware of that. In fact I want to make arrangements to move to single rooms for another, oh, month, and by then something should be settled, I should think. Don't you?"

"Don't give me your light and airy voice, Maggie. You know very well that you must give an answer to Mr.

Brown on the town property. I wish you would say yes to his offer today."

Maggie scanned his face. It was the face of her earnest lawyer with her best welfare at heart. She saw nothing else there, and she made an intuitive decision right then. "Tell him no, I don't want to sell the town property."

Dennis was astounded. "Maggie! Why are you spiting yourself and putting yourself in an untenable position financially?"

"I don't know. I just don't feel that I should sell the *Morning Call* site."

"All right, Maggie. Pretty soon you'll drive yourself so far into the ground you may have to take the only way out."

"What is that?"

"Accept my proposal, of course."

"I couldn't possibly, Dennis. Not even in the most adverse of circumstances."

"This is not the place to talk about it, Maggie. And you don't know what the future will bring."

"No I don't. Is *that* a threat, Dennis?"

"It's a wise word to a wise woman who might be wise to cooperate occasionally."

"I see," she said. *Cooperate*. Exactly. Cooperate.

God, if only she had the *Morning Call* morgue to rummage around in. All the answers had been there, she just knew it. All she had now were tenuous threads, amorphous connections that didn't make sense. And they all centered around one thing—no, one person— Frank.

know about everything.

"I knew about Reese," she said brokenly. "Frank knew about the northbound ... k because Reese told

Chapter Seventeen

Her refusal to . . . cooperate . . . must have somebody hopping, she thought. Something had to happen,
and soon. They were starting to lay track on Danforth
land now, and they were getting close to the moment
when they had to veer off and begin grading down around
Logan's property.

She felt a tension shimmering in her bones. It was as if
she were playing some kind of cat and mouse game with
them, where the cat knew where the mouse was hiding,
and the mouse knew it would be swallowed up any minute
and still gamely dashed around, taunting its tormentor.

She was doing that. She didn't know who the
tormentor was. It could be Mr. Brown, it could be
Dennis, it could be Reese. It could even be Madame
Mother. Maybe it had always been Frank, she didn't
know.

But she knew, she was absolutely sure, that Frank had
looked into it, and he had not turned up in Colville on
some peripatetic whim. Frank had come because Denver
North was coming, and Frank had bought as much land as
he could on the route to Cheyenne because he was sure
he would have a commodity that Denver North eventually would want to buy.

And then he had been killed, and he left it all to her, the person who least wanted to sell.

It didn't make sense.

She waited for someone to approach her, to threaten her, to make an overture of some kind so she could see what she was fighting. All she knew was she was fighting Mr. Brown's determination, Dennis's deadly desire to have her, and Reese's easy profligacy with her money.

Nothing happened. No one approached her. No one said a word except what Dennis told her that morning.

But she knew now that her indecision had nothing to do with her being irresolute; some intuition held her back, and she trusted it implicitly. She would find the answers, and then she would know what to do.

"You cannot mean to move me out of this suite," Mother Colleran protested angrily. "The desk clerk just stopped me and handed me the keys to some little dingy room on the third floor. There has obviously been some mistake, Maggie."

"No mistake," she said mildly. "We have another week of luxury before the money runs out."

"I don't believe you. Frank's estate must have been enormous. You were running a business from it. You paid salaries from it. You—"

"I can't support you and me and Reese with no money coming in, Mother Colleran, it's as simple as that."

"You can sell the Colleran land."

Maggie shook her head. "It is amazing to me how *everyone* wants me to sell that land. It's almost as if you think you're entitled to a piece of the profit."

Her mother-in-law's eyes flickered and she turned away abruptly. "Don't be ridiculous, Maggie. Frank left it to you. I just don't think he intended for you to waffle around the decision for so long."

Maggie felt another little jolt of perception. The old crow didn't think Frank *intended*...? "What did Frank intend, Mother Colleran?" she asked casually.

But her mother-in-law had caught the inference. "He certainly didn't intend for you to walk around here destitute when you have something that will bring you enough money to live comfortably no matter what you decide to do."

"And you," Maggie said pointedly.

"That's beside the fact. I'm not at all important in terms of this decision."

"You're right about that," Maggie muttered, and her mother-in-law pretended not to hear her.

"You have to do what's best for yourself, Maggie, always remembering that in spite of the fact that the newspaper is gone, you are still Mrs. Frank, and Mrs. Frank does not live in dingy hotel rooms parsing out silver like she was a recluse."

"Indeed. And how does *Mrs. Frank* live?"

"She lives like Frank lived, comfortably, open-handedly, with status—"

"And with the good advice and comfortable companion-ship of her beloved mother-in-law," Maggie finished acerbically.

Mother Colleran stared at her. "Really, Maggie, there's no cause to get nasty. You don't have to take me into account at all."

"I don't," Maggie murmured. "However, at the moment, I have not made a decision, and we will vacate these rooms in another week and make the best of things until I do decide what to do."

"Well, I hope to tell *you*, Maggie, that Frank never would have dawdled around being virtuous about it. What good is the land now anyway since the fire?"

Another little jolt. "Oh, I don't know. I suppose it's possible to reclaim the pastureland. I could marry Logan

331

and we could build a real nice spread on that land . . ."

Her mother-in-law's face contorted in the most terrifying expression Maggie had ever seen, murderous, driven beyond all restraint—and then it was gone. "So you could, Maggie. It's yours to do with what you want, of course. But I tell you, I will never live in the same house with that man, Maggie. *Never*. Think about it."

"I've thought about it; it appeals to me enormously."

"Even if you could have Reese," demanded her mother-in-law.

"Especially if that were possible."

"Well, I won't stand for it, Maggie, I just won't. That cowboy, that roughshod farmer, that . . ." She flounced into her room, and slammed the door, and still her voice came out at Maggie, muffled, writhing with imprecations.

Maggie sighed. Madame Mother certainly hated Logan. She wondered why.

So now he was a boarder at Melinda Sable's, and though it cost him a premium price, Reese was glad to pay the freight to be able to pretend to seduce Melinda Sable's luscious body every night. She wasn't Maggie, but her attitude was exactly right; playful, reluctant, bold, and submissive all at once. In his wildest fantasy, he saw Maggie living in this very house and begging him to visit her in her room in that same tantalizing tone of voice.

Her naked body was a constant image in his mind, and he ached with a rock-hard determination to possess her. He wanted her at his feet, totally beneath him, at his mercy, vanquished. He wanted to hear her ripe lips murmur sweet compliments of his mastery.

She was primed for the taking. She swore she didn't want him, but she wanted no one else. She only wanted to rut in every conceivable place with the cowdog, but he

332

knew his eventual domination of her would wipe the memory from her brain.

She needed only one night with him. He was not Frank, a man who had not appreciated the temptress he had had in his very own bed. No, he adored the audacious sensuality he had seen the cowdog incite, adored the brazen need that compelled her to demand to be taken whenever her desire kindled.

To have a woman like that, wanton, ripe, willing, without having to approach her with a hundred dollars in his hand . . . He invariably stiffened with anticipation every time he thought about it. Maggie in the hands of the cowdog; what did he know about satisfying such lust as Reese had seen in her?

He knew nothing about Maggie's profligate sensuality. Only Reese Colleran could replace the husband who had abandoned her. It was the one thing he had come to Colville for, a decision he had made long before he had ever seen Maggie's voluptuous body. And now he could have that *and* Maggie's hot receptivity too. He kept remembering the first time he had seen her, from the hill above the church. And invariably when he thought about Maggie, he saw in his mind's eye the first time he had unwittingly spied on her.

The memory always aroused him unbearably. At those times it was good he had Melinda Sable's body to bury himself within. Even now, as his quiescent member spurted to life, he was halfway out the door, seeking surcease from his ravenous need.

But Melinda was busy this day. Melinda was sweet; she patted him gently on his face and stroked his throbbing erection. "You know there's a sweet little girl in the room down the hall, Reese. Brand new; you might want to try her. I've been waiting to give her a really powerful man. She's a friend of Maggie Colleran's, Reese. Her name is

333

Annie Mapes."

"I know what I'm going to do."

Logan turned at Maggie's statement and sent her a long considering look from across the room. He was all muscular cowhand today, so much so that Mother Colleran had bolted from the suite when he arrived, fresh from riding with his herd to pasture upland.

They hadn't said more than a couple of words to each other after her departure. It was almost as if they felt shy with each other.

He smiled at her gently. "I knew you'd figure it out, Maggie."

She shook her head. "I figured some of it out. Not everything. And do you know what it's really about? I *think* it's about Frank. Isn't that unbelievable? After all these years. The man won't stay buried."

"Colville keeps him alive," Logan said. Much to his detriment, he thought. He knew she was reminded of Frank in one way or another every day, whether it was by her courtesy address or by something Frank had done. He didn't see the townspeople calling her "Mrs. Logan." Not at all.

"*No.* Listen, Logan. He looked into it. Frank looked into it. Remember, I said my bloodlines are very good. I said I was sure Frank looked into it. Didn't anybody think it was odd that someone like him wound up in Colville? Do you see? I said the same thing to Reese. He wound up in Colville, too."

"They looked into Colville?" he said, puzzled. "They . . . Frank . . ." he searched for the connection, "Frank . . . .knew about Denver North."

She let out a breath. She wasn't imagining it; it was a possible, even logical conclusion. "And the first thing he did was buy that tract of land—how many thousand acres?—right on a direct line north to Cheyenne. He came to buy land and sell it."

"Well, fine. And he stayed."

"No. No. That's the part I'm still working out. I still don't understand why he willed it to me. Do you see? He never expected he wouldn't realize an enormous profit on it. But even so, there was his brother and his mother and even Dennis. Why me?"

"Maybe Dennis knows why."

"Dennis would never tell me . . . now. Every time I think about what has happened since A.J.'s death I have this mad feeling that it is all deliberate."

He didn't protest her statement.

"Don't you?" she demanded.

"But you say it's connected to Frank. How? Where?"

"It's crazy. Reese comes to Colville. He wants to see his mother, he wants to be my friend. To help with the paper. And that happens right after Harold Danforth and I tangle about the railroad. Right? And then Arwin is telling me that people are saying I'm antirailroad because I want to get more money for the land I have. Then the for-hire notices appear in a place over which I have no control. The paper. More suspicion. Then Reese practically proposes to me. A.J. is mysteriously killed and Reese immediately steps in. Mr. Brown comes on the scene and begins making offers few can refuse. I refuse him. The sheriff then as good as accuses me of murdering A.J., except he can't find any proof and he only has a theory. I run a story about the miserable worker accommodations up at the track site, and two days later, the office burns down. Suddenly I have two pieces of property to sell and the only bidder is Denver North. And that is on top of Dennis proposing to me at least twice, and Mother Colleran urging me to sell. I had a feeling that A.J. had been killed so someone pro-Denver North could take his place, and I could be framed for murder so that I

335

could be gotten rid of, clearing the way for the sale of the Colleran ranch. You're right, it sounds crazy."

"Or," he said soberly, "it sounds like a conspiracy."

A conspiracy. At his words the tension in her diminished. She wasn't quite demented then. She had an ally who thought the things that had happened were not exaggerations of her imagination. She felt a sweet gratitude for his discernment. He had handed her a possibility, something solid to work with, to work backward from, because the first words that leapt into her mind as he said it were "Who? How?"

"Everybody. Nobody. People you don't even know, if Frank and Denver North are the focus of all of this."

"But the end result has been this enormous pressure for me to sell, and circumstances have made it imperative that I consider selling."

"But who stands to gain the most, Maggie?"

"That's just it," she said unhappily. "Me. And only me."

And then she didn't know what she was going to do. The very idea of a conspiracy was both potent and frightening. It meant she had more than one enemy; it meant she couldn't attack lest she were gunned down from behind.

Like Frank. Like A.J.

God, how she kept coming back to that, too.

Had the same person murdered them both?

Another connection. Five years apart . . . how was it possible? How could those two deaths be linked?

The net tightened still more.

She felt a jangling fear that nothing she did would be enough to save her, that she would be sacrificed to the maw of somebody's greed.

Whose greed, when she was the only one who would benefit?

She was consumed with a racing need to take some kind of action.

"Nothing to your mother-in-law?"

Logan's voice pulled her back from her scattershot thoughts.

"Nothing. Nothing to Reese. Nothing to Dennis, although only he is empowered to act for me when I do sell." *Only* he, she thought. He hadn't been in Colville then. He had come on Frank's summons from San Francisco.

Her mind raced ahead. If Frank had brought him to Colville, he must have written to him. What if he had written letters about Denver North? He bought up the land with no intention of ranching whatsoever, she could see now in retrospect. What would she find in a letter that she didn't know already?

She didn't even care what she might find. The thought was she could *do* something, she could move, she could take action.

"Logan I want to break into Dennis's office."

He didn't move a muscle. He didn't try to dissuade her. He smiled his slow, gentle smile. "Any time you like."

They watched Dennis's office all day from the front window of Bodey's store.

"You two ain't no decoration, hanging out there like that," Arwin said.

"She's at loose ends," Logan explained. "This gives her something to do with her time."

"I know a hundred things she could do better with her time," Arwin said tartly, thumping his hand down on a stack of *Colville Clarion*s. "Like this rag, for instance.

337

You just lookit this. And you tell me, Maggie Colleran, that this town don't need the clear eye of the *Morning Call.*"

"The *Morning Call* is in mourning," Maggie retorted. "This town has gotten exactly what it wanted: a positive picture of the beneficent Denver North." She turned her head to peer out the window again. "That man must be chained to his desk," she whispered to Logan.

"He always struck me as being extremely dedicated to his work," Logan said. "And you," he added without expression.

She jumped. "I suppose he is. After all, *two* proposals. Oh, there he is . . ."

"Hell, heading straight for here. Damn, duck Maggie. Arwin, get that back door open, and hold him here."

"Whatever for?" Arwin protested, bewildered by their sudden unorthodox departure, but they were gone by then, sliding along the side of the store and racing across the street to the building where Dennis had his offices.

"There's a back entrance," Maggie whispered, pushing at Logan until they were out of view of the front windows of Bodey's store.

The rear staircase was narrow and dank. "Second floor," Maggie directed, "in the front."

They pulled up in front of a frosted paned door with Dennis's name lettered across it in gilt.

"This looks like it," Logan said, grasping the knob.

"You didn't expect it to be open?" Maggie said in disbelief.

He grinned at her. "Maybe I did. So now we break in."

"What with?"

He smiled again and reached into his pants to unsheathe a small knife he wore strapped to his belt.

"I never noticed that," she said, awed by his cleverness.

"You were too busy noticing other things, Maggie. All

right, let's see if I can spring the lock." He inserted the blade between the door and the molding and moved it upward until it hit something solid. Then he removed it and reinserted it so that just the tip of the blade pressed against the lock catch, and pushed against it gently. "It's giving, just a little. Another . . . You have to coax it sometimes . . ."

"And you're so good at that."

"You noticed. There!" He swung the door in. "Check the window, Maggie. The last thing we need is him climbing back up the stairs now."

"I don't see him. Damn, he could have gone to Arwin's to get some supplies or something. No, wait, he's going on down to the hotel. Good."

"All right. I'll keep watch. You look."

She rubbed her hand over her face. "I wish I knew what I thought I was looking for," she said plaintively, as she tackled his filing drawers.

Nothing was locked. And nothing was coherent.

"You would think he could have made things easy for us," Maggie said ungraciously, as she raced through the drawers trying to find one piece of paper that related to her or to Frank.

"I don't understand this," she whispered finally. "There's a mountain of paper and nothing that makes sense. Nothing pertaining to the estate."

Logan came and looked over her shoulder as she sifted through a pile of papers, scanning each in grim comprehension. "It's a smokescreen, Maggie."

"I don't understand."

"I mean, this is supposed to look like he has a closetful of clients, but look . . . the dates, the descriptions. Not Colville cases, Maggie. Look. How is that kind of legal action possible here?"

"Damn." She shoved the drawer closed. "Where else?"

339

"The closet," Logan said from his post back at the window.

"He has a strongbox," she said suddenly, as she rooted through the closet. There were a couple of boxes of papers there, too, but nothing relating to Frank, nothing about her. "He must have stored everything at the bank." She shoved the boxes back into the closet, with a sinking feeling of defeat.

"Damn, we learned absolutely nothing."

"I wouldn't say that," Logan whispered, cautioning her to silence as they crept out of the office and closed the door carefully behind them.

"I would," Maggie said gloomily as they exited onto the street.

"Maggie, you just didn't put everything together the right way. What we learned was that Dennis doesn't have any other client but you, and it makes an awfully strong case against him that he's asked you to marry him *and* he's urging you to sell."

She would be wise to cooperate occasionally, Dennis had said. An implicit threat, she had thought. Dennis had never been her friend, her confidant, or her advisor.

What had Dennis been? A man reaching to control a great deal of money through her, but a man so desperate for it that he would stoop to killing and arson?

A conspiracy?

What did she have to offer him that Frank could not have given him upon the sale of the property once the railroad had arrived? Dennis would have shared in the profit, surely.

"Maybe," Logan said thoughtfully, "Dennis wanted you and the money and the hell with Frank."

Her heart sank. "He must have been damned disappointed at how independent I am. He could never

340

persuade me to do anything he wanted me to do. How did he think he would convince me to marry him and give him management of Frank's estate and the proceeds of that sale?"

"You'll have to ask him, Maggie."

"I'm sure he'll be . . . frank," she said satirically. "It still doesn't quite piece together."

"No, it doesn't. It's one possible explanation."

"I don't like it."

"It's a start."

"I think I have to do something drastic."

"And I know something drastic you can do, too, Maggie."

Her eyes softened. "I'd love to say yes."

"So say yes."

Wasn't it tempting? She would marry him to smoke out the conspirators and have his luxurious lovemaking for the rest of her life.

"Yes to perpetrate a plot?" she asked doubtfully.

"Yes because you can't live without what we have together," Logan said firmly.

"Without working out any details?"

"Details take care of themselves, Maggie."

"I couldn't do that, Logan; it wouldn't be fair."

"To who? You? You can't presume to say what would be fair to me. You know what that is already, without my telling you."

"But I have to . . ."

"I know, I *know*. I'm waiting, Maggie," he added, flicking her cheek. "Maybe that's all *you* have to know."

She had her own plan, her own plot; she didn't need *him* to carry it out. She didn't need anything but her own courage, because this was the thing she had told Logan she had decided to do.

341

She went to Dennis's office first thing in the morning. He was there, busily turning papers, absorbed in work, or so it seemed.

But now things were different, Maggie thought. Now she had an inkling of how things were really. Dennis was a potential adversary, and she was wary of him now as she sat across from him.

But he didn't sense anything different. "I'm happy to see you here, Maggie. What can I do for you?"

"I believe it's time to make a decision about the Colleran property."

He nodded. "That is a wise decision. I recollect that Mr. Brown offered you twenty thousand and said he would neither dicker nor make you another offer. Are you ready to take that offer?"

"Actually, I'm not," Maggie said boldly.

"Oh? Then you have nothing to discuss with me, Maggie. The fire has made the price a debatable issue."

"My very thought," Maggie agreed cheerfully.

"And you do understand my fee for negotiating the sale will be fifty percent of the proceeds?" Dennis added flatly, intending to shock her.

He did. "I didn't understand that at all," she said slowly. "That does throw a different light on things. It really does. All right, Dennis, consider this. My offer to you is the equivalent percent of the dollar amount that you can get for the acreage. In other words, if you can get fifteen dollars an acre, I will pay you fifteen percent of the profit. Or thirteen. Or twenty if you're wily enough to negotiate that. I will tell you that I won't pay you half on any terms whatsoever, and you would do well to settle for my offer rather than not have me sell that land at all."

She saw she had caught him totally off guard. He had sincerely believed that he could coerce her into his exorbitant terms.

"Even if I am the only one who can negotiate

for you?"

"You can't negotiate if I don't want to sell, Dennis. Think about it. You know my terms now, and you can't bamboozle me into thinking the land's worthless just because someone burned it down. Nor will I allow you to accept what is ostensibly Mr. Brown's offer, and then pocket the difference between that and what you really asked. Are we clear?"

"You'll regret this, Maggie."

"You could come away with as much as a hundred thousand dollars, Dennis. I certainly wouldn't regret *that,* if I were you." She rose and went to the door, then turned to face him. His expression was ugly, frustrated. "You have to agree, Dennis, I'm being extremely co-operative."

"And damned foolish," he growled, but she didn't wait to hear that. The die was cast now, and she had to sit back and wait to see who turned out to be snake eyes.

his tone.

It set her hackles up. "Oh, I see. It had to be your way or not at all, is that right?"

Chapter Eighteen

Logan stayed at the hotel. He had a feeling, a damned bad feeling. Maggie was probing, striking out, and someone was bound to get in the way, someone connected somehow to the railroad. If he were really demented he might think, as Maggie was beginning to, that everyone in town might be connected to the railroad.

On the other hand, Frank, Mr. Brown, and Dennis Coutts were enough of a mouthful to swallow for anyone, even Maggie. And the possibility of collusion sounded like a fairy tale.

But he was dead certain sure that if she announced that she were to marry him, there would be hell to pay. Dennis had asked her twice. Reese had made noises about it. Reese . . . he couldn't figure out Reese. Reese had been hanging around for weeks, and barring the time he had spent in Maggie's newsroom, he didn't seem to have any discernible occupation other than keeping his witchy mother out of Maggie's way.

For which, he imagined, Maggie had been duly grateful. But when it came to that, he was still Frank's brother, still entitled to share lodgings as her brother-in-law, but what more? What more had he intended when he came rolling into Colville? Maggie? Had his sights really been set on Maggie?

And had he known about the money? Mother Colleran had known about the money. He didn't like what he was thinking. It was as if Reese had been another threat coming from the opposite direction with the same purpose in mind: Maggie and the lure of the profit from the Colleran land.

Reese had come and things began to happen. Up until then it had only been Dennis with a clear field to Maggie and the profit.

And who had engineered the murder, the fires, the necessity to sell out to Denver North—which of them? And from which of them was Maggie in the most danger now?

Maggie saw a familiar face on Main Street as she came briskly out of Dennis's office. "Annie," she hailed her, and Annie Mapes looked at once startled and happy that there was a familiar face in a week of strange, forgettable faces.

"Maggie," she cried breathlessly as she hurled herself across the expanse between them and threw herself into Maggie's arms.

"So you're in town now," Maggie said, hugging her, patting her shoulder, standing her away so she could look at her. But Annie did not look happy. She looked thinner, wan, with circles under her eyes. Her hair was untidy but her dress was immaculate—and costly—Maggie thought.

"I'm in town now at Melinda Sable's, just as I told you I would do," Annie said defensively. "It's . . . nice. It's clean, and she's got it decorated real nice, classy. And she doesn't force you to do anything you don't want to do."

"I'm sure she doesn't," Maggie said comfortingly.

"I can have guests in my room—besides the regular guests, I mean. Would you like to see it?"

Maggie hesitated. Would she? Was she just the slightest bit curious to see how she lived, the woman whom Frank chose over her? The woman who somehow had the wit, the guile, the theatricality to keep him by her side until the day he died . . . ?

"Of course I'll come," she said warmly. "Now tell me about Sean," she added, as she took Annie by the arm and they began walking toward the other end of town.

"They're working down around Logan's property now, Maggie. They're going to slide around Gully Basin and then back up to our land. What *was* our land. When Sean sold, you know, we divided what we got. I have some money now, so I could leave at any time. It's just that Sean . . . I couldn't leave him, not till the project's done, because he's spending his money faster than he makes it. He may need me, and I may need more money too. Look, here we are, Maggie. Didn't she fix this up nicer than any other house on this side of town? You'd never know that it wasn't a boarding house. In fact, she does have some real renters that have rooms on the other side, where they don't see the comings and goings. Upstairs, Maggie, right down the hall to the end."

She threw open the door there, and Maggie stepped into a pale blue bower, a perfect setting for Annie's coloring, all lace and satin, with pale blue curtains and a blue Chinese carpet on the floor.

It was nicer than anything that Annie had ever had, even at home growing up with her folks. The room seduced even her with its elegance, femininity, and peacefulness.

But it was a room designed to make an impression on a male visitor too, Maggie thought. She couldn't forget that. It was designed to present a picture of luxurious feminine willingness.

"It's very nice, Annie. I hope this is really what you want."

"Even if it isn't," Annie said spiritedly, "it's better than I had."

And Maggie had no answer for that.

"Did you ever meet Melinda?" Annie asked curiously.

"Yes, once."

"She's not hard."

"No. She seemed very practical, very tough-minded," Maggie said with a faraway note in her vice.

A door slammed down below, cutting off her next thought. Annie didn't need to know that Melinda had suggested that she, Maggie, had a peculiar kind of talent that was well suited to a place like this. She wondered what kind of room Melinda might have put her in. Not lace and satin and pale blue, like this. Something strong, radiant. Red. Velvet. Her imagination was running away with her.

"I should go."

"You won't forget me?"

"We're still friends, Annie," she said sadly, because she knew it would become a friendship that could only be clandestine once Annie became known for what she was.

"I'll show you down," Annie said, and led her out into the hallway. The staircase curved downward sinuously into an entrance hallway. Off of this was the parlor, and as they made their way downstairs, they could hear voices, one thick and loud, one murmurous.

". . . bitch, bitch, bitch . . ." A grunt followed this, and then a soothing feminine voice. And then, "I've never had a day like this . . . damn goddamn . . ." Another grunt. "Damn her for messing me up . . . like . . . that . . ."

Annie cringed. "Oh no, oh no," she whimpered, her

voice tinged with fear. "It's him. *Him.*"

"... hold still, bitch ..."

Maggie caught the frantic note in her tone. "Who? Who is *him?*" she demanded, clutching Annie's arm because she thought she already knew.

"A man I had the other night. He was a terror. He was wild. He wanted ... .he wanted Melinda. He's having ... Melinda ..."

They reached the bottom step with Annie clinging to her tightly. They couldn't miss the sight in the parlor. Melinda Sable lay on her back, stark naked, on the floor, her legs in the air, and pounding away at her, fully dressed, was Reese Colleran, in a frenzy of anger and resentment. Money lay scattered on the floor all around them.

But there wasn't enough money to remove the glazed look from Melinda Sable's eyes.

Reese looked up and saw Maggie, her expression of total revulsion, and he felt like choking Melinda because she wasn't Maggie. Then Maggie was out the door and he pulled himself away from Melinda, pulling up his trousers hastily, and went tearing after Maggie, out into the street and back down toward the hotel.

Oh Maggie, he vowed, you will pay for this. You will. You saw me ravaging you in my heart after you had savaged me, and I will make you pay for that. I know just how!

Emotion pumped through his veins with the same force with which his manhood had taken Melinda, and even that was not enough to give him the wind to catch her as she raced away to find sanity, to find Logan.

Melinda and Reese, Melinda and Frank, Maggie thought to the pounding of her footsteps as she ducked down side streets in an effort to elude Reese. It was all of a piece, and maybe all men were the same. Maybe even Logan had taken the plunge into the reassuring depths of Melinda Sable's sex for the asking price. She would never know, but at the moment he represented everything that Frank and Reese were not. She needed him desperately to wipe away the sight of Reese on top of Melinda.

It was hell, it was sheer hell, and she didn't know if she could even live through it. It was her worst nightmare come true: that Melinda could take anyone from her, everyone, that she was not woman enough to hold a man by her side.

And she was not fast enough. By sheer will, Reese gained on her and gained on her, never allowing her from his sight. Finally she felt him grasp her arm tightly and jerk her to an unbalanced stop.

"Walk slowly now, Maggie."

"All right, Reese." What could she say to this man who was in the grip of some unholy emotion that was still reflected in the timbre of his voice. She had no choice.

They walked slowly, and he took several deep gasping breaths to calm himself.

"You have to let me explain."

"There's nothing you have to explain to me," Maggie said shuddering. She couldn't help it, and she knew he felt it and that it fired him up all over again.

"You will listen," he said threateningly, and she turned her head away. "And now you see why, Maggie. You're such a bitch."

It was like he had turned on her. She never dreamed he was capable of such resentment. It poured out of him in waves as he hauled her into the hotel lobby and up the steps into the suite, locking the door behind him.

He thrust her onto the sofa and pulled a chair up beside her. "This is why, Maggie. Don't you see? You won't give yourself to me, even though I know what a whore you

350

are. Oh, yes, I know all about you, Maggie," he added tauntingly at her horrified expression, "and I've been aching for you ever since I got here. Even now. You think that Sable bitch could take your place? She's a convenience. Men have conveniences when they can't get what they want from their bitches at home."

"Reese, you are talking nonsense," she said firmly, as her mind raced wildly. "You're upset about something, obviously. I don't care if you pay Melinda Sable for her time and energy, truly I don't."

"I only do it because I need you and I can't have you. But right this minute I could have you."

She sucked in her breath. "You won't do that."

"I won't do that, you're right, and you know why, you scheming bitch? Because you double-crossed me. Because there was hell to pay because of your goddamn double-cross, and you don't deserve all the pleasure a *man* can give you. But you're not going to see your cowdog any more either, Maggie. From now on, you're mine. And I will take you. I will! You'll moan and beg for me. But not tonight; tonight I have to make amends for your treachery. Tonight I have to make other things right, and then I can take you, and give it to you the way I give to Sable." He reached out and pinched her arm and then jerked her to her feet and pushed her into her room. "I'm locking you in, Maggie, until you make the right decision."

As she fell onto her bed she heard the door slam shut and the key turn. She looked up at the window and she saw that someone had boarded it up from the outside and that there was no light. There was a metal grid with a lock like a screen over the inside of the window.

His words suddenly registered: ". . . until you make the right decision . . ." Someone wanted her to make it badly, badly enough to insure her cooperation by these very crude means.

351

Cooperation again. Decisions. It was all connected, it had to be, and the end result had driven Reese just a little crazy. More than a little crazy. Her treachery. What was her treachery that she should be imprisoned like this?

And where was Logan with his pronouncements of danger and his theories of conspiracy. He had scared her half to death and now it was all coming true.

What had she done to precipitate this?

And then she knew: she had told Dennis she was going to sell the land for as exhorbitant a price as he could command from the greedy corporation.

It was the only change, a catastrophic change, but to whom was it a signal that she was involved in a double-cross, if the only one who needed the land were the railroad?

The answer was so simple it was like a beacon of light revealing the track.

Mr. Brown and Denver North, who had only wanted to pay her twenty thousand dollars for that land. And now she was asking five hundred. A damned double-cross, she thought, and not hers. Not her treachery, not her conspiracy. And Reese was involved in it somehow.

She sat on the bed and thought about it. The hours crept by, and she had no idea whether it was daylight or dark, nor could she figure out just how Reese figured into things.

A long time later she heard footsteps and a knock at the door.

"Well, Miss Maggie." Mother Colleran, triumphant and condescending.

"Good evening, Mother Colleran. Have you brought the water and the gruel?"

"Oh, you stupid girl, making light of all this. Why couldn't you just have done what you were told?"

"What I was told?"

"You should have sold the land sooner, Maggie, and

352

none of this would have happened."

"How do you know, Mother Colleran?"

"I know."

Interesting, Maggie thought. "Well, Mother Colleran, I've agreed to sell it now, and for a fairer price."

There was a long pause. "How *much* fairer?"

"Lots."

"Enough for us to be comfortable again?"

"Enough, even, for you to have a separate income."

Another pause. Money was seductive to that old bat. Why hadn't she known that?

"Do you mean that?"

"There's no guarantee that Denver North will pay my price, Mother Colleran."

"*If* they pay your price?"

"I mean it. But only on the condition you settle back in San Francisco."

A long pause once again. "Frank wouldn't want me to leave you, Maggie."

"But I'm going to marry Logan Ramsey," Maggie said with great conviction, and she thought at the moment that maybe she even meant it.

She heard a choking sound. "If you put it in writing, I'll, I'll let you go."

"Get me a piece of paper."

A moment later it slid under the door.

"I need a pencil."

"No tricks," Mother Colleran warned, as she opened the door a crack and threw in a pencil.

Maggie wrote furiously. "I'm ready," she called, and the door opened again that cautious inch.

"Let me read it."

Maggie thrust the paper into her hands. "I promise, contingent upon the sale of the property known as the Colleran ranch, to settle upon my mother-in-law a sum in the amount sufficient for her to maintain herself comfortably in a separate household, the only two provisos being that she remove herself from Colville, and that she release me from this room per our agreement," Mother Colleran read.

"You have to sign it too," Maggie said.

The old woman looked at her maliciously. "Anything, Maggie dear. Give me the pencil." She scribbled her name at the bottom of the paper and Maggie snatched it back.

"Now we walk out to the desk, Mother Colleran, and we give this paper to Miles for safekeeping, and he can only give it to a lawyer of our mutual choosing."

"You said *nothing* about that."

"Well fine, I'll tear it up and go back into the room. Why should I share anything with you, after all?"

"All *right*."

They walked carefully side by side to the lobby and gave the signed sheet to Miles who folded it into an envelope and wrote Maggie's instructions upon the back.

"I haven't seen you," Mother Colleran said. "I hope I never see you again." And she turned her back on Maggie and walked back into her suite.

Maggie watched her go and then carefully made her way out onto the hotel porch.

And stopped dead.

Converging on the hotel from different directions were Reese, Mr. Brown, and Dennis. And following hard on Dennis's heels, Logan zigzagged in and out of the shadows.

She ran. She didn't even know where she was running until she was a long way from the hotel. The only place she could safely go was back to Melinda Sable's.

Such a safe place, she thought, skirting around crowds of men standing outside the saloon. It was a usual

354

night . . . the bar was crowded, the poker tables were tight, and someone soon was going to let off some steam.

She slipped up onto the veranda of Melinda Sable's house. A maid answered the door at this time of night. A polite maid, who told her plainly that Annie was busy and she didn't know if Maggie were allowed to wait.

"Oh course Maggie is allowed to wait." Melinda drifted into the entrance hall on hearing voices. "Hello, Maggie. Have you come to take me up on my offer?"

Maggie sank onto a little bench that backed the curving staircase. "I'm running away from Reese. He's a little single-minded these days. Aren't you offended?"

"I'm never offended by hundred-dollar bills, dear Maggie."

Maggie felt offended. "I shouldn't have come here," she murmured. "I needed a place to hide; I thought of Annie."

"You think they won't follow you here? Reese will wind up with me as usual tonight, and worse than ever because he can't have you, Maggie. But I don't mind. I think in a way it kind of completes the circle: Frank didn't want you and desired me; Reese is desperate for you and can only settle for me. Very balanced, don't you agree?"

Maggie rubbed her hand over her face. She was so tired now, and not up to bandying words with Melinda. She was sure her brain ached from trying to figure out the different combinations of events that could have ended in her sitting exhausted in the hallway of Melinda Sable's house.

She knew some kind of resolution was coming. It was only a matter of time—a matter of moments, as the door knocker thumped resoundingly against the paneled door.

Reese pushed his way in. "There you are, Maggie."

"I think I am." He was calmer now, she saw, but no less single-minded. He was alone, and she wondered where Dennis and Mr. Brown were. She wondered what Reese was going to do. Surely he wasn't going to drag her from the house, or worse, drag her upstairs and force himself on her.

There was a glitter in his eye that told her he was but a step away from doing just that. There was no one to stop him; Melinda had melted away, leaving her to confront him alone.

"So, Reese . . ."

"It's very simple, Maggie. You must come back with me and negotiate personally with Mr. Brown."

"Why is that, Reese?"

"Because he is not going to accede to your outrageous price, Maggie, and I'm the only intermediary who can bargain for you now."

She felt like her head was going to fly right off of her body.

"Did I hear you right? *You* are *Mr. Brown's* agent?"

"You heard right. And he is a man who doesn't like to spend a lot of money unnecessarily."

Maggie tried to gauge how far she could push him. He was very edgy, but no more unnerved than was she. He wouldn't listen to reason, she thought, and he might be pushed too far by her reneging on the negotiation altogether, but it was the only tool she had for dealing with him.

"Then he and I have nothing to talk about," she said quietly.

"No, no Maggie, you don't understand."

"I guess I don't," she said. "We have nothing to talk about, Reese. Mr. Brown's offer has always been too low, and apparently my price is too high, and from what you say we have no means to meet somewhere satisfactory to both of us."

356

He didn't listen, just as she knew he wouldn't. He was right on the edge, and he started speaking to her slowly as if he were dealing with a dim-witted child.

"Let me explain it again, Maggie. You must come back with me and together we will negotiate with Mr. Brown."

"Dennis is the only one who can negotiate for me, Reese. You know that."

He flew into a rage. "No, no, no. Damn it, Maggie. I had a job to do and I came here to do it, and you are not going to screw it up for me. You almost did tonight. We're both very lucky Mr. Brown will see us tonight, you hear? And you better not do anything to ruin it for me."

She saw a glimmer of an answer in his incoherent words. Just a glimmer. It might be prudent, she thought, to go with him to see Mr. Brown. Mr. Brown knew the answers. She was sure of that now.

"Well, Maggie Colleran. Here we all are together," Mr. Brown said, settling himself on the sofa in their suite. "You know, of course, that Reese has been my able assistant all these weeks. No? Oh my, yes. Reese is employed by Denver North, Mrs. Colleran. At a handsome salary, I might add. His job was to get you to sell at a profitably low price for us. But it didn't quite work out that way, did it, Reese? Well, not yet at any rate. Did you say something, dear Mrs. Colleran?"

"No," she said sharply, but she knew she had made a sound of comprehension. Reese . . . Reese had spread the gossip; Reese had arranged the notices . . . Reese had set the fires. She knew Mr. Brown was watching her and reading everything as it came to her, because her consternation was written clearly on her face.

"Devalue the land, my dear," he explained gently.

"But not for *you*," she said crisply. "You weren't fool enough to think that I would assume that."

"I had hoped. Reese got people to wonder who would buy the land now. Nice touch, don't you think?"

Reese, with a charm that was nearly as charismatic as Frank's. Reese, with his treacherous fingers lighting the match that incinerated all her hopes and dreams.

"Oh yes, we needed by then to put you in a position to force a choice, Mrs. Colleran. It worked out beautifully, actually. The whole thing went. There was nothing you could salvage, and you had to begin again."

"And the *Clarion?*"

"Set up by Reese, funded by the company, of course. I was surprised you didn't see that right away, Mrs. Colleran."

But A.J.?

"Why Reese?" she whispered.

"Oh my dear Mrs. Colleran. Reese has always worked for the line. How on earth do you think that scoundrel Frank even heard about the proposed northern expansion?"

Another blow. Low . . . breathtaking.

"He bought into Colville, my dear; he bought the paper so he could drum up support for the track, convince people that it was a good thing and that they needed it, so that we would find a most receptive environment when we arrived. And didn't he do a good job?"

"Except he didn't count on Maggie reversing all that public awareness with negative publicity," Reese put in raggedly. "He would have killed you, Maggie."

"So someone killed him," she shot back. "I don't suppose you know who it was?"

"I can't pay your price of course. Twenty thousand dollars is as high as I am authorized to go," Mr. Brown said, ignoring her question.

"Then we have no more to talk about—until you consult with your superiors," Maggie snapped. "And do be aware please that only Dennis Coutts can make any offers, counteroffers, or refusals. This is by the terms of Frank's will and it's immutable."

"The bastard," Reese muttered.

"We will handle it." Mr. Brown said soothingly. "You may go, Reese. I must assume that Mrs. Colleran is not receptive to listening to any more explanations." He left reluctantly. "Such a biddable employee, Mrs. Colleran. But ruthless, truly ruthless. I was truly hoping that you would be responsive to his suit. A woman like you could bring out the best in a man."

"Yes, but how would that have fit in with Denver North's plans?" Maggie asked caustically.

"Oh, that. Well, Reese was to have received a sizable bonus if he brought you and your land into the Denver North fold."

A shot rang out—then another. They jumped up simultaneously before Maggie had even a chance to comprehend what he had just told her. They dashed out the door together through the lobby into the crowd of frightened spectators who stood surrounding a body on the ground.

She knew it was Reese before she even looked—and that he had been shot in the back, like Frank, like A.J.

"Ain't it coincidental you're right here on the spot, Maggie?" Sheriff Edson murmured as Doc Shields and several helpers bore the body away.

She turned on her heel and stalked away from him. When she returned to the suite, Mr. Brown was gone and Logan was waiting in his stead. She walked into his arms and let him hold her a long, long time.

"I know who killed Reese," he said, stroking her hair.

"I know almost everything."

"I know about Reese," she said brokenly. "Frank knew about the northbound track because Reese told him. Reese worked for them. Reese . . . oh, my God. Reese . . ."

"Maggie," he whispered, cradling her head. "It's almost over, almost. Come to my room, Maggie, and let me hold you through the night."

Chapter Nineteen

"He accepted fourteen fifty an acre, Maggie. I thought you'd be pleased. Unless you want to jockey back and forth with him?"

"I assume you will find pleasure in your fifty thousand dollar fee, Dennis?" she asked, not answering him.

"It's enough to make a start somewhere else," he said, and did not look at her.

"That's fine then," she said.

It was late afternoon of the following day. Maggie had slept in, upset by the sudden violence of Reese's death, exhausted by all the emotional revelations, and consumed by the knowledge there was more yet to come.

"When will you leave?" she asked, as she signed a paper he placed before her.

"Within two weeks. We need to make out the contract of sale between you and Denver North and give them time to wire the money here. There is no other business I need to wind up."

"No, Frank was your only client, wasn't he?"

"Yes, he was."

"And you drew up the will?"

"I drew up the will."

"You have to tell me, Dennis, why did it all come

to *me?*"

He smiled grimly. "I thought you would have figured it out, Maggie. It came to you because *I* wanted it to. I dissuaded Frank from changing the will. If everything had gone to his mother, or to Reese, or to that Sable woman, I would have had no control over it whatsoever, and in point of fact, they might have sold the land long before it could have commanded this much money. It was a very marketable asset.

"And then of course, it occurred to me that Frank might never die before he consummated the deal, and he would get everything and I would get nothing.

"So you see, Maggie, I arranged it so he got nothing and I got a chance to try to convince you to marry me so that I could get control of the property."

"A gamble, Dennis."

"Not as long as you weren't married and you hung onto the land. You were the only one, Maggie, who was stable enough to understand what it all meant, because you didn't care about the money. At least not then. That was a very lovable trait, Maggie, because I felt I could pick up what meant nothing to you, the property, and give you the security to keep on with the paper."

"You killed A.J."

"I won't admit that. But I did feel that a power of attorney from you, if you were in a situation where you couldn't negotiate once Mr. Brown came to town, might be very beneficial."

"And Reese," she added tonelessly.

"My dear, Mr. Brown would never have met your price while Reese was alive, and I never would have gotten my excellent fee. Edson will never prove anything, Maggie, about either you or me.

"Just remember, Frank had always been a lucky son of a bitch. He brought me along on his coattails. I decided to ride solo on the last trip, Maggie, but I did my best for you, always. I loved you, Maggie. I meant it when I said I wanted to marry you. I really did believe, from what Frank wrote to me, that he very well would have liked us to marry, but I know you can't believe that after his rejection of you. It doesn't matter now anyway.

"I'll complete our business and leave town. There's a release form in Frank's client agreement with me that will take care of the provisions of the will, and then you'll be free to find a new lawyer."

"All right, Dennis, I trust you on this. You'll just walk away, a richer but hardly wiser murderer."

"You hate that, but you can't do anything about it, Maggie. Don't try."

It was a warning, and she knew she wouldn't breathe a word of it, ever. When he left, the whole thing would die.

"Mother Colleran, I trust you're settled comfortably for this week in your room."

"I hate it. How much money are you giving me?"

"We haven't chosen a mutual lawyer yet. Perhaps you want to investigate that for me."

"I want the money. I know that Brown agreed to pay you a great deal of money and I want my share."

"You will certainly get a share, Mother Colleran. It will be worth it to see you embark on an exciting new life . . ."

"Hogwash, Maggie."

"Why did you let me go?" she asked suddenly.

"I want the money. I never had money, Maggie, ever. They kept me bound to them, both of them, by the fact that I was dependent on them for an income. If I could have gotten control of that land, I would have sold up in a minute. Reese told me to put pressure on you. I thought he would make it possible for me to leave this place. I want to leave here so badly, Maggie. Don't deny me

363

the money."

"I promised," Maggie said, feeling just a little sorry for her. She was an unattractive old woman who had held a monster up on a pedestal for such a long time. Where would she go? How would she live? She had a fleeting desire to want to know, and she squelched it.

Mother Colleran would be just fine, wherever she went; money would ease her way, and her unruly mouth would do the rest.

They buried Reese the day after, in the cemetery, beside Frank. Mother Colleran held onto Maggie with two clutching hands, and dry sobs racked her body. Maggie couldn't cry and she couldn't make the old lady let go, couldn't find either remorse or sorrow about Reese's death, couldn't forgive Dennis for his slavering greed.

He had been the one to play the double-cross. Frank had trusted him and all he had seen was the golden promise of the future, if only Frank could be gotten out of the way.

Conspiracies. Two separate conspiracies with one end, one aim: to marry her and sell the land for a fat profit that would pad their pockets and cheat her on every level possible.

No sorrow for Reese; he had known exactly what he was doing. He was a pawn for Mr. Brown, nothing more, nothing less. He had lied, sought her affection, stolen her home, burned her property, all in the name of cheating her out of the rightful value of her land. Whatever bonus he might have obtained by marrying her, he would have earned it, especially when it was weighed against what Mr. Brown might have had to pay.

No, Dennis couldn't let Reese cheat him out of his fee. By no means. As though Maggie would have had no say in the matter and would just have laid down and allowed Mr.

Brown to roll right over her with whatever offer he happened to come up with next.

Stupid men. Stupid, stupid men, always wanting to hold on and push and direct and tell a woman what to do.

She looked at Logan, who stood across the graveyard plot from her, and she wondered how like them, really, he was.

She saw Mother Colleran off on the stage to Cheyenne the following week. They had settled on an amount between them with Maggie's new lawyer, and the old lady was satisfied with her stipend and willing to sign a release that she would not apply to Maggie again for money.

She was glad to go, and in that waning moment just before the stage set off, Maggie felt a pang of affection for her, as if their enmity had existed on an entirely different level altogether.

And then the driver swatted the horses with the reins, and the cumbersome coach gave a jerk, and the stage lurched forward and moved briskly out of town, with Mother Colleran waving a handkerchief until long after it could possibly have been seen by Maggie.

Maggie stood watching the coach as it disappeared down Main Street.

All the ends are tied up now, she thought. Her money was in her hands, to use as she would. Logan waited for her at the hotel, as Mother Colleran did not want the cowboy seeing her off as well. She still had the property on Main Street to sell or leave vacant as she would.

She had all the answers that she ever wanted to know.

She had everything and she had nothing, and on the day that should have been the happiest of the past months she felt uncertain and unsure, and as if she did not even want to make that one step that would take her into a certain future with Logan.

She knew why. For all his loyalty and patience and understanding, she still didn't know that he wasn't the same beneath the skin as Dennis or Reese.

She didn't know whether, if she fell into his arms, he would change like a weathervane, blowing this way or that.

He had stayed so much in the background, just loving her and giving her the room she needed, that she wasn't sure at all that once he came into the foreground he wouldn't take her over completely. Or that he didn't want her the way the others wanted her: for the value of the dowry that was now held in the bank in *her* name.

He walked down Main Street to meet her, certain that she was having second thoughts about everything.

But that was Maggie. How did a man love someone like Maggie, with her fierce independent spirit and her utterly feminine surrender to him? He was almost sure what she would say to him the moment she saw him. She would say she wasn't sure, she didn't know. She wanted to wait. She wanted him.

He knew. Here was a beginning, not an ending, and yet she would see it as an ending with no beginning.

He wondered whether he ought to even try to convince her otherwise.

He saw her in the distance, serenely walking toward him, her curly hair tousled by the wind, her dress plastered against her slender body, her eyes searching the street, searching—he knew it—for him.

He caught her in his arms, and she pushed him away slightly. "You know Logan, I was thinking . . ."

Oh those disastrous words, he thought with a groan.

"But you see I hadn't thought . . ."

He didn't even know what she had or hadn't thought. This was crazy; she had to make up her mind about him

366

one way or the other. He just could not love her enough for both of them.

"I just think I need a little more time."

He could have predicted those would be her closing words.

"Fine," he said shortly. What could he do, after all, in the middle of the afternoon on Main Street? The woman, for all his ravishing pursuit of her over the last weeks, still did not know her own heart.

And then he looked at her and thought she knew indeed. She had to heal, she had think, she had to remember. He had to not push, but he was going to find it very hard to go back to the ranch with only his cook, housekeeper, and ranch foreman for company.

She needed this distance, he thought, and maybe just a little disinterest on his part, maybe just a little less encroachment on her freedom. He didn't know.

In his heart of hearts, he wanted her to come begging.

She watched them break ground on the Colleran land at the invitation of Mr. Brown, who seemed excessively pleased at the price he had paid and the pace at which things were proceeding.

She was conscious of the supreme irony of it. The man now considered her an associate with whom he had done business. She wondered how she would feel as she watched the fields being torn up and filled in and the markers laid for the trackworkers when they got there.

"The future, Maggie Colleran. You put Colville into the future."

Yes, she thought and where did I catapult myself? Right into limbo with no home, no work, no Logan, who had been suspiciously absent from her life in the last week or two. She had garnered a great deal of gossip by her bold sale, not a lot of "I told you so's" when rumor of the price got around.

"Not a good move, Maggie," Arwin said, shaking his head.

"I had no choice," she said stonily, but she wondered whether everyone was aware that was the case. And why was it their business anyway?

She stayed at the hotel and rented Dennis's former office just to have a place to go to sit and think.

A waste of money, the office and the hotel room both. She could have been with Logan, except that Logan didn't seem to want to be with her anymore.

She would not beg him.

She had thought he wanted her. By every evidence that she could understand, he had wanted her, and his desire was white-hot, burning out of control, equal to hers. He had come for her all those weeks ago, he had come and she couldn't understand why he now stayed away.

She spent a great deal of time wandering around the *Morning Call* building site. She knew Jean was working for the *Clarion*, a base disloyalty, he told her, he knew it, but where else was there for him to go?

She saw in his eyes after that that he had lost all hope of her, that she would never forgive him for his defection.

But she felt defeated too, how could she blame him for anything?

One day she rode out to Logan's ranch, but no one was there.

Another day she saw him in town and they greeted each other awkwardly. She saw the heat in his gaze and she knew that he wanted her, and she waited for him to ask, but all he said was, "How can I ask you to choose between your new freedom and me?"

He wondered when she would learn that she could have them both.

*   *   *

368

And now the nights grew hot as spring crept in. Sultry sometimes with the yearning for someone's arms around her, and a body rigid with all the possibilities of the long night ahead.

She felt herself responding to it, falling headlong into a shattering desire for what could not be quenched without that one perfect body beside her.

He was right, she was wrong; there had to be other ways besides her rigidly one-sided way that denied them both the thing they most wanted.

Other ways . . . oh, God, she remembered how he had enticed her with that very phrase, aroused her curiosity and her voracious femininity. How he had shown her those other ways, how he had denied himself for her to show her the nature of her desire and the infinite variety of ways to fulfillment.

Other ways.

It didn't have to be *her* way.

How did she go to him and say, I want it to be *our* way?

She thought she had thrown away the chance.

Melinda Sable said, "But there's no one in your life right now, Maggie. You might come and stay with me for a while and see how you like it. That little Annie Mapes is working out very well."

This was the worst, thinking that Logan himself would stoop to paying someone for that sensual surcease he had been denied by her. What if he did?

Oh God, that body in someone else's arms? Not *hers?*

She was getting crazy, she was dreaming of him at night and all the things they had done together. She remembered long hot kisses and a long, hot, other part of his anatomy. His legs. Wrapped around her. His hands . . . all over her . . . Everytime she created it she shivered with memory. She wanted it again.

She remembered telling Mother Colleran she was

going to marry him.

She hadn't meant it; she had wanted to aggravate the old witch. And she had wanted it to be true.

What had held her back?

As she wandered aimlessly through another spring day, she couldn't think of a single thing. Soon they would drive the cattle to market, unless Denver North had a loading dock and a connecting line ready by then, and Logan would be gone for the three weeks or so that it would take to get the cattle to Cheyenne and sell to the best buyer.

Three weeks lost to *her*. Why couldn't she make an overture? It was as if they were strangers, and all because she could not quite make up her mind.

"I wish you had come sooner," she had told him on that magical day after the burning of the ranch pasture. She wished he would come now.

He didn't come, and this wanting and waiting were searing in their intensity.

Her nipples ached for his caress. She yearned for his hard maleness filling her. She needed the feel of his muscular body surrounding her. She needed his kisses.

She could be a wanton and seek him out, and only for that, but was that all she wanted?

No—she wanted all that he offered, and it suddenly occurred to her that perhaps she had nothing to offer in return.

She stared at the vacant lot, an inkling of an idea playing around the edges of her mind.

Was it that the person she thought she was did not exist any more? She had had newspaper bred in her bones by her father. She had been the lady editor, the newspaper lady, the woman who ran the newspaper business, and all of that was gone now.

Was it necessary for her to be that in order for her to be something else?

These became troubling questions to her, shunting aside for a moment her adamant desire.

If she could find the answer to that, she would know what to say to Logan.

She felt like all these important pieces of her life depended on each other, and that only she had to make these choices.

It didn't have to be so, she thought. She could be everything she needed to be, and she could belong to Logan as well, and he to her. She just didn't understand the thing in herself that would not let her give in to it.

She could have the paper again, she thought. It could just *be*, and she wouldn't have to run it, she wouldn't have to fight because there would be no Arch Warfield with his mythical contract trying to scare her into doing what he wanted. She could start fresh, with her own hand-picked people. There would be no A.J., but she would remember him every day of her life. And there would be a renewed sense of vigor in the startup of a new project, one that would not be shadowed by the presence of anyone she did not want in the press room.

There was so much. She felt it welling up inside her like a bubble, as if this were the answer she had sought and didn't know where to find before now.

She had the money, she had the resources. She could do it, and if she could do it, she could give herself to Logan forever without a qualm.

The sooner she did it, the sooner she would be in his arms.

He was a man with a restless need and there was nothing that could satisfy it but the luscious body of the woman he loved in his arms.

371

Where was she? Out trying to figure out how to juggle some mystical freedom with the thought of living with him and being his wife.

It was laughable. Crazy. He knew she was going crazy for him the same way he was for her. It seemed insane that she would deny them both because she needed to find yet another answer to another unsolvable question.

The problems would take care of themselves, he had told her, and he firmly believed it. She could not.

But leaving her alone had not made her so hungry that she had come to seek him out.

If anything, she had stayed more firmly entrenched in town, and he wondered what the hell she was doing there.

What if there were someone else, another man holding her and kissing her, wanting her with almost as much volcanic passion as he did?

What if she felt that he had not kept his promise to pursue her until he overcame her every protest?

He had not done that. A man had to be a saint to put up with the fact that every objection he overruled yielded still another protest.

He felt at wits end. Desire and exasperation had mixed into something akin to a feeling of just letting it be, let it nurture itself until it rooted in something real and positive that they could make grow.

And how did he plant that seed? he wondered.

And then he thought, *maybe he had.*

It was a very easy thing to set into motion. Maggie got an architect and a plan, and before she knew it, she had engaged a construction crew to begin work a month hence.

She was filled with it. She was Maggie Colleran again, active, alive, in charge, and it was all hers. No one could take it away from her.

372

She couldn't even analyze why she phrased it that way. All dangers and threats were past. She needed only to reconcile with Logan and she would be whole, complete.

It was now her move, and she willingly made it by driving out to the ranch this one last time. Logan was out in the pasture branding calves, and there were more men around the place than she had seen before

She felt suddenly out of place, a step out of time. The only times she had ever visited him here of her own volition were on the weekends when he had made arrangements that his men be elsewhere.

She hadn't even thought about the fact there might be work in progress. She had thought only of herself and the news she had to tell him.

And now she had to wade through fifty or more roughshod cowboys to even see him. Somehow it didn't seem fair.

Or did he see her? In the shimmering heat of the afternoon, he bent over a chute with a hand at the ready to grab the branding iron that was being stoked a few feet away from him. Sweaty with the fire and the heat of the day, he was totally beguiling to her. He was rapt in his work and his shirt clung to his arms and chest and back. She could see the moisture dripping from him, and each nuance of movement as he lifted his arm, grasped iron, and set it against the calf's haunch.

The hiss and the stench disgusted her, and still she stayed, her eyes riveted upon him, his movements, his intensity. She had come for that and nothing would deny her.

No one commented on her presence until the first round of calves had shot through the chute. Then she heard a low, rough voice tell him, "Hey boss, you gotta visitor."

He took off his hat and lifted his eyes, and he saw her immediately, beyond the ranch hands. With slow, deliberate motions he gave instructions to his crew and then walked over to meet her.

What did he see, she wondered, but she knew how she had dressed for him: as elegantly and lightly as possible, in her thinnest dress with the minimum of undergarments, a minimum of everything, including words.

"Hello Logan."

"Maggie.'

He took her arm and led her over to the shade of the porch where they could be both cool and private.

She hadn't dreamed they would be so stiff with each other. His sky-blue eyes were guarded, and if he were happy to see her, she couldn't tell. He couldn't find words to say to her, nor could she find a way to begin.

Finally he said, "We're branding today. It'll be a while."

"That's all right," she said tentatively. What if he told her to come back tomorrow?

"Do you want to stay?" he asked after a moment.

"I'd like that, yes." She was hesitant. Did he *want* her to stay?

"You can go inside. It's cooler. Mrs. Martinez has probably left by now . . ."

"It's all right. I'll be fine. Really."

He turned away and she entered the house. It was very dark inside, very cool. Different from the last time she had been here. A different feeling—not warm. As if he didn't want her anymore.

So here was a long afternoon at home, if she were with him, if she were not the Maggie Colleran that needed *activity*, and being in *charge*, if she were . . . his wife.

If she weren't so intensely self-absorbed.

What would she do in this house all day?

She wandered through it looking for clues. In the kitchen, Mrs. Martinez had set out clay pots filled with dirt all set in a row in the sun-filled window. Outside,

Maggie could see a freshly hoed rectangle of dirt for her garden. Laundry flapped from a rope attached to the house. Fruits and vegetables ripened on a table in preparation for Mrs. Martinez' cooking or preserving them.

Yes, these were things she could do. The beds would be changed, the mattresses aired. She would make quilts to cover them and stuff pillows to lay on. She would sweep and sew and knit socks in the winter, except she did not know how to knit socks or sew or make quilts.

She didn't like to garden, and she didn't know a thing about preserving vegetables, and she didn't know how she thought this was going to work.

"But there's always the housekeeper, Maggie," his voice said behind her, and she jumped.

"I know that," she said, but she hadn't thought that he would consent to a housekeeper if indeed he were thinking of taking a wife.

"Problems take care of themselves." he added, stamping into the room and covering the floor with pasture grit, oblivious to its cleanliness. "We have a nice indoor pump, built the house right around it, Maggie. I was thinking about things even then. Excuse me." He pumped the water and dunked his head under it when it gushed out, and then reached for a towel to blot his wet face.

Then he stripped off his soaking shirt, and rubbed the towel all over his chest and arms briskly.

The sight of his naked chest mesmerized her. She swallowed convulsively as he leaned against the table, folded his arms across his chest, and leaned toward her with that particular bend of his that signaled he was really listening.

"Maggie?"

"I . . . um . . . I'm here," she said tentatively.

"Finally," he agreed, with just a trace of acid in

his tone.

It set her hackles up. "Oh, I see. It had to be your way or not at all, is that right?"

"No actually, it had to be a way that satisfied both of us, Maggie, but you weren't around to help me find that way. You were in town finding your own way, and I assume, because you're here, you have."

"It was an idea," she said stonily. "It doesn't matter now." Like ice water, his attitude was. He was like ice. Utterly indifferent to what she had gone through and how much she had needed him. All he cared about was that she had not been around for *him*. "Anyway, this is a waste of time, Logan."

"Waste my time," he said.

"I don't think you're really prepared to listen."

"I see. You came here to get angry, to accuse me of doing all the things you've been doing so you can have an excuse to just walk away, right Maggie? You want back to town, you want no commitment, no sharing, because then you won't ever have any control. Nothing, except, if it's offered, all the sensuality you can handle. That's not sharing, that's self-gratification."

She slapped him. "You bastard. And you've been thinking all these weeks that the things I feel most deeply about are just some sort of way to get out of giving you an answer to whatever questions you choose to ask, when *you* choose to ask them. Oh no, Logan, you're not going to dismiss those feelings so easily, as if I don't have a right to them and they're not *real*."

"That's good, Maggie, let's hear about how *real* they are, how many hours you spent soul searching, weighing your precious freedom against whatever you want from me, as long as it's not something that will bind you to me with any permanence."

"You stupid fool. Who needs to be vilified for this, permanently?"

"You do, or else why are you here?"

"I'm here—"

"No," he broke in roughly, "You're here for *this*," and he reached for her and pulled her to him violently until she was hard against his naked chest and could hold her chin at precisely the angle where he could delve into her protesting mouth most deeply.

Only . . . for *this*, she thought, her mind swimming with sensation as he plundered her mouth in a way that seemed wholly new and different to her. One touch, one kiss . . . she hated him for waiting so long in a place where words were meaningless and only the cataclysmic touch of the senses held any weight.

She ran her hands over his chest and shoulders as she met every kiss with the abandon of someone long denied. Who had ever kissed a woman like this before? Only he. He was the only one. Together they had invented these kisses solely for their own delight.

No words, no words. There was only sense and sensation, the slide of material to bare soft shoulders, the caress of a hand that had never felt the thick sinewy muscles of a man's forearm—ever. His soft soft touch removed every last garment she had worn. Her nakedness pressed into the rigidity of him, still clothed, still elusive. His mouth sought the kisses she had withheld from him all these weeks, never having enough, always seeking more of the nectar of her sweet mouth. And his hands, his hands sought the ways to enfold her, caress her, possess her, and when that was not enough, he lifted her into his arms and carried her to the table, the long rectanglar table, and laid her on it, sweeping away the ripening vegetables for the taste of her ripe body.

And now he could possess her everywhere, could feel the shock of her greedy fingers seeking him out, wanting to hold the thick thrust of his manhood in her hands and press her lips against the luscious tip of it. He braced

377

himself against the table and let her have her way, knowing hands playing all over every hard inch of him, her mouth taking its fill of him. . . .

She knew what she was doing to him, and with one sensuous foray deep into her satin heat he repaid her in kind. She writhed against his fingers and signaled her readiness.

"Oh Maggie!" Her nipples enticed him as her hands undressed him further. He touched, he stroked, he kissed, he sucked at them.

He climbed on the table and in one hard stroke he mounted her. They lay together, bathed in the sunlight on the kitchen table.

"This gets tricky," he whispered.

"I love it."

Hard against soft, soft against hard. Exquisite, deep, holding. And then hard brisk thrusts; hard, hard, hard; his mouth, hard, seeking; his arms under her, lifting her buttocks to meet his thrusts, to come tighter to him, deeper, circling, pulsating, wrapping herself around him voluptuously, seeking his virility, his tongue, her depths, the creamy satin slide that burst in the very center of her being . . . just . . . like . . . that . . .

"Oh yes," she murmured against his lips. "Oh yes, like that . . . Oh, more . . . oh yes . . ."

Oh yes . . . he shuddered violently as he spent his desire deeply into her feminine core.

He held her.

"Ummm, Logan?"

"Maggie?"

"We're on the kitchen table."

"Did you notice that?"

"It's hard not to."

378

"Poor Maggie; you're between a rock and a hard place."

"In more ways than one," she retorted tartly.

"Not too comfortable?"

"I *was*," she temporized.

"Yes," he said softly. "I was too." He eased himself away from her and had a moment's tempting vision of Maggie raising herself to a sitting position, the long line of her body as seductive as Eve.

He lifted her off the table and carried her naked into his bedroom.

"Why should I dream of you here, when you are here?" he asked whimsically, settling himself in beside her, body to body, nakedness against nakedness.

She nestled herself tightly against him.

"Did you dream of me?"

"Every night, every day, every way. Why did you need to do this, Maggie?"

"I wish *I* understood," she said slowly. "Do you realize for how long Dennis had been trying to run my life? *And* Mother Colleran? It just seemed like once they were gone there was nothing, not even the paper. It would have meant coming to you dependent on what you could give me. I didn't like it."

"And yet it is the way of things," he said with just a trace of irony in his voice. He didn't touch her now. All those little prickly feelings were right on the surface with her. The point was she had come, and he needed to know why. Why she had come, he thought, might be more important than why she had stayed away. It would set the course of their future—if they had one.

"Not my way," she said staunchly.

"But I knew that."

She took a deep breath. "So—I'm rebuilding the *Morning Call* office."

"What!"

379

"I'm going to publish a newspaper."

"I see," he said with no inflection in his voice. But he didn't see. He saw more fruitless nights alone without her. He saw hurried liaisons once again wherever they could grab a moment's privacy. He saw only weekends relegated to one day of complete isolation from anyone else and anything else. And he could see nothing beyond that, not marriage or children or a life he could make with Maggie if she were to be managing things the same way.

She had another master, and he wondered if he could give her up to it again. He slid one hand idly along the undulating curves of her body, as if the contact would reconnect him with her.

What was she asking him to relinquish now? Could he live without the voluptuous heat of her body? Could he give her back to running a business and still keep her? Could he, and could he . . .

The answer was, and he knew it well now, that he would do whatever was necessary to have Maggie.

He became aware of her hand shaking him urgently. "You don't see, Logan, really. I want to be with you, all the time. I'm not planning to live in town, I want to live here, and I'll go to Colville every morning, and I'll hire the best people so I won't have to kill myself to get the damned thing published, and I'll—"

He covered her mouth with his hand to stem the flow of all her plans. "Is that really how you want it, Maggie?"

She pulled him toward her confidently. "No, how I really want it is with you."

He proposed again one bright day as they watched the framing for the new *Morning Call* building being raised.

"I've come for you for the last time, Maggie. I want you. I want to marry you."

"I want to marry *you*," she said. "Will you marry me?"

"I can't wait," he answered fervently.

Three weeks later, in the church where Frank had been memorialized, Maggie Colleran married Logan Ramsey in a simple ceremony to which they invited everyone in town. Afterward they celebrated with a lavish wedding luncheon on the front lawn of the church.

And Maggie felt happy and loved; she was Maggie Ramsey now, not Mrs. Frank, not ever again. No one had the nerve to even mention what Frank Colleran might have done. But Colville knew how to enjoy a party; Maggie and Logan were their own, home bred and home settled, and on the day of their wedding the townspeople gave them their support and affection.

In the end, Mr. and Mrs. Ramsey decided to spend their wedding week on the ranch.

Martinez and the boys were herding the cattle up to Cheyenne. Denver North was proceeding approximately a month behind schedule, and Colville was growing by leaps and bounds as Mr. Brown gleefully wrote up notices of the new western boom town and inserted them in newspapers from New York to California.

The new *Morning Call* building was nearly sided and was waiting for the plasterers. Maggie cheerfully hired Jean away from Arch Warfield and set him to work supervising the construction crew. Annie Mapes had left town after Sean was shot dead in a drunken barroom brawl, and Melinda Sable shamelessly recruited likely young women from the newcomers in town attracted by Mr. Brown's advertisements.

But all these things were forty-five minutes away from the ranch where Logan held Maggie tightly in his arms in a secluded little world all their own. She felt secure and whole and at one with his weight pressing into her and

381

holding her fast. She loved his weight on her, and the way he fit so perfectly between her legs. She never got used to it, the sensual arousal, the erotic penetration, the movement, the motion, the explosion of joy. Each time it was different, with other ways, other words, other joy.

He had found a new way to pleasure her. Not really a new way at all but rather a communication as old as nature and yet wholly new to them. He came to her honey source so gently and forcefully at the same time, spreading her legs, seeking her with his tongue, caressing her in this new delicious way.

She twisted to find him, to hold him, or kiss him, or something wonderful to show him how much she loved this new wondrous expression of his love for her.

He shifted himself to give her the utmost freedom to explore his surging manhood with the same desire with which he explored her.

She was all silk and satin, lush to the touch. He felt her mouth, her tongue coming at him with the same insatiable fervor with which he approached her, with the loving, passionate desire to discover everything about him there was to know.

There were no barriers now; they had each other as completely as if they were one. His kiss seduced her, had her demanding more. Her succulent exploration of him nearly sent him reeling over the edge. How potent was her mouth on him. The knowledge of Eve caressed him knowingly in just the right way, with just the right touch.

And when she bore down against him he knew what he had to do to bring her to completion. Her writhing movements complemented her own torrid caresses. She felt the turbulent release coming, coming, and she enfolded him deep within her velvet mouth. Together they pitched headlong into a tumultuous culmination, all the more sensational for their intimate radiant trust of each other.

The heat spiraled downward almost unendingly in completion of this erotic demonstration of his complete love and desire for her. And then he wrapped himself around her as if he would never let her go.

One day, not too many weeks after the wedding, the stage from Denver drew up to the Colville depot with a wrenching halt. It carried a lone passenger, and in the early evening hour only Arwin Bodey, who had come to pick up the mail, saw her.

"Mother Colleran?" he demanded in disbelief.

"Hello, Arwin," she said airily, just as if she had expected to see him.

"What are you doing here?" he asked cautiously. He felt he should ask, at any rate, because he was the one who was going to relay the unwelcome news to Maggie, and not too soon either.

"Oh, my dear Arwin, I have been consumed with guilt for ever leaving Colville and abandoning Maggie. So self-centered of me; I must have gone mad after Reese died, I swear, to think of leaving Maggie alone with all those new people coming to town and her so eligible and wealthy. I came back to chaperone her of course, Arwin, and to make sure she makes the right decision about her future, and not wind up with that smelly cowboy. Arwin? Did you say something? *Arwin?*"